WHEN I'M IN YOUR ARMS

A KELLY

When I'm in Your Arms by A Kelly

www.akellyauthor.com

Romance, rethought

Cover by Amro Ashry

ISBN:

978-0-6482463-3-6 (Paperback)

78-0-6482463-5-0 (ePub)

978-0-6482463-4-3 (Kindle)

PRAISE FOR A KELLY

"*When I'm in Your Arms* is a terrific work of erotic fiction with emotional depth and expertly drawn characters that are rare for the genre." - Self-Publishing Review

"A daring erotic romance. It's a truly entertaining read filled with steamy scenes, complicated characters, and narrative twists and turns to keep you guessing." - Independent Book Review

"The sex is phenomenal. But it isn't just about the sex, this is a gripping tale of a woman's attempt to navigate the labyrinth that is the human heart." - Jo Niederhoff, San Francisco Book Review

ABOUT THE AUTHOR

A Kelly is a fearless romance author. Her stories will make you rethink love, taboos, and the ugly and the beauty of human relationships. She has travelled the seven continents and met people from different walks of life where she draws inspirations from.

A Kelly - *Romance, rethought*
Social media handle: akellyauthor

To all hearts who have been the light to others in their darkest hour

PART I

ANDREA CURTIN

MY BOY

MAY 2003

I FELT big inside the Roman Colosseum. The hypogeum spread wide beneath my feet but it was no longer unconquered. I had trawled the secret passages only people with certain privileges could access: corridors bearing flakes of original paint, dungeon walls plotted with man-inflicted scratches, pillars battered by violent traffic. In between the smell of algae and sediment rock, there were whiffs of rustic odour. Blood, my nose told me. Imaginary, but apt; the earth was chilling inside those tunnels. It swallowed me whole then spat me out, and I was reborn into the past. Within that time the faded blotches around me undried and became the blood of men. They were the entertainment, and such entertainment was the ultimate indulgence.

Exploring those secret passages was a dream come true; a far cry from my previous visits when more than half the complex had been off-limits. Protected areas, dangerous structures, and major preservation work. Necessary for the city and historically urgent in the context of humanity, but it had been irritating. My interest had little to do with archaeology. I just liked tales, tales of Roman men – the subjects and objects of dominance and torture.

I reached out to thank the man who had made this visit happen. Marco DiAngelis accepted my hand as if taking me away for a dance. A leading man in his own right, Marco was no tour guide. He headed the recently-concluded Colosseum restoration, and therefore had those certain privileges to open or close a gate. Despite his authority, what he had just done could've landed him in hot water if word ever got to the mayor. But he would do almost anything for me.

I knew it. And I used it. And I was prepared to deal with the aftermath.

The casual handshake slowly turned into a possessive grip as his gaze intensified. I was all sweaty and stinky, yet he wanted to––

It was like dodging a fly eager to get into the warmth of my mouth as I angled my face to escape his kiss. Growing up in Sydney I'd had my share of swallowing flies; not this time.

Marco robotically stopped. 'Andrea,' Marco said. 'My *bambolina*. If only...'

From the corner of my eye I noticed my husband, Chris, in the distance, walking to join us from a restroom break. Marco withdrew and instantly changed into a friendly Roman historian boasting about the majesty of the Colosseum. Still, he couldn't help glancing at my low neckline. He then moved on to exchange best wishes with Chris, who was now standing next to me. Smiling apologetically, Marco made the excuse of being late to a meeting and left.

'Wow! You must know that guy very well. He let us see everything!' Chris said as we exited the complex.

I had anticipated that comment. 'Yeah, that, and... tit for tat, I suppose,' I said with a hidden grin.

'How much did you pay him?'

'Nothing.'

'What? Is he single?'

That assumption.

What man could resist the daughter of a Singaporean stewardess and a Polish mountaineer? A triathlon athlete and lifeguard who was once the Northern Beaches' fastest woman on sand (and almost landed a modelling job with Speedo)? Marco certainly couldn't. He and I had met eight years ago; I was fourteen. A rogue period, I called it. I was a clerk at my parents' travel agency. When I was by myself, I'd ditch my trousers, wear short shorts and sit with my legs crossed. If a handsome customer came in, I'd freely bend down to open the drawer or stretch to reach that one travel brochure at the top shelf just so I could show my midriff. At the time, Marco was a manager at the Italian National Tourist Board. I wasn't attracted to him, I just wanted to attract him (he was a fly then, which would've made me... a Venus flytrap?).

I didn't mind using my beauty to make men bow. But as a wife I didn't want Chris to think that. So I glared at him, telling his assumption about Marco's interest in me was silly.

'I've gotta ask!' he innocently responded.

Despite Marco's romantic intentions and his lingering soft spot for me, his effort to show us the Colosseum's secrets hadn't exactly been free. 'Tit for tat' it was, borderline bribery. I had singled out Marco as the man to deliver my dream when I heard about his appointment to the restoration project, but I had to make him deliver without money involved (I don't hand out hard cash) or anything of an amorous nature. I wanted to give him a reward that I could consider ethical. Maybe it was meant to be, because out of the blue my boss at the music shop (my other job) mentioned a Paul McCartney concert at the Colosseum.

'Forget about the free concert!' I'd told Marco then. 'You'll have to camp for days to get good seats. I'll get you and your wife tickets to the *benefit* concert.'

'*Imposibile*!' Marco dismissed. 'Even I can't afford it.'

He could've. Typical Marco. When he'd had to return to Rome after wrapping up his Down Under assignment, he swore we'd be together again. I tried to chance a free flight out of him every time we spoke on the phone. Despite my seduction, he'd *bambolina* me and say, 'In time, I will get you here'. Marco would do anything for me, unless he had to open his wallet.

'Not at all impossible, Marco. In return, just a small favour. When I come to Rome, treat me like I was from the History Channel or Natgeo.'

I had worked three jobs to pay for the tickets. I resisted nights out and maintained a thrifty lifestyle. Chris had said then: 'How much do you need to fly to Rome? Haven't you saved enough? I can contribute, you know.'

I had dreamt about seeing the Colosseum in its entirety since I exposed my underage mind to Mother's favourite book: *For Honour and Entertainment: The Real Gladiator Story*. But my desperation to get to Rome this time had come from another place: I needed a distraction from our son, Christopher Jr. Chris figured it out eventually, so he stopped asking questions.

I shielded my face from Rome's harsh sun. I flashed a grin at Chris before confessing: 'I gave Marco the concert tickets.'

'What?' said Chris. 'So they weren't for us?'

'Come on, you're not a fan of Paul McCartney!' I said, stroking his arm. 'Rather than money, which he might've used for something stupid, I paid for my experience of a lifetime with another – for him and his wife. And along the way saved a few kids from being killed by landmines.'

Chris rubbed the top of my head. Touching my cropped hair felt like petting a West Highland Terrier, he said. I liked it this short – no matter how much Chris (or the wind, or anything) tried to mess it up, it always stayed perfect. I didn't even own a hair dryer.

Chris's fingertips moved along my crown; half massaging, half pinching. I wriggled away. 'Sorry I kept you in the dark. You know me, I like a bit of drama.'

'Mrs Sarina Curtin...you are full of dramas, but I love you for that,' he said touching the tip of my nose.

Sometimes Chris called me by my middle name. Odd, I'd never liked 'Sarina'; it sounded like a department store. On the other hand he was rather fond of it, so every now and then I let him.

'So, tell me, was it worth it?'

'Every penny. It always intrigued me, you know. Were those gladiators really proud of what they were doing? Or was it just to make a living? Or was it just to fulfil the Emperor's and the people's desires? I won't know the answer, of course, but being there just gave me perspective.'

'I can understand that.'

He'd never know what my perspective was. *Hard men in chains, loin cloths, sweat and blood...*

'You're a history buff yourself, Mr Army Guy.' Chris had been in the military for sixteen years. He retired shortly before Christopher Jr was born six years ago.

'Yeah. Modern history, I suppose, World Wars and that,' he said. He leaned on me. 'You smell good, by the way.'

I had forgotten – Chris's gift. So Marco the fly had probably smelled Chanel when he didn't hesitate to kiss me. 'Did I smell bad before I wore this stuff?' I sniffed myself.

I'd probably smelled like coconut – all I cared about was sunscreen and moisturiser with a beachy feel. During school days I'd preferred to stay plain and hang out with boys who didn't care how I smelled. I used to get into fights with them so regularly that the nurses at the medical centre had nicknamed me 'Bruisey Andie'. Now my left hook might've lost its strength, but my beauty routine hadn't changed much.

'No! No! You never smell bad,' Chris rebutted my statement. 'It's just that I like the scent of No.5 and I wanted it on you.'

'I see. I like it, too!' I said.

I did, honestly.

Chris rubbed my arm then kissed my hand. 'Lucky me!' he said.

We joined a group of locals waiting to cross the road. The Fiats, the Vespas, the smoky buses were whooshing past us one after another. When we started crossing, Chris held me close as if bullets had been raining on us. Over the top. But it made me wonder: Why hadn't he protected Christopher Jr. like this? Didn't he see our son was headed for the street? And that that car was going to hit him?

It wasn't Chris's fault. I was the one who should've been watching Christopher.

Now under Rome's harsh sun my head hurt from the continued self-interrogation: What could I have done to prevent the accident? What should I have done? How had it gone so wrong?

I shook off my thoughts.

Think Colosseum... swords, spears, open wounds, broken bones, beasts, fire, water, loin cloths, hard men in chains.

A tingle in my belly—

Ancient Rome aside, I'd always loved hard men like my Chris. Teenager's lust. Too eager, too soon. We got married following my pregnancy, barely two months after we'd met. I was sixteen, he was thirty-one. But I had never regretted it. I'd loved my son. And I was always thankful for Chris. Although unprepared and overwhelmed by the baby's arrival, my husband had always been by my side – and after my baby was cruelly taken away he had been *on* my side, despite his own grief and people burning me at the stake for being the worst mother in the neighbourhood.

Once again I stopped my runaway thoughts.

Think Colosseum... swords, spears, open wounds, broken bones, beasts, fire, water, loin cloths, hard fighters, chains, leather, loin cloths...

We continued north, following the tramline. Soon the Colosseum was out of sight.

A man's shout slapped my ear, '*Al ladro!*' and a ball of commotion rolled behind us. I turned around. Two men came out of a convenience store chasing a boy who was running towards us. The boy made a quick turn and, right before my eyes, he bolted across the road. He caught the toe of his worn, dirty sneaker in the gap between two cobblestones and was brought to a stop just as a courier van was speeding up the road.

A starter pistol went off inside my head. I sprinted towards the boy, knocked him forward to the other lane, and cocooned him with my own body just as the van swooped past my arching back. Soon another vehicle dashed towards us from the other direction. The ground shook. Whatever machine was about to batter me, I wasn't letting him go.

I would've had time to do this to Christopher had I not been distracted...

When the tyre screeches stopped among the honking noises, I opened my eyes. '*Stai bene*?' I said huffing, my palm on the boy's cheek. His gaze was soft. Despite the hostile men coming for him, the boy had no fear. Was this just a game to him? Perhaps he played it every day and he knew the cat would never get the mouse. For a split second he flashed a smile – for saving his life or simply for the hug? Then he slipped away from my embrace and all I could see were his bony legs limping across the road. Five, six steps and he disappeared behind the traffic chaos.

'Andrea!' Chris's voice thundered above the anger and distress around me. 'Andrea... oh my God... call an ambulance!'

I forced myself up, but my ankle was jammed under the tyre of a small truck. A gash ran along my left arm from elbow to wrist.

I sat up as straight as I could, periscoping my head to see the other side of the road where the boy had run to. I spotted him behind a wall of spectators. Two policemen passed him by, assessing the traffic and running towards where I was lying. Then there were two more coming from another direction – they had no interest in the cars piling up on the street; their eyes were scanning the shops and footpath, hunting low. And they found the boy. Soon one swing of a baton landed on his body. And another... and another...

'Nooo!' I cried. With all my might I tried to free myself.

'Andrea, stay here,' Chris said. He blocked my view of the gruesome scene. 'He's not our son! He's just a thief.'

I LOOKED at the photo of Christopher Jr. in my wallet. He was sitting on his dad's lap, hands on chin, half smiling; he wasn't quite ready for the shot when everyone said *cheese*.

I wept quietly. Behind the half-open bathroom door I watched Chris brushing his teeth.

Realising I was looking at him, Chris turned around. 'Are you comfortable there?'

'As comfortable as I can be with a cast and a bandage,' I replied.

'Let's go to sleep,' Chris said as he finished in the bathroom. He took the wallet away from me.

I still wanted to stare at Christopher, I'd rather feed myself with pain than sleep in hollowness – and my husband couldn't understand that.

In the dark, Chris's pre-slumber huffing reverberated across the bed. He lay on his side facing me and as his breathing settled into a series of soft, flat whispers, he turned around. His sleeping routine was quick, simple – while I would stay in a coffin position for hours thinking about Christopher, trying to recall what had distracted me the day that my son ended up in the middle of the street.

Even in Rome I dreaded the night-time. I wanted my wallet, I needed to see that half smile again, and then maybe I'd go somewhere outside, away from my whispering Chris.

I groped for my crutch. The sheets rustled and the bed shook.

'What are you doing?' Chris said.

'I need air.' I limped towards the door.

'Jesus... Andrea!' He slipped his arm under my armpit and carried me back to bed. He put the crutch away from my reach.

'How old was that boy you think?'

'Seven, eight,' Chris said, spreading the blanket over me. He rubbed my crown and kissed my forehead.

'He was so tiny...'

'Might be older. Italian kids, they're forever kiddy. Like Tony's son. I mean, Franco is twelve but he looks eight or nine to me.'

'He was only a boy. He probably stole some lollies because his parents never gave him any.'

'That could be his story.'

'How badly do you think they beat him?'

'Don't talk about that boy any more, please.'

'Did his parents even care?' I whispered.

He cringed. 'Seriously, Andrea, you want to talk about this now?'

He knew where I was going. We weren't in our own bed, yet I couldn't help starting the fire. Our sometimes-dormant, sometimes-constant argument: were we bad parents? Was that why the accident happened? Was I not meant to be a mother?

Was that why Christopher's little brother didn't even make it into this world? Chris would say it was a miscarriage, I would insist he was stillborn (I carried him for 26 weeks – Christopher's brother was *stillborn)*. At the end of it all the argument would come back full circle: we were bad parents, I was not meant to be a mother. At least that was what I thought Chris believed when he said, 'It's just not meant to be.' So he never wanted to try again.

I pulled myself up, leaning on the biggest pillow out of the six we had in our bed.

I observed my husband's sleeping routine once more. When his pre-slumber huffing turned into three consecutive blows of air, I saw three candles on a birthday cake, floating somewhere inside the four walls of the hotel room. The candles were blown out one by one. Christopher Jr., dressed in denim overalls, was sitting on Chris's lap. A colourful cone hat towered on top of his head, crooked and loose. I took a lot of pictures, including the one I kept in my wallet.

We opened the gifts while people ate the cake and drank lemonade. Then I let the kids play in the front yard. In fact, every adult was in the front yard. It was a no-alcohol party and everyone was adequately attentive, so I don't know how Christopher managed to get past them all and end up in the middle of the street. All I could remember was that I wanted to get Chris's attention: *look at Christopher, he's so happy on his new tricycle!* But my husband was somewhere else, gazing at something, at someone, out there. In the background a car engine closed in and faded. Then there was another, a bigger car. I turned around and saw that Christopher couldn't stop his runaway tricycle. Before I knew it, I found everyone circling around my son who was lying motionless next to his tricycle. He was bruised, grazed, but didn't look too bad. I didn't understand why he never woke up.

'Was it true they couldn't save him?'

Chris didn't respond – eyes shut, body still.

I had a closer look at that handsome face... he was really asleep.

I could never forget the accident like he had. I could escape from it; but here there was no work to be done, no phone calls to be made. Memories of the Colosseum had been replaced by the boy in the street. I inched towards Chris. He could be my comfort tonight. I kissed his neck, and slowly moved my hand down to his groin. I rubbed him bashfully. Then I stroked him harder, then vigorously.

Like an aggravated snake, Chris sprang out of bed. He was about to hiss at me but in the end he simply shook his head, took a pillow with him, and headed for the sofa.

HEART LOST

MARCH 2015

THE CROSS CITY Tunnel flickered in front of me like an out-of-focus 3D game. Driving past midnight, after a sleepless 14-hour flight (and terribly bumpy in the last hour), I wished I'd listened to Chris and got a taxi home.

I sipped my energy drink. Two weeks had gone like a flash. My first trip to Dubai, running in high heels every day as a retail consultant, hunkering down in one shopping mall after another. One night I hadn't even realised the city had been hit by a sand storm until I was on my way back to the hotel. Piles of sand barricaded buildings and buried kerbs. Some roads were closed because the storm had created dunes across them.

Sand storm – a curtain of yellow smog – just like what I was seeing at the moment. The tunnel didn't usually look this yellow. They couldn't have changed the lights so it was probably my tired eyes. I tapped my cheek to stay alert.

The road branched and I almost missed my exit.

I slapped myself this time.

Useless energy drink! And I paid an airport price for it.

As the yellow became even more yellow, I thought about the turning point that had happened on that trip. The grand opening of a babywear boutique. The owner, Rachel Santarossa, had whipped me hard like no other client, and I liked it. But the job itself had whipped me in a different way. Holding those tiny clothes in my hands, smelling the baby fragrances, feeling the blankets with my fingertips – I had to turn the shop into a happy place, yet it was a constant reminder of my dead sons. I'd done it without shedding a single tear. I had survived the trial indeed; in fact I had triumphed. Time heals everything, they say. Maybe this was the start of it.

I no longer worked multiple jobs. Four years ago I set up my own retail consultancy firm. I typically worked 70-hour weeks, and more if I was travelling. Chris had been telling me to slow down, but my career was a runaway train and I didn't intend to stop it.

The exit to the Western Distributor was in sight.

Home. Soon.

A tingle deep in my neck compelled me to roll my head. I shook my shoulders and stretched my neck. The tingle persisted, and now it crawled to the surface. My skin burned, my ears were full of buzzing bees, and my jaw was locked. The overhead sign said Anzac Bridge. Then everything turned black.

Cars around me trumpeted past like an out-of-sync fanfare. The blackness came and went, but I still struggled to see where on the bridge I was exactly. The railing running alongside me blurred. I felt a slight rock then heard a screech along the passenger door. With all I had I fought my veering car.

That was too close. I almost stopped breathing, I almost let go of the wheel.

I slowed down, but kept driving. A police car would turn up behind me any time now. What would I tell them?

I navigated away from the main road, heading towards my home neighbourhood. I looked around. The flashing red and blue never arrived. There was only the darkness of night, and the lonely driveway ahead of me.

Chris was fast asleep. I couldn't remember the last time I saw him. We'd talked on the phone once when I was in Dubai – for ten, fifteen minutes. And even before then I'd only seen him for a fleeting moment; he was either getting ready for bed or snoring away on the sofa with a history book covering his face. It scared me that I kind of liked our separation.

In the shower I slathered myself with rose oil. Plane odour; it made me reek of old upholstery and soap alone wouldn't do the job.

Having moulted all my travel smell, I tiptoed to bed. The street light shining through the blinds drew horizontal lines on Chris's face. That handsome face, duvet-covered chin, even in sleep he looked like he was smiling.

After barely a couple of hours' sleep, I woke up drenched in cold sweat. The light shining from the outside window looked distortedly yellow. My neck was burning again and my chest felt caged. My arms jerked, trying to reach my husband.

'Chris....' I moaned.

The big man turned to me. He murmured, 'Hey, honey...'

'Chris...' My voice faded. 'I'm not feeling so good...'

I SIPPED my hot chocolate and smiled at Chris. For the last two days – 48 whole hours – he had stayed with me. That was more than the combined time he had seen me in the past three months. My husband, my man, my friend. I found his presence ambiguous. He was like a broken pillar in our relationship: it stopped the ceiling from collapsing completely, but it didn't give enough support to keep it up either.

'Did Sophie ring at all?' I asked.

'Jesus, honey! You just had a heart attack and you're worried about your assistant?'

'*Mild* heart attack.'

'Goodness me, you're impossible.'

'Well, I'm trying to delegate now, aren't I?'

'And she's good enough to run your empire?'

I was about to shove the words 'heart attack' at him – because he was going to give me one right now. In the end I simply squeezed his hand, silently telling him I'd be okay.

'Silly question, but is there anything I can do?' he slowly said.

The only thing Chris knew about my work was *retail*. But then I had an office, not a store; I ran around, talked to people, but never sold a thing.

'Sophie will handle everything just fine,' I said. 'Hey, while I remember, do you need my help on your tax this year?'

'Don't! Don't remind me of that! And don't remind yourself of that!'

I didn't apologise for asking and I waited for him to say more. Last year Chris had been on the verge of bankruptcy; his fitness studio was in trouble because of unpaid taxes and penalties. Financially it was resolved, but it was still a sore point for him.

'Sorry,' Chris said. 'My taxes are in order. I'm good.'

'All right,' I said and looked around the room. 'What am I going to do now?'

'You really need to slow down,' Chris said, handing me a couple of aspirins. He sat next to me and whispered, 'I've missed you.'

'What are you going to do with me if I slow down?'

'We can go on holiday, a cruise perhaps?'

A cruise? A good idea if I'd been retired. But I entertained him anyway: 'To where?'

'The Bahamas, Mexico, wherever. We can go to the Yucatan Peninsula, you've mentioned the Mayan pyramids a few times.'

I smiled at him warmly. He remembered. I cancelled my thought of him being ridiculous. The Mayan pyramids, I would love to go there; although like the Colosseum, it wasn't for archaeological reasons, I was more interested in their bloody rituals and tribal wars.

'Yeah?' He rubbed my arm.

'I don't know...'

'You're not keen on cruises, are you?'

'Well... generally not, but Mexico sounds good.'

'We fly there then?'

'Chris,' I said. 'I don't want to go away.'

'If you stay here you're just going to keep working.'

He was right.

'Slowing down makes me think of Christopher.' I looked around the room. 'And his brother.' His cot would've been there in that corner, surrounded by mess of toys and all things babies. 'It's like I'm stuck in this dark room. Funny thing is, I can see – but only sadness.'

Chris bowed his head. 'I know I've caused you to be like this. You want to avoid me, avoid us, so you work insane hours, and now you're ill. I thought I'd lose you. It's all because of me.'

'Stop that!' I said observing his glistening eyes. 'Why is it your fault?'

'You know why,' he said desolately.

'You know what, I think I've been feeling better about Christopher.'

'That's good to hear. But you still want another baby, right?'

'Maybe in time I'll cope with it better,' I said, 'and stop nagging you.'

Chris looked into my eyes.

'Do you hate me, Chris?' I responded to his stare.

'No. How could I hate you?'

'Am I disgusting? You know, when you saw me bloody that day, on this bed...'

'Andrea... no! It's not that!'

'You never touch me any more. You don't even try.'

Shaking his head, he sighed: 'You know why I can't.'

'No, I've never understood.' I waited for him to say 'it wasn't meant to be' and I was ready to crucify myself by saying *I* wasn't meant to be a mother.

'Honey, I love you with all my heart, but I can't do it.' He held back for a few seconds, then he explained to me, slowly, 'Touching you, making love to you, makes me feel guilty, makes me afraid, what if it happened again?'

By now the crucifixion inside me had started, but Chris' dreaded sentence never came out. Instead he put his palm on my cheek: 'It's not you, I swear. It's me.'

'Do we adopt, then?' This had been on my mind.

'You know it's not a solution.'

'Why not?'

'It wouldn't be the joy that you want. I wouldn't love the baby like it was our own, Andrea. Would you?'

I was about to say *I would*, adamantly, but I saw the truth in Chris's statement. 'So what choice do I have? I just have to keep working like a maniac.'

'Look, to anyone else I'd say let's get a divorce––'

He had never brought this up before, but I had thought about it and I wasn't surprised he had, too.

'––but for the hundredth time, I *love* you, Sarina.'

'Don't, please...' I sighed. 'I don't want a divorce, either, Chris. We've gone through a lot together. But, if you want me to slow down, it isn't gonna work.'

I wasn't going to change. I wanted *him* to change. He wouldn't, I knew, but if there was one thing I'd learned about my

Chris: he always tried.

He said, 'I will, I guess, do some soul-searching. Maybe somewhere within me I still have that courage to make you happy again, the way you want to be happy.'

HEART FOUND

NOVEMBER 2015

CHRIS'S SOUL-SEARCHING concluded almost nine months after he'd said he'd try. And his solution was to take me on a cruise. Not quite to Mexico, but to New Caledonia.

Despite my opinion about cruises and holidays in general, I had looked forward to this one. At first the joy felt unreal – like I was on drugs, but not quite drugged. But through a quick soul-searching of my own, I managed to make sense of why. One – in between the time of my heart attack and the news I would be taken on a cruise, I had fallen ill so many times I couldn't work; two – I'd missed the beach; and lastly – Chris had organised it with smiles and energy that belonged to the Chris I'd known before Christopher's death. He'd showed such belief that what he had in store would make me happy again. I wished he had picked Christmas; he could've, but he blamed the high prices. I think he'd just wanted to avoid kids (and Santa, and Rudolf).

From our stateroom balcony I watched the ship separating itself from the dock. Chris was hugging me the whole time. Then we headed to the pool, massaged sunscreen onto each other and tried different cocktails. In the late afternoon Chris dragged me to the gym to play personal trainer with me.

Afterwards we went to the spa, followed by a four-course dinner. I slept like a log for the first time in a long time.

'Hello sleepyhead!' Chris said as I entered the bathroom the next morning. He was brushing his teeth, smelling of cedarwood oil – shiny and naked.

I reached for my toothbrush and impishly swayed my hip, nudging him to make room for me at the sink – less than half the size of what we had at home.

He tickled me and I let myself fall on him as he wiped his mouth with a flannel. While his breath smelled of fresh mint, my mouth was still daubed with the remnant of lamb jus from last night. But I didn't care, I kissed him and ran my fingers on his well-oiled chest.

He didn't resist.

I was wearing nothing under my bathrobe, I lifted my left leg, leaned on the sink and reached for his cock. It was only semi-hard but I couldn't wait, I was in such a heightened state I had to have it inside me.

'Andrea!' Chris barked and pulled himself away from me. 'Jesus! I don't want your pussy!'

We were both stunned by what he said. I thought he was going to apologise but instead he dragged me out of the bathroom and said, 'Just let me brush my teeth in peace!'

I sat myself on the bed. Fuck him! I shouldn't have agreed to this cruise. There was no downstairs bedroom, there was no office to escape to. He didn't want my pussy. Why the hell did he bring me here? What the hell did he find in his so-called soul-searching?

I had to get out of this place, or at least out of this stupid stateroom.

I headed to the pool. My husband didn't want me, maybe someone else out there did. People were smiling, with soft good-morning gestures. Surely, they thought I wore a bikini underneath my bathrobe. Well ladies and gentlemen, boys and girls, *surprise!*

Uniformed gapes surrounded me. People swam away as I tore through the pool like Moses parting the Red Sea. Mothers covered their children's eyes, men froze, women scowled.

'Ma'am! Ma'am!' A lifeguard stopped me in my tracks. 'You can't do this, ma'am.'

I didn't say anything.

He wrapped a big towel around my body, still in the water. He was hesitating, anticipating that I would retaliate. But I just followed his lead and got out of the pool with the water-hungry towel hanging off my shoulders. Soon two other lifeguards, two security personnel and a service person gathered around me. The service person, the only female in the fence of crew, quickly covered me with my bathrobe. She put her arm around me and off we went to the doctor's office (while the fence of crew followed me like a ring).

I asked for Chris as soon as I was with the doctor.

'He will be here soon,' the doctor said. On his gold name badge was printed: Dr Reuben Moss.

Chris took ages so I decided to go ahead and do the examination and blood test without him. The doctor was satisfied that I wasn't drunk or on drugs. I just told him it was insomnia and that I wasn't aware of what I had done.

'We don't want any trouble, okay, for you or for everyone else,' said Dr Moss.

Perhaps I could've been charged with indecent exposure. Maybe if I were a guy I would've been.

'I'll prescribe you with something that will help you sleep. Keep it low-key from now on, yes?'

Low key? Indeed. I intended to keep my clothes on for the rest of the cruise.

Chris finally showed up, terror-stricken. Before we returned to our room, he had a one-on-one with Dr Moss. Probably the doctor advised him to put me on a short leash. Six days a prisoner... lucky we weren't in Mexico.

'Why did you bring me here, Chris?' I said as soon as we were alone in our room.

'Andrea, what were you thinking?'

'I wasn't thinking anything.'

I was preparing myself to be interrogated: *Why? Do you think you're that attractive?*

But he simply hugged me, and kissed my forehead. 'I'm sorry about what I said earlier. I just didn't like what you did.'

'Why did you bring me here?'

'Look, I know I've been unfair to you. I've been a jerk. I told you I wanted to make you happy again,' he said. 'There's something, a proposal, sort of, that I wanted to tell you on this cruise.'

'I guess I've ruined the moment?'

He shook his head gently. 'This is as good a time as any,' he said. 'Sarina...' He sighed. 'I know I haven't been a good husband to you. I've been thinking hard over the past few months. It might sound crazy... but I think I can make you happy again, at least, a *little* happier.'

I really didn't know where he was going.

'Here's what I'm thinking: you go and find another man who can fulfil your needs—'

'What?'

'We're still together as a couple, but you, and whichever guy you decide to be with, are together just for sex.'

'Is this what you meant by soul-searching?'

'Straightforwardly, yes.'

'Why is it suddenly about sex?' I said.

'You might not want to admit it, but it is about sex as much as you wanting a baby.'

I bet he thought I'd just proven that myself.

He continued, 'Just think about it. Back in the early days, you said you wouldn't be able to live without sex.'

'It was a lifetime ago! Everything is different now. I'm different.'

'Not that different,' Chris defended his argument. 'I haven't made you feel that way, you don't feel fulfilled; and you became frustrated, you fell ill, you do crazy things.'

'It's not because I haven't had sex, Chris,' I said. But the scene at the swimming pool soon reminded me how lame my answer was.

'Truthfully, you hating me—' he continued.

'I don't hate you...'

'Let me finish, you hating me, is it just because of Christopher? Because of the miscarriage? Or is it because you *hate me*? Hate me for not being a good husband? Say we adopt, do you honestly think the presence of a child would make you happy and say *I want nothing more*?'

'You're crazy, Chris. Where did this all come from?'

'One of my friends confessed to me about his situation. He's gay, he couldn't satisfy his wife, they were both unhappy, so they agreed to have an open relationship. He goes out with his lover, she goes out with another man, yet they're still together because they still care for each other.'

'This is too much.'

'You don't have to say yes or no now.'

'And with this arrangement... you're going to be with another woman?'

He held my hand. 'No. I don't need another woman, as long as you're still with me. Maybe in time I would reconsider the baby. But now, or for the foreseeable future, I can't. I don't want to promise something that I can't keep. I can't see you suffer again... No, no.'

'You're professing a tragedy even before it happens.'

'I'm still traumatised by it all, Andrea! Please understand that. I held him in my arms, I held both our children in my arms. And they were lifeless.'

I'd been wrong. He hadn't forgotten; everything about Christopher and his brother was still as vivid in his head as it was in mine. So I just cried with him and I suddenly felt this indescribable closeness, it was like he was my husband again.

What Chris sensed in me was outrageous. But I never thought about sex the way he'd laid it out. Before today, to me, sex was just an urge, and an urge like that ought to be *killed* if it was only you who wanted it. But all this time this urge had been killing me instead.

For what Chris had revealed, his willingness to make me happy, I admired him immensely. In his soul-searching, perhaps he had revisited how our relationship started: everything about us back then was sexual. Within the first few weeks of our meeting, we made love every night; all day when it was a weekend. And yes, I told him then that I wouldn't be able to live without sex.

But what about my longing for motherhood? Would it fix itself and disappear if I felt like a woman again? Would the bleak hope of another baby that Chris had hinted at ever become real hope?

Maybe one step at a time, just as Chris suggested.

'Promise me, think about it,' Chris said.

Here, on this ship and on the beaches of New Caledonia, I would have all the time in the world to think about it. On a normal day I would've been cynical, but right now I felt ... excited.

TRIP TO THE BUTCHER

JANUARY 2016

I SHOOK my shoulder-length hair as I inspected my new do in the mirror. Behind me, my hairdresser Jordan was brushing away loose clippings from my neck.

'So, what's your plan for the rest of the day?'

'I'm meeting a friend for lunch,' I said. 'Then we might do a bit of shopping.'

'Nice.'

Man shopping – I bet he wouldn't have guessed that.

I was running late so I power-walked to the Portuguese restaurant where I was meeting Leanne, my friend of twelve years. We had met at a neighbour's auction; at the time Chris and I had been struggling to sell our house following Christopher's death. With Leanne's help, 49 Minchinbury Avenue finally found a new owner in a young couple who'd fallen in love with its cottage charm. When they were told about the incident, the woman simply said: 'I believe life goes on. We're not planning to have kids so hopefully his spirit will be kind to us.'

Close to the restaurant I spotted Leanne. 'Lee!'

'Your hair! How fab!' Leanne said.

'Jordan,' I said, helping her to push open the thick wooden door.

'He does my hair, too, but it never looked as good as yours!' Leanne pulled a curl down between her eyes.

The waitress sat us down and we ordered a jug of sangria.

'You're okay now? Not dying?' Leanne said.

'I'm an ox!' I said. 'How's life for you, these days?'

'Still contemplating a divorce, Barry and I.'

'I'd say sorry, but I know you're miserable with him.'

'Meh to him! Hey, in the meantime, you know, I've been trialling this new thing.'

'What new thing?'

'Male escorts.'

'Shit! Really?'

'Is it that shocking to you?' Leanne reacted to my gaping mouth.

Yes, I was shocked – not because Leanne was doing it, but because she'd beaten me to it.

'I thought you were the most open-minded Asian I knew!' she said.

Asian. Sometimes I wished I looked totally Polish. Without make-up I'm often called Chinese even though I have round eyes with visible creases on my eyelids (some people thought I'd had plastic surgery). Technically I am half Chinese, but I never feel it.

'Sorry! I didn't mean to be a judgemental so-and-so. It's just that I never thought you were the type,' I said.

'I've tried a few. They were gorgeous, and it was out of this world.'

'Does Barry know?'

'Meh! We're divorcing, Andrea! He wouldn't care.'

'He's a small-time dick but he cares about you.'

'Well, he himself has been paying for hookers, so I've committed no sin.'

'Oh, so he didn't have an affair?'

'You don't count hookers as affairs?'

I shrugged.

'At least he didn't try to deny that he's an arse, you know, he didn't throw things back at me. I respect him for that.'

'So he told you?'

'I found out and he didn't deny it. And he took full responsibility. He confessed, yeah.'

'Were you jealous?'

'At first. But now, with a platoon of hunks to pick from, the husband and wife thing... felt like nothing to me. Sex with no strings attached is a hundred times better.'

'Huh...'

'Mark my words, Andrea Curtin,' Leanne said.

'Any recommendations?'

Leanne choked on her sangria. 'Now... that's something I wouldn't think I'd hear.'

I looked around and whispered, 'Chris told me to, you know, have sex with another man.'

'Really?' Leanne leaned back and frowned. 'Part of a role play? He's into that sort of thing, is he?'

'No, he just wanted me to have... urm... a fulfilling sex life with someone else, I suppose.'

Leanne knew almost everything about me, beyond Christopher's death – the stillbirth, the lack of intimacy in our marriage, even my New Caledonian moment of insanity. She smiled wide and said: 'Good on him! Now that's a man! That's a *man*!'

'Do you think he's having an affair?'

'Your Chris?' Leanne paused. 'Have you been getting that vibe?'

'I don't know,' I conceded. 'Well, he goes out most Thursday nights...'

'And you're usually out with me Thursday nights!'

'Yeah... true.'

'Do you know where he goes?'

'Not really, probably the usual blokey places. He likes to go out with a friend of his, they used to work together. Hate that guy.' Kenneth Reid – one of Sydney's flies, though I had never been his Venus flytrap. 'Well, I don't think Chris is having an affair. I freaked out when he told me to find another man, but he sort of made sense.'

'Oh, he made perfect sense!'

'I don't want to pick up some random guy at a bar or somewhere, you know. Maybe... maybe an escort is the answer? What do I do?'

'I'll give you the number of the agency that I've been using. The guys are clean, you know – regularly tested, safe, always, and like I said, they're gorgeous and they're there just to please you.'

'I can't believe I'm doing this...'

Leanne reached for her phone and gave me a number. 'Well, happy new year!'

CARNIVORES

FEBRUARY 2016

I ARRIVED at an apartment complex in Circular Quay feeling I'd left something behind – like one of those dreams where you forgot to put on your shoes or underwear. In business, covering all possibilities made me feel confident to make a choice. But applying the same principle to choosing a man to have sex with had sent my head spinning: What makes a good client? What makes a good escort? Will it be as great as Leanne proclaimed? If this guy is an arsehole, will the sex still be mind-blowing because he's that good?

Leanne would've said I was being silly, but...

One stiff step at a time, I was finally one knock away from meeting my escort.

'Andie!' Alban, the 30-year-old Mediterranean jock, greeted me with a cheek-to-cheek embrace. I'd picked him for his muscle and his intense eyes. He claimed to be straight, approachable and fun, extremely fit and always ready to please. What he flaunted in his ads represented how he was in the flesh, although he wasn't as bulky as some of his photos showed.

'Wow...' I commented on the waterfront views. With the rate I was paying him, multiplied by maybe five or six clients a month, plus tips, I guessed this was the kind of luxury he could afford. I wondered where the bedroom was.

'It's really nice to have you here, after exchanging texts for like two weeks, was it?'

'Sorry, I must've been annoying.'

'Oh no, not at all! I love texting with you. You're always pleasant, and funny. This way, please.'

We got to the bedroom. I almost didn't want to step inside. 'Umm… Alban, this is the first time I've done this. Please tell me if I do anything I shouldn't.'

'Andie…' He held my shoulders lovingly. Then he shook his head looking straight into my eyes. 'I wish all my clients were like you. Don't worry about it. Okay?'

I smiled.

'Just one thing: I usually take payment in advance.'

I pulled out an envelope even before he'd finished his sentence.

'Oh, you don't have to be so quick!' He didn't take the envelope. He took my hands and invited me to sit on the bed – two high pillows, all in white linen, with a green blanket spread across the edge.

Once I sat, I flashed the envelope at him again and he put it on top of the chest of drawers in the corner of the room.

'Thank you,' he said, and came back to me. He leaned forward, very close to me. 'Just relax, okay. I'm here for you. I want you to have a good time. Leave everything to me. If you want me to drive, that is.'

I smiled again.

'Would you mind if I asked you to have a quick shower before we start?'

Thanks to the heads-up from Leanne, I had come prepared with my own shower cap, towel and everything else as if I was on a weekend away.

There were candles in the bathroom. I took a couple of minutes to wash and dry myself.

Time to grab what I'd come here for. Or --

I could take a few more moments to enjoy the vanilla scent.

I let go of the door handle and took a step back. The reflection in the mirror mesmerised me. It was as if I was staring at somebody else – flawless figure, ample breasts, perfectly shaved bikini line. A woman ready to welcome her man. I hadn't thought twice when I bared it all to dozens of people on that New Caledonian ship, yet it horrified me to do it for one man – the man on the other side of the door who was supposed to see me naked. Did I fear him? Did I fear the sex? Did I fear myself?

I put my underwear back on.

Then my dress.

As soon as I pushed the bathroom door open Alban greeted me, though he seemed briefly bewildered.

He quickly put his arms around my waist and whispered 'Did I tell you you're beautiful?'

His hands followed my waistline until his fingers met above my belly button. He kneaded my satin-clad flesh upwards and stopped at my breasts. Then he withdrew. He took off his top, presenting himself to me.

His chest – unbelievably smooth and shiny. His tan was natural and he had bulges in all the right places. Slowly I landed my fingers on his biceps – so hard, so tight. Then I placed both my palms on his chest, hand-printing him.

He kissed my neck. 'You're very, very beautiful. I'm so lucky.' Then he proceeded to my shoulders while discreetly unbuttoning my dress.

I took a deep breath, closed my eyes, and leaned on him. I should've been turned on. He was exactly my type, and this was how I wanted to be touched. I forced myself to feel something... something other than:

His arms felt like Chris's.

His chest felt like Chris's.

And he kissed like Chris...

When he arrived at my cleavage I withdrew.

'Sorry... shouldn't I have done that?'

'No... it's not that... Umm...'

'What is it, Andie?'

'It's not... umm...' Then I sighed and said, 'Alban, you're wonderful. But I can't do this. Please don't be offended.'

He knelt in front of me with a reassuring gaze. I wondered if this had happened to him before – clients bailing out at the last minute. He didn't seem surprised.

'Hey, it's okay,' he said, and rubbed my arms.

And that felt like Chris, too.

I buttoned up my dress hastily. There he was, my dream man. He was still smiling; perhaps hoping I'd calm down and pick up where we'd left off, perhaps he wanted to be as accommodating as possible so I'd try again with him next time. Whatever it was, I didn't want to tell him goodbye, but I didn't know what else to say.

'Hey, how about we go out for dinner?' he proposed.

I still didn't know what to say.

'A *friendly* dinner,' he added.

Effective damage control.

I nodded and took his hand.

AS I HAD EXPECTED, when I told Leanne about what happened with Alban, she laughed and the word 'silly' came up. Not silly at all! It surprised me how a twenty-minute sexual experiment could drain me that much. Fortunately Chris was out of town for three days so I could have some quiet time to recuperate.

'You can't just give up after the first one!' Leanne said. 'You said yourself he was lovely. *You* need to do a bit of homework to make yourself ready.'

'I don't wanna work on it. I'd rather work on my real work.'

'Oh, don't be so pathetic.'

I wondered how Leanne could forget about her husband and move on to having sex with another man just like that. Maybe she was so resentful of Barry that there was no such thing as emotional connection any more: being husband and wife meant nothing, she'd said. I, on the other hand, still saw Chris as *my Chris*, my husband, despite our relationship telling a different story.

I was still thankful for what Chris had done. That rogue period had started when I was twelve years old, puberty had barely hit me, yet I trapped boys like the jaws of Venus flytrap. I swallowed flies, even cockroaches – boys, adults; they were all the same. They'd wanted my pretty face, and for those who hadn't known my real age, they'd wanted my whole body, too. But Chris was different. I was a lump of humiliation when he found me – the night when a swarm of flies feasted on me. He didn't want me as a possession; he took me in his arms to rebuild me, with the strongest of protection and the kindest of hearts. And with that he ended that rogue period. He was the rock that became a cornerstone of my life – until we lost Christopher and his brother-to-be.

None of my losses were Chris's fault. But I blamed him for what I felt – he'd never left me stranded, yet he'd hardly given a helping hand. He'd just stood there, always neutral.

Yes, that was Chris, always neutral.

Not this time. He'd taken a stance: he wanted me to be with another man, for the same reason as when he found that pile of rubble. He wanted to rebuild me. He'd spelled it out. If I chose to stay sexually frustrated then it was on me. Maybe – just maybe – I should try again and stop blaming my husband for my misery.

I resolved to stop being an arse myself.

JAKE WAS A WELL-BUILT Italian in his early thirties. Based on our communication leading up to the session, what struck me was his straightforwardness. His messages had no fluff – *yes we can do that; see you Sunday.* He had asked me about my expectations and he really dressed up for it: leather and metal, Spartacus skimpy.

He said in his profile 'only for ladies 18-65, bad boy good looks, passionate, gentle, but can be wild when called for'.

Maybe as a result of my gladiator theme request, he was clearly on the wild side today. As soon as he opened the door for me: *bang bang*. He didn't give me time to um and ah about anything. He grabbed me, he kissed me, he spun me and restrained me against the wall. I surprised myself by how readily I stripped for him as soon as he stripped himself. His bang-bang style was indeed contagious.

Then I was spun again and this time I ended up leaning back on the kitchen bench. A few quick kisses, and away he took me to the sofa. He rubbed himself on me, looked at me hungrily, then in a flash carried me to the bathroom.

The shower was running above us. He was standing behind me, me leaning on him. He slathered my skin with rose oil (he'd asked me my favourite oil) and he rubbed my body from shoulder to chest, from chest to groin.

I smiled, drowned in my own fantasy: this man was a fighter, he just rescued me from the chamber of an aristocrat, and—

Just as I thought we were going to settle in one place for a while, I found myself in his arms, being carried to bed, still dripping wet. Well, this could count as being rescued... But *bang*

bang, he was suddenly on top of me. He ripped open a Durex with his mouth and put the rubber on with impressive efficiency.

He nudged my thighs to make room for his hips. As soon as I felt him knocking, I sat up.

He felt like Chris.

LEANNE'S VOICE blared on my mobile phone speaker while I was browsing the *backpage* site. As she repeated the whole silly thing, I randomly opened a few links in the adult entertainment section.

'He gave you permission! There's nothing to feel guilty about!'

'It's not guilt... it's just... I couldn't feel them,' I said.

'What do you mean? They're both beefcakes. What could you not feel?'

'It's not about the meat!'

'You just weren't turned on! You've been picking the wrong men. Too hard.'

I was such an open book.

'And too old!' Leanne added.

'Old?' I frowned. 'They were younger than me.'

'Yeah, old.' Leanne said. 'I can find you another agency if none of Amanda's men are good enough.'

'It's not that,' I emphasised. 'I just couldn't do it.'

'You just need the right man,' Leanne insisted. 'Next time you look, think of bunnies, not GI Joe.'

'You really are an advocate.'

'You don't know what you're missing if you don't try.'

'I tried!'

My clicking turned indifferent. I cringed at a nude photo of this body builder guy, sticking up his arse and pulling down his cock. Another guy posed in a shower, body hair all over. I mean, I like hair, I *love* hair, but this guy was a Yeti. The next link took me to a man in a cheap suit blowing a kiss. With 'you won't be disappointed' promises, those men were probably more interested in pleasing themselves than their clients. Perhaps that was what you got with independent escorts. Even though it hadn't worked out for me, at least Amanda's men had class.

'Third time lucky, how about that?'

I didn't respond to Leanne as my attention diverged to what was loading on my screen after I clicked *European twink at your service.*

'Lee, I'll call you back.'

Hi guys, I'm Lucio. I'm a 23-year-old European guy. 180cm, 70kg. Versatile. Tell me your fantasies. Me, my body and my nice 7-inch tool will satisfy all your desires.

He hit me in the chest: those big blue eyes – soft yet striking; bushy brows, straight and low – masculinity at face value. His hair was dark and thick; his body wasn't quite a gladiator type, but it was toned and mildly golden. If he was auditioning for a modelling job, I would've hired him on the spot. His shorts hung just low enough to show the top of his pubic hair. I almost touched my laptop screen.

Oh my...

The photos, which he had clearly taken himself, were of his reflection in the mirror. He was standing in front of a sink; Listerine, body lotion and soap was scattered on each side of the tap. The expression on his face was like a sad teddy bear in a Kmart toy aisle wearing a bib saying 'Take me home'. Maybe this was how he scored sugar daddies.

Despite the timidness on his face, the man demanded to be looked at, to be told your story, to be felt, to be invited into your world. His stance was bold; his shoulders drawn back, his neck straight.

I enlarged another photo. He even looked good with his shirt on. Then he was topless again and this time his shorts were pulled even lower. But from where he stood and with the angle of the photo, the body lotion tubes on the sink strategically covered the parts I wished I could see right now.

This man knew how to tease.

And I couldn't resist.

Hi Lucio, do you provide services for women?

PART II

FREDERICO LOWE

MOTHER AND GRANDMOTHER

(SOUTHERN) WINTER 2004

AS SOON AS Mother and I arrived in Sydney, she warned me not to steal.

'If you do anything stupid I won't bail you out,' she said as we were leaving the airport terminal.

I just nodded. But stealing wasn't stupid. I only stole to eat.

'This is not Roma. The police here won't take money,' she said. 'Not that I have money.'

I nodded again although she didn't see me.

I wished we'd taken a taxi but Mother took us to the train station instead. It was so bloody cold. Not that I liked the stinking hot days in Rome this time of year, but it was nasty cold down here.

On the train, surprisingly, the air made me sleep. Bursts of warm wind from the air conditioner caressed my hair while the carriage rocked gently. The seats had proper cushioning – thin, but better than my saggy bed. Peace. Rest. Until Mother unceremoniously slapped my shoulder and hauled me out of the train.

'We need to change trains, come on! We don't have much

time!' she said, rushing ahead with two matching suitcases in tow; one big, one small.

My legs felt like jelly from being folded while I slept. My suitcase bounced behind me as I tried to keep up with Mother. Just my luck, the lift to the other platform was not working.

'Shit shit shit!' Mother kept charging towards the stairs. The wheels of her suitcases beat violently against the tiles as she mercilessly dragged the trunks up the steps.

We made it to our connecting train but my legs felt like smashed jelly now.

'Don't you fall asleep again,' Mother warned. 'We're not too far now.'

I did want to go back to my peaceful, *choo-choo* sleep – but by now I was wide awake.

We arrived at this weird station called Macdonaldtown. We were surrounded by massive sheds, like an industrial estate, but no one was working. My legs had recovered from their state of jelliness but I dreaded the walk ahead. No car waiting for us, no sign of Mother going to a bus stop or anything. Knowing my luck today, it would probably be a long walk.

Surprisingly, on the other side of the train station there were houses and Grandmother's place was in fact only five minutes away. It was a tidy, two-storey house. My legs suddenly felt strong at the thought of being home – and this home looked to be a place I could get used to.

Initially Mother had wanted to stay with her stepbrother (her dad's son with another woman). She said she had helped raised him and he was pretty well off now. They had fought on the phone at the airport; in between Mother's barking, all I heard was a heavy male voice saying 'No, Alex!' repeatedly. Two of her sisters were in Sydney – they'd refused her too. The other one was in Perth so she was useless.

When we arrived at her door, Grandmother was stunned. I

thought it was because Mother looked so different. But after the long stare, the first words Grandmother said were: 'Fuck off, Alex!'

I'd say Mother was wise not to tell her we were coming. I was surprised none of my aunts or uncle had told her about our arrival. Grandmother would've barricaded her place and we would've had to spend the night homeless probably.

The two women shouted at each other for a while. But it all turned soft when the argument became about me.

'He's your grandson. He's only ten, for fuck's sake!' Mother said.

And I looked at Grandmother so pitifully that she couldn't say no.

The next day Mother and I went to a government's office to change our names – to make it official that Father was gone from our lives.

'You're my son, okay? Not his!' she said after leaving the office. 'What's your name?'

'Frederico.'

'Yeah, yeah. Frederico who?' She was annoyed.

'Frederico Lowe.'

'Good. Who's Matteo Sabato?'

'An arsehole,' I said.

'Good!' she said.

Father had always blamed someone else for his misfortunes – not just blamed, but punished as well. And he had a lot of misfortunes: food poisoning from a dodgy dinner out, losing his job, catching a cold, losing money, and so on. Of course, when I say he blamed 'someone else', I mean he blamed Mother. But once I was out of my toddlerhood I became 'someone else' to blame, too. He hit us for his misfortunes, he also hit us for nothing sometimes. So, yeah, credit to Mother, 'arsehole' was a fitting description.

'Why didn't you change Frederico as well?' I asked her.

'I gave you that name.'

Mother was born in Sydney. She grew up here, too. Pity she had problems with all – I mean *all* – of her relatives. I had hoped I might've found a few boys my age that I could call family in this new city, but nope, not meant to be. We were alone, just like in Rome. Mother said a few times that if Grandfather had been alive I would've been his favourite grandchild. If only...

Despite growing up bilingual (Mother had taught me Aussie English all right), during our early stay, Grandmother couldn't understand me very well so we didn't really converse much. I thought it was her poor hearing, but other people struggled to understand me too.

'Find him a school, will you?' Grandmother told Mother.

So she did. I might as well die. I'd rather have been beaten up by my arsehole father than sit in the classroom. At least back in Rome I still had friends like Giorgio who had always listened to me and said everything would be okay. I'd written to him but he'd only replied twice, and I'd never heard back from him again.

When it got really bad, I thought of the kind woman who had saved my life last summer. She'd whisper in my ear, '*Stai bene*?' and take me away. We should've gone to China and I might've found her there. Not this metropolitan shithole.

UNCLE D

FALL 2006

'I'M IN HERE,' I said when Grandmother knocked on the bathroom door.

'Well, be quick about it,' she replied. 'I need to clean.'

Grandmother grumbled out in the corridor, still sweeping or scrubbing or something. It sounded like a rat clawing at the floor.

I blocked out the noise and continued my business. That kind woman was behind me, smelling like flowers. Her firm arms were around me and her chest was pressed against my back. She was wearing a low tank top and her skin brushed against my shoulder.

Then she rubbed my crotch. 'Don't stop...' I whispered in my head. I tried to picture her face, but it was sketchy. But I could see her big eyes. Those eyes... if we ever met again I would've recognised them.

I floated to cloud nine drenched in her and my own sweat. My knees weak, I was blissfully landing back to earth, but I soon crashed. Two nasal voices were yakking in the background like a bad opera. Then one got closer. The knob turned. The lock was loose.

What I heard next was a witch's shriek.

Grandmother soon joined the Cruella deVille lookalike who had one foot in the bathroom and the other on the corridor floor. Both women were stumped having caught me wanking over Grandmother's not-so-shiny toilet bowl. Actually, I was finishing off and in panic I let go of my *Signor Primo*, and the fluffy toilet mat under my feet copped the brunt of its drip.

'Alex!' Grandmother called Mother and slammed the door shut. 'That boy of yours! What's wrong with him?'

I jumped into the bath, closed the shower curtain, and squatted there as the three women engaged in a heated argument outside. I cried.

Grandmother had never had a son, so I figured she didn't know what boys do. And Mrs Cruella DeVille turned out to be my aunt who'd just come from Perth. She probably didn't have a son either.

A decision was made to kick me and Mother out. Mother wasn't terribly upset. Maybe she had earned enough to afford a place of our own. I was thankful, too. Those two had always argued, and when they did, they sounded like the two fighting stray dogs that used to live on our street in Rome. *Wawwwaawwaawwaa waawwaawaaa...*

Mother took a few pieces of jewellery with her. She said they were gifts from Grandmother. Then she took me to this shop called 'Cash Converters'. She got me to stand outside by the entrance, minding our suitcases. People stared at me like I was on lookout while Mother was robbing the shop. About half an hour later she walked out, her hands busy stuffing cash into her wallet.

Our new place was about a twenty-minute walk from a station called Stanmore. It was a boxy brick building with three storeys of apartments on top of garages on the ground floor. Without saying anything Mother started dragging her suitcases up a flight of stairs with that familiar violence. I just stared at her from the courtyard.

Oddio. Seriously?

'Come on, Frederico!' she said.

My legs felt like jelly even before I took a step. When Mother said 'top floor', the state of jelliness reached its peak. As soon as I got to the front door I was ready to fall.

A man called Darius Rossi was waiting for us. Mother handed him money and the apartment was ours. Darius said it was cosy. Cosy my arse. It was a birdcage. The living room had a two-seater sofa, a small coffee table and a chest of drawers (no TV); and the room was packed with just those few things. The bathroom could only fit half a person; there was nowhere to hang the towels (or anything else) except the shower rod. There was only one bedroom, with a door that had a habit of opening itself.

I wished we'd stayed at Grandmother's.

Once all our things were in, Darius handed me two dollars and said, 'Go and get some lollies.'

'Say "thank you, Darius",' Mother said.

'Call me Uncle D,' he said.

'Thank you, Uncle D.'

I didn't want lollies, I wanted a donut from that divine-smelling bakery we'd passed on the way.

'It's two fifty, thanks!' the girl at the bakery said.

I gave her $2.

She grinned bouncily and asked, 'Have you got 50 cents?'

I shook my head, then looked at her pitifully. She said she'd let me off, just this time (although in the following weeks I kept returning if I saw her, and got away with paying only $2 until she didn't work there any more).

It was a chilly afternoon, but I didn't want to go back to the birdcage yet, so I walked aimlessly as I devoured my donut. I wondered what sort of kids lived in the neighbourhood, but all I could see was old people. I had the last bite of my donut and licked my fingers to the last grain of sugar.

When I got back to the birdcage I heard Mother moan and scream from behind the half-open bedroom door. It was a different scream from what I'd been used to, when that arsehole Matteo had been in charge. I never understood Mother. She'd worked so hard to get away from a man, and now, just like that, she threw herself at another. She could've at least cleaned this place so we could live in it. Why look for pain?

Mother and Uncle D took their sweet time and it had turned really windy outside so I decided to linger in the living room and ignore the strange bedroom noises.

All the furniture in the apartment was ancient. There was only one window behind the sofa and the curtains were full of holes. People who'd lived here previously had left a few things: a hammer, a mug, a few hotel pens, a table lamp and some cables. I looked in the drawers hoping to find something valuable. The chest wobbled because of its uneven legs (or the uneven floor). All the drawers were empty. But one leg close to the wall didn't make a woody noise – there was something stuck under it. I crouched. Surrounded by an army of baby cockroaches, I noticed something rectangular and black.

It was a notebook. I pulled it out, shook it, beat it against the wall and blew on it to get rid of the dust and bugs. The remaining cockroaches on the floor started crawling around the room. I climbed up on the sofa.

The book had a fake leather cover. On the inside cover was written: *Property of Daniel Lucio Nanini*. In the first few pages there were sketches of naked superhero/sci-fi-looking women done crudely in blue ink – their faces looked like lizards; their hair bloomed disproportionately, like the singers in Mother's CD covers; and their breasts looked like giant melons. I tore the sketches out. With a Holiday Inn pen I struck the name (although I quite liked 'Lucio') and wrote: *Frederico Luca Lowe.*

My first possession – I didn't know what I'd do with it yet. I wouldn't draw in it. Maybe I'd write things that I'd never say to anyone. Yes, it would be a good place for secrets.

Suddenly Uncle D and Mother came out, giggling. From her droopy eyes and panting, I didn't think cleaning would've been in Mother's agenda today.

'Oh, you're back!' Mother said.

Yeah... I didn't need an hour to buy lollies!

Eventually Mother did clean up the apartment (only after seeing the cockroaches approaching the bedroom). I wished I had my own bed. The sheet we were sleeping on smelled funny. I wondered how and when Mother would wash it because we didn't have a washing machine.

Past midnight I caught Mother crying. She went to the bathroom several times, clutching her lower stomach. 'Frederico...' she whispered. I pretended to be asleep. When she started to huff and wail, I got up. She said her back hurt as she drew her hands from her stomach, slowly. I would have asked her what was wrong, but I didn't want to know.

'Could you press here a bit? It usually makes it better,' she said pointing at a spot in between her shoulder blades. I pressed. She stayed silent. I pressed harder, she sighed with discontent. Her hands were on her stomach again. I took a gamble and massaged the small of her back instead. If it was her stomach, perhaps pressing her back on the same level might've help. She didn't respond. Out of frustration I pressed her with my fists. 'Fuck!' she said and jiggled away from me. She looked at me and exhaled long. 'Shit, Frederico.' She exhaled again. 'How did you do that?'

I just stared back at her. Whatever problem I'd fixed with my fists, she fell asleep soon after. Would've been nice if she'd said thanks instead of fuck.

The next morning I woke up on the sofa. Mother had moved me. Through the door I saw her stripping the bed violently and clumping the sheet into a bag.

For the next few months Uncle D came and visited Mother regularly. Sometimes he brought us nice food and he would always give me money with that same line: 'Go and get some lollies', even when it was raining cats and dogs. He also found a new school for me. It was still bad, but not as bad as the first school Mother put me in. The big boys at this school were way friendlier. When I had a bad day, I just hung out with them, played games at the arcades or ran around the streets, happy. I didn't have to fantasise about that kind woman any more, and for the first time in this city, I fit in.

2/9/2006 Met with Adam and Frost from year 11. They love me

SAM

SUMMER 2007

I BEGGED Mother not to send me to summer camp that year. I sucked at everything, and people enjoyed watching my blunders. Water stuff was the worst of all – kayaking, swimming, rock-jumping – I wasn't born to be in the water. In saying that, out of water I sucked too. Back in Rome I'd thought I was a fast runner, but here the guys ran like Olympians (or maybe they just showed how slow the Italian policemen were). Even the girls did better than me. 'Join the cooking challenge, *Francesca*!' my classmates would tease.

But Mother said I wouldn't learn if I didn't go. I had to be tough. I had to be a strong boy. Didn't she know that I wasn't a boy any more? And I was never going to be strong?

'I worked hard for this, you know!' Mother said.

And I couldn't refuse. She did work hard to pay for the program (and for that new backpack). I looked into her eyes and stopped arguing.

The first day it was the same story. I got laughed at, I finished last. This year was particularly bad because everything was about water. Water. Water. Water.

On day two they said there was going to be a rock-climbing challenge. I used to climb with Giorgio back in Rome, and I was good at it (but knowing my luck it would probably turn out I was overrating myself). The torrential rain ruined the day and the challenge was postponed.

I really wanted to win this one, or at least show I could compete. Later that night I sneaked out of the dorm to practise. I scaled the wall with little difficulty. No safety, no light, no fear. I got to the top with only the overhang left to take on. I'd never done overhangs, but this was my chance. I reached out my right hand and grabbed a big rock in the middle of the overhang, then I moved my left leg to a smaller rock under it. I swung my left hand to another big rock close to the edge of the overhang. At almost the same time I let go with my right hand. But the big rock was like a cup, and it was full of water from the rain. Caught between the choice to grip the watery rock to hang on or use it to propel myself directly to the top, in the end I did neither.

I fell to the ground sideways. My left arm and leg broke like twigs. *Cazzo!* I got up slowly but the pain was unbearable. Out of nowhere a group of boys gathered around me. Seeing my muddy clothes and muddy everything, they laughed.

I forced myself to stand up, but my leg gave out.

A tall boy came running towards me, bursting out of the wall of bemused boys.

'Frederico! What happened?' He knelt beside me.

'Nothing,' I said. I'd noticed him around but how he knew my name was a mystery.

He shone his torch on me, head to toe. 'Bloody hell! Look at your arm, look at your bloody knee!'

They bloody hurt.

'What's going on here?' Mr Truss, the PE teacher, turned up.

'Get back to your rooms!' he roared, and everybody but me and the mystery boy dispersed. 'Sam?'

'Frederico had an accident, sir,' Sam said. 'He needs help. He broke his arm and probably his knee, too.'

'Oh my God!' Mr Truss said after he'd examined me.

'It was my fault,' Sam said. 'I took Frederico here to show him how to win tomorrow. I shouldn't have done that.'

Hell! Why would he have said that? I had no time to think about it. Another teacher, Mrs Lincoln, soon joined us and called an ambulance and I lost my chance to ask in the chaos that followed.

Over the following weeks Sam spent a lot of time with me at the hospital and at home – more than Mother did (she said seeing my casts made her want to break me into more pieces).

When I was well enough to travel, Sam took me to his house. He had a lovely house with a swimming pool. His mother was lovely, too; she made us orange cake and lemonade.

Sam taught me how to swim; he made me feel safe in that pool of his, always encouraging even though I looked like a cat on cocaine. We also played video games and sometimes I crashed at his place. I would always wake up with a blanket over me. I thought his mother did that, but one night when I was half asleep, I realised it was Sam; he even gave me a kiss.

Following the summer camp, Mother disappeared a lot. I still heard noises in the bedroom but it wasn't Uncle D. It was a different man every time, although Mother still moaned and screamed the same way and came out giggling at the end of it. Some nights when I really wanted to sleep I rang Sam and he'd let me stay over.

One night during the school holidays we watched *The Matrix Reloaded* in his room after a steak dinner his mother cooked us. She let us eat on our laps while slumping on Sam's giant beanbags (to Sam this was a treat; the family had always eaten dinner at the table). I could actually cut the meat, and when I put it in my mouth... miracle! Now I understood that Aussie beef ad when it said 'melt in your mouth'.

'Did you watch the first one?' Sam asked me.

'No.'

'I so love Neo.'

'Yeah, he's cool.'

'So love Neo.'

My eyes caught a woman onscreen with huge cleavage, black hair, and big eyes. 'Hey, who's that?' I asked.

'Fuck me!' Sam chuckled loudly. 'Frederico, the quiet one, turns out to be a MILF guy.'

I squirmed.

'That's Monica Bellucci,' he said. 'You like older women, huh?'

'What? No!'

'Or is it because she's Italian?'

'No!'

'Come on!' He elbowed my shoulder.

'No! She just reminded me of someone. A woman in Rome, she was so kind to me. She was Chinese though.'

'You're freakin' delirious. How could she look like Monica Bellucci if she's Chinese?'

I was delirious. That kind woman didn't look like Monica. She was Chinese, but not quite Chinese because she had big eyes, like Monica. And her hair had been short; she looked more like a guy, definitely not like Monica.

'Won't blame you if you wanna fuck her,' Sam said, pointing at Monica's shiny tight skirt.

'Shut up! Not like that.'

'So you like girls?'

I actually didn't know. I'd never fancied any of the girls at school.

'How about Mandy, Veronica... or... Kimmy?'

'They like you,' I said. They did; in fact, an army of girls at school liked Sam.

Sam posed like Mrs Ewing, our English teacher – shoulders straight, hands clasped together at his belly. He said, 'Imagine Mandy...'

Yes, she was pretty.

'... would you want to hug her, kiss her, cuddle with her...'

Still a question mark.

'...and put your dick in her?'

Eww! If you put it that way then *I don't like girls!*

'No!' I said trying to erase Sam's question from my head.

Now I told myself to imagine that kind woman. Would I want to hug her and kiss her and cuddle with her? Yes, I smilingly thought. And if I had that chance I would say thank you for saving my life. But having my *Signor*...urm... dick in her? No! I didn't want to do all those things that would make her scream.

'I like boys,' Sam said.

I stared at him. Meanwhile, Sam's cool man Neo was doing his acrobatic stunts on the TV screen behind him.

'You're a beautiful boy,' he continued. He touched my elbow and stroked downward to my wrist, then he softly scooped my palm and drove it under his shirt, over his chest and then down to his crotch.

Wow! Mine had never been *that* bulky. Sam was bigger and older than me, but his was like a massive, thick chunk of wood. Would two more years of growing up take mine to that level? I didn't think so.

That bulky thing – I liked touching it; it was comforting,

amusing and rewarding. It made Sam smile and sigh like he was flying free. And the best thing was, Sam did the same to me. He sent me to cloud nine and beyond. It marked the end of my flying solo.

1/2/2007 Sam and I did it

PETER

FALL 2009

SAM LEFT ME. He moved to the UK when his dad got a new job. I didn't think I was in love with him (he might've been with me), but the day before he flew to London we both cried like proper lovers – heavy tears, desperate kisses, please don't gos, promises we'd never forget each other. For a few weeks we stayed in touch, but then it stopped. I guess he must've found a new love.

I lived a friendless life for months; sleeping 12 hours a day, talking non-sense to Mother, crying over Sam, crying over myself. One day Adam and Frost, the older boys from my school I'd befriended a few years earlier, dropped by my place. It was past midday, I was barely awake. 'Pie face!' Frost said as he wiped dried saliva off the corner of my lips.

The guys told me about their Uni life – how they were doing grown-up stuff, preparing for their future. They introduced me to one of their mates Peter who was studying to be a doctor (he looked like a proper doctor already). The four of us hung out a lot, but I still missed Sam and our magical time together.

One day Adam caught me crying. I didn't say why and he didn't ask, he just gave me this small plastic pouch with white stuff in it.

'It will make you feel better,' he said.

I just stared at it.

'Snort it!' he said. 'Like this.'

I watched him and then had a go myself. It was like breathing straight from the exhaust of a Roman bus. It sliced my nostrils and burned my throat. I sneezed and coughed. But a few seconds later... miracle. I didn't miss anyone. Warm air caressed my hair. I was rocked gently. A fast train to bliss. It lasted a few minutes, then I couldn't remember anything.

That shit called ice soon became my best friend.

One day Mother found my stash.

'Fuck, Frederico!' Mother said. 'Where did you get this?' Then she snorted it, like a pro, and pushed me out of the bedroom. She used it all that day. From then on I was obliged to share with her every time Adam replenished my supply (he was filthy rich and had no problem with me only paying him peanuts for it).

'Junkie!' Mother called me every time she found me using. Yes, that was me, but the way she said it made me feel like I was a thing she could toss around. I hated the word. And I hated her hypocrisy – she used too, but she seemed to see herself as another class of junkie, as if it was a status she was proud of.

At the height of my addiction (although I never thought it was an addiction), Peter started to pay attention to me. At first he acted like a concerned GP, but then he began to take care of me, like Sam had.

'Frederico...' Peter would take me in his arms. He'd put a cold compress on my forehead, feed me soup, hug me when I was shivering, and say no when I asked for drugs. 'You can beat this!'

This went on for a while. My addiction was now to both ice and Peter. One night we were alone. Peter had just nursed me through another episode. I looked at him and for once he didn't have his doctor face on. How I wanted to prove that this train wreck could be his greatest lover. Peter read my expression. My breath stank but he kissed me. We stripped ourselves naked and we tried to make love. But I couldn't get it up.

'Hey, hey,' Peter said when I started crying. 'It's okay. We'll do it next time. You see, this stuff is bad for you. You can beat it. I'm here for you.'

I desperately wanted to feel that magic again – boy to boy – and Peter was such a gentle soul. Slowly I managed to crawl back, cutting down one week at a time.

In my sober time we finally did it. Making love to him was more than magical. Nothing else had existed in the world but us; he was like my soulmate. He kept telling me I was beautiful, how he needed me, how I kept him going through the tough days of being a med student.

But bloody Mother. One night Peter drove me home after a movie. We heard noises in the kitchen. Mother had stabbed herself in the gut. Her zombie face gazed at me, blood spreading across her dress.

'Frederico...' she sighed.

I wanted to push the blade into her further and finish her botched attempt. But she was my mother – so I held her hand and said everything would be okay.

At first, despite the fact he had a heart of a surgeon, Peter was more shaken than I was. Rather than the event itself, I think it was the fact that it was my own mother that shocked him. A son like Peter wouldn't believe a mother could ever do that. After a few minutes though, it was like his super power suddenly returned. He told me to ring triple zero and did all the medical things to Mother.

After Mother's suicide attempt, Peter left me. I heard he even left medical school. What a tragedy. I couldn't help feeling responsible. I stopped using completely, and for every sober day I said, 'This one's for you, Pete!'

Besides, after Peter was gone, whenever I was high I'd see Mother lying on the kitchen floor, bloody, and calling my name. The drugs were no longer a train to bliss. I realised her act mirrored what I had wanted to do to myself – only I'd never made it a reality. At that time I feared death more than I feared life.

JERRY

JULY 2010 - JANUARY 2012

After being absent for months, one morning Uncle D showed up. Mother had been sick (in a junkie sense) but when she saw Uncle D, she had this energy out of nowhere and thought she was Sophia Loren. She squeezed his crotch and mumbled *ti voglio da morire* in her over-ripe accent.

Uncle D set himself free and said to me, 'You'd better get a job, son, or I'll kick you out, both of you.'

'Don't you ever threaten my son!' said Mother. Sophia Loren no more.

Uncle D was about to slap her, but I stood between them – something I'd never done with that arsehole Matteo. Mother was a bad creature, but as long as I was around, no one would hit her ever again.

Mother couldn't sustain herself after saying just those few words and she ran to the bathroom and puked. Fuming, but apparently unsure what to do, Uncle D left.

'Oh, look at you!' I said to Mother. The bathroom floor had started to look strange if Mother *wasn't* on it. I helped her up, wiped her face with a wet towel, and guided her to bed.

'Frederico...' she sighed.

'I'm here,' I said, pressing on the usual spot between her shoulder blades. Over time I had found a few more points on her arms, neck, shoulders and head that soothed her aches and nausea.

'Frederico...' she whispered and went to sleep.

The next day Uncle D came again, surprisingly, to apologise. He offered me a job at his cheapskate construction company and I had no choice but to say yes. I carried wood all day in the wind, in the cold, sometimes just wheeling rubbish. Most of my earnings went to Uncle D and to Mother's treatments. She overdosed a couple of times, then Adam stopped supplying that shit so she was craving; and then she caught pneumonia – and herpes – from some guy. Stupid Mother! Although I considered it lucky the guy had given her herpes, not a baby brother or sister.

The work at Uncle D's development site broke me. My muscles ached every day, and sometimes I had to skip dinner because there was no more money left. When this happened, usually I was like a junkie myself the next day – delirious and faint. Within two weeks I lost eight kilos, and one day I collapsed onto a half-dry concrete floor with planks of wood raining over me.

The fall really broke me – collar bone snapped, shoulder tendon mushed. And it left a permanent scar – a nail from one of the wood planks had pierced my left cheek, narrowly missing my nose.

Mother was nowhere to be seen during all this. Well, she was there, but she spent most days in the bedroom, snorting ice (not sure where she'd got it from) and smoking weed. She worked at a supermarket three days a week, but that was mostly to fund her habit.

Uncle D didn't kick us out; he even paid for my hospital bills. He didn't let me go back to his construction site so I found myself other jobs – shopkeeping, cleaning food courts, waiting tables. Not as back-breaking but it wasn't enough, especially with Mother catching all sorts of new illnesses on top of her out-of-control herpes.

One night Mother begged me to give her that pressure-relieving massage until she fell sleep. I cried doing it. She didn't know I was ready to die; my own body ached so badly from standing all day, serving weighty plates, scrubbing floors and carrying tonnes of rubbish out. And I still had to take care of our piling laundry. This time of the month was worst. Hearing me complain one day, Mother had simply said, 'Get over it, Frederico! Women have periods. Otherwise I wouldn't have had you.' Then she puffed her weed. I wished she hadn't had me. What was I to her? Not a son, not even human. She never thanked me for anything.

After sulking and burying myself in despair, I decided something had to change. I flicked through an old newspaper to find a miracle job. And I did. 'Masseuse wanted. Competitive rate. Training provided.'

When I arrived at the parlour, a tall, slim woman with overly big breasts greeted me unenthusiastically.

'I need a job. I saw this ad.' I showed her the newspaper clipping.

She showed me a 'fuck off' face but I looked at her with such desperation that in the end she called the manager.

The manager was a short woman, but her biceps could break any man on a massage table. She pulled my hands. 'These ain't made for pleasure,' she sneered. 'For Halloween props, maybe.'

'Please, I am good.'

'And what's wrong with your—' She pointed at my left cheek.

Cazzo! That nail scar had got infected, and the way I'd bandaged it was far from elegant. 'Nothing. Just...'

She laughed. 'Burst pimple, huh? Go home, boy.'

'Please... I need the money,' I said and looked at her even more pitifully.

She sighed and called a woman named Jerry.

Jerry was transgender; stocky and tall, but beautiful. She was also the friendliest out of the three.

'Do you think he can help you?' the manager asked Jerry.

'What d'ya mean?' Jerry frowned.

'I don't know, can he do something for you?'

'You wanna work here?' Jerry asked me, looking at the newspaper clipping. She pointed at her shoulders: 'Show me!'

And I did.

'How old are you?' she said, leaning back into my hands as I worked a knot out of her right shoulder.

'Eighteen.'

'Huh... how old are you?' she asked again, clutching my wrist as if trying to gauge my pulse like a lie detector.

'Eighteen.'

'Gosh, you're such a twink!' she said and let go of my wrist. 'What's your name?'

I pulled out my best massage move on her neck while thinking hard. 'Lucio.'

She offered me a job as an errand boy, with a promise that I would be trained to be a masseuse – someday – and I was even promised a lucrative career. It wasn't much different from what I did at home; cleaning bodily fluids, being told off, and being surrounded by junkies. From time to time Jerry would let me smoke with the girls at the back of the parlour, and I quietly took in the things that happened behind closed doors, according to those girls: body slide, ATM, tie and tease, rimming...

A couple of weeks later Jerry taught me some proper massage techniques. It was therapeutic but mostly erotic. She warned me: 'Give them pleasure, treat them like a king, but your rear grommet is off-limits, understood? And make sure your genie doesn't make its way into someone else's bottle.'

As I had promised, I was good. I was *really* good.

Word spread and within a month I had become the parlour's most sought-after masseuse. I prided myself as a genuine pain reliever, although without my pretty-boy look I wouldn't have gone this far. A lot of my clients liked to be massaged while lying on their backs (with the girls the men were usually faced down) because this way they could see me move, they could stroke my hands, and their eyes could follow my crotch.

Some of the others got jealous and tried anything to get me out of the scene –twisting my arm; purposely giving me large and rough clients; one of them even tried to give me food poisoning. But Jerry was always there to keep everyone in their place. And I was always safe.

One night I took a new client on – he was all grey, not overly handsome, but really charming and reassuring. He moaned at every press of my hand. When it was over he praised me like no one else had done, then he sat up. He touched my bare chest. He said he'd give me $100 if I was willing to strip naked for him. It was a no-brainer.

25/7/2010 – not a career, but I earn heaps more

6/8/2010 – my uniform: tight fake leather briefs

18/8/2011 – this guy Max, we touch each other

PABLO

MARCH 2012 – SEPTEMBER 2012

I SURPRISED myself by how long I survived at that parlour. I guess the money kept me going even though it drove me crazy. I'd never seen so many cat...no, dog fights. Those ladies didn't muck around, they took each other on like fighting dogs. Besides, cats don't fight. My two tabbies in Rome had shown nothing but love to each other.

I'd kept the no-sex policy (loosely), but one night on my way home from the parlour, Max the grey stopped me on the street and asked if I'd like to come over to his place. It was another no-brainer.

When we got to his home, Max rang his regular escort. Pablo was handsome, tight, and willing to do anything. I expected meanness from him, like those jealous girls at the parlour. Surprisingly, he welcomed me; role play or not, he made me feel comfortable around him, and Max. He even seduced me like Sam had. With his Spanish accent, he was unbearably hot.

At the beginning Pablo and Max just wanted me to watch them do their thing – and I earned $50 for half an hour just doing that. After a few romps Max got bored. He offered me $100 if I let him watch me come while Pablo and him had their foreplay. This routine kept him content for a while but before long he demanded a threesome. Pablo started with giving Max a blowjob while Max rubbed my dick. I released a loud sigh and that made Max withdraw from Pablo. Max grabbed me and fucked me hard. It felt like a knife but I didn't dare scream – I just kept moaning the sexy way.

The grey man had endurance like a horse. My moans stopped as I cried silently. To my surprise Pablo immediately seduced Max away from me, saying it was his turn. And Max fucked Pablo even harder; he tied him up, gagged him and spanked him. Pablo earned $900 that night and I got $250.

It was Pablo's thing to be a sub, he told me. He kept saying, 'It's just a game, Lucio. In time you will learn. If you're playing the right game, and playing the game right, you'll earn it. And soon you'll start enjoying it so much that you crave it!'

Pablo might've convinced me he had fun in those romps, but what he'd done that night, when he seduced Max to get him off me and offered himself, he did out of fear.

I'd thanked him when he handed me the cash. 'We don't want you end up in hospital, do we?' he said. I looked at Pablo then and I was sure that had happened to him.

Doing it with Pablo had given me a head start in the world of escorting. He was generous with his advice. I wasn't sure why – I was supposed to be his competition. He seemed to like me, not like he wanted to be my boyfriend or anything (he had a steady boyfriend back in Spain), he just couldn't help taking care of me. He was also diligent in enforcing protection. 'Never do it bareback, Lucio!' he kept telling me. An expert in making men intoxicated, he always found the right time to put the rubber on without interrupting the flow (he'd slip a condom under the pillow, or under the blanket, or anywhere within his reach during the action). And I learned.

Pocketing $250 a pop was a godsend considering I was

earning $25 an hour at the massage parlour. As I scored more clients, I quit my job at the massage parlour to do escorting full time. Things also got easier and more natural for me. I learned how to read men (and got used to their sweat and grunts) and gave them what they couldn't get elsewhere. Pleasure – top, bottom, soft, rough – oh yes, pleasure was the priority and everyone had different preferences, but one thing never changed: 90% of them were married and they wanted *safety*. And I gave them safety; I told them it was okay, their requests were fine, it was just a need, and I was there to provide a service and no one would know.

Once I was able to afford nice clothes and dinners out, I started dating a few guys. Arthur the plumber, Liam the advertising man, Brendon the rugby player – but they ran away as soon as they knew what I did for a living.

While my 'career' was taking off, Mother's condition had become my number one enemy. She tried to kill herself again, although she didn't get hurt this time (she dropped the knife before she could even move her hands). Then her herpes attacks got nastier. Many times I thought of abandoning her, but she was my mother. So I sought help. Despite the 'flexible payment plans' the rehab facility offered, it was still going to cost a lot. Caring for Mother had forced me to work shorter hours. The only way I could survive this was to get higher pay for fewer hours.

One night I braced myself to contact Max and offered myself alone. He agreed and so I played Pablo's game and let Max use me as he liked. As long as he paid, I'd take it. I also started offering this service to other clients and the money soon flowed in. Max and I did it for about three months, until Pablo found out. I remember it was a stinking hot day, Pablo drove me to a junkyard. He dragged me to a hidden corner. He had a piece of wood in his hand, ready to swing it at my face. But I looked at him and begged, and begged, and in the end he let me go.

'Go far!' Pablo said. 'I don't want to see your stupid face ever again!'

12/1/2012 – Pablo, Max and me - weird session

16/2/2012 – Now I know pain.

31/4/2012 – Am I brave enough to do it alone? Yes. I am. And Max doesn't hold back

22/9/2012 – Pablo almost killed me

JERRY'S LADIES

JANUARY 2013 – JULY 2013

WORD GOT out I stole Max from Pablo so I moved my work away from the city and took limited calls only in the west. By now money from my short-lived prosperity had run dry. I came back to the massage parlour, hoping to get my old job back.

Jerry was now the manager. At first she shook her head, indicating she wouldn't give my old job back, but then she said: 'I think I have a solution.'

'I'm listening.'

'Women.'

'Huh?'

'Bloody hell, Lucio! Put your brain to work from time to time!' she said. 'WO-MEN, escorting *women*!'

'Oh!'

'A growing market,' Jerry said proudly. 'There's a lotta lonely rich women out there who could do with some cuddling from a top cut like you.'

'So... just cuddling.'

Jerry gave me a hopeless sigh. 'Imbecile! You fuck them too! Just one thing, you need to be more attentive, you need to put extra effort in to make them feel extra special. Listen to them, agree with them, cry with them, laugh with them. Make them feel beautiful. They will remember every detail and they will reward you for it if you do it right.'

By reward, I hoped she meant *tips* – not praise or job satisfaction.

'With that look, and those eyes, women will melt, Lucio,' Jerry said. 'Give it a go, I can introduce you to some ladies if you want. I'll tell them to be gentle with ya.'

And gentle they were.

My first lady was in her mid-forties, very attractive, and as Jerry said, very rich and lonely. We had dinner and talked like best friends, but when we were in her hotel room, I froze. She made light of my cock-up and gave me more champagne. When she thought I'd calmed down, she undressed herself and drove my hands to her breasts.

'I'm not your mother. You can at least pretend you like them.'

'Sorry.' I withdrew my hands.

'Don't you wanna do this?' Her line gave me a choice, but she put my hands back on her breasts.

This time I learnt. I massaged them – a little gentler than I would a man's buttocks. The nipples got in the way but touching them made her delirious. She caressed me, kissed me and as I tried to catch up I was already on top of her. She moved my hands along her body, showing me how she wanted to be touched. I was sure Jerry had told her to teach me these things.

She said: 'Look at me like you wanna be with nobody else.'

I did. Then she grabbed my dick and shoved it into herself.

Whoa... glide in, glide out. I could save a few bucks from not having to buy lube.

'Do you know why we call this "getting laid"?'

I was going to shrug and let her do the talking, but she waited for my answer. 'Um... because I lie on top of you?' I said.

'Yeah... you put your body on me.' She put her arms around

my arching back. 'Not do a harbour bridge.' Then she pulled me close. 'Let me feel your weight. That's how you make a woman feel safe. It's not muscle, it's not hardness – it's that perfect weight.'

She took a deep breath and nudged my pelvis. I continued gliding my dick inside her as she moaned, licked her lips and sighed. Then she stopped. 'Have you ever heard someone say "I was faking it!"?'

I stared at her blankly.

She laughed. 'Try again! I *was* faking it.'

And so I tried.

'It's not dancing, Lucio. *You* follow the lady.'

And I tried.

'Deeper...' She crammed my bum towards her.

It felt like a warm wet sponge was wrung around my dick. I could've enjoyed it if she'd stopped saying she was faking it. Faking it my arse! All those loud moans and screams and the writhing... she was delirious. She just wanted me to do it again and again. In the end she admitted she came.

'Next time you'll get it first time.' She winked and paid me $800.

On her second visit we genuinely had fun. My skinny frame, she said, was an asset. 'You see, you can get into the nooks and cranies that big men can't,' she said after I fucked her from behind while she lay in the foetal position, with her thighs barely apart.

The next romp she asked me to perform oral sex on her. If done right I would give her the pinnacle of female orgasm, she said. She made me see her pussy up close as she explained the different spots.

I nodded.

'I bet you've forgotten what I told you already, but as long as you know where my clit is, you'll be fine.'

And I started by kissing her inner thighs. She had put some pleasant-smelling lotion there. I pecked her pussy – that body of pink flesh, with folds and dots. It glistened. I expected it to taste like a guy's pre cum... I pushed my tongue in... it was actually thinner, and slightly sweeter.

'The tip of your tongue, Lucio! Not a camel lick.'

Tip only – got it.

She moaned.

'Imagine the head of your dick...' She breathed in and huffed. 'All that sensitiveness... condensed into a spot the size of a...'

She screamed as I flicked her clit – that spot the size of a pinhead, full of things that made her delirious. I never saw anyone pump their hips so high when they climaxed, and I'd never been so highly paid without having to bruise.

'You're a good learner Lucio. Unlike my know-it-all husband.'

Jerry's other ladies were nice people, too. They were all generous and from the way they dressed and splashed out, I knew money was no object for them. Another perk, I was always well fed with those fancy pre-sex dinners. Some of them asked about my personal life, some of them didn't want to know. Those who knew about Mother's illness paid me more voluntarily.

Suddenly doing it with women wasn't so scary any more. In them I had found this 'fine line between pleasure and pain'. Being fucked as deep as they demanded me to, surely it hurt, but that was the gold they hunted for. As long as you looked into their eyes – they'd feel loved.

I wasn't sure about this being a growing market, though. My female client base never grew. It was always Jerry's ladies. Apart from my first lady, I always did the same things over and over – and they came the same way each time. Pleasing them had somehow become like maths – one plus one was always two.

It was easy money, but I still preferred men.

CJ

SEPTEMBER 2013 – JULY 2014

'FREDERICO!' Mother shouted. 'Come back, you! Don't be like your father!'

But I left her. Those nurses would suss her out. How, I didn't care. I'd worked hard to pay for her junkie mess, harder than she ever had for my summer camps.

Since I'd experimented with Jerry's ladies, I'd slowly crawled back to get a slice of my original market – horny men. I heard Pablo had gone back to Spain. Max was still around, and still happy to see me. It took me a while to get used to the pain again but money always helped. And I always survived.

Going back to this man-to-man business surprisingly filled me with dread. Money flowed in but dealing with these men's demands, both manly and sissy, drove my dick to think retirement. I still had a few romps with the ladies, but not regularly.

Too many bills to pay, I sucked up the dread and kept going – sometimes with the help of ED pills. I rented an apartment closer to the city. My landlord had bought the large one-bedder outright, and I dealt with her direct, so with my charm I managed to rent it cheap. Having my own place meant I had an option to host my clients, too. Mother still lived in the birdcage but a lot of the time she was a resident at the rehab centre.

One of my loyal clients was CJ, a handsome gym junkie who smiled a lot. It was like his body had an oversupply of endorphins (he'd told me, 'When you exercise you produce endorphins; and endorphins make you happy.'). He took me to his gym once – I shouldn't have gone. 'This should be easy for you,' he said as he corrected my pose, readying me to do some arm curls. I couldn't lift the damn thing more than three times. We tried another exercise, another machine. But I sucked at everything. Summer camp all over again. At the end of it CJ hugged me, wiped the sweat off my forehead and kissed me. 'This stuff isn't your thing, huh?' he teased. 'Let's go back to your place.'

When people say don't judge a book by its cover, that was CJ. He was a meat pack, but in bed, if Max was a lion who'd shred you to ribbons, CJ would've been a mama tabby who'd lick her kittens clean and keep them warm. He kissed on the lips, hugged with a seductive sigh, and he penetrated me (even 'fucked' sounded too harsh) like he was needling silk. He had a thick 9-inch dick, yet it never hurt.

Over time his motherliness spilled outside the bed. He began to read me like a best friend. 'Hunny-bunny you look awful. What's up?' he'd said, one day. That was the day Mother overdosed herself again. He gave me $1000 on his next visit after I told him about Mother. Then he began to take care of me like we were a couple. One day I cancelled our appointment because I had a cold. He insisted on coming over. He played nurse for two days, and paid me for it. He sent me parcels and vouchers for Christmas, and a Tissot watch for my birthday.

So I had become his best friend, too, the escort way. When we met we didn't always have sex (giving me a breather from those pills). When he cried in my arms: 'I love her. God I swear I love her' – a familiar line – I always replied: 'I'm sure she loves you too.'

These men paid other men for something their wives couldn't give. It was a transaction, fair and square. It wasn't cheating. It had nothing to do with love – these men never intended to leave their wives or start a new life with someone else. It was a need. It was being human.

'She'd never understand,' he sobbed. Another familiar line, to which I responded with a kiss, telling him I understood, and he was safe with me.

When CJ and I had sex, I asked myself if he was as gentle with her as he was with me. I believed so. His wife, like other wives whose men looked for sex elsewhere, might've noticed something was up otherwise. Sneaking around hurt CJ, I could see it. But she might never realise, though their relationship would've been ten times better had he been able to open up to her. But what woman could take it? He might've wanted men sexually and perhaps married her to appear 'normal', but I believed his love for her was real.

I sympathised with CJ, but it wasn't my problem to solve. He had his life and I had my job. All I could do was to give him the service he asked for.

CJ's regularity and generosity allowed me to upgrade Mother to a more expensive rehab after she ran away from the first one – apparently one nurse was stealing from her.

But good things never last. After enjoying a comfortable life for a few months, my regular clients started to depart for various reasons – guilt catching up with them, getting found out, relocation, money trouble. All of my clients were now one-offers, except for CJ.

Mother was happier in the new rehab. For the first time in a long time I could actually see a person's face instead of a zombie's. I tried to save money by moving back to the birdcage, but it was still tight – and I couldn't save any more with Mother's soaring treatment bills.

One night the last good thing was about to come to an end. 'Lucio, hunny-bunny,' said CJ, 'I think from now on we should take it easy for a bit.'

'Have I done something wrong?' I asked, putting on my pitiful face.

'Oh no, no, no. You're great. It's not you. I'm getting really busy now with travel and all that.'

'So we won't see each other regularly any more? I can travel with you.'

'I guess we'll have to see,' he said, and kissed me. 'Maybe... we can meet again in three weeks' time?'

And three weeks turned into a month, a month turned into two. I was broke, and seeing Mother's ever-rosier face, hearing her saying thank you to me (which made me feel human again), I couldn't bear taking her out of that rehab. Besides, CJ couldn't have dumped me just like that! So I braced myself to contact him:

'A promise is a promise.'

'Lucio? What are you playing at?'

'We'll meet this week, and next week, and continue with our old routine, or I will tell your wife!'

'You son of a bitch!' CJ said. 'Just let me go, okay?'

'Oh yes, I can let you go, can you let me go?' And I sent him a naked photo of myself.

We went on to see each other every week or as I told him to. But over time I started feeling sorry for him. He looked older and older each time we met. Once Mother was out of rehab, and once I got some of my old clients back, I decided to let him go. Still, he told me he wanted to see me again despite him complaining I'd blackmailed him.

With increasing demand (apparently my look was 'in' at the

moment), I jacked up my rate and this time CJ conceded he couldn't afford me. Finally he let me go.

Sort of.

He still texted me every now and then, saying he missed me and asking if I had a (cheaper) friend he could hire. 'A newbie is fine,' he said.

I kept wondering how his relationship was with his wife – were they still doing it, or were they estranged? Once again I felt sorry for him. A need is a need, and this man couldn't satisfy his.

Some things were just meant to be. Maybe CJ was a good guy who deserved some happiness. Out of the blue, I received a text from my old friend (enemy) Pablo. Back from Spain, he had a proposal for me. He admitted he'd been struggling. He had tried modelling, then porn; and when nothing worked out he tried *construction*. Even Pablo the hunk couldn't survive it.

'Let me do threesomes with you like the old days. I'll be the partner who cops the bruises and you get all the nice stuff,' Pablo said.

And he was even willing to negotiate his rate.

I declined his offer, but I did promise him something else. 'I'll talk to this guy. He's a nice man. A total gym junkie like you. He's not into spanking and hard fucking. But hey, you've gotta play your game, right?' I said.

7/9/2013 CJ WHOA... *generous biceps, generous tips*

31/10/2013 I think CJ is addicted to me

18/11/2013 Nathan's wife is a bitch

23/12/2013 Why did Jeff have to leave?

5/1/2014 I had to do it. CJ doesn't like it, tough luck! He's a rich bastard.

26/3/2014 I think CJ cried. I can't keep doing this.

1/7/2014 Pablo and CJ – a match made in escort heaven

ROB

22 FEBRUARY 2016

I STUCK out my bare butt in front of the mirror to check the damage after tonight's session. Bruises of all sizes peppered my cheeks and thighs. Bloody Rob! Now I would have to nurse and disguise them. My next client could only see perfect baby skin – not bumps and blemishes. Hopefully they would clear completely by the time it was Mardi Gras so I could still wear my sequined blue thong without disgusting anyone. I shouldn't have let him paddle me for as long as he had. But the guy had paid extraordinarily well; it would cover a few days of income from other clients (who paid the exact rates, not a cent more, and asked for the sun and the moon) – so I could afford to take a break to recover. Besides, these days Rob was the only client who was into giving *me* a happy ending, a reward somewhat worth suffering for.

Still, it hurt. Rob's voice was torture in itself (and it would usually keep playing in my head for days) – the way he wanted me to say, 'Thank you, sir!' 'Yes, sir!'... unbearable!

I carefully lowered myself onto the bed. It was a pain in the arse, literally. I reached for a tiny plastic sachet from the bedside table.

My old friend.

I put it in my palm, clenched a fist, opened it, clenched it, opened it, as if I could make it appear and disappear like magic.

The sachet – a quarter-gram of ice given to me free by Pablo (probably of a lower grade; nothing good comes free).

I tore the corner of the sachet, thinking...

For the past couple of years I had been escorting on and off, following the money cycle – earning, spending, broke, earning, spending, broke. Tonight I was in the 'earning' stage. Mother had been clean for a while following the rehab, but she relapsed.

I looked at the powder in my palm. Maybe I should give it to Mother. She'd been nagging me for it. Well, more than that, she'd been threatening me. 'I'll kill myself, Frederico!' 'I'll get it myself with or without your help!' But as far as I knew, she hadn't got hold of any behind my back, and she certainly hadn't managed to kill herself.

At the moment *I* needed this shit.

So I snorted it.

For the next few hours I might be able to forget about Rob and his voice. And I might also forget about Mr G from yesterday, a 70-year-old man whose only request was to have me lie on him for half an hour... and another session the day before, with a fella who fucked me hard and then watched me shower while he was grunting endlessly (phlegm, snot and all). And the one before, and the one before...

It was a big ask to expect the mediocre-quality drug to make me forget all those. I might need to pay for the real thing.

But I would like to think myself wiser. My days with Peter hadn't disappeared from my mind.

Regardless of what people told me about ice, promoting or condemning, the bottom line was that I didn't like it. It had been my friend because I hadn't had an alternative. Discovering the world of escorting had been the substitute to that – men liked me, they praised me, they couldn't resist me. Now, the question was, if this world had become demandingly boring, then what? Those ED pills, I'd been popping them like candy.

Should I call it quits? What would I do instead?

The same questions every night.

I shifted myself to the middle of the bed and lay flat on my back. My new city apartment had the space I'd always wanted: a large living room, two generous-sized baths, two bedrooms – one for myself and the other for work. If I quit now, who'd pay the rent? No way could I go back to the birdcage. And the only thing I was good at that could fund my lifestyle was being Lucio. So I decided to toughen up.

Right on cue, my mobile beeped with a message from Rob:

Hey Lucio, you good for Fri?

What's an escort to say? An escort would start hinting that he needed to take it easy for a bit. Rob had been booking me every week, sometimes twice, for the last two months. He didn't always spank me; what concerned me was his desire to be close to me like CJ had been. Every professional escort knew that was a sign of attachment. Some of them would stay away from these sorts of clients.

But it was Rob. I shouldn't answer Rob's request as an escort. In his eyes I was his lover, and a lover never says no.

Of course. See you then.

How long could I go on? Being fondled, fucked, beaten for money? Was there anything more to it? Yes, I liked it when they said I was beautiful, when they said I was the best. But when the sessions were over, what was left? Maybe I should start posting on ladies' sites. I'd never done that; all of my female clients had been introduced by Jerry. And they were all right.

What was it that people say? A change is as good as a holiday? Maybe I should go back to becoming a ladies' man.

I pondered.
No, I still preferred men.

A WOMAN NAMED ANDIE

27 FEBRUARY 2016

I WAS GOING to tell Rob I'd only see him once a fortnight, not more. But I couldn't. Perhaps I was secretly addicted to him.

Once more I scrutinised my butt in the mirror. The bruises from last week had pretty much cleared, now I had to start over.

But that could wait. Right now I simply wanted to have a bite to eat. I grabbed a frozen pizza and watched the ultrathin dough, topped with cheese and bacon, spin behind the cloudy microwave door. My mobile beeped. Bloody Rob!

But it wasn't him.

Hi Lucio, my name is Andie. Do you provide services for women?

After all these years, having copped everything from sweetness to pain, for the first time I felt scared of getting a new client. Despite my recent thoughts of becoming a ladies' man again, I hadn't done anything yet to re-enter that market, so this woman must've got my details from my current *backpage* ads. Why did she pick me? No woman had ever contacted me directly. Did she know Jerry? No, then she wouldn't have asked if I serviced women.

What was an escort to say?

Of course. I prefer women, actually ;)

I watched the phone screen, waiting for the three dots to appear so I knew she was typing. But nothing came through.

The microwave dinged and I snatched the pizza out. I took a bottle of Peroni from the fridge and sat down.

Halfway through the first slice, I received a reply:

Great. I'm Eurasian, 34 yrs. Are you okay with that? If yes, are you available Sat 5 Mar?

I typed 'see you then', but... no! Not that Saturday.

I am fine with that. Unfortunately 5 Mar is Mardi Gras. I will be out in the afternoon. I am available before noon. Is this good for you, Andie? Or maybe another day is good for you?

There was this sensation jumping up and down in my belly, and it wasn't gas. I wanted her to say she couldn't make it so I'd escape the meeting, but at the same time I felt like chasing her. Being wanted by men satisfied my ego, but I'd been wanted by so many it had become a bit blah. Being chosen, by a woman, out of those other ridiculously handsome straight escorts – and not just for Jerry – made me grin like a teenager. Had I found my lucky charm? Somehow someone had heard me when I said I needed a change.

Morning is fine. 10-11am?

That is perfect for me, Andie.

See you then. Have a good night.

You have a good night, too, Andie. See you soon ;)

22/2/2016 – Txt from a woman Andie. She wanted me. So happy.

PART III

ANDREA CURTIN AND FREDERICO LOWE

ANDREA CURTIN: BOLTS AND NUT

2 MARCH 2016

'HEY, WHAT'S UP?' Chris said when he found me home before him. I was immersing myself in the pages of Hollywood affairs.

'Nothing.'

'Yesterday you finished early, today you--'

I was about to interrupt: *You complain if I finish late, you complain if I finish early.*

Chris said, 'Let me finish: Today you even finished earlier. And you didn't work last weekend. I am impressed! I love you being around, you know. But...'

There was always a *but* with Chris.

'... you look so glum! You miss working crazy hours, huh?' Chris said dismally.

Glum? Ever since that fateful click on *backpage* I'd told myself work could wait another day. I felt okay being home alone – musing Lucio's photos, looking into his eyes, touching my laptop screen wishing I could erase those body lotion tubes covering his privates.

Glum? Maybe I didn't want Chris to see me roll in all this

excitement. It was like he had the short end of the bargain. I'd never asked what I could do to make him as happy as I was now.

'So, I'll never win?' he added.

'Chris... what do you want?' I said. 'I'm always miserable, you know that.'

'So, haven't you found your Mr Right yet?' Chris asked me nervously.

I chuckled. 'You could've just asked, you know!' I said. 'Don't need to be so cryptic with the introduction!'

'Yeah... you might say that, but if I'd asked you: "Hey, how's your sex life these days?" You'd tell me to go to hell.'

If he'd put it like that, yes, I would've said go to hell. And I had told him to give me space in the earlier days of this escort experiment (when he'd asked me every day how it was all going). I closed the magazine in my hands and looked at my husband: 'I couldn't do it.'

'Really?' he said, concealing his smile.

'I met with them but I couldn't *do it*.'

'Not sexy enough?'

'Oh, not that. They're sexy as, but it just didn't feel right,' I said. 'It was like... I don't know... like I'm doing something bad.'

'Well, I suggested it to you.' He sat next to me and put his hand on my thigh.

No other men were better than my Chris, that hand was hoping. But at the moment there was someone better than him. Every time I looked at that man's photos: *you and me, Lucio, you and me*. Under the blanket, I imagined it was me and him. When I was naked, it was him in me. I was not much of an actor, the only way for me to conceal my unruly inner-self was to put a mask of glum. So when Chris was around, he wouldn't have to feel second-best.

'I know, but, those escorts, they were men, like you, you know,' I replied.

'I don't understand.'

'What do you think of a gay escort?'

'What? Why would you want a gay escort?'

'I don't know.' Truly, I didn't. I picked Lucio because he drew me; he was like a beautiful toxin which held me subdued with no hope of recovery. But I had to give Chris a reason. 'Someone neutral, or... not that, someone that I could have sex with, with freedom, you know, knowing that it would strictly be professional.'

'You wouldn't sink that low, would you?'

I thought he'd welcome the news that he'd still be the only real man in my life. 'What do you mean?'

'You want to have sex with a gay man? Have you thought about where his cock has been? Get real, Andrea!'

'Oh...w-w-well... every escort's cock has been everywhere!' I said. Chris was about to leave the room. I stopped him by saying, 'I guess sleeping with another straight man just felt wrong.'

'You think those straight escorts would fall in love with you, pursue you, and complicate things?''

I hadn't anticipated that comment.

'No offence, you're very, very attractive, any man would want you. I'm your husband, for goodness' sake! But you know what I mean? These guys, they just want your money.'

'Why don't I sleep with you?'

I didn't know if I meant what I'd just said. In my mind Lucio was a man I would a hundred per cent do it with – I wanted him like he was my destiny. His photos, the two-dimensional him, had wallpapered my brain and heart. I couldn't see anything past those teddy bear eyes, mildly golden chest and barely covered crotch. Now, face to face with my husband, reality hit. Chris didn't deserve the short end of the bargain, he shouldn't be number two.

'Sarina...' Chris said, and took my hand.

That hand, the same hand that had rescued me from an orgy pit where a swarm of flies had mercilessly feasted on me. One summer night I had surrendered completely to my then-sports-star boyfriend, stripping for half of his football team *for fun*. They were gentlemen on and off the field (my little brain said), they had boundaries, and Jim would watch out for me if any of them ever crossed the line. Little had I known, my supposed protector, the mighty Jimbo's idea of fun was pimping me to all of the boys in the room. He'd watched as Greg, Ant, Sonny, Hillsy, Rock and Ton grabbed me, tore my underwear, and toyed with me, until I managed to slide free from under Ton's body (the full-back was so drunk he couldn't pin me down) and throw myself out the window. I landed on a pile of mulch and screamed for help. There was nothing coming, apart from thuds of boys' feet landing on the same pile of mulch I was lying on. Soon enough I had felt their groping hands trying to recapture me.

Then *that hand* had pulled me up, taken me away from the web of humiliation and placed me behind his wall of solid muscle. Everybody crawled back, converged to one side and stood still. They knew who he was: an army major living next door, a mixed martial arts instructor; no Uni football players could've ever been his match.

I blinked away the memory and took a deep breath. 'I couldn't do it with any of the escorts because I realised I still wanted you.'

'Come here, you silly!' Chris hugged me.

'Why don't you want me any more, Chris?'

'Andrea... I still want you,' he said. 'Well... you know what, let's try again.'

My lips parted, my heart raced.

'I can't promise when, but soon, give me time and we'll try again.'

After staring at each other for a length of time, we sealed the commitment with our tears. It was what I'd wanted but it somewhat hurt. As soon as he fell asleep I reached for my phone:

I'm so sorry, Lucio. I can't see you. Please cancel my appointment. Enjoy the Mardi Gras. I'm sure you'll have fun. Will think of you when I see the parade.

I tiptoed out of the bedroom anticipating a response.

Hi Andie, you don't have to be sorry. May I see pic of you? I am curious. No worries if you don't want to, I understand. Wishing you a good day, Andie ;)

I smiled at Lucio's words, imagining his teddy bear eyes. I wanted to ask him: 'How can you "prefer" women if you are gay? Or are you bisexual?' (His ad hadn't seemed to indicate that was the case) 'Have you ever fallen in love with a client?'

But desiring another man, gay or straight, wasn't the right thing to do even though I was, surprisingly, deeply sad letting Lucio go. Chris had always been number one, but he wouldn't be a lover like Lucio as I'd imagined – not after what we'd been through. With my cancellation message, I had let go of my chance to be a woman again – the way my younger self had tasted, this time better and wiser, because I trusted the man I'd give my body to. On the other hand, I *had* given myself a chance to be a woman again – the way husband and wife were supposed to be, and the way I saw myself now: a mother.

Still, it was not easy letting go of something that you were sure of getting. I contemplated sending a photo of myself to Lucio. Which one? The one from a work do last week? Or maybe I should take a selfie right now in my night gown. And he might say I was beautiful.

But I simply replied:

Best not with my photo. Wish you all the best.

I came back to bed, facing Chris. I caressed his cheek. He

had passed his pre-slumber routine and now he was huffing like a whale. Then he turned around. Faintly I heard my phone beep from inside my handbag in the living room. After tossing and turning I decided to have a look.

May I ask why you changed your mind?

I smiled. Somehow I was flattered that he didn't want to let me go easily. Then I thought of Chris, my Chris. I typed:

I think I shouldn't do it. Hard to explain, but that's basically it. I'm married. I hope I haven't offended you in any way because I think you're a good guy.

I pressed 'send' too quickly. I wanted him to know how apologetic I was, and my decision had nothing to do with him, but soon I felt silly about my remark about him being a good guy.

About five minutes later, a reply:

I am not offended, I am just asking coz I was happy to have a woman as a client. I usually have men who are married like you, you know. If you change your mind you can still contact me of course.

Perhaps he thought I was worth pursuing because I was half Asian, and he was one of those people who believed Asians had a lot of money – like the landlord of my previous office and even Leanne herself, being a real estate agent whose buyers were 80% Asian. Or perhaps he was desperate for a female client – or desperate for a client full stop. But he put it all so simply – being married and engaging an escort was absolutely okay, a lot of his clients were in the same situation as me. And I believed it. My husband had actually said that, too, and I almost changed my mind. Those teddy bear eyes...I wanted them to see me.

And so I was starting to type: *Luci—*

Backspace backspace backspace backspace

As my fingers were hovering and hopping between letters without typing anything, I heard a voice from the bedroom: 'Honey?'

I quickly typed: *Thank you* and switched off my phone.

ANDREA CURTIN: UNICORNS AND RAINBOWS

6 MARCH 2016

DJ Marcellus got the 'Glitter Nation' party running with Timomatic's *Parachute*. The beat shook the ground floor of the city department store, which was filled with shoppers meandering around during the extended trading hours. The event was to promote a new line of bold, theatrical and audacious shoes to keep the spirit of Mardi Gras alive.

Half a dozen topless waiters waltzed across the floor with trays of champagne in their hands. The burly men resembled a masculine version of the Playboy bunnies – bow ties, white cuffs, black tuxedo pants – sexy and obedient. I knew them all, I helped recruit them (more like auditioning them; 72 applied, six were chosen as Satyrs and one was chosen as their master, Dionysus).

Taking up about 40 square metres, the roped area was jam-packed with the young and hip – girls, boys, women, men, straight, gay – and then there was me and Chris.

The head waiter, Jason, approached me offering more champagne. Unlike the rest, he was wearing a white tuxedo, no shirt, white bow tie, and white pants.

'Hey Jase, or should I call you Dionysus?'

'That's the weirdest thing,' Jason said. 'I'm in a tux so I'm hardly a Greek god.'

'I know. Sorry for the last-minute theme change. But you look dapper,' I said, still clinging to Chris who had been keeping quiet since we arrived. 'Jase, this is my husband Chris.'

'You two are my favourite couple!' Jason said. 'Love your dress, Andrea, and those boots! You're killing the look!' Then he glanced at Chris who was in between smiling and looking away. 'Well, I'll leave you two lovebirds alone, enjoy the party!'

Chris examined my red sequined boots. 'Do you like what you're wearing?'

'Ummm... for a one-off event like this, yeah, why not? Not the most comfortable, but fun.'

Chris nodded with disinterest. When I put my palm on his cheek, he kissed my hand. Sipping his champagne fast, he looked around, watching the waiters chatting away, flirting, serving and spreading the good time.

'They're incredibly handsome,' I teased. 'But none of them is as handsome as you, of course.'

'Does that gay escort you talked about look like them? I really hope you have better taste.'

'What?'

'Look, Andrea, I'm sorry but this is just not my thing. You stay, okay? I'm gonna go home and chill.'

'Oh, Chris... I'm sorry, I thought...'

'It's okay, it's okay. You stay. Have a good time. I'll be fine.'

'You know what, I'll come with you. Timomatic and Will.I.Am aren't exactly rocking my world, they're actually giving me a headache.'

Rap music, bass thuds and free-flowing champagne weren't exactly Chris's thing, I knew. But I thought coming to this party would help him see my world (and give him a summative answer to his question: *what do you do exactly*?) and show him we could have fun together despite what had happened. Last night we had tried to make love but it had ended with Chris sleeping on the couch, fuming, and me seeing the end of the road.

'I don't want to be humiliated like that again!' Chris had said as he was putting on his shorts.

'Chris! You're my husband, how was it humiliation? It's our first time in a long time. You're just nervous. There's nothing to be ashamed of.'

'What's next? Counselling? Sex therapy?'

'We agreed to give it a go...'

'Yeah, clearly I can't do it! You had the easy part, just lying there looking pretty...'

'You just can't stand looking at this, can you?' I chucked the sheet which Chris had tried so hard to keep on top of us the whole time. I stood up. 'You're expecting blooming teenager's breasts? A tighter pussy?'

He shook his head. His lips were pressed together, drawing a flat line on his face.

'If I'm such a turn-off, well, how about this, you don't have to touch me, we just do IVF?'

'Jesus, Andrea! Listen to yourself! *IVF?*' he said. 'I wank and off you go? I can't have another child! And I won't try again.'

'Oh, I know, you still believe we shouldn't be parents. Or *I* shouldn't be a mother. Huh? When you saw me bloody... It wasn't meant to be? Right? Isn't that what you always said?'

'Think what you like!' he said, and took a spare duvet with him downstairs.

Last night and this evening were different scenes, different conversations, but the vibe was the same. I watched Chris stepping off the party floor in a rush. I knew I'd said stupid things, but I was in a mess as much as he was. Quickly I said goodbye to the schmoozing crowd and the waiters around them, then I flashed to the department store exit to re-join my husband. Grabbing his arm, I begged, 'Chris, please, I'm sorry. I just thought it would help you chill, you know, after last night.'

'Andrea, how could that help me chill?'

'I know, silly me.'

'So, you're into that kind of thing now, huh?'

'What do you mean?'

'First a gay escort, now it's a gay party?'

'Hey! That party was my work. It was a project I accepted, and I don't discriminate!'

'Whatever.'

'Yeah, let's go home.'

Chris led the power-walk through the city streets, dodging people and cyclists. I knew he was hoping I'd lose him, knowing I was wearing a sky-high pair of platform boots. But I bit away the sting and kept at his tail. We passed shop after shop, and suddenly Chris slowed down, then stopped. His face was red, but not from the workout. A couple of ATMs had been decorated for Mardi Gras.

'Hate all this sissy bullshit! Thought it was over yesterday!' Chris yelled. 'Where are straight people supposed to draw money from?'

'They're just unicorns and rainbows!' I said of the decorative patterns. 'Take it easy, will you? You might offend some people.'

He huffed.

The walk to the carpark had never felt so long. As we were waiting at an intersection, on the other side of the road a young pregnant couple kissed each other. The man was all over her, rubbing her belly, and she was so beautiful.

'I wish you could understand,' I whispered, holding my tears.

Chris let out a heavy sigh. 'I wish *you* would understand.'

I let go of my husband's arm and walked away. Where I'd go, I didn't know – I just kept walking.

Then a yell roared from behind me. It was a voice I'd never heard, but there it was, Chris's voice, fiercely blustering at me: 'You do what you want! You want a homo dick? Fuck that bullshit gay whore! And why not have his baby, too!'

I didn't dare turn around. How many eyes were looking at me? How many hands wanted to slap his face for such a slur? One of the hands was mine. The more he mocked the boy I'd chosen, the deeper my urge; the deeper my hatred for the man I had once loved.

I still didn't know where to go, but I knew who to turn to.

Hey Lucio, Andie here. Not sure if you remember me. Well, I changed my mind again. Are you free next Saturday?

ANDREA CURTIN: THE RELATIONAL TRANSACTION

10 - 12 MARCH 2016

SIX MONTHS ago I'd helped set up Coeur Blanc Lingerie in Singapore and it created a sensation. '*Watch out, La Perla!*' the press had said. The merchandise was delicately Parisienne, the store design was exclusively Andrean. Fixtures, interiors and staff uniforms were all white, only the lighting and the merchandise gave colours to the store. For the grand opening I insisted all staff wear what they sold under their uniform, and tastefully style themselves to make sure the customers knew it ('If your garters don't show, your skirt's too long' 'Top buttons? What top buttons?'). It stirred an outrage from a women's rights group who claimed it was exploitation blah blah. But the girls themselves loved the idea, and the customers loved it even more.

The customers... back then I thought of them as 'others', like those wives of the super-rich, or female investors who commanded men in and out of the boardroom. Like Rachel Santarossa, the lady whom I worked with in Dubai and now owned a babywear empire in the Middle East. Not me, no. But now, with a man to impress, I *was* one of those customers.

Thankfully Leanne was with me, otherwise I would've told

myself my plain black bra and briefs were good enough for Lucio.

We declined assistance when the boutique lady approached us.

I meandered along the sparse display units, going from one island to another. The lighting was focused, and so was the boutique lady. Every time I picked up an item, I'd feel a spotlight shining on me: *oh, she wants to wear it to please her husband,* or perhaps the lady had a scandalous mind: *it's all for her secret lover*.

'So... what should I be? Naughty? Demure? Sporty?' I asked Leanne.

'Just be yourself, hon!' said Leanne. 'Now, you've found your man, the next thing is to claim your freedom. You don't need to pretend you're perfect. Although I'm sure you are! But you know what I mean; you don't need to please anyone but yourself. Those guys won't make you feel bad even if you fart in their face.'

I burst out laughing, attracting the attention of the boutique lady. 'I don't know what myself is! What's me?'

'Are you that damaged?'

'That's it! I'm damaged!'

'Shoosh!'

'Damaged, horny, lost...'

'From what you've told me he seems like a pro. Not a part-time newbie who doesn't know how to make a conversation, just goes in, pumps and bye.'

'Have you got that sort?'

'Once. Before I knew Amanda. You get a bad apple every now and then, just like all things in life,' she said. 'Hey, show me his photos.'

'No!'

'How are his assets?'

'Well, there were no naked photos of him. They were all tasteful! No OTT butt exposé or distorted close-up of his cock.'

'Did he say his size?'

'180cm, 70kg.'

Leanne took a pair of panties and formed a bulge behind the crotch with her fist. 'Hmm?' she winked.

Once more the boutique lady gave us her full attention.

'Why does his size matter?' I said.

'You're paying him for his cock, don't you wanna know? I won't take less than an eight-inch.'

'A man can have a twelve-inch for all I care. If he doesn't have anything else to offer then that's a waste of a foot-long.'

'Well, all right. Let's see how this one goes.'

'Now... give me ideas!'

'How about these?'

'Too dominatrixy.'

'Huh... true. Laces and eyelets...' Leanne said browsing through the fixtures. 'These?'

'Not bad.' I took the purple satin bra and panties set from Leanne's hand and imagined myself in them. 'It's a bit too conservative, no?'

'Conservative? Woohoo! Never thought you'd say that. Okay...'

'I like these,' I said, showing Leanne my find: white, delicately lacy, low cut.

'Wow... yeah... that is sexy. Not sure if you're going to look like a bride though?'

'A bride? Geez!' I frowned. 'Look: no rubber, no clips, no sliders. All lace. Sultry?'

Leanne softly hummed *Like a Virgin*.

'Shut up!' I said.

'Put them on.'

I disappeared into the changing room.

And my friend continued humming the song. 'What's his name?' she asked from the other side of the curtain.

'Let's just call him L.'

'That's not very romantic.'

I kept quiet while putting on the ensemble. I did feel like a virgin, but in an erotic way – like I'd been saving myself for someone special.

'You done? Let me see!'

I came out fully clothed.

'Eh? You didn't like them?'

I gave her a pouty smile. 'I want *him* to be the first to see.'

'Welcome to paradise!' Leanne said.

I HAD ARRIVED at Lucio's apartment massively early and now I was lingering in the lobby, in front of the watchful eyes of the concierge girls (the building was partly serviced apartments). When it all got too much I decided to let Lucio know I was here, even though I was still early. I walked out – past the first glass doors to the mailbox area, then another set of glass doors to the intercom.

'Come on up, Andie. Level 12.'

I didn't say anything. I was looking at my reflection in the glass doors and soon *Like a Virgin* played in my head.

Why had I chosen a white dress, too?

I looked so wide!

Mirror... where's a mirror when you need one? As far as I remembered I hadn't looked like that when I left home: the long-sleeve chiffon-cotton dress hung perfectly, hugging my waist, flaring just below my knee. I chose stilettos to give myself that extra height so I didn't look like Humpty Dumpty.

Glass distortion, I assured myself as the doors slid open. A view to the lobby slowly divided my reflection before wiping it completely. Once more I passed the concierge girls.

I stopped in front of a wall of mirrors: *Am I beautiful enough for him?*

Well, *he* had to be beautiful for me. I was paying him for that.

Since that Mardi Gras weekend, my shower time had doubled. Not because I was scrubbing for longer, but because of my post-shower mirror stare. Standing naked, I'd ask which part of me turned Chris off? My face? Boobs? Tummy? Butt? Thighs? Or was it just his fear of getting me pregnant that overwhelmed him? One step at a time, he'd suggested. But I'd wanted it all at once – sex, pleasure, the divinity of husband and wife, a baby. I was so thrilled by his 'try again' proposition that I'd forgotten to ask what *he* had wanted.

That was my mistake. But why had he pressed his lips when he'd looked at me naked? It drew a flat line on his face for half a second, followed by his eyes narrowing. He might as well puke. Then he smiled, and he smiled. His hand hurriedly switched off the bedside lamp as he lowered himself onto me. His kisses were plenty but quick. He rushed to cover us with the sheet before he loosed his boxer shorts. He'd tried. Oh he'd tried. But he couldn't get it up.

Alban and Jake, had they really been good actors when they'd said I was beautiful? That their cocks rose instantly the moment they laid eyes on me? How about those flirts and advances that came my way from business associates, random men at restaurants, guys on flights?

It was just Chris. My Chris who no longer desired me. One step at a time – to where, really?

Once again I'd abandoned my hope to be a mother. But it didn't mean I had to come out empty-handed. Lucio, the man of my dreams, would please me like there was no tomorrow. And I intended to be as irresistible as his best male client was, if not more. Or I could aim higher: to be more desirable than his real boyfriend. Escorts mixed business with pleasure, not with love. *Let's see about that.* I would find that spot in his body, in his heart, in his mind, wherever, in whatever way, to make him want me more than anything. Venus flytrap talk? Perhaps, but this time I was trying to attract a bee. If a gay man, let alone an escort, was ever to fall in love with me, what would Chris say?

From the reflection in the mirror I saw the concierge girls staring at me. I had no idea how long I'd been standing here. I marched to the elevator. A toned, skinny girl rushed from the entrance, calling for me to hold the elevator. Quite tall for an Asian, although still shorter than me; she looked to be Thai or Vietnamese.

'Thanks!' she... or rather... *he* said. He was a pretty ladyboy in short shorts and tight tee, with a fake Chanel bag. He could've been a dancer, but from the way he pouted his lips and placed his hand on his bum, dare I say, he was likely an escort. 'Have a good day!' he said as he strutted out of the elevator on level 6.

On level 12 the elevator doors opened. I almost didn't want to step out. But my uneasiness was soon replaced by warmth when I saw a handsome face peeping out from the third door down. I wished I'd had to walk further to his unit, but I took it as a nice surprise.

His facial features looked exactly the same as in his photos, but boy, he was a lot skinnier, *a lot*. I didn't think his photos were touched up. Maybe they were old photos, or maybe he'd been ill? Or maybe it was just a case of the camera adding five kilos.

'Andie?'

'I'm here!' I said cheerfully. I noticed he'd buttoned his shirt wrong and his hair was damp, sticking out on the right side of his crown while the rest of it was flat.

'Yes, you are...' Lucio said studying my face. He paused.

Isn't he supposed to say something? Nice to meet you, or you're beautiful?

But he stayed paused. His lips trembled. Had he said anything else right now, his words would've come out choppy.

And he didn't even give me a hug or a peck on the cheek.

I flashed a lopsided smile. *What's his game?*

Lucio smiled back and invited me in to sit in an armchair in the living room.

I crossed my legs, put my bag on my lap and took out a white envelope. The neckline of my dress plunged as I bent down to put the envelope on the coffee table. Earlier I'd sprayed the envelope with my perfume.

'You know the trade,' Lucio said staring at the envelope, then my hand.

'I've been with a couple.'

His face went slack. He glanced towards my eyes, but quickly stared back at my hand. 'Lucky them. I wish I was your first,' he said.

My preconception said these working men would do and say anything to make their clients feel good. But was Lucio trying to act innocent? Or be cutely clueless? Unlikely. No escort would've acted lost and disappointed like that. Was he put off by me? If so, I would've thought he'd start being excessively cheerful and full of praise.

Finally he stopped avoiding my eyes. For a minute we stared at each other.

So this was what it was like being with a really young guy. Part of me felt I was taking advantage of him. He was probably doing this so he could finish Uni, or to simply live. But he was offering a service; perfectly legal, perfectly justifiable. And along the way I was helping him with his education, or life.

'Do you want me to have a shower?' I asked.

'Hmm? Urrmm... no, no.' He shook his head. 'Just relax.

Make yourself comfortable,' he said, his eyes wandered aimlessly again. Too early in the morning (those eyebags!)? Boyfriend trouble?

'Would you like a drink?' he offered.

'What do you have?'

He paused as he stared at the fridge from where he stood. 'Italian beer?'

I chuckled. 'No thanks.'

Silence, again.

'What's your limit?' I asked.

He flushed.

'With you, no limit,' he said. For the first time I saw ease in him. 'You really know the trade. What's *your* limit?'

'No spanking.'

'Right...'

'No... back door stuff.'

'Right...' Lucio said and walked behind me. He pulled my hair behind my ears, massaged my shoulders and pressed his face against my neck. 'Anything else?' he whispered.

His Adam's apple vibrated against my skin. I curled towards the source of the vibration – and he swiped his lips on my ear lobe. He wrapped his arm loosely around my neck. I cradled his right bicep between my ear and shoulder, rubbing my cheek against his flawless skin.

'No... I think that's all,' I softly replied.

'You smell good,' Lucio whispered.

And he smelled of something – not a cologne or deodorant, it was his body scent. Thousand Islands dressing? Not quite. Cider? Maybe. I couldn't decide if I liked it, but it made me want to taste that smell.

He unzipped my dress far enough to open the neckline, then pushed both sleeves down simultaneously, exposing my shoulders and the top of my chest. I bloomed; not a Venus flytrap, but a white lily who'd seen the sun for the first time. Now the 'sun' was gently squeezing my breasts. I looked up, Lucio's head was slightly above me, which meant his chest was right behind me. I closed my eyes imagining that chest... Why imagine? It was right there...

My lips were looking for it but the backrest was shielding his flesh.

Still occupied with my quest to blindly find his chest, I didn't realise Lucio was now in front of me. He presented himself plainly. The smoothness, the innocence. Every now and then his body scent drifted past me. It could take me forever to figure out what it was, and to finally taste it.

How long is an hour?

Before I ran out of time, before anything changed, I grabbed what he offered. I used all my fingers, and my lips, to explore his bare, honest torso.

'You're my first,' I confessed. 'I didn't do it with the others.'

'Oh...' He squatted to meet my eyes. 'Lucky me...'

'Be gentle, please...'

Yes, I wanted him to be gentle because of who he was. He wasn't made to play rough. And with him I had become fragile, too. I didn't want Spartacus. I wanted his twink heart, to guard and foster, so that it'd never break.

'I will take good care of you,' he said and guided me to stand up. He unzipped my dress all the way this time. The skirt fanned around my feet. He pressed my hips then slowly moved his right hand up along my spine. When it arrived at my neck he pulled me to him and we effortlessly kissed.

Lucio gave in to my embrace. I could reach the whole of him, there were no muscles resisting, no wall of meat buffering my advancing body. He lifted me up. I flung my arms around his neck as my legs hooked around his waist. His defined hip bones poked my thighs. I looked at him, and he responded with a reassuring stare: *I will take good care of you.*

Once I was lying on the bed, Lucio delicately took off my heels. With my foot resting on his shoulder he rubbed my calf and thigh – so attentively, as if he were polishing a precious statue. He squeezed my ankle and gave me a little glance, asking for permission, but he went ahead and kissed my toes anyway. The tickle almost made me kick his mouth. Tittering, he went on. And just as I was about to smack his face, he stopped and let me settle.

The interlude marked the end of playtime. He was now crawling on top of me like a leopard on a hunt. Soon the prey would be in his claws, but—

He looked at me, not in admiration or lust, it was doubt. I hovered my fingers over his face. To the left of his nose I found a scar – it was like a star had been carved out of his cheek. A feeling burst in my heart but I was too afraid to articulate. Silently I promised him something absurd, irrational and ridiculous.

I must've caught his attention. Suddenly he stripped himself with conviction, then peeled the remaining layers from me. His palms felt like magnets to my nipples. He kissed me generously, more than any man ever had. Then he lay low. Nipple on nipple, crotch on crotch, he rubbed himself against me. Between the comforting moves he dropped his weight on me, forcing me to gasp. When he let me breathe again. I couldn't help open my legs wide, inviting him to enter. But he put his finger on my lips and softly shook his head. Instead he squeezed my breasts as if trying to make my erect nipples point even higher. Then he sucked them.

My knees jerked, my legs flexed restlessly. Lucio pinned my thighs in place. Now I had nowhere to release the rising heat, so it stayed within me, stretching my skin, tingling my nerves.

Lucio finally pulled himself away from me. He watched me huffing and puffing. Satisfied, he kissed my lips. His fingers weaved through my hair, caressing me like a lover. My stretched skin eased, my tingling nerves settled. It was as if I was sharing the trapped sensation with him, and we both reached the equilibrium between crazy and calm. Was it how lovemaking was supposed to be? Instead of sprinting all the way, we paced our hike, and before reaching the peak, we let ourselves roll back half way down.

I asked Lucio a silent 'what's next?'. He looked at me intently. He put his finger on my lips again, and this time he slid down until his chin touched the line where my inner thighs met. He nudged me open. Then he bowed low. I jolted when I felt his tongue. He looked up. Seeing my smile he continued. The lapping action I had expected was never forthcoming. Instead he probed me and used my own wetness to help him tease my clit. I writhed and made him lose the spot. But he came back and found it again, and again. I scrambled to find something to hold on, the best I could do was clutching the sheet. As I climaxed his hands slipped under my clawing fingers like silk, disarming me to open my palms to him. Our fingers interlocked. We were one, and he hadn't even entered me.

Lucio crawled up beside me. He caressed my hair for a while – quite a while that I relaxed and thought that was it. Then he took a deep breath and crawled on top of me. My breasts were squeezed, my belly pressed. The restriction – such an arousal. He moved his hips down and let his cock drop between my parting thighs. His cock head kissed my pussy, and I let him in. His coral blue eyes kept looking at me; when I tried to escape, he followed me, questioning. And I kept replying with my own eyes: I was fine. With every visual communication, he moved deeper. He was gentle as he had promised.

He smiled sweetly. 'I'll make you happy. I will make you remember.'

Before I could process his remark, he pushed in with one long glide until his pelvis couldn't move any further. I arched my back but my hips didn't shift an inch. This man had more than turned me on, he made me feel weightless, beautiful, natural. *How?* Did I just strike it lucky that I'd hired the right man for the job this time?

With Chris, it used to be good, great, I thought, but not like this. Lucio wasn't my teenage dream, this man was my reality. I had fantasised him as my destiny, now the destiny was in my hands. I'd suddenly grown up; just with one lesson – this was what making love should've been.

What would Chris say about this?

Chris... my Chris who... *No!* No more of that flatline. This was my moment and no one could ruin it.

A cold kiss woke me. I shouted something, my throat felt dry.

Lucio's face was so close to me, so close. He begged me to look at him.

Teddy bear eyes... Tell me this isn't an act.

'I'm here,' he said – almost crying.

'Lucio...'

And I could look into his eyes without inhibition. This man had filled more than just a sexual void; he had freed me. I'd told Chris before our New Caledonian cruise that my life was like a dark room. Right now I was still in that dark room, but it was lit by the star carved out of Lucio's cheek. With him it felt legitimate. I didn't owe him anything, it was fair. It was my right to be pleasured by a man. And this man knew women... or he knew me, at least, and despite his initial fear, he seemed to enjoy it too, immensely. His irises looked smudged, his eyelids drooped. He certainly hadn't looked like that when we started.

I cried out as he entered me once more. His presence had replaced my grief, the union of our bodies had given honesty back into my heart. It might not last, but for the moment he was every bit the manly figure I had unknowingly longed for.

I almost relaxed. But when I opened my eyes, ready to wrap up the action, my man was still moving, ready to go inside me again.

'Don't tell me you've had enough,' he teased.

I just breathed out rhythmic silences. *Have I?* I could've gone on, but I wasn't used to this; every single thing I'd expected was realised – and he was willing to give even more. Perplexing. No outcome, in business or pleasure, had ever been 100%. But this... this was beyond a perfect ten.

I closed my eyelids hard. I couldn't help crying, although I didn't exactly know why.

'Andie...' Lucio whispered. His hands still held on tight to mine. 'I'm here for *you*. Have I done something... or have I hurt you?'

I slipped my palm away from his grip and put my arms around his shoulders. My upper body lifted, halfway between letting go and hanging on. I swore his eyes were teary. I swore he wanted me. So I pulled him to me, I seized him so nobody else could have him. He was no longer a series of photographs wallpapering me. He had gone inside my heart, without knocking, and he dwelled in it. A moment ago my head hadn't dared to articulate that absurd and ridiculous promise; it could now: 'You're the only one I'll ever desire.' With what he had given me, it felt like a betrayal to make love to another man. And I almost said it in his ear. But it was only sobs that he heard.

'Turn around,' Lucio said. 'I'll give you a massage.'

'No,' I sighed. 'Just lie with me.'

As my tears dripped onto his bare chest, I stroked his

pectoral muscles, almost scratching them. He in return ran his fingers through my hair.

If something is too good to be true, it probably is. This happiness with Lucio – *what's the catch?*

I wondered, and wondered, and I could find none. After a few breaths I fell asleep.

When I woke up Lucio was still lying next to me, watching me.

I sat up. Time.

'Quarter to eleven,' Lucio said when I started looking for my watch.

'Oh... I thought it was later than that,' I said.

'Is that a good thing?'

I smiled. 'Having more time with you *is* a good thing.'

'Really?' he said, caressing my cheek.

'What if I slept in? Would you have woken me up?'

'Nnnooo. I would've charged you overtime,' he said casually.

I laughed. 'Happens a lot, I suppose, someone losing track of time because they're too... umm... what's the word... intoxicated?'

'A lot of them, yeah. I'm the time keeper. Usually I leave it up to them, whether they pay extra or not. I don't want to rip them off.'

I swung my feet out of bed. 'Gonna have a shower.'

'Let me hold you one more time,' he said.

I took his hands and pulled him up. He hugged me and breathed into my skin, from my belly right up to my chest, then he let me go.

In the bathroom I grinned victoriously. They told me money couldn't buy happiness. What total bull.

And those same people might argue that what I had now was not happiness; it was an illusion, true happiness lies within you... *Well, fuck that!* Happiness, today, was Lucio letting me see that star in the dark; and he didn't even know it. It had a price. It could be short-lived. But at this very moment happiness was in my hands.

I mused over Lucio's body lotion – the twin tubes covering *that part* on his photo. Molton Brown – the brand of choice to many gay men, I'd read. How could he know so much about women if he was gay? I opened it to sniff – he wasn't wearing it this morning.

Now I had seen all of him, but life was still too unpredictable. If this was to be my only encounter with him, at least I would take with me *his* mysterious scent – not some man-made potion they put out on the shelves. I still couldn't decide if I liked it, but I wanted it, and it would stay with me as a memento.

FREDERICO LOWE: ANDIE

12 MARCH 2016

THE PAST HOUR and a half had been a blur. I remembered rushing to look as perfect as I could in 20 minutes after I'd overslept, then the intercom rang. She took forever to come up, then I saw her face. Inside my head there was this ping-pong match – should I do it? Could I do it? And then I smelled her perfume – a wonderful time machine. When I was a boy on a dusty Roman street, her body had blanketed me, and I had felt safe for the first time. Now I was a man the scent provoked me in a way no other woman, or man, had done.

Andie was in the shower now. Her handbag was on the armchair. I could look for her ID, but somehow I didn't want to. In time I might find out.

She was all dressed up when she emerged from the bathroom. None of my female clients *ever* came to me wearing a long-sleeve dress. But the dress was perfect on her, she looked mysterious in it (beautiful, too).

My task to please her was over. As she packed her bag I paused to take in who 'my client' really was. So her name was Andie. It suited her, although I wasn't sure it was her real name.

No more boy's cut; her brown hair flowed softly to her shoulders. I couldn't decide if I preferred the original her, or the current her. She looked great, but she was missing her masculine side. And she wasn't Chinese, she was Eurasian, that was why her eyes were so big. Was it her dad or her mum who was European? Could she be half Italian like me? She'd said *stai bene*.

Before she headed to the door I caught her hand. 'Let me hold you – just once more.'

She let me.

I rolled up her sleeves. No sign of the arm muscles she'd shown wearing that singlet. But they were still the arms that had protected me – a filthy boy, a thief – and she got hurt for it. Yes, she bled for me. I remembered the gash. Why she had done that, I might never understand. Not even my own father would've protected me like she had. That arsehole, what did he know about protection? He would let other kids beat me up at school without reason. '*Essere un uomo*!' But I wasn't a fighter. The fists had never made me a man.

I ran my fingers along her skin, up and down, up and down. They had been a stranger's arms, a tourist's arms, some woman's arms. Now they had become *her* arms. I looked for the spot where that gash would've been – and kissed it. It really upset me that I still couldn't thank her when she was right here in front of me, in my arms.

I breathed into her. And she whispered my name – the one that I advertised. She said it so beautifully, her full lips puckered pronouncing the end of it. I imagined how it would've been, hearing her sigh 'Frederico...'

What if this was the last time I ever saw her?

I grabbed her waist gently and touched her face. She took a deep breath, then thought for a second. I'd caught the same expression on her face earlier when she was in the lounge chair.

Damn! What did I smell like? In that 20-minute mad rush I'd been in two minds about putting on my Molton Brown or spraying Calvin Klein, but in the end I hadn't put anything on. Perhaps I'd been sweating too much after the ED pill from last night. Damn!

But she simply breathed into my neck, up to my cheek, then kissed me on the lips.

I palmed the back of her head. She obliged to my pressing. She sucked my lips and I felt her tongue in my mouth. And she would've felt my growing dick against her belly. She had changed since I first encountered her. It was still her, but a better her. I didn't need her muscles, I didn't need her protection; it was my turn now to give her safety.

We withdrew, we panted. There was barely a millimetre between our faces. My palm was still on her.

'Thank you for taking care of me,' she said, and slipped away.

What sort of persuasion would I attempt now?

In the end I refrained from going after her, getting in her way and demanding an answer as to whether I'd see her again. She couldn't know who I was, not now. I hoped I had done enough to make her want me more, to make her remember me – not as a boy, but as a man.

I reached for the envelope on the coffee table: $450, $100 more than my rate. I smiled, not for the money, but the smell of her perfume. I *would* see her again.

ANDREA CURTIN: THE AFTERMATH

14 MARCH 2016

I COULD FEEL myself putting on my Cookie Monster's look – eyes as round as they could be, pupils pulled in, almost cross-eyed.

'Huh?' Leanne smirked. She looked like a cookie.

My lips pouted, then parted, then shut.

'So?' she said impatiently.

I fidgeted. The mint-cucumber water rippled in the jug in front of me. 'Yeah, yeah, it was good,' I said, nodding quickly.

'You can do better than that!'

I locked my shoulders together. 'It was brilliant!'

'Wow! So he was as handsome as your dream prince?'

'He was. It was like... he knew me.'

'Those guys are clairvoyants, I tell ya,' Leanne said. 'How big is he?'

'What? Umm... I don't know. I didn't see it.'

'What were you doing? It wasn't just dinner, was it?''

'No! We did it! Well, he was... I couldn't take my eyes off of his. He has captivating eyes – blue, deep, a bit... I don't know, daunting. I just couldn't help looking at them. Before I knew it he was already, you know.... When I woke up he had his boxers on.'

'You fell asleep?'

'He was cuddly.'

'It was safe, right?'

I thought so. He did say it was safe – in his ad. How careless of me not to check!

'I guess you're the emotional type and not that into cocks?'

'Why? His organs are not the most important thing but I like cocks as much as you do. If you really need to know I shall observe it next time!'

'Aha... that was actually my next question,' Leanne said. 'When are you seeing him next?'

'Dunno.'

'Don't you need to book in advance?'

'Do I?'

'He's not that busy, is he?'

'I don't know. I don't have his diary,' I said. 'Okay. Next week. How about that?'

'My, my, he was *that* good, was he?'

'Eww... I don't want to look desperate,' I said. 'How often do you see those guys?'

'Once a month, or if I get lonely, once a fortnight.'

I watched the water jug, counting the mint leaves. His smell, his touch, and *that kiss* before I'd left... I couldn't wait a month, not even a fortnight.

'Look at me,' Leanne said.

'Hm?' My eyes were still on the mint leaves... five, six, seven...

'Look at me!'

I did.

'Something happened...' she said.

'Yeah, I fucked someone.'

'Since when did that make you put on a funny look?'

'What?'

'When we sat down, you looked at me like Bugs Bunny.'

'Can't I be happy for once?'

'Happy, yes. But... never mind. I guess good sex makes people crazy in different ways.'

I looked at my friend intensely.

'Remember it was just sex,' she said.

'Of course!'

I looked at a text from Sophie. 'I'd better get back. This Singaporean client is really freaking out about everything. When things are on time, he's freakin' out. When things are a bit late, he's freakin' out. When things are really late he'll go ballistic!'

On the way to my office I texted Lucio: *13th Apr, 2 p.m. Are you available?*

ANDREA CURTIN: CYCLES AND ANNIVERSARIES

13 APRIL 2016

THE SMELL COMING from the kitchen filled me with guilt – I knew what that smell meant. From halfway down the stairs I could see the dining table: a bowl of mixed berries, two plates of buttermilk pancakes with cream on the side and cutlery wrapped in red napkins – all spread beautifully. And then there was Chris.

He was busy wiping the kitchen bench. Since that Mardi Gras weekend we had barely talked. He'd been away, I'd been away, and we hadn't slept in the same room. Why did he even bother?

'Happy anniversary,' Chris said when I joined him. We gave each other a quick peck on the lips. He knew I'd forgotten. The 13th of April had slipped my mind many times before.

'You're in a rush?'

I smiled. 'No, it can wait. Let's have breakfast,' I said, and put my phone on silent.

'A historic breakfast,' said Chris, recalling his first ever cooked breakfast with me eighteen years ago. He smiled and smiled.

And I broke down sobbing in front of my plate of pancakes. That Mardi Gras night he'd smiled to mask his disgust of me, now he smiled to mask his sadness. What were we celebrating exactly?

Chris came to my side and leaned on my shoulder. I forced myself to stop crying. I cut a piece of pancake and put it in my mouth.

'It's still as good as ever,' I said.

Chris walked back to his chair.

'Are you busy tonight?' he asked.

'Ummm... no, I shouldn't be.'

'I booked a table at Verve for 7 o'clock. Is that okay with you?'

'That's nice,' I said. 'Of course I'm okay with it. It's our anniversary.'

My phone flashed missed calls relentlessly but I kept my attention on Chris. 'One of my friends said they served the best seafood linguine.'

'If you have to go, that's okay,' said Chris.

I hesitantly finished my last pancake and gave Chris another peck on the cheek.

'Where have you been?' Sophie said to me. 'Jude was cursing and swearing like crazy! The mannequins that came this morning were the wrong size.'

'What did you say?'

'I rang Troy and asked for redelivery.'

'And?'

'Everything is under control.'

'Good. You're brilliant, Soph!'

'For the opening of BB's at Bondi Junction, Lauren wondered if you could come over and supervise the installation of the feature wall. She needs it to be ready before 4 o'clock.'

'What?'

'Actually, she wanted you to *create* the feature wall. She wouldn't trust anyone else to do it.'

'I'm not painting!' I said. I did a one-off painting job at Lauren's first shop but that had been because the painter had botched it and they only had two hours before the guests arrived. It was must-do damage control at the time. On any other day I would help out (Lauren was my first client and she had hooked me up with a lot of big businesses), but not today – *not this afternoon*. 'Tell Lauren to trust Siva to do it. I'm busy this afternoon. And I have to leave early tonight. It's our anniversary and Chris has booked a table.'

'Oh! Happy anniversary!' said Sophie.

I smiled for formality. I really wished Chris hadn't. That fancy restaurant. What would we talk about?

Right now my heart kept asking me if it was 3 o'clock yet. I would cry in Lucio's arms – the tears I'd stopped in front of my plate of pancakes. I would tell him what Chris had done this morning, and what he had done on that Mardi Gras weekend. I would ask him if I was wrong not to want my husband. Lucio would say it was okay, wouldn't he? Out of any day, on the 13th of April, I'd rather be with my escort than my husband.

Suddenly my stomach pulsed. I rushed to the ladies' room.

Shit!

I'd never really paid attention to my monthly cycle since we stopped trying for a baby. Even with Chris's recent hint that he would try again, it'd never come to a point where I felt the need to track my period. It came when it came. But with Lucio in the picture I would have to now.

I came back to Sophie dismally. 'What the heck, tell Lauren I'll be there at about two.'

'Cool. I'll let her know.'

L, sorry... something came up. Can't meet.

And I rang Chris to cancel dinner. 'I'm not feeling well.'

'No worries,' he said. 'I'll see you at home then.'

CHRIS WASN'T around when I got home. I kept myself awake to wait for him. Maybe I'd say sorry for cancelling dinner, maybe I'd just smile at him and he would understand. On my third can of energy drink:

L, can I call you?

And we spoke for hours. I told him what Chris had done this morning. I cried – the tears I'd stopped in front of my plate of pancakes. And I told Lucio what Chris had done that Mardi Gras weekend.

'You are beautiful, Andie. If he doesn't know that, he's blind.'

And I asked him if I was wrong not to want my husband.

'Not wanting your husband is just a feeling, Andie. There is no right or wrong. I think your husband loves you. He just doesn't know how to show it.'

And I begged Lucio to kiss me. He did. I could hear him breathe through the phone. He felt so close I could feel his lips. Then he played with me. He said for the first time a woman's body aroused him, like there was no room for anything else in him but me. My breasts, he said, were the most beautiful things he'd ever held, and having them in his hands felt like he was holding my heart.

'Lucio...'

'Andie, I'm close.'

'Give it to me...'

I clutched my phone, my arms outstretched.

And I felt his cum smearing my cervix. I came too. Next month I would be late. Then I would start to show... then...

It couldn't happen – even if he had been here with me. Something would be waiting around the corner – to crush me, to tell me it wasn't meant to be. 'Why?' I cried. Lucio asked if I was okay. He kept calling my name like he was about to lose me. But I continued crying, moaning at reality, and asking why.

When I woke up it was already sunrise and my phone battery had run flat. When my phone came back to life I saw a text from Lucio:

You have every right to be loved. You're beautiful, you're incredible.

I checked the downstairs bedroom and there was no sign of Chris.

L, I'll pay you next time I see you.

FREDERICO LOWE: ANDIE

27 APRIL 2016

ANDIE CAME out of the elevator. That face, those big brown eyes. What she had revealed in her call that night had given me hope. If I made the right move, she *could* be mine. Someday. Not now.

I greeted her at the door wearing only a pair of low-cut jeans, showing the waistband of my black brief shorts. I didn't want to waste time unbuttoning a shirt. Today I wanted to drive at a different speed; as soon as she arrived, I'd make her mine – only if it felt right. As always, I would follow her lead.

And Andie unashamedly responded to my hint. The door hadn't even closed behind her, and she glued her hands to my chest. With a devilish grin, she played with my pecs as if trying to extract the almost non-existent muscle. She smelled me, then she cocked her head and looked at me. I had a feeling she didn't like my Molton Brown.

Her phone rang.

'You're a busy woman,' I said.

'Sorry, I should've switched it off.'

'Naughty!' I picked her up and carried her to bed.

She giggled.

'But you're special, you know that?' I caressed her face.

She just sighed.

'So you chose red this time?' I said, commenting on her dress.

'Yeah... you prefer white?'

'Anything on you, I prefer.'

Andie gazed at me as I took off my pants and briefs. It was her turn to be stripped, but the fabric clung tightly to her body, no zip, impossible to take off unless I ripped it apart. What was an escort to do? I rolled her skirt up to her hips, pulled down her lacy underwear and lay on top of her. I liked the idea of making love to her half-naked.

Her face was radiant. She smelled different today, same perfume, but her body smelled different. Her parted lips told me she was ready.

Her head popped up just as I prepared to enter.

'What's wrong?' I said catching her squinting at my crotch. I knew she meant to be discreet, but she failed miserably.

'Safe, always,' I said taking my hand off my dick, showing her the rolled base of the condom.

And she blushed. She turned her head to escape my gaze, but at the same time she still tried to look at me. In the end she just squirmed. In my eyes she was a divine being, but this was a moment of her being so human. It felt so simple. We were just two people doing silly things. I wanted this simplicity to last forever, but back to reality, Andie, *my client*, needed a little something to feel back at ease. I reached into my bedside drawer. 'If you don't trust me, we can use this.' I swung a dildo at her face.

She instantly blushed again. 'No! No! Put that away!'

I persisted with the veiny, bulbous rubber, it was now almost touching her lips. 'You never used one of these?'

'No! Put it awaaay!'

She used my chest as cover to escape the sight of the toy. 'I want *you*. I want your nice seven-inch tool,' she said.

'Yeah?' I nibbled gently on her ear.

She called my name, the one I advertised. With that I scooped her up and carried her like a belly pack. I pinned her against the wall and forced myself into her. Her eyes were burning. Her legs clung to my waist so tightly, I could only move inside her, nowhere else.

I turned around. The wall was now a metre away from me and I was her only support.

'*Llévame*,' I said in between my heavy breaths. Romantic to say, and aren't French words supposed to be a turn-on for women? A pair of ballet dancers might've invented it. *Carry me,* she said. I would bear Andie's weight and carry her anywhere she wished. But at the moment, I kept telling myself not to drop her.

As Andie's body slid down bit by bit, I suspended her with all my might. She clung to my shoulders, giving me a chance to propel her up and drive myself into her further.

Push after push, I started to regret my experiment, but the sight of my woman getting totally intoxicated, oblivious to my struggle to keep everything together, gave me that extra rigour – enough for the final stretch.

And I released myself. In those few seconds she felt as light as a feather. And I surprised the both of us with my howling as I came. With the very last drop of energy I laid her gently on the bed, then hurled myself down next to her.

That had been an impossible position; I shouldn't have had enough upper body strength to pull it off, but I had Andie – my better half, then and now, in Rome and here, in my escort world and in my real world. I was glad it was her who had helped me get there; although my excessive puffing eventually forced me to admit openly it was my first time.

'Never before?' Andie said in disbelief.

'You're the only client I could lift like that.'

A cheeky laugh. 'Well, I can't imagine you doing that with another man. But another woman? Come on! Are they all bigger than me?'

'I don't talk about my clients with a client.'

'Oh, come on!'

'No, no.'

'All right!' she said and played with my nipples. 'I guess even for a stud, there is always a first time for everything.'

For a while I enjoyed the gentleness of her fingertips. It sent me to a different state of relaxation – somewhere in between sleepiness and an afterglow. When she pressed harder it was a hit right to my heart... but I quickly cut short my own blissful moment. I said, 'Hey... I'm supposed to please you, not the other way around.'

And she said sweetly, 'It pleases me, playing with you.'

I took her hand and kissed it. I turned sideways, locked my eyes on hers while my fingers crawled down her crotch. I was expecting her hunger to show again, and I would give her more, although I was still spent.

Secretly I was thankful when she told me she wanted to talk.

'We have time, don't we?' she said, continuing to play with my chest as we lied flat on our backs, side by side.

'Of course.' I smiled, giving the floor to her.

Strangely, at the same time the urge to enter her again overwhelmed me. I nudged myself up. She bit her lips and opened her thighs wide, giving me a peak. I wanted to get close but her knee kept me in place. Dammit, Andie! She was pink and in full bloom and I couldn't wait to be in her warmth. But I stayed true to my principles. If it was a conversation that she was after, then a conversation she'd get.

She giggled at my defeated face as I slid down to lie flat again. Then she stretched like a cat.

'Ugh...' I groaned as she unexpectedly sat on my belly.

'So, where do you hang out?' she asked. She slid backwards so she was sitting on my thighs. Then she bent forward to rub her lower stomach lightly against my pubic hair.

Usually when a woman client wanted a conversation, she'd ask if I was bisexual, or if I had a boyfriend, which I'd avoid answering by saying, 'It's complicated. Believe me, you wouldn't want to know.'

Rubbing her thighs, I responded: 'A few places in Oxford Street, Kings Cross, and sometimes The Nest, at Potts Point. But compared to other escorts that I know, I don't go out that much.'

'The Nest? Sounds very... birdy...'

'What's that look?'

'No, no. Just an interesting name, that's all.'

'It's very exclusive. There's no ad, no listing. You can't search for it. You won't find it on your own. You have to be invited to be a member. A member can take a guest, but the process is long and there's no guarantee you will get in. And you can only go there as a guest once.'

'Oh... right,' she said. 'I might've heard of it, from somewhere...'

'A good girl like you should never have heard of it.'

'Is it a strip club? Kinky, fetish kinda strip club?'

I smiled, half-nodding and half-shrugging.

'Is it a gay club?'

'Well... yes, but I've never heard that straight people are banned. I've bumped into a few ladies, and they *seemed* straight. As for the guys, no, all gay,' I said. 'And, no, I won't take you there.'

I could see her picturing man in cages hanging from the ceiling, cocks and balls flapping, bulb-like posteriors swaying.

She rolled herself off me and lay back down. 'Do you really have high libido?'

I chuckled. 'You don't ask a man that!'

'I can ask you anything, right? I'm paying you,' she said gleefully.

There is a myth that male escorts have unusually high libidos – otherwise how would they get it up on every occasion? She'd probably heard or read that in her search.

'I'm normal,' I replied, 'or I'd like to think that I am.'

Now I asked myself that question, because at this moment I wanted to be inside her, pumping, pleasing her – and myself – constantly. And there was nothing normal about it.

'Look at you! You just want to do it... yeah? Bang bang!' she said.

Yes, bang and my defences crumbled. 'It's all your fault!' I said, and this time I sat myself on her, then I tickled her sides. 'You always turn me on.'

She screamed. 'Wait! Wait! Let's just cuddle for a wee while longer,' she said.

And a cuddle she got.

'You know, you said you preferred women. Was that true?'

This time she'd more than stripped my defences. I didn't prefer women – Jerry's ladies felt like work, just like men.

'You think I lied?' I said.

'It did cross my mind.'

'I prefer women. I never had a bad experience with a woman. But I've had some with a few men.'

She didn't buy it. Those big brown eyes were demanding I explain further.

I took a deep breath. 'Well, I prefer women because they're more understanding, they respect me more.'

I was telling the truth to a certain degree, but when I'd said *they*, I really meant *you*.

'Men can sometimes treat me like a slave and they just assume I like it. And I guess with women it's easier to draw the line. I won't fall in love with them,' I said and noticed her blinking quickly, 'whereas with a man... sometimes I want him to be more than just a client. But of course it could never happen.'

I sensed Andie was still not satisfied with my answer, but she let it go and moved on to another topic: escorting couples.

'No, I haven't done it,' I said. 'Heard about it. I guess the most straightforward scenario is a threesome. The escort can please one of them or both. Sometimes couples just want to see how others are doing it, you know, when things between them aren't working.'

Andie went quiet, apparently contemplating something. Then she dropped the bomb: 'This thing... what I'm doing with you, it's actually my husband's idea.'

The bomb exploded in my chest. My thoughts of her being an unloved, sexually-unfulfilled wife instantly changed to that of an adventurous woman who had such deep trust in her kinky husband that she'd have sex with another man for him. But what was that phone call about? She'd clearly said her husband thought she was disgusting. Had she been drunk? Despite the chaos going through my head, I said calmly, 'He's a brave man.'

'He's a good man. It's just so complicated between us.'

'Relationships are always complicated.'

'I cancelled the first time because he freaked out.'

'Not surprising. If I was him I'd be afraid of letting you be, let alone sleep, with another man. Do you want me to do it with your husband, too?'

Andie vehemently said no. Based on that, I assumed she'd been seeing me behind his back. The hope was still there, some day, she could be more than just a client.

Then there was long silence.

I knew she wasn't ready for another round of action just yet, but I wanted to remind her why she hired me in the first place. I threw myself at her.

'I'll pay you overtime! Are you bored of me talking?' she said, wriggling under me. She wasn't trying to get away, she just wanted to rub herself on me.

'Did I say anything?'

'Yeah, you said: *I'm bored, Andie, let's do it! Please please please!*'

Deep down, having to hold off the action disappointed me – or disappointed my dick. Was there a different kind of testosterone? When I was with a guy, no matter how long I was denied cumming, I had never felt like this.

'I just don't want to leave you unsatisfied when the time is up.'

Andie laughed. 'I'm a woman,' she said. 'I enjoy conversations as much as sex.'

Conversing in bed wouldn't quite cut it, I thought. So I suggested dinner at a nice restaurant.

Once more she rejected me.

'I know a lot of people who like to hang out around here. I can't...'

I simply smiled at her. If she wanted to stay in bed, so be it, but I wanted her to be on me. So I invited her to lay her head on my belly, which she did with enthusiasm. Finally something!

'What do you do?' I asked, playing with her hair. 'If you don't mind me asking.'

'I'm a retail consultant,' Andie said, placing her hand on my balls.

I took a deep breath. 'And what is that?'

She chuckled. 'Well... I help store owners, or managers, to make their stores look good, and make things work for their customers, basically. New stores, old stores, making money, losing money. Any kinds of stores. I advise them on display, layout, merchandising, customer service...' And with that, she rubbed my dick.

I sighed. 'Customer service...'

'You would've passed my training with flying colours.'

'Really?' I started to pant, trying to keep myself under control with her hand persistently arousing me.

'Yeah. Speaking of customer service, do you always clean-shave?'

'Umm... I always have a bit of beard and moustache.'

'No, I meant, your chest and your arms and your hmm hmm.' She touched each part.

'Oh... that. Yes I do.'

'Really? Is that what gay men prefer? I find it a bit too smooth.' For the first time she challenged what I had.

'With my clients anyway, they like it smooth, yes.'

'What does it take to make you keep your hair?'

I shuddered, partly because she suddenly let go of my dick, partly because of the question itself. 'I don't know... you don't want me to shave?'

'For an overnight session?'

'Tempting. But a lot of my clients wouldn't book me with hair.'

'What happened to customer service? Am I not special enough?' she teased me, then said emphatically, 'I'll cover the cost.'

I would've done it for free, but I couldn't be that man yet. I said, 'My hair grows slowly. You want to cover my income for the whole month?'

'Hmm... true... I don't think I can afford that,' she said.

I grinned. 'I'll do it for you.' I hoped she took it as an act of goodwill from me to a special client.

Andie showed me her guilty face. 'No. You don't always have to give in to people's demands, you know.'

'I know, but you're not just some people.'

'I'll pay you double for the overnight session.'

I hesitated for a moment, but I accepted her offer.

It was well past sixty minutes, and she hadn't asked for sex again, but I saw the fire in her eyes. This time I followed my instinct. I started kissing her again and whispered, 'This one's on the house.'

Without resistance she opened herself and I sent her to heaven once again. She didn't cry this time, she just closed her eyes and smiled. I kissed her lips, they parted. I stayed inside her as I held her in my arms. When I withdrew she was already asleep. She shivered when my body was leaving her. I quickly covered her with my blanket and tiptoed to the bathroom.

Seeing she was still fast asleep after I cleaned up, I carefully opened her handbag and checked for her driver's licence:

Andrea Sarina Curtin

And she was thirty-four as she'd said. There was an empty photo compartment on the right side of the wallet – it looked as though something had been pressed there for a long time but had just been taken out. I scanned her address and memorised it. As quickly as I got it out, I put the licence back inside her wallet and her wallet inside her bag.

I wrote on a page of my diary:

Andie, my name is Frederico Lowe. You saved my life when I was a little boy

I wanted to put that note inside her bag. But I struck my own writing and tore the page to pieces and threw them in the bin. I went and sat next to Andie and watched her, recalling the conversation we'd just had. So her husband had freaked out. He still wanted her, yet he didn't want to touch her because he found her disgusting. Was it just Andie overreacting? Or were they so estranged that I could steal her from him?

A moment later Andie woke up. She didn't have a shower

this time. She gave me a long hug, pulled her skirt down, then looked around.

'Looking for this?' I dangled her red G-string.

'Lucio!' she giggled. She put her heels on, gave me an envelope, glanced at her underwear in my hand and walked away. 'Keep it.'

The envelope still had the same smell, but the money she'd put in there was far too much.

'Andie I can't accept this,' I said, stopping her from opening the door.

'I owe you for that night, remember?'

'Andie...' I grabbed her waist.

And just like in our previous meeting, she breathed into my neck then moved up to my cheek and kissed my lips. I cupped my hand behind her head and this time I didn't let her go when she wanted to withdraw. How I could make her world perfect. That night on the phone she had revealed her desires. She'd sobbed uncontrollably when she talked about babies – I couldn't make out what she said exactly. Whether she'd overreacted about her husband, I didn't know. But if I had connected the dots correctly, the bottom line was that her husband couldn't give her what she wanted most: sex and a baby.

How I looked forward to the overnight session. Maybe then, if the time was right, I would reveal who I truly was.

ANDREA CURTIN: MY CHRIS WHOM I HAD LOST TOUCH WITH

5 MAY 2016

I CAME home to a beeping washing machine, and to Chris rumbling in the laundry room. I peeped in. He was unloading a big pile. It seemed that the whole of his underwear drawer was in the basket. So wherever he'd gone to in the past week, he hadn't done his laundry.

'Andrea.' He heard me walking up the stairs.

'Oh, hey,' I said. 'I'm just going to have a shower.'

He caught me up. His hand reached out to me. I couldn't remember the last time we'd had a physical contact.

'Can we sit down?' he said.

That hand.

That face.

I hugged him. The wall of muscles pushed me back when my arms squeezed it tight.

'I missed you,' he whispered.

The feeling (as Lucio had put it) of not wanting my husband still lingered, but I had made peace with it. And with that I had made a little room for Chris, my Chris whom I had lost touch with.

I responded with a caress on his cheek. 'What do you want from us, Chris? From me?'

I had got the long end of the bargain. Lucio's touch and words had made me wake up with the glow of a fulfilled woman every day. Now I wanted Chris to have something, too. Something other than misery.

'I want us like this. At this moment. I want you like this, Sarina.'

This, a fulfilled woman, was the product of a business transaction. A transaction conducted by a man I knew might just be a great actor. But my heart wore a different lens. The fulfilment was the fruit of a real relationship between me and Lucio – Lucio the clairvoyant, the sex god, the shrink, who had empathy strong enough to put my broken heart together; and me, who let him be the permanent resident of my heart. The money was simply a means to make my happiness legitimate for everyone else (Chris, if he ever found out; Leanne; and mostly Lucio himself – he'd surely ditch me as a client if he found out I was falling for him). The money meant I could say: 'It was just sex.' 'It was just a service.' 'Chris suggested it.'

If *this* was what Chris wanted, then he'd better pray that Lucio was in it for the long haul. Chris didn't know, possibly wouldn't ever know, dependency existed between an escort and his client's husband. Up until now Lucio had always been available – when I texted he'd reply within minutes, my appointment times were always okay, he always answered my calls. Sometimes it seemed he'd drop everything for me, or maybe he'd do that to all his clients. Just like I told my clients that they were my best client. But anything could happen; at some stage Lucio might get a career break and become, perhaps, a successful model or movie star; or he might find a sugar daddy and retire. Then what? I would once again be in pieces, and Chris would get his misery back.

Maybe one step at a time.

For now I would give Chris my happy self, my loving self, as he deserved.

I kissed him. 'We don't have to try again, Chris.'

'Sarina...'

'Please, be honest with yourself, with me. Just because you're my husband, it doesn't mean you have to do only what I want.'

'You mean it?'

'Of course.'

'You know I love you more than anything?'

I nodded.

'In time I might...'

I put my fingers on his lips. 'It's okay, Chris. It's okay.'

ANDREA CURTIN: SHINY SHORTS

2-4 AUGUST 2016

I WAS ready to board the plane bound for Singapore when a phone call came from my prospective client. All cancelled – our upcoming appointment and the subsequent store revamp plans that we'd agreed on. The client had every right to do it, everything was verbal, but this was the first time I had been majorly screwed over. As Leanne said, like everything in life, sometimes you get a bad apple. Still, it didn't give me comfort. It was a total lapse of judgement on my part. Although I stayed polite throughout the whole phone call with the business owner (who was insincerely apologetic), I went home fuming.

Expecting Chris to be tucked in bed either reading or falling asleep while reading, I was surprised to hear giggles in the bathroom. I eavesdropped, my husband was talking like a little boy. 'No, I wouldn't wear them! ... Yes it's gonna be fun ... Your bulge? ... No, no, I'm keeping my trousers on.' He could be talking about some rendezvous at a beach where everyone else would be wearing budgie smugglers, but it wasn't that kind of conversation. As I heard him saying goodbye, I quickly ran back downstairs.

Chris was white-faced when he found me in the kitchen. 'Aren't you supposed to be on the plane?'

'Well, my dickhead client didn't want me any more, and they only told me half an hour before boarding,' I said, stirring my hot chocolate.

'That was rude,' he said.

'Exactly!' I said. 'Coffee?'

'No ta,' he said. 'Sorry to hear that, but hey, lucky me, I get to see you tonight.'

I plopped two marshmallows into my mug.

'Shower time,' Chris said. He was about to kiss me but I instinctively pulled myself back.

'Have I got bad breath?' Chris said.

I quickly composed myself. 'No, no, sorry!' I said hugging him tightly with a culpable smile. 'I just didn't expect it.'

And we kissed before he headed upstairs.

When I heard the shower running, I tiptoed into the bedroom and found Chris's phone on the bedside table. I went through his call log. There was no record of the call taking place a few minutes ago.

'Huh...' I murmured. In fact his call log was absolutely clean. Just as I was about to put the phone down, a message came up from someone called Pub:

TN Sat my dear? Btw I'm hard R u?

How I wanted to read the whole conversation. But finding a new message magically turned into a read message would be a tell-tale sign to Chris that his phone had been tampered with, and the water in the shower had stopped. Soon I heard him whistling. I quickly put the phone back.

In the kitchen I sipped my lukewarm hot chocolate and from behind the island bench I watched some uninteresting TV show. Then Chris came down to say goodnight – towel-clad. We kissed again and I touched him like a loving wife would. Once he disappeared upstairs I threw myself on to the sofa and kept watching the uninteresting show until around midnight.

Chris was asleep when I slipped into the bedroom. I groped to find his phone and quickly went into the bathroom with it. I tried to unlock it, but the PIN I knew no longer worked.

SOPHIE BACKED out of my office where I was cursing and swearing at the computer.

'What is it Soph?' I yelled when I caught sight of her leaving.

'Nah, nah, nothing important,' Sophie said.

'Sorry, I'm a bit cranky,' I said. 'I'm going to Singapore again next Thursday.'

'So Aaron changed his mind again?'

'Seemingly so. And his offer is too good to miss, and he signed something on paper this time. So... I decided to give it another go. Stupid, right?'

Sophie tentatively shook her head.

'Yeah. And I'm cranky because of that.'

'Right...' said Sophie. 'Okay, I'm going to drop this off to Karin, and if there's nothing else I might just head home straight after.'

'Sure. Thanks for coming in on your day off, but I really needed you.'

Sophie winked at me. 'Take it easy, boss!'

Alone, my mind drifted back to Chris and his giggling, and that message from Pub. But a phone call of my own short-circuited my trail of reasoning.

'Lucio, what do you want?'

'Hey Andie! How are you?'

'I'm okay. What do you want?'

'Umm... just calling to check, is Friday still good for you?'

'Yeah, yeah,' I said impatiently. 'Anything else?'

'Umm... no. Sorry to bother you.'

'See you then,' I said and hung up.

My tummy churned. It hadn't felt right since this morning. And I should've known better to avoid curry for lunch! As I sat impatiently on the toilet, I thought about what I could do to snoop more on my husband.

I got changed in the office and went to Chris's fitness studio as casual Andrea, donning a loose shirt, a pair of skinny jeans, a pair of glasses and a pony tail. I couldn't disguise myself even if I'd dressed like a babushka.

I peered into the fitness studio like a callow school girl trying to find out if her sweetheart had been a two-timing lover. My husband was in his singlet, showing off his biceps, and he was wearing a pair of shorts, shiny and subtly bulging in between his thighs. He smiled, corrected his client's posture and then started instructing him intensely. I could imagine him saying: 'One two three four five six... hold... hold...'

Is it just Chris being a hands-on coach?

In front of Chris's bending body the sweaty boy was struggling to sustain the weight, panting into his instructor's chest. He must've been in his late teens. I bet the boy liked the smell of the man in front of him, *my man*. Did he go to Chris's gym looking to bulk up or to get fucked?

Chris still wasn't satisfied with the boy's performance. He held the boy's upper arms, explaining something, maybe about how arm muscles work. Then they both laughed and the boy slowly nodded. And he tried again. The neckline of Chris's singlet drooped even lower, the boy could've bitten it and ripped it off if he'd wanted to.

My stomach churned once again. I needed to sit down or I'd start drawing attention with my contorting. I hurriedly returned to my car and headed back to my office.

Surely I was wrong. I kept telling myself that as I stared at my office wall. How could he have made love to me so passionately when I was sixteen? Twice, three times, four times a day? Maybe I had made myself unattractive, or life had made me unattractive. Surely, Chris wasn't that shallow?

I loosened my pants. I really wished I hadn't had that curry.

Once more I concluded it was just my distorted perception of him. Pub was just his mate, nothing more. And that 'hard' word was just a joke. And that boy at the gym was Chris's client, nothing more. Still, I needed to satisfy my curiosity, and I consulted my fountain of knowledge.

L, how do you know if a man likes another man?

I lay flat on the sofa next to my desk. Waiting... but the answer never came. Perhaps I'd ask him in person tomorrow – and we could have all night to discuss the topic.

Then a thump hit my lower stomach, from the inside. I ran to the toilet and sighed. It wasn't the curry after all. I almost slapped myself for forgetting this time of the month. Again!

FREDERICO LOWE: OVERNIGHT WITH ANDIE

4 – 10 AUGUST 2016

SHIVERING, I tucked myself into bed wishing the all-nighter with Andie had been tonight. I would've had her for warmth (even though I was supposed to be her warmth, I could've taken advantage of the cuddling) or I might've even been sweating by now from all the action. It was 2 a.m.; I had been working since 11 a.m. yesterday, but I was still wide awake. I reached for my diary. Entries had been sparse – no other clients were worthy of any mention but Andie.

22/2/2016 – Txt from a woman Andie. She wanted me. So happy.

28/2/2016 – Why Andie? Why? Only she knows.

Now that I knew why she'd cancelled then, I wrote a note: *husband's idea, but he freaked out*

11/3/2016 – It was that kind woman ... she was different but she's still that woman. She cried when she peaked. I could've cried, too. What have I done to deserve her???

And I touched my own writing wishing it could make her come alive right now.

13/4/2016 – she wanted to see me again but cancelled. Something came up?? An excuse or the truth??? ~~Maybe husband found out!~~ We had phone sex, but she told me she wanted a baby and her husband didn't??

27/4/2016 – My red hot Andie; happy, relaxed, a bit wild

16/5/2016 – Andie cried in my arms. She wouldn't say why, but I knew.

6/6/2016 – Magic. Untying her ribbon was like opening a present. But she still didn't want a massage!!

6/7/2016 – Damn Andie! Something came up again??? I want to see you! Now!

18/7/2016 – My Andie, glowing. Something, there's something.

3/8/2016 – Andie so grumpy on the phone!

5/8/2016 – (placeholder for allnighter yay!)

L, how do you know if a man likes another man?

No... was her husband gay? No! I looked at Andie's message in dismay. When a wife started catching a drift, it was never a good sign.

About an hour later I received another text:

L, sorry have to cancel Friday.

For any other client, fine. But I didn't want to let Andie off easy.

Something popped in my head. I counted the number of days when she last cancelled, and the cancellation before that... and I felt as forgiving as a man could be. And I wanted her to tell me. I replied:

Why?

Something came up

I don't believe you.

And my phone rang. A courtesy call? Or was she angry at me?

'Lucio, please... I... I have a meeting interstate,' she said softly.

Either she was a lousy liar, or she wanted to tell me the truth she unknowingly put all her guards down and became a lousy liar. I would've sounded like that when I made an excuse to give summer camp a miss.

Why didn't she tell me? Did she think I would've been put off by her period?

'If you don't come I'll shave,' I said and took a selfie of my bare chest and my legs, including my feet. A lot of my clients liked my hairy feet; one of them openly told me they felt like loofahs when I gave him a foot job. I knew she wouldn't be able to resist.

'Lucio! Shit, you're argh... no I can't!'

She really didn't want me to know, and didn't want me to see her this time.

I cradled the phone and reached for my diary: *5/8/2016 – ~~(placeholder for allnighter yay!)~~*

I added: *cancelled –*

I was going to write 'period' – but that word reminded me of Mother. So I wrote *untouchable* instead.

Despite my disappointment, I understood. But I wished she'd told me the truth like I was her real man. Real couples talk about this thing, right? I would've loved to have her in my arms, any time of the month.

Then I looked at my previous entry: *3/8/2016 – Andie so grumpy on the phone!*

And I added: *PMS.*

'Don't shave, please... please... you know what, I'm going to Singapore in four days. Come with me.'

I didn't say anything. I was still wondering why she tended to book me when she was... femininely unavailable?

13/4/2016 – she wanted to see me but cancelled. Something came up?? An excuse or the truth??? ~~Maybe husband found out~~! *We had phone sex, but she told me she wanted a baby and her husband didn't??*

I added: *untouchable*

27/4/2016 – My red hot Andie. Happy, relaxed, a bit wild I added: *now I know why she smelled that way*

6/7/2016 – Damn Andie! Something came up again??? I want to see you! Now! I added: *untouchable*

'I'll pay for everything. Lucio?'

18/7/2016 – My Andie so glowing. Something there's something. I added: *now I know what that something is.*

'Yes, yes, I'll come with you. How long?'

'Three days.'

I sighed. How much would that cost? Maybe not a lot to her. If it was someone else, I would've soaked it up like a sponge. But this would be her money. For what? My hair wasn't worth that much. I said slowly, 'Andie... that's okay, you sort out what you need to do and I'll see you back here in Sydney.'

'Lucio... But...'

'I won't shave, I promise.'

'Okay. I'll see you back in Sydney next week,' she said. 'You didn't answer my text earlier.'

'Hmm... I don't know the answer, Andie. I guess a man in love with a man is the same as a man in love with a woman.'

THREE DAYS later I received a text from Andie:

L, please come to Spore.

Behind the letters I could see her sulking, even crying.

Andie you ok?

If you're free pls send your details to lisam@tvb.com.au. *She'll sort out your flights.*

I'll pay for it, Andie.

L, don't be silly. I am paying.

She'll see my real name. Don't really wanna do that.

And Andie never replied. A couple of hours later she rang.

'Do you want to know my real name?' I answered.

'So... Lucio is just a trade name.'

'Are you surprised?'

'Umm... Yeah, I guess so. I can't imagine you with any other name. So what's your... Umm... I like Lucio.'

I didn't say anything.

She continued: 'No. I don't want to know your real name. I'm giving you my credit card number.'

I disinterestedly wrote the numbers Andie was dictating to me. Frederico, Lucio, would that make a difference? Not to her, but to me, it's who I am. I wished I could've at least heard her call me *Frederico*, and she didn't even need to know who I really was. But then she wouldn't have meant it. She might even find it a turn-off. She liked Lucio, she'd said so, emphatically.

'You trust me with this?' I asked.

'There's not much on the card, you won't rip me off.'

'Not enough for a business class ticket?'

'Nope.'

She texted me the details of her return flight.

'I'll book it now. See you soon.'

'Don't forget to tear up that piece of paper you wrote the number on.'

I chuckled. 'I thought there wasn't much in it?'

'I know. Still, it'd be a pain to deal with fraud if someone else found it.'

I WASN'T QUITE sure if Andie was the type who would get all warm and fuzzy when she saw a man with flowers. With a bouquet of white roses hidden behind my back, I knocked on her hotel room door. I heard her steps after my first knock.

'Lucio!' she said and hugged me round the waist.

'Hello, gorgeous,' I said, kissing her and gripping her shoulder with my free arm.

She flinched.

'Hey, you okay?' I asked.

'Yes,' she smiled. 'It's nothing... I hurt my shoulder.'

'And your knee!' I said looking at her bandaged leg. 'What happened?'

'Ah, just me being... me. I fell down an escalator.'

'Andie! That's what happens when you work too hard.'

'No pain, no gain.'

'There's no gain in falling down the stairs!' I said, hooking my arm around her waist. 'You need to think about your health, you know.'

'You sound like the nurse at the hospital.'

'It means I'm right,' I said, and swung my other arm around to present the flowers. I trembled; I, a veteran escort, trembled as I held out a bouquet of white roses to my client.

'Oh! Lucio!' Andie said. Her expression was of shock rather than being shyly blown away like a girl on Valentine's Day.

'Hope these will cheer you up.'

Slowly she cast a smile, the widest smile I'd seen on her. She stammered, one unfinished word after another, in the end she just hugged me again and said a simple thank you.

I hugged her back and she flinched once more.

'Oh sorry... sorry...' I said. I had a peek under her shirt: a bruise as wide as my palm spread from the top of her left shoulder. 'Andie... this looks nasty!'

'It's not as bad as it looks, believe me.'

'No bang then?' I winked.

'Do you think I flew you here just because I was horny?'

'I'm your escort.'

'If I was horny I could've easily picked up someone local. Singapore isn't short of handsome and hairy men.'

I shook my head, chuckling. 'I guarantee you wouldn't wanna be with any of them.'

She gave me a smirk of defeat.

'So, why did you fly me here?'

'I needed a trusted companion.'

'You trust me?'

Andie bowed her head, then she stole a glance at me. 'I do.'

I was about to let it all out but she blew my chance.

'And I want to do other escorty things with you that I can't back home. Like... dining out.'

'Right. You must know, escorting, well, for us men anyway, it's 90% a bed-based business.'

'Business, huh?' She rolled her eyes.

Apologetically I pressed myself onto her, hoping to stop her train of thought triggered by that 'b' word.

She trailed her fingers down my throat, from my Adam's apple down to my collarbone. 'You always know how to tease,' she said, staring at a few curls poking out of my first two open buttons. She unbuttoned two more... and more curls revealed themselves right in front of her nose. She glanced at me, briefly holding her breath, apparently thinking. That look when she smelt me. Damn! Was my deodorant too strong?

She carried on unbuttoning and took off my top. She inhaled sharply then nibbled down from under my chin down to my collarbone. And so she arrived at my chest. Her mouth puckered as if she were ready to suck the sex out of me, from everywhere. She dug her fingers through the curls in between my pecs, on my pecs, on my stomach, down to my crotch.

Then she too took her top off, pressed her own chest against mine, and rushed to unbuckle my belt.

'So, you are horny after all.'

'Of course I am,' she said, taking off our remaining clothes. 'I *need* you to fuck me.'

'Right...' It was the first time she'd used the 'f' word.

'Because—'

'I'm your escort.'

She shook her head. 'Because you're mine, for now. And because I can,' she whispered. 'But you really have to be gentle this time.'

'I'm whatever you want me to be,' I said, and slowly gripped her waist. 'And trust me, I'm good with bruises.' I walked backwards and let myself fall into an armchair in front of the study desk, facing a mirror. I invited her to sit on my lap, then let my dick in.

'Lucio.' She sighed and leaned forward.

She clutched me, she panted, she gasped, she gnashed her teeth, and she really brushed herself against me.

I put my palm on the back of her neck and watched her body move in the mirror. The bruise tattooed her shoulder like blue roses, and the cuts underneath looked as if she'd bled from the thorns. But she didn't seem to feel any pain. She rose and fell in a rhythm – gracefully, calmly, deeply. Then she moaned – unsatisfied. Soon she abandoned the rhythm, and she raged and thrashed her body against me.

I wasn't sure where she was going. She bent her neck backwards like she was unconscious although her lower body was still pushing against me aggressively. She was going too fast.

I gently lifted her up.

'No, no, no, don't stop!' She opened her eyes and panted.

'Shhh... Who said anything about stopping?' I said, spinning the armchair away from the mirror, and turning her around. 'Lean back, Andie, lean on me,' I said.

And she moaned hungrily as my hair tickled her back. I gently entered her again, and placed my hand on her pelvis to keep her in place. This time I moved. And she followed. I put my other arm around her chest and squeezed her breasts, forcing her to lean back even more.

'Lucio…' she said and brushed her spine against me like a bear rubbing its back against a tree. And with that, she roared.

I kissed her bruise and her cuts. I wished I'd been there to hold her when she was hurt. I felt the pain, which reminded me of the gash on her arm that afternoon in Rome. I was about to whisper: *Andie, you saved my life when I was a little boy…* but before I could, Andie came. It wasn't like any other climax, she screamed – loud and devastating, and I watched it all from behind her.

She panted, swallowed, and panted again. Then she got up and stood tall in front of me. I watched her eyes scanning me: my dick dangling over my balls, wrapped in a filled condom, then my hairy chest and crotch. She didn't stop there. Instead, she knelt down, kissed my pubic hair, drowned her nose in it and rubbed her cheek. Then she moved along the top of my thighs, licking every single strand of my hair, left and right.

'My God, you're beautiful,' she said.

'What is it with you and men's hair?'

'I don't know. It just drives me crazy.'

'So that's your thing, huh?'

'Maybe, call it a fetish, but I'm sure it's not that weird.'

One of Jerry's ladies had a shoe fetish – at the time I'd thought she was wild: licking my loafers like ice cream. But Andie's desire for my hair was out of control!

'It would be hard for me to keep this up,' I said playing with my own chest hair.

'But you're my escort.'

'I know,' I said dismally.

'But you're someone else's escort, too,' she said calmly. 'Don't worry, I will let you shave – some day.' She winked.

When she tried to push herself up she groaned in pain.

'Hey... Be careful.'

'I think the painkillers are starting to wear off.'

'Come, let me put some ice on it,' I said.

'There's an ice machine down the corridor,' she said.

After cleaning myself, I quickly put on my clothes and grabbed a plastic bag. I came back with the bag filled with ice cubes.

'Good?' I said, pressing the ice bag to her shoulder.

She moaned.

'I wish I had my magic bruise gel,' I said. 'We escorts swear by it.'

Andie turned, her eyes full of sorrow. 'I guess sometimes you have to play rough?'

I regretted what I'd said. 'Part of the job,' I said, anticipating more questions.

But she simply touched my face and gently kissed me. 'When I was stumbling down that escalator – it was a long and steep one – I thought it was my time. And I was fine with it. I never feared death. But then I thought of you when everything started to blur. Not my husband, not anybody else. *You.* And I told myself: "No! I don't want this to be my time." And I begged someone, I don't know who, just begged, for a chance to see you again.'

I kissed her neck while fighting my urge to tell her who I was.

'Why you?' she asked.

I let go of the ice bag and knelt in front of her. 'You wouldn't just go without seeing my hairy chest, hairy crotch, and hairy everything else, would you?' I quipped.

She laughed and put her chin on my crown, smelling my hair.

'Somehow I didn't end up at the bottom of the escalator,' she said. 'An old man saved me. He's 82, he told me. And he was little, but boy he clung on to me for dear life.'

'I should thank him.'

'He'd just smile at you and say, "*Méiguānxì Méiguānxì*" just like he did to me,' she said.

'What does that mean?'

'It means "it's okay, it's okay".'

'So what's your plan for the rest of the day?'

She shrugged.

'Don't you have business to sort out?'

'Well, who says there's no gain in falling down the stairs?'

I cocked my head.

'We'll check out of this city hotel and check into a beach resort in Sentosa. We can swim, suntan, and eat as much as we want and drink cocktails until we're drunk.'

Swim?

'Right... Asian food paradise here, I suppose?' I said.

'Yeah. And I've got the right company.'

'What's your favourite food?'

'Well, funny enough, my favourite Asian dish isn't actually Malaysian or Singaporean. It's Indonesian. It's called Satay Padang. Padang is a place in Sumatra, the home of all things spicy.'

'Aha.'

'Let's go pack up,' she said.

'So that's it, we're just going to eat and get drunk?' I said omitting the 'swim' bit.

She smirked. 'No, we can fuck as much as we want, of course.'

'How about a massage? It's to die for, I swear,' I said.

'You always promote it hard, your massage,' she said.

'I'm not all about my hair,' I said.

'All right, I'll take you up on it,' she said, 'and you, sir, you can stay topless the whole day.'

'Wow… after all my massage persuasion, I'm still all about my hair…'

'I'm afraid so.'

'So, things will never be the same after I shave?'

'I'll never see you the same way,' Andie said with a straight face. Then her stomach rumbled loudly and she burst out laughing.

'Let me guess… You haven't eaten all day?'

'No, I haven't,' she said, and put her arms on my shoulders. 'You will always be *my Lucio*, hair or no hair.'

I took a deep breath.

'SURPRISED YOU DON'T fly business class,' I commented as I was perusing the airline magazine on our flight back to Sydney.

'No. Premium economy is good enough,' she said. 'Thanks for sorting out my bags earlier.'

'You don't have to thank me for that!'

'I just want to show appreciation, you know. I'm not used to having help when I travel.'

'Your shoulder is hurt, and besides, I'm your…'

'Escort, yes, yes.'

'Actually I was about to say *man*, I'm your man for the day so it was a manly thing to do.'

'Ooh, that's sweet.'

'I will pay for some of the expenses, Andie, it's only fair.'

'No, no. I'm your client, Lucio. I pay for everything,' she said.

'I can't bring up the e word yet you brought up the c word.'

'Well, because I can,' she said. 'Seriously, I'll pay. Don't tell me you thought of contributing because I'm a woman.'

'No, no. It's just that you've been too nice to me.'

'Having a nice client, isn't that what every escort hopes for?'

'Yes.'

'So chill out. Just enjoy.'

'I know this is all business, I get it. I get it. But you must know, I take good care of my clients. And tell me I'm sexist, but the truth is, because you're a woman, I care for you even more.'

'I'm a big girl.'

I took her hand. 'Andie... there's something I want to tell you.'

My throat dried.

'You're the best client I've ever had,' I said in the end.

She grimaced, indicating she didn't buy it. But she didn't grill me, instead she put her head on my shoulder. As she tried to find a comfortable position, she flinched.

'Hey, maybe you should take your painkillers now,' I suggested.

'Good idea,' Andie said and reached for her tablets. 'Flying always reminds me of my parents. My mum was a stewardess, a Singapore Airlines stewardess. My dad is Polish, but he's lived in Australia since he was little. She met my dad on a flight after he'd climbed Everest. He was battered – frostbite, broken knee and everything.'

'Wow... Your dad climbed Everest?'

'Uh huh,' she said. 'He was being a total sook when he flew back. The whole flight he couldn't stop trying to get attention. My mum, well, it was love at first sight. She had already fallen for him by the time he stepped onto the plane. She took care of him and he became even softer. They had their first date the next day after they landed in Sydney.'

'How romantic!'

'My dad was handsome when he was young, I must admit. I've seen his photos. Not so much now,' she said. Then she studied my face: 'I wonder how you'll look in your sixties?'

'I'll still be handsome,' I said.

'Huh!'

'Will you still see me when I'm in my sixties?'

She looked at me. 'I doubt it. I'll be in my seventies by then and I bet you wouldn't want to see me that old.'

I caressed her cheek. I would see her that old, and more. I would make love to her again and again...

'My nipples would look like a pair of raisins,' she chuckled.

... no matter how grey and crinkly she was. Suddenly the thought of growing old together with Andie filled me with pain – beautiful pain. How safe the future would be. On this plane, I wished I could tell her that, and the other things a legitimate lover would say. All I could do right now was release my pain by doing what Lucio the escort could do. I grabbed her breasts and squeezed her nipples – her nipples that would turn to raisins someday, but they would still be the sweetest things I'd ever taste. I pulled up the armrest between us and lifted my hips towards her.

A stewardess passed us by and turned her head in embarrassment. By now I was kissing Andie passionately, my left hand was on her thigh, the other still on her breast, all fingers spread. Andie quickly withdrew.

She chuckled. 'Well, you'll still be a stallion in your sixties, I'm sure, and you'll still look youthful.'

'You bet. I'm a twink, remember?'

'Funny that, I always wonder about that word. You are handsome, sexy, well, ridiculously sexy, but I don't – well, I don't mean it in a bad way, but you don't look like the other, umm, twinks that I've seen.'

'Huh! You've been shopping around!' I said and put on a sorry face. 'Haven't I met your expectations?' I asked.

'Oh, not like that, Lucio. No one, I mean, *no one* even came close. You're not like the others. You're the best. You're perfect.'

'That's my Andie,' I said. Then I enthusiastically added, 'And no one else has hair like me.'

She laughed and I squeezed her shoulder. Her laughter turned to a yelp.

'Oh... Sorry, sorry!' I said and kissed her lips. 'Did that make up for it?'

Blushing, she nodded.

Another stewardess went past, discreetly glancing at us.

Andie yawned. 'Can I sleep on your shoulder?' She nudged herself towards me.

'Of course.'

'It's nice to have the row to ourselves. Doesn't usually happen when you travel alone. Usually there's always someone at the other end.' She leaned over to my side, then sat up again. 'Umm nah, I'd better not.'

'Why?'

'Before we even reach Darwin I would have killed your shoulder.'

'That's ok. Squeeze me, bash me, kill me. Make me earn it!'

'You've more than earned it,' she whispered. Then she inched towards me trying to find a comfortable position. 'When it's quiet, could you ask for an extra blanket? I know they're busy preparing supper now, and they'd hate to be bothered with puny things like an extra blanket.'

'I'll keep you warm.'

'I know. But I still need another blanket. Their blankets are fluffy.'

'What's up with you and fluffy things?'

'Comfort.' She smiled and placed her head back on my shoulder.

As the crew were pushing and pulling their trolleys to serve supper, Andie's eyes drooped and her head slowly slipped off my shoulder. Half-awake she put her head back in position, and then she slipped again, several times, until she fell completely asleep with her head dangling in between the bottom of my shoulder and my elbow. I gently moved her head to my lap. No resistance. I nudged her bruised shoulder to stop it from scrunching and then spread my own blanket over her as she shuddered.

'Andie...' I whispered.

She stayed non-responsive.

'Andie,' I whispered as tears came down my face, 'my name is Frederico Lowe. You saved me when I was a little boy. We were in Rome––'

I let out a sob. 'You may never know who I am. You will run away if you know. Yes, you will. That's okay. I can be your Lucio forever. But know this, I will do anything to make you happy, keep you safe.'

I'd seen all of her sleeping faces, but this one broke my heart. She was there, but she couldn't hear me. I was trapped, in between my Andie and my secret. Tears dripped from my face; they fell and glowed on her cheek. Each drop was a confession – one for my name, one for who I was. For that she looked like she was smiling.

I wiped the tears off her and off myself as a stewardess approached me and asked whether I wanted fish or beef.

'I'm not eating, thanks,' I said.

How I dreaded the days that would follow. True, I hated having so much hair everywhere, but I also loathed having to shave and become someone else's escort.

PART IV

THE STORM

ANDREA CURTIN: THE NEST

31 AUGUST - 1 SEPTEMBER 2016

THE LAST TEN outfits I'd bought were all dresses, and the last five pairs of shoes were all stilettos. No shirts, no suits, no pumps, no boots. Not exactly the latest fashion, but it was my own new trend. I only decided to take stock of my recent purchases after Chris, of all people, had commented on my choice of new clothes.

'Sorry I'm late... problem with a delivery,' I said to Chris, who was already waiting at the table having his wine. We were at Monola Tapas for a dinner date.

'No worries. Don't be so stressed,' said Chris. He got up and kissed me.

'Can I get you anything to drink, ma'am?' a waiter asked me.

'Just water, thanks,' I said.

'What? No no no,' Chris said to the waiter. 'Bring her your best pinot.'

I laughed. 'All right, pinot it is.'

I nodded as I looked around the expansive dining area: exposed brick walls, Spanish art, splashes of red on the pillars and ceiling. As my gaze swept across the room, a burst of laughter from a table on the far left made me turn in my chair, and from the corner of my eye I knew Chris was looking, too. I repositioned myself to face him. 'I've been wanting to come here.'

'I know.'

'Good of you to set this up.'

'The least a husband can do,' he said. Leaning back, he threw a smile at me. 'I like you in dresses. And you're... happier. And you ordered water? Anything I should know about?'

'No. It's probably just a phase, you know, mid-thirties... time to change style. And be happy.'

'I'm glad,' he said. 'Look, Andrea —' He took my right hand as my fingers were flicking the edge of the menu. 'I know we've decided...'

I was about to cut him off but I let him continue.

'You know... I was kinda glad you didn't actually do it with those escorts. Honestly I couldn't bear the thought of you making love to another man.'

I wanted to crush the menu now. 'It would've just been sex. How can you make love to a stranger?'

'Do you want to try again?' Chris said squeezing both my hands this time.

'Chris, don't do this to yourself, don't do this to us,' I said.

'I *want* to. Please give me a chance. You still want it too, don't you?'

That handsome, hopeful face. Not quite Lucio's teddy bear look, but I wanted to make that hopeful face a happy face again. I didn't anticipate I'd have to make a decision at this dining table; before those tapas plates came, even before my pinot came.

And so we wined and dined like a couple who had weathered a marital storm and come out stronger than ever. With every cheer, with every adoring word my husband spoke to me, I tried to figure out how this would fit in my new world – the world full of dresses and stilettos, filled with the joy of *making love to a stranger* called Lucio.

The waiter came to refill my pinot. The burgundy liquid flowed into the crystal glass and behind it was my rosy-faced husband. His eyes flashed to the left side of the room. The waiter standing next to me was blocking my view. I didn't know what caught Chris's attention, but there was another burst of laughter.

'And you wanted water?' Chris said watching me gulp my wine.

I chuckled; it must've been my fourth or fifth glass. 'This is very good wine.'

What was Chris's motivation for tabling this 'try again' business? Just guilt or was he genuinely on a path to starting a family again? On top of that, how would I feel when the time came to sleep with my own husband? It could be tonight, it *would* be tonight. Now I wished I'd made an excuse to get out of this dinner.

I put on my impressed face as the waiter carefully placed a plate of mantecados in front of me. How fast was dessert served! In an hour or two I would have to turn myself into the wife I should be. Yes, I had another man on my mind, but I'd never thought of it as a sin. My conscience was clear. The real question was, after tonight, after the next round of togetherness, *should I keep Lucio in my life?*

As Chris excused himself to go to the bathroom, I turned my head towards the table at the far left and had a good look. The four men were enjoying their Spanish beer and making their way through the paella in the middle of the table. It wasn't their loudness that attracted me, it was Chris's eyes that had led me to them. They were all attractive men, but one stood out, the wide-eyed boyish brunette in a blue Lacoste polo and tight jeans. His eyes were intense, his lips full and his smile was deadly. He reminded me of someone, from a while ago – when Christopher Jr. was still with us – somewhere at Minchinbury Avenue.

I SWAYED LEFT and right as Chris helped me negotiate the dark path to our front door.

'We forgot to fix it, honey!' I said. The patio light had exploded after the heavy rain yesterday; the leak above it had turned into a waterfall.

'I'll do it tomorrow,' Chris said.

Having no sense of exactly where I was standing, my foot tripped on the door mat. I shouldn't have had the dessert wine after all, but I needed it. Now I was happy for no reason. Chris, on the other hand, looked as sober as he always was. His face beamed when he turned on the living room light and without warning he picked me up and carried me to our bedroom.

It's time...

I bounced on the mattress. *Our bed* – a square piece of foam, something to lie on for basic biological reasons. Now, with Chris on top of me, I didn't recognise where I was. Lucio's bed felt like home.

Chris took off his shirt. The light coming through the window shone on him. His army body was still there for me to see. He was still my type, and I *could* still make love to him. He wriggled out of his pants, and finally his underwear.

'Chris are you sure?' A stupid question right after I saw him rock hard and breathing like a man with proper sexual desires. But I had to ask.

'Of course,' he groaned. 'Are you?'

I had to turn that hopeful face into a happy face. 'Yes.'

Chris moved slowly, gracefully. I remembered. I hadn't usually felt the initial push, it was only when he was inside that

I knew my man was ready. He had always started gently and shallow, I remembered. He was as constant as clockwork.

I lifted my head slightly so I could reach his lips. My legs opened wider as I pulled at his shoulders and wrapped my hands around his neck. My strangling was a cue for him to begin the next part. This part would shake me, hurt me, rip me apart. I would've *craved* it if Chris didn't give it.

'Are you sure?'

'Uh huh,' I gasped.

And he paused half way, but he was still hard. My old Chris. This was indeed his old self. The big man, he'd always hesitated, scared to hurt me. But I wanted him in, all nine inches of him, even though it hurt. I slapped his bum.

He groaned and pushed his cock all the way. Then he restarted his clockwork.

I screamed, the way I'd used to. After more than a decade of being an unloved wife, this should be heaven. But it shook me in a different way. The Spartacus love had become ancient, yet I couldn't picture Chris and me in a different way.

Once again Chris pulled out. And once more I slapped his bum. With his cock dangling and him on all fours, he looked like a bull at the height of his mating ritual. I grabbed his cock and put it back in me. I growled, and he responded. He pushed his cock as deep as he could, and the clockwork climbed to a speed of a bullet train.

I screamed louder. Hurt me! Rip me apart! *That's my Chris.*

Chris's eyes were shut. His mouth gaped, no flatline. *Who is he imagining?*

Sarina, he mumbled.

That hurt, too.

And he came.

Both of us panted – together, concurrently.

Chris kissed me again and again. I was back to being happy

for no reason. I was not an ordinary wife; I was not like any other wives who were mad at their cheating husband. For I was a cheater, too, but a virtuous one; because my husband had wanted me to, because it had made me a better wife – a wife who would understand if her husband was gay, but who could give herself when he asked for it. And this wife had the capacity to do it all because she herself was fulfilled, thanks to a 'stranger' called Lucio.

He fell asleep while I was still lying on his chest. When the vibration in my head subsided I started to feel a settling, pleasant sensation – it was over.

Will there be another one of these romps? Tomorrow? The day after tomorrow?

Should I stop seeing Lucio?

Being skin on skin with Chris took me to this void where my ability to think diminished completely. Carefully, I removed myself from his embrace. The shower was made for thinking so I was heading that way. But before I reached the bathroom I caught Chris's phone lighting up.

Pub: *Missing u my dear! Wasn't the same without u. R u good this Thu?*

Had I thought I understood my husband's homosexuality? It had felt different when I'd imagined it, when we were fucking. Now, seeing those words lit up...

I made up my mind: No, there wouldn't be another one of these romps with him, and no, I wouldn't stop seeing Lucio.

THE OPENING PARTY OF LOH & Ven's first Australian shop looked over the top from the outside. Splashes of deep red, deep purple and silver clashed against each other. And there were sparkles everywhere. But there was no such thing as over the top for Karin Loh, the co-owner, jewellery tycoon on the rise, and my childhood friend. Karin grew up in Australia but left for Hong Kong when she was twelve. She followed in her mother's footsteps in gold trading before moving on to precious stones.

'Woot woot!' Leanne said when she saw me approaching. She was waiting on the street, having a cigarette. 'You look bloody stunning. Turn around!'

I turned and sashayed on the footpath: midnight blue velvet gown, plunging at the front, plunging at the back, tight on the hips and bum.

'You look hot too!' I said.

'I *am* feeling hot!'

'Sorry to keep you waiting.'

'Your heels are getting higher and higher! Louboutin?'

'Indeed.'

'Why didn't you get your man to come?'

'He's got a meeting, I told you.'

'No, I meant your other man.'

'Oh, him?' I said. 'A lot of people at this party know Chris. So no talking about my boy.'

'Your boy *toy*,' she said.

'Shh!' I said, as we stepped into Karin's glittery shop.

'Wei!' Karin greeted me. For a while when we were kids she used to call me Andrea, but as our families started hanging out together, we called each other by our Chinese names. 'Aren't you a goddess!'

'Congrats, love! You'll be the next Van Cleef and Arples,' I said. 'Ling, this is Leanne, my date tonight.'

'Welcome, Leanne,' said Karin. 'Where's your hubby, Wei?'

'Well, the invitation said I could only bring one person.'

'Oh, you're bad!' said Karin as she showed us around. 'Hey, look at this. Recognise the silverwork?'

'Perfect! You did go with my suggestion!' I said. 'Theo is the best mirror and silver artist around.'

'Kar!' a guy called and motioned Karin to the back room.

'Sorry, guys,' Karin excused herself.

'Andrea!' a voice called me from behind.

Kenneth Reid? That fly! I never understood how he and Chris could be friends. They had worked together as personal trainers at a city gym before Chris set up his own and Kenneth set up his health food business. 'Ken! Fancy seeing you here,' I said.

'I worked with Karin in recruitment,' Kenneth said. 'I do HR stuff too these days.'

'Oh?' I said. An odd one to branch off from health food. 'So all these smiley faces behind the counter are the fruits of your consultancy.'

'Pretty much,' he said and winked at me. 'Chris here?'

'Oh no, he's got a meeting he couldn't get out of. Actually, he's meeting Joe. His office is just next to yours, right? Are you still in St Leonards?'

'Oh, yeah, yeah,' Kenneth said. 'Shame! He'd let go of the opportunity to be with his gorgeous wife?'

I rolled my eyes. 'I've got a date, you know.' I pointed to Leanne.

'Wassup, guys?' Leanne said.

'Excuse us,' I said and walked away with Leanne. 'Hate that guy.'

I felt a nudge on my shoulder. It was one of the guys I'd seen running around.

'Are you Andrea?' he asked.

'Yes.'

'Kar needs you in the back,' he said.

I followed the man. A few metres before the entrance to the back room I passed a group of men where Kenneth was the centre of attention. His silver shirt made him look like a glow worm. I heard him say, 'I was the last one out tonight. Joe wasn't there. I reckon he's at The Nest again havin' a geewd time.'

The group laughed, unaware of my presence behind Kenneth's mammoth frame.

'Rumours though, right?' someone responded.

'No, mate,' Kenneth said sipping his champagne. 'He'd asked me about the place. Quite a while ago. I don't know how he got his membership in the end, but he's in the circle, ow yeah! Thursday night. People like him, where else would they be.'

I quickly went inside to find Karin.

'I want you to have this.' She handed me an intricately carved Chinese style jewellery box.

'It's beautiful, thank you.'

'Open it!'

'There's something inside?'

'Yes, you silly! Of course there's something inside.'

I gasped looking at the pink diamond pendant. 'I can't accept this. This is too much!'

'It's a gift, you have to take it! Come on, you've been very generous with me. I'll be offended if you refuse.'

We were about to start a conversation about diamonds but the run-around guy called Karin once more and I made my excuse: I told her Chris was sick.

THOSE WEREN'T JUST RUMOURS, I knew. Kenneth was a fly, but he wouldn't lie about something like that. The 'vibe' Leanne had brought up when I'd asked if she thought Chris was having an affair, now it was more than a vibe. It was like bit by bit his skin peeled away, revealing another Chris. It made sense to me now that he didn't want to touch me. Were Christopher Jr. and his brother's deaths just an excuse for him to not have sex with me?

Hey, you've reached Chris Curtin...

'Bastard!' This was the second time I'd heard that greeting. I tapped at the steering wheel. Earlier when I'd found the garage empty and the house as dark as a cemetery, I had waited, hoping my husband would turn up. But it was now close to 11 p.m.

Once again I searched online for The Nest, gay club, exclusive, Potts Point, but nothing came up. Lucio was right, there was no information whatsoever about it. Only vague mentions of it, nothing that I didn't know. I tossed my phone and drove off.

Half an hour later I arrived in Potts Point. I'd rarely set foot here. The crowd made me dizzy. Every big man looked like Chris. Reluctantly I dialled the only person whom I hoped would help me.

'Andie?'

'I hope I'm not interrupting.'

'No, of course not.'

'Hey, that club you mentioned, The Nest, where is it in Potts Point exactly?'

'Andie? Don't!'

'I'm going to find it with or without your help. So you might as well tell me.'

'Andie, it's not a place for you.'

'Would you tell me, please?'

'Where are you now?'

'I'm somewhere... just came off Victoria St.'

'Go home, please, Andie. It's not safe there.'

'Fine. I think I know who can help me.' I hung up, parked my car and approached a group of skimpily-dressed ladies congregating around the fire exit of a massage parlour.

'Well, missy, this ain't a place for you,' one of them told me. She was wearing a leopard-print bra top and leather skirt. Her legs were stocky and muscular, elongated by the oversized platform heels. 'Is that real Chanel?' she continued, observing me while playing with her platinum wig.

'Hi ladies!' I said politely. 'You might be able to help me. I'm looking for The Nest.'

Silence. The girls looked at each other.

Another one of them told me in a heavy voice, 'Huh... if you don't know where it is, you're not gonna get in.'

'Please...' I begged.

'Your husband *is* probably there,' said another one, followed by laughter all around.

'No, just looking for my friend.'

'Well, ring your friend and ask them to take you there.'

Finally one girl spoke up, in a real lady's voice, loudly, 'That way!' She pointed to her left. Her friends were gasping and whispering. She continued, 'Walk about 10 minutes, go through a lane next to number 79. Another 5 minutes, and you should see a steel door on your right. Looks like nothin', but it's there.'

'Thanks.' I sighed.

'I reckon you won't last with those stilettos. The path's uneven, up and down, potholes and shit.'

I left them giggling. Past the lane the street was poorly lit. The stench of old beer, piss and weed filled the air.

Out of nowhere two men appeared in front of me. They pushed me back into the laneway. One of them could've been a bouncer, but the other one looked a bit too skinny to be one.

Soon I was cornered.

'Ooh la la...' one of them said.

'What do you want?' I said. I tried to make out their faces. The big man positioned himself behind me, his arm around my neck. 'Hel–' I tried to yell but a fat palm gagged my mouth.

'Ooh la la indeed...' the skinny man said. He pushed his hand under the neckline of my dress and started groping my breasts. 'Nice boobs...'

'Check out her bag,' said the man who was gagging me.

His friend shone a small torchlight into the bag. 'Oh yeah, what have we here?' He opened the jewellery box Karin had given me. 'Is that real diamond?'

I tried to nod.

'I'm going to let you speak, if you scream, I'll break you.'

I gasped. 'Yes, it's a real diamond. Take it, take my money. Just leave me alone.'

'I want your things, and I want *your thing*,' the skinny man said.

'Do you think she's a real woman?'

'I bet she is. But you can never be sure these days... Only one way to find out...' The man crouched and ran his fingers up my legs, from my calf to my thigh. I kicked him aimlessly. I drew all the energy within me to break free but I couldn't even wriggle. Where was my youth? I used to fight boys and win. I tried one last swing of my leg, it reached my attacker's upper thigh but the sharp heel got caught in his key pocket. The man grabbed my ankle, twisted it, and fiercely moved up to probe me.

My cry was muffled.

The man's finger was sliding inside me. Behind me the other man's cock was growing. Through the loosening gag I mumbled, 'No... please... let me go...'

'Would be nice to fuck a real cunt.'

I bit the fingers that were gagging me and screamed: 'Help!'

'Fuck!' The big man gripped me tighter.

'I will break more of you,' he said crunching my chin.

I was wriggling with all my might as the man was unbuckling his belt. My phone rang. *Is that Chris? Is that Lucio? Leanne? Whoever, please help!*

The man stomped on the buzzing phone.

'Now, where were we?'

FREDERICO LOWE: THE NOTORIOUS LANE

1 SEPTEMBER 2016

MY CLIENT JIMMY almost lost his pair of oversized golden horns as he grooved to *It's a Sin*. He was one of the many Nesters who got lost in the celebration for everything Taurus. Apparently customer reports showed there were more members who belonged to this star sign than any other, so every first Thursday in September the club would throw a bull-themed party, including a stunt show and rodeo competition. Funny they would celebrate being Taurian in September – some said it was because September was the month of virgins, and honouring their members during this month would encourage them to reminisce about that feeling, when they were with that someone special for the first time. But a more reasonable explanation was that the owners were high when they came up with the idea.

Jimmy endlessly body-searched me, begging that I tell him he was my first, over and over. When *Careless Whisper* came on, he clung to my waist with one arm, while his other hand was firmly on my crotch. Soon his lips ravaged my face.

Time was almost up. I gently ushered the 40-year-old away

from the dance floor. Five minutes to go, time to wind down and wrap up the action. No overtime tonight – not even an extra minute. I still had one more client to entertain, but usually with Jeff it was a pleasant encounter.

'One more!' Jimmy begged and ordered a shot of tequila.

As Jimmy gulped down his drink, Andie's name flashed on my mobile screen. She didn't usually ring. I ditched my black horns (I looked more like the devil than a bull when I had them on). I was prepared to offend any client for Andie so I answered.

Andie greeted me politely, but her agitation showed as soon as she finished her first sentence. While listening to her, I mouthed 'Good night' to Jimmy and left him at the bar grooving with himself; he probably didn't even know I had left.

'Andie? Don't!' I said regretting I had ever mentioned The Nest.

I ran out to Victoria Street as fast as I could. There were two entrances to the club accessible from that street. One was through another club's basement and there was no sign of her there. I felt weak. *The notorious lane.*

When I got to the archway, I could make out a man's back. He was with two or three more people, all jumbled up in one black blob against the dark wall.

To my horror I heard Andie's voice.

'Let her go!' I said, running towards them. No one would be threatened by my warning, I knew; all I hoped was to buy time.

The man turned to me and said, 'Walk away, boy! You ain't seen nothing.'

Slowly I made out what was inside the black blob. A man had his arm around Andie's neck, forcing her to lean on him. He was so fat I could've mistaken him for two people.

'Let her go!' I stepped closer, a punching-arm length from the skinny man. A sunken face, with eyes that weren't quite with himself.

The man jerked his hips and zipped up his fly.

No. No. No. He couldn't have done it to my Andie. Had I had a knife I would've cut his dick right now.

But I had nothing. One delirious skinny man, I'd come out okay, but against both men? I just needed to give Andie a chance to escape; I would take a beating for her, any time.

I dodged the skinny man's punch. When he was still dealing with his dented ego, I kicked him and pushed him away. I slid through the gap to get to Andie who was still being strangled by the fat man.

Seeing his partner on the ground, the fat man let go of Andie to deal with me.

'Andie, run!' I ordered.

But she just leaned on the wall, shivering, looking around for something.

'Andie!' I cried. 'Run!'

An arm like a swollen python twisted around my neck. In front of me the skinny guy was up, maximum fury, ready to finish me off with his torch. But before that happened noises swarmed from behind us. The ruckus quickly turned into a scene like a witch hunt – shrieks and bellows broke the air, torchlights shone on us.

'Here! Here! Those thugs are here!' a heavy voice rose above others.

As my attackers retreated, I glanced back. The menacing figure of a tall, sturdy woman came into view, and soon more crowded around her, with a couple of bouncer-type men on either side of the group.

'Get outta here, Stick!' the fat man yelled to his partner and soon both of them fled.

'Get them!'

'Come back, you cowards!'

The hostile crowd gave chase, leaving me alone with Andie.

'Hey, you okay?' I ran to her. She clung to me silently. 'Are you hurt?' I touched her face. She turned away. 'Look at me, are you hurt?'

'No,' she said, feebly pushing me away. 'Just leave me alone, let me go home.'

'Come on, I'll walk you to your car.'

But she didn't move. She looked around the laneway as if she had just arrived there: the wall, her handbag and her crushed phone, and the spot where she was pinned.

'Andie?'

She suddenly let go of me and collapsed as her feet failed to support her.

I caught her. 'Hey, what is it? Do we need to go to the hospital?'

She shook her head and sank to sit on the ground.

'You can tell me, I promise I...'

'No, they didn't,' she said.

I hugged her and took a deep breath. I exhaled. Thank God thank God thank God.

'Come on, we should get out of here. Can you walk?' I said as I gathered her things.

Hopping on one leg, leaning heavily on me, she blindly followed my movement.

'Where did you park?' I asked as we got to the main street.

'I don't know...' She was shaking.

'It's okay. Let's stay here a while.'

Hugging her under the street lamp I could see her bare back. Her arms were resting on my shoulders. I stroked her nape and I felt the tension within her ease.

'I told you it ain't no place for you, missy!' the woman who'd led the chase earlier came back. 'Are you all right?'

Her attention soon shifted to me.

'Bloody hell! Lucio!' she exclaimed realising who I was.

'Jerry,' I said.

She said, 'So... *you* are the friend that she was looking for at The Nest?'

'Goodnight, Jerry,' I said. 'Thanks for your help.'

'We're just looking out for each other. There have been a few attacks lately. Sharon was hit on the head three nights ago. Those cowards!'

'Did you see where my friend parked her car?' I asked.

'Not far from our ol' fag station,' Jerry said. She wanted to go on but as I said 'Thank you, Jerry,' again emphatically, she got the message and left us be.

'I'll get the car for you, you wait here, okay?' I said to Andie.

'No, please, don't leave me. I'll walk with you,' she said hugging me tighter.

After about 20 minutes of hobbling we found Andie's car. She slumped in the driver's seat.

'Can I stay with you for a minute?' I said.

She nodded.

'Andie...What were you thinking?' I said.

'I was looking for my husband. Gossips don't lie.' She took out her wallet, and between some cash and crumpled receipts she pulled out a photo. 'Here. Do you know him?'

A man in an army uniform, it looked to be an old photo. I clipped the photo with my thumb and index finger to have a closer look. Soon my palms were sweating. This, *this* was her husband? I was ready to vomit. No. Not him. So the safety I'd given him was at the expense of Andie's tears. How could I have said he wasn't cheating? He definitely didn't deserve her understanding! And the babies she mentioned in her cry that night? My stomach heaved but I tried not to react.

Although I did react when she said: 'Right... so he is famous within the circle then.'

'Look, Andie, it is what it is. I know men. It's just a need.'

'Just like my need when I'm with you?'

'Maybe, but may I say perhaps it's even shallower than that,' I said. 'Andie, I have faced this situation many times with my male clients. Just keep it to yourself. Trust me, it's easier that way.'

'How is it easier?'

'You'll see.' It hurt to say it; it wasn't going to be easier.

'Is he your client?'

'No.'

'Do you know him?'

'I've seen him around at The Nest but I don't know him, no.'

'He was there, he was there, I'm sure,' she trembled. 'Let me go home.'

'You can't go home like this. What would you say to him?'

Andie looked at herself: the neckline torn, her skirt shredded. 'He won't know. He's not home.'

'Well, he's not at the club either.'

'You were there?'

I nodded.

'Was that the way to the club? Or have I been fooled?' she said.

'It was the right way, well, the long way, but one of the ways. It's hardly used because it's on street level. The club owners don't really like that. It's notoriously dangerous there. Did the girls tell you to go there?'

'One of them did,' Andie replied. 'Maybe they wanted to flush out those bastards. Used me as a bait.'

Fuck that girl! I glanced at my ringing phone – Jeff – I rejected the call. 'I can give you the key to my apartment and you can freshen up there, I can't come with you...'

'That's okay, Lucio. I have my work clothes in the back,' she said. 'I can wear the jacket when I get home, if he's there.'

My phone rang again.

'Sorry, I have to take this.'

I answered the call in a cheerful Italian accent. 'Tesoro... I'm so sorry, yes I am late... I'm in hospital... I had an accident.... No, no. Nothing serious... Thank you, thank you... Ciao.'

'You didn't have to do that.'

I reached out my hand to take the car key out of the ignition. 'I'll drive you home. You're not okay,' I said, and carried her to the passenger side.

She didn't resist.

'You want my husband to see you?' she said.

'No, no! I'll stop somewhere, close enough to your place, and you can drive from there.'

As we were leaving Potts Point, we passed a couple of police cars. The two thugs, their faces bloody, were being handcuffed and herded away by four policemen. Behind them some of the people giving chase were being arrested, too.

'Look at me, bastards!' Andie said, winding down the window.

I flicked the central window lock and stretched to pull her hands from tapping the glass. 'Andie, no, you don't want the police to find you now,' I said and gradually sped up.

'I don't care!' she said. 'Let everyone know! Let my husband know! See what he's done to me!'

'I know you're upset,' I said. 'But perhaps you need to take a step back. Making a rash decision to punish your husband doesn't usually end well.'

'You're experienced in that, I suppose?'

'I've had a client who got found out by his wife.' Nathan, whose wife I'd once called a bitch.

'How did she find out?'

I sighed. 'He was caught.'

'You two were caught?'

'No. He was caught... you know, masturbating in the bathroom and calling my name.'

Andie flinched and shook her head.

'Sorry.' I continued: 'They had an ugly divorce, they hurt each other along the way. But it didn't have to be that way. If only they could see beyond this stigma of cheating, affairs, infidelity. Paying for a service is none of that. You have a need, you pay for it, fair and square. I don't know about his wife, but I know he loved her, he really loved her.'

I pretended it was Nathan's wife sitting next to me. Even with that I still wished I could stop the car and just vomit.

'What is love, Lucio?'

How could I do this to her? I looked at her sympathetically. She knew the answer. Her face tightened, her skin would tear and let out the words she was dying to say about love.

She gave me that answer: 'Love? It's just an ad. It's broadcast in a beautiful, irresistible way, yet it leads to emptiness. It's short-lived, useless. By the time it's gone you've spent so much of yourself – you pay for it excessively. You have no more to give. And you're broken to the point that you don't know who you are any more.'

And it broke me to hear her say that.

My little finger nudged hers. She stayed cold. I turned to her, demanding she look at me. I said, 'When you love someone, you will do anything to make them happy and safe, I mean, *anything*.'

She did look at me. I wasn't sure if she believed me, or simply wanted to believe me, but I felt a level of positivity in her stare. 'How could that man make his wife happy when he was fucking another man?' she asked.

'It was just sex, Andie.' My ego wished she could understand. But she was his wife, she had every right to be mad.

'So you're on his side.'

'I'm not taking sides. I just don't want you to make a mistake like other wives.'

'He's not a bad man,' she said, shaking her head a little. 'He was my hero once. And when I thought of him, I thought it was love. But I never knew exactly what it was. And I don't know if he still loves me. Whatever that means.'

What she said made me doubt myself. What was love exactly? I knew what it had been to Nathan as he'd spoken of it, but to Andie's husband? How did he love her? Had my service to him altered how he loved her?

'I guess love is different to everyone,' I said. 'I don't know if your husband still loves you, but I'm sure he doesn't want to hurt you.'

'He's a good man,' she murmured. Then she took a deep breath and sat upright. 'You're right, I'm not like any other wives. I will let it go this time.'

For a while Andie was in her own world. She pressed her face against the window and watched the footpath running beside her, one rubbish bin after another. Suddenly she broke down.

'Andie...' I pulled over and took her in my arms.

'He made me do this,' she said, rubbing her crotch harshly. 'I wouldn't have been there if it wasn't for him! Why didn't I fight back? They were so disgusting! So dis-gus-ting!' she cried and stretched her already tatty skirt away from herself.

'Andie, Andie, stop,' I said, gently pulling her hands towards me.

'There wasn't even anything there – rocks, bricks, an old pipe, a wood plank, or *something*! When I saw them coming for you, I just wanted to smash their skulls.'

She'd still tried to protect me even when her own life was in danger.

'You're safe now. I promise. Everything will be okay.'

She looked at me. I could see her husband's face inside her eyes. He didn't deserve her. Was I the force that ruined her marriage? I had never intended to be, but I would be glad if I was.

ANDREA CURTIN: EVERYTHING WITHIN THE SPACE OF HUMANLY GOODNESS

1-2 SEPTEMBER 2016

TWO STREETS away from my house, I asked Lucio to stop the car. He hurriedly hopped out and came to my side. I whimpered as I tried to stand up.

'Come,' Lucio said, gesturing to me to grab his shoulder. 'It looks very swollen,' he said surveying my ankle.

'Just a sprain. Painful, but I guess I'm just a wimp.' Having him to lean on, I wanted to be a wimp.

'Andie, you're not a wimp,' he said with his hands firmly on my waist. 'I'll help you tidy up. Where's your jacket?'

I indicated the back seat.

He held the jacket for me and I pushed my arms into the sleeves. I watched passively as my escort did his best to hide the tears on my dress. He wasn't supposed to be my escort tonight, but he was, and more.

'I'm sorry you had to cancel with that client.'

'Don't worry about it. You're more important,' he said, still fiddling with my dress.

'I'll pay you. I've ruined your night.'

'Andie!' He shook his head. 'Please. I'm just doing what any other human being would do. Time isn't always money, you know.'

I was looking for a word that described gratitude, fondness, respect, romance, closeness, longing, honesty, kindness. But tongue-tied, vocabulary-poor, in the end I simply said, 'Thank you.'

He gently thumbed my lips, trying to get rid of something around them, perhaps dried blood, or smudged lipstick. Then he brushed my under-eyes with his sweater cuff and ran his fingers through my fringe.

'It's fine, Lucio,' I said. 'So, where to now for you?'

'I'll take a taxi back to Potts Point, get my car and then I'll go home,' he said. 'Good night, Andie.'

I rubbed my cheek against his when he gave me a peck. It was hard to say good night when I still wanted to explain my feelings of gratitude, fondness, respect, romance, closeness, longing, honesty, kindness – everything within the space of human goodness. Earlier he was going to give me his apartment keys and I'd refused – could I change my mind now? The night would be so much better...

But I drove off and watched Lucio's reflection in the mirror – getting smaller and darker – until I could see him no more.

I went around and around my neighbourhood, waiting for the light in my house to go out. But after an hour the light was still on, and I was fading. Much as I'd hate to face Chris, I didn't want to be a victim of a car crash – not tonight, after what Lucio had done for me – or even worse, making someone a victim of a car crash.

I said a silent hello to the lonely driveway. I reached behind the seat and pulled up the bottle of champagne Karin had given me at the party. After a few gulps of the bubbly, and sprinkling some on my dress, I hopped out of the car with an after-party smile. I almost fell as the pain on my ankle stabbed me up to the knee. Leaning on the bonnet, I slowly stooped to feel my injury and examined it under the patio light. Lucio had been right when he said it was very swollen. But I soldiered on, keeping my after-party smile, and opened the door.

'Hey, how was it?' Chris said lying on the sofa, eyes on the TV.

'Yeah it was fun,' I said.

When he finally turned to see me: 'Jesus what happened?'

'Got a bit tipsy, Leanne and I... we fooled around, she was trying to pull me over to this handsome waiter. But I ran away, and I fell down. I didn't see the gap between the footpath and the road.'

'Andrea!' He cringed as he smelled me.

I walked away from him. 'I'm going to take a bath. Back soon.'

Half an hour later I joined my husband who was still fixated on whatever he was watching. Disguising my limp, I tried to keep his attention on the TV. 'Ah, *Apocalypse Now*,' I said. 'No wonder you're still awake.'

Chris smiled, pulling me closer to him. 'That's better!' He kissed me.

Helicopter noise, explosion after explosion. Not long after we started cuddling Chris fell asleep. I stared at that handsome face. *Who else has he been kissing?* I recalled what Lucio told me – let it go. It had sounded impossible at the time. But now that I was with Chris, with *that hand* on me, maybe I could. I nudged myself carefully out of his embrace and spread a spare duvet over him. I hobbled upstairs and sent a text to Lucio:

Thank you again, L.

I'D SQUEALED when the physio was bending and mending my

ankle earlier this morning. I usually had high pain tolerance, but this time I had truly become a wimp.

Kept awake with a fever last night, with my ankle swelling like a beetroot, I had been going to take a day off today. But I decided to go to work when Chris said he was taking a day off, too.

I sat at the edge of the bed in my underwear, struggling to put on my stockings. Half my body was pulsing with pain and I dreaded having to face the people I had to see today, but I couldn't be with Chris for the whole day either, despite deciding last night that I would let go and forget about what he'd been up to.

Then I heard a knock on the door.

'I'll get it!' said Chris from downstairs.

Too late for me to get to the door first, I raced to make myself decent instead.

'Chris! Is Andrea around?'

Karin.

'Is she okay?' I heard her asking Chris.

I hurriedly came downstairs, hopping on one leg, hanging on to the railing. 'Hey, Ling!'

Chris looked at me. 'A bit hungover I suppose, but she's fine.'

'You didn't drink that much last night, did you?' Karin said.

'Not as much as she'd like to admit,' Chris winked at Karin. 'I'll leave you ladies to it.'

I ushered Karin anxiously into the living room. She asked, 'I went to your office and Sophie said you took a day off. Are you okay?'

I nodded.

'The police came to my shop this morning,' Karin said.

'What? Why?'

'There was a robbery or something? And they found my gift to you!'

'Ssh... Chris doesn't know,' I concernedly responded. 'I got mugged.'

'Oh my God, Wei!' Karin said. 'You're hurt, aren't you?'

'No. No. I went for a drink at Potts Point after your party. Got a bit drunk and went to a spot I shouldn't have,' I said. 'What did the police say?'

'They wanted to know who the pendant belonged to. They saw the Loh & Ven brand on the box. I said it was a gift for a friend. I promised I'd make you go to them to give a statement within 24 hours. Otherwise I'll be in trouble and no doubt they'll come looking for you,' Karin said.

'Right... I'll go to the police before I head to the office,' I said.

ANDREA CURTIN: THEN THERE'S THE 9TH OF SEPTEMBER

9 SEPTEMBER 2016

'Go home, Soph,' I said as I was ignoring yet another call from Lucio. It was relatively early for us, 9 p.m., but I could see my assistant was falling asleep.

'How about the invoices?'

'They can wait till tomorrow,' I reassured her. 'Go home.'

'All right, if you're sure. If you need anything, I'll be in the bath.'

Another call from Lucio. Much as I longed for him, I wasn't ready to speak to him again. I was imagining his face, probably worried. Those big blue eyes would be blinking after each ring.

Reluctantly I answered.

'Andie! Finally! Are you okay? I've been ringing you since yesterday. Where—'

'I'm okay, Lucio.'

'Where are you?'

'Still at work.'

'Can I see you?'

I paused. 'No,' I whispered.

'Why?'

'I see you, not the other way round.'

'Andie, I just want to see you're okay – after what happened.'

'I told you, I'm okay. Good night, Lucio.' I hung up.

The business card for Detective Constable Alex McCann was still on my table, lurking right under the monitor; it had been there for almost a week. Tonight I was able to scrunch it and toss it in the bin – it was over. I had given my statement, and thank goodness in the end I didn't have to appear in court. A lot of people had been mugged by those thugs, so there were other more significant and willing key witnesses to testify, and that was enough.

I stared at my computer screen. My calendar was full but I'd rather focus on my misery – bring it all to the surface, dwell on it, feel sorry for myself, and cry all week.

Misery 1: The near-rape in the lane – it had felt like being ravaged by Greg, Ant, Sonny, Hillsy, Rock and Ton. It was over with the officials, but I was still ruing what I hadn't done to those two thugs. I could've kicked those men's balls, bitten their fingers off, gauged their eyes, but no, I'd been completely helpless. I had been asking for it, yes, and it was all because of Chris!

In a funny sense I was thankful that I couldn't fight those two losers, that Chris wasn't there to rescue me. In the end I was rewarded with everything within the space of humanly goodness. A man called Lucio.

The notorious lane incident: A misery? No.

Misery 2: Chris. My Chris who was no longer mine. No doubt he'd been fooling around with someone – who, and in what form, I didn't know yet. He hadn't been mine for a long time. It made sense he didn't want to touch me, I told myself again and again. I just wished he had been truthful. I would've understood. I was hurt, but in the scheme of things the wound was superficial. It was more like a punch that had fired me up, got me motivated, and spurred my impatience to uncover the truth about my husband. Was this a misery? Not quite – it was a challenge.

Misery 3 –

The 9th of September.

Today.

I opened my drawer, it was time to see him again after I had taken the photo out of my wallet. Christopher Jr, in his denim overalls. And his dad was behind him, smiling. I couldn't find another photo to replace it. Christopher was always with Chris in pictures, and I didn't want to see Chris in my wallet.

I stared at the empty leather chair in front of me. I wished someone was there, sitting attentively while I told them about today being Christopher Jr.'s birthday. Christopher would've been a young man now – handsome, naughty but polite, a heartbreaker; he might've been an athlete, or he might've joined the army.

Maybe Leanne would hear my story again – for the twelfth time.

Maybe Chris, if I could see past his lies.

Hesitantly I called a number.

FREDERICO LOWE: ANDIE'S OFFICE

9 SEPTEMBER 2016

ANDIE WOULDN'T ADMIT that night at the notorious lane had traumatised her, oh no, she would act tough, no men could've ever destroyed her that way. But I knew inside she was breaking, and she herself might not realise. So I tried to get to her as fast as I could after receiving her call.

Andie's office was still fully lit, although it looked empty from the outside. The red room was full of knick-knacks and there was a display of a miniature shopping strip by the window; there were all sorts of shops on that strip – from a candy store, café, boutique, to a warehouse-style building that looked to be a furniture emporium.

As soon as I knocked, Andie appeared from behind the partition and limped over to open the door for me.

She led me into her private office. 'Thanks for coming. I'm sorry, I haven't got cash...'

'Andie! I'm here as a friend.'

She shook her head. 'No, you can't be my friend. I'm paying you to be here.'

I stopped insisting; I could refuse payment when the time

came. 'You've been crying,' I said, gently lifting her chin. I peeped under her scarf: a long bruise laced her neck. 'Does it hurt?'

She nodded weakly.

I looked down. 'You're wearing heels?'

'I've got to look good, injured or not,' she said, and raised the hemline of her pants, revealing the heavy strapping around her ankle. 'But they're killing me. I don't know why I still have them on.'

'Come here,' I said, guiding her to the sofa. Next to it was a bin, half filled with empty energy drink cans. I squatted and removed her heels carefully. Slowly I massaged her foot, and very gently kneaded her ankle over the strapping.

'Don't stop,' she sighed, leaning back, eyes closed.

After about 10 minutes she touched my hand. 'Thank you, Lucio.'

She wanted more, but tonight she seemed to be feeling guilty about everything I did for her.

I joined her on the sofa.

'I will get the money tomorrow. I can—'

'Andie! Forget about the money!'

She stopped arguing and nodded. 'Good night then.'

'You didn't ring me because you were after a foot massage. What is it you wanted to tell me?'

She contemplated what to say next. 'It's been a tough day.' She trembled. 'Yeah... tough.' And welled up. 'I just needed someone here.'

'I'm here.'

'Yeah... and I'm glad.' She looked around, inspecting the four walls around her as if looking for an alternative source of comfort to the man sitting next to her. She couldn't find any. So she let herself fall onto me. Her lips were pressed against my T-shirt and with a muffled voice she said, 'Just stay with me.'

'Of course.'

'Tell me everything will be okay.'

A common tell-me request along with 'Tell me I'm beautiful', 'Tell me I'm the sexiest man you've ever met'.

But unlike with my other clients, I meant what I said: 'Everything will be okay, Andie.'

'What if it isn't?'

'Then I'll make it okay,' I said. *Oh yes I will.*

I had noticed her doubts when we were together. She was tossing up between the possibility of me saying things truthfully, and the thought I might've only told her what she wanted to hear. But tonight she gave me a gaze of trust. Maybe her desperation drove her to trust me. Whatever it was, right at this moment I saw her putting everything she was in my hands.

'I had a son, Lucio,' she said, withdrawing from my embrace. 'He died because of me.'

So I hadn't been wrong about her losing a baby. But I had misread her earlier tonight; after all, her desperation had nothing to do with the incident at the lane.

'Today. Sixteen years ago. Car accident,' she said.

I pulled her back into my arms, very close to my heart. My heartbeats would soothe her pain, at least a little, just like hers did when I was about to be road-killed. Now I understood her protection. I couldn't fill her son's place, but only I could understand her loss. She'd told *me* that many years ago, with her embrace.

For the first time I felt my existence had meaning. I'd been a part of Andie in a deeply intimate way, beyond sex and longing. But what would she think of me if I told her I was that boy? When she'd run across the road, had I simply reminded her of her dead son? Or had she thought I *was* her son?

'I wanted another baby, we tried, but he was stillborn.' And she broke into sobs just like she had on the phone that night. 'I wanted another baby so badly... but my husband didn't.'

That army face. I thought long and hard about what I was going to say. 'Maybe your husband just needs time.'

'No, time is up.'

'I'm sorry.'

'Christopher would've been nineteen today.'

That made me realise how long it had been since that day in Rome. 'He was a Virgo, huh?' I said.

In between her sobs she beamed at me. 'Yeah, he was.'

'I haven't lost anyone, but a friend once told me he lost his twin brother when he was six; he drowned trying to save him. He said to me that every time his brother's death started to weigh on him, he felt his presence, like Tinker Bell sitting on his shoulder. *Campanilla*, that was what he called him. The guilt never left him, but every time he saw that shining light on his shoulder, he felt all right. No matter how briefly, he felt that his brother's spirit gave him a break from his sorrow.'

I waited for her reaction. It might've been too childish for her.

'That's a beautiful story,' Andie said.

I wanted to tell her: And only a few months after I heard that story from my friend Giorgio, I met the most beautiful human being... and now here I am, holding that beautiful human being in my arms. But I swallowed those words and asked her instead, 'Have you ever felt his presence?'

Andie thought for a while. 'Sometimes, yes. But it scares me, so I... funny that... I tried to drive him away. He makes me sad.'

'Maybe you should think of him as Tinker Bell, well, if that's too sissy, maybe Peter Pan.'

She chuckled. 'You always know what to say.'

'I always try.'

'I never talked about him like this,' she said, contemplating.

'I have this fear of hearing him say: "I hate you Mummy", "Why didn't you save me Mummy?" ...'

'Hey, hey, Andie,' I said as she started to shake. 'Don't do this to yourself. Whatever it is, no son would ever say that to his mother, not to you.'

'I want to forget about him,' she said, showing me her son's photo.

A beautiful boy. I almost cried myself. I covered her husband's face with my thumb and said calmly, 'You can't forget about him, he was your son.'

'That makes me sad, too. Wanting to forget about him.'

'In time you might accept what happened. Believe me, it takes time.'

'I hope you're right,' she said gloomily.

'I know I am,' I said, 'because I'm an escort, and an escort is always right.'

She put her head on my chest once more and closed her eyes. 'I don't want to go home, but I don't want to stay here either.'

'Are you up for a drive?'

She looked at me. 'Where?'

'To the stars,' I said and carried her, barefooted, out of the office.

ANDREA CURTIN: MINCHINBURY AVENUE

9 SEPTEMBER 2016

THE NIGHT SKY above the Bouddi National Park spread like black velvet sprinkled with silver sequins. 'I've never been here before,' I said, head tilted up, hand on Lucio's shoulder, moving clumsily as I tried to hop-spin to soak up the magic.

'One of the best star-gazing spots in New South Wales,' Lucio said, catching me as I almost fell.

'Stars... remind me of Christmas. When I was a kid Dad always let me choose a tree topper. And I always picked the same one, year after year: a silver star made of pearl wires, sprinkled with crystals. Mum was always picky about colours. If the topper was silver, the other decorations had to go with silver. So our living room would look like the Milky Way.'

I slid down, dragging Lucio to sit on the sand. I put my head on his lap. 'Oh, look! That one is so bright. Maybe it is Christopher.'

Or maybe it was the one that was carved out of your cheek.

I reached out and stroked the scar to the left of Lucio's nose.

'Is that his name?'

'Yeah, Christopher Jr.'

How and why I could readily open up to him and believe each word he said, I didn't know. His friend, Tinker Bell, the stars. He didn't try to pretend he understood, he simply told me how his friend coped with his loss and guilt. And when he said he would make it okay, he indeed had made a good start of it. Right now he was a friend to me, a dear friend, much as I didn't want to admit it.

Maybe one more request tonight would make me feel truly okay.

'Lucio… would you… would you drive me?'

'You want to go home?'

'No, would you drive me to my old house? Where he died?'

Lucio looked me in the eye: 'Are you sure?'

'I want to.'

I could hear him say *are you sure* again, but in the end he just nodded, carried me to his car and off we drove to Minchinbury Avenue.

Lucio's hand was on mine most of the journey. I didn't know what this would bring, seeing the street again, but I had to do it and I felt better that Lucio was with me.

The suburb hadn't changed that much. The playground had been upgraded, some trees had been chopped down, and a couple of new houses had popped up, but apart from that, the neighbourhood was as I had remembered it.

'This was the house.' I clenched a fist then hugged myself as if a cold wind had just blown against me.

Outside was 20 degrees, the dashboard indicator said. The smell of French vanilla had somehow intensified now that we were stationary. I observed the house, recalling the day we brought baby Christopher home from the hospital and the first night we slept together as a family under that roof. It was a night like this. 'It still looks the same. The gate is still the same,' I mumbled.

I paused for a minute or two, putting together the bits and pieces I could fetch from my memory – fast forward three years past Christopher's first night at home. As I looked at what was around me, the picture was becoming clearer, and fuller. I remembered more than ever.

'I was watching him peddling his tricycle around the driveway, round and round,' I said, smiling. 'It was our gift to him.'

I huffed then continued, 'Other kids were praising him, circling around him, chasing him. I was there,' I said, pointing at the front patio. 'I remember I was leaning on that pillar close to the driveway. Christopher was all smiles. The other adults were gathering around the garden, everywhere, some of them near the gate, some outside the gate. We left it wide open. Just like that,' I pointed decisively at the open gate.

'Chris, my husband, was standing there near that hedge,' I said indicating the other side of the garden. 'He looked so happy watching Christopher. But... between looking at my son and my husband, I was distracted. Chris was immersed in a different kind of happiness, it was like... he was dreaming. He wasn't looking at Christopher. Then I heard... I might've heard a car coming but it wasn't the car that hit Christopher.'

I paused.

'When I looked back, Christopher wasn't where he had been, he was zooming past the open gate, probably excited that he could go so fast... but it was too fast. He whooshed past people's legs... and he was on the street in no time, and a white van hit him. It didn't make a big sound. I only heard people screaming. Then everything went quiet.'

I was about to hop out of the car, but Lucio seized my hand. 'No, stay here,' he gently said. 'Stay here.'

And I stayed.

'What did Chris see?' I was asking both myself and Lucio. 'He was standing there…'

Then I looked at the adjacent house. He could've been looking that way. Yes he had been! The Conways. There *was* another car, I'd heard it. A sedan pulling out of the driveway, and that was what Chris was looking at: the driver, Vinnie, the handsome 21-year-old. Or it could have been his father, who was equally charming…

My hand robotically flicked the car door open.

'Andie, no, please stay,' Lucio said, holding my hand tight.

'I need to find out.' Who was my husband falling in love with back then?

Lucio kept his grip on me. 'No, you have to let it go.'

I was about to say I couldn't.

But, Lucio was right. The Conways might not be living there any more, and even if they were, what would I say? *Was Vinnie driving the car that day on Christopher's birthday – 9 September 2000, at around 2p.m.?*

As I looked at the man sitting next to me, for the first time I saw a possibility – if I did let go, I might just find something good enough to start a new life for, a life without fear of Christopher, a life that I'd been desperate to have, with – this man? A family – with this man? My mind twisted, my heart contracted. Absurdity took over. The Lucio effect. It wasn't the first time. But… could it be? Could it be?

I came to his side. He pushed his seat back as I spread my legs on top of him. I unbuckled his belt, unzipped his pants and pulled his cock out.

'Andie?'

'Give it to me.'

He kissed me and I sucked his lips. I kept sucking as my hands unbuttoned his shirt. I scratched his chest. Not enough muscle to play rough, but it could absorb my pain, my tremors, my fear. How could he know so much? How could he *feel* me? It wasn't just because he was a pro, *surely*. No escort in the world would've made me feel so understood.

He reached for the glovebox.

So not tonight.

Of course not. It would never be any night.

I smiled at him ruefully. But soon his kiss wiped the sulkiness off me. He took my hands away from his chest, interlocked his fingers through mine, and guided both our arms to stretch up. He pinned my palms to the car roof with his. And so he gave me what he could, not a new life, but comfort, safety and pleasure. And that was enough, for tonight.

'*Sayang...*' I said.

The foreign word gave Lucio permission to take me out of my sorrow. His seriousness faded. 'What is that?' he said, touching my nose, expressing his bemusement.

I moved myself back to the passenger seat and pulled a few sheets of tissue. I used one to wipe my face and passed the rest to Lucio. 'It means "dear, darling" in Malay. My mum used to call me Sayang when I was little.'

'That's a nice word,' he said as he pulled away the condom and cleaned himself. I didn't think he'd come. 'You called Christopher that?'

'Actually, no, I never called him that.' I surprised myself. 'But I called my first dog Sayang,' I chortled. 'I was four or five. He was a black lab. I guess that's why I never called my son that.'

'Cute,' he said. 'So I'm your dog?'

'Nooo! It's just... I thought... you're dear to me, you know. Even though I'm your client you're my escort, that sort of thing. I really appreciate what you've done.'

'I can be your dog if you want me to.'

My eyes widened. I had seen those men who wore pig and

dog masks and walked on all fours, pulled by a leash; Leanne showed me them one day.

'*Awoooooo! Woof woof*,' he howled, barked and then started nibbling my neck.

I laughed and looked at Lucio lovingly. 'How much do I owe you?' I really didn't mean monetarily, but I was curious what he was going to say. He didn't say anything. He clearly wanted to, but in the end he just kissed me.

So we left Minchinbury Avenue slowly.

'You learned how to drive in Australia, right?' I teased. He had been driving one-handed while his other hand had been glued to mine. 'Remember two hands on the wheel?'

He laughed. 'I'll stop holding onto you, if that's what you want.'

I ummed. 'I like your hands, it's like you can do so much magic with them... but I think you should put both hands... on the wheel...'

'As you wish,' he said.

We hadn't reached Sydney but I was anxious about the end of the journey. I didn't want it to be over. But what Lucio had done for me tonight would go on beyond the remaining kilometres. A new change had just taken effect within me. I wasn't free, but I was able to smile as an honest person.

It was approaching 3 a.m. I started seeing the haze blanketing the city, it was grey, but it was bright. It looked out of place. In fact, everything looked out of place: the dashboard looked hazy, my own hands looked hazy and even Lucio looked hazy.

'Andie?' Faintly I heard Lucio calling my name. Or so I thought.

Gradually I felt heat around my neck, then my head went empty, and so did my chest. Then the cagey feeling.

Not another one...

I gasped for air, scrunched my chest and said, 'Lucio...'

In between the ringing in my ears and everything else, I heard someone crying, and he said he knew me, and his name was....

Then everything turned black.

'IT'S NO LAUGHING MATTER!' said the doctor who was called Dr Wheelan. 'You nearly died, again!'

He had made himself abundantly clear about me being close to death, ever since I opened my eyes in that hospital. But there he was... going on and on about it. Grumpy old man!

'Third time you might not be so lucky,' he said.

'I feel all right, maybe it was just lack of sleep, too much V,' I said.

'Huh... yeah, energy drinks... don't ever touch those again!' Dr Wheelan said, writing something on the clipboard.

'Can I go home... soon?'

'No!' Dr Wheelan snapped. 'You're going nowhere tonight. If everything is okay by midday tomorrow then maybe we'll let you go. *Maybe*.'

I sighed, my eyes on Lucio's face – it was pasty white, probably from hearing 'almost died' repeatedly.

'All right, for now, I'll leave you be. Dr Richardson will come around later this morning,' the doctor said. He was about to leave, but decided to have a final say: 'Be prepared to be lectured again.' And he smiled as he left the room.

I chuckled.

'You don't seem to take this seriously,' Lucio said flatly.

It was the first full sentence he'd spoken since I woke up.

He continued, 'Why? The doctor was right, you know.'

'I've heard all that before. And yeah, I should take it easy, but I don't know how to.'

'You should call Chris,' Lucio said.

I cocked my head. 'No, I want you to stay, please.'

'You looked surprised I said that.' Lucio frowned.

'Yeah... why would you want me to be with Chris?'

'I always want what's best for you,' he said, and squeezed my hand. 'He needs to know you're here.'

I nodded and reached for his hand.

He played with my fingertips saying, 'I thought I was going to lose you. You were so cold. And what was that about, the doctor said *third time you might not be so lucky*? You've had this before?'

'I had one a while ago now. It was nothing, just a mild heart attack.'

'Andie! You *can't* have a heart attack! Or anything! Anything that might kill you.' And with that Lucio hugged me. 'Please!'

How I loved how he felt. In sickness or in health, his hug felt amazing.

'Whoever you are, you're the best thing that could happen to me, at least tonight. Thank you for everything'

'I always want what's best for you, like I said.'

Lucio stared at me. He stared and stared.

'Lucio? What's wrong?'

'Umm... nothing, nothing. I just want you to know that I will do anything for you, as a friend.'

'Let's not go that far, eh?' I smiled. Although I sighed long, and shook my head repeatedly.

I wanted to escape his stare, there was something persistent in it, something that demanded I understand but I didn't want to know what it was. I reached for my phone, which had stayed in silent mode since I left the office. I rolled my eyes: four missed calls from Chris.

'You know Andie... you remind me of someone,' Lucio said, half murmuring.

I frowned. 'Don't tell me it's your mother!'

He didn't say anything.

'Who is it? A gorgeous actress?'

'You know—'

The phone vibrated in my hand.

'Chris...' I answered.

'Andrea where have you been?' Chris's voice blared.

'Work. What's up?'

'No, you haven't been at work! I rang Sophie, and I came to your office, and I rang Leanne and Karin, no one knew where you were!'

'I'm fine, Chris. You don't have to babysit me.'

'Andrea... I didn't mean to. I just... I know what today is, or yesterday was.'

He hadn't usually remembered.

'I just wanted to make sure you're okay,' Chris said softly. I could hear him welling up.

'I'm okay, Chris.'

'Please come home.'

'I'll see you tomorrow, okay?'

'No, please, come home now.'

'Chris... I'm... umm... I'm in hospital.'

'Andrea?'

'I was walking aimlessly... you're right, I was... I wasn't in a good place. And I just felt unwell.'

'My God! Why didn't you call me? Why didn't the hospital call me? Did you have...?'

'It wasn't as bad as the first one. I told the doctor not to ring you. I didn't want to worry you, it's nothing. I'll be out tomorrow.'

'Jesus... Which hospital, Andrea? I'm coming there now.'

I tried to think which hospital. I looked at Lucio who was

mouthing *Prince Albert*. 'Umm... Prince Albert. I'm fine, honestly.'

'Sarina...' Then I could hear him sigh. 'Please don't say you're fine. The first time was very hard, okay? But at least I was there. This time... God, you were by yourself! Please don't let me lose you. I'm scared. I'm telling you, I'm scared. I'll see you soon. I love you.'

He loved me. My husband loved me.

I looked at Lucio – the other man who didn't want to lose me. I scowled, trying to hold my tears – I didn't want to say it but in the end I told Chris the words: 'I love you, too.'

Lucio kissed my forehead as soon as I hung up. 'I should go,' he said.

'Thank you for everything tonight.'

And Lucio left with his head down.

FREDERICO LOWE: MY SWEET ANDIE

18 SEPTEMBER 2016

I DIDN'T THINK Andie would see me so soon. She'd been out of hospital last week, then I'd received her text late last night asking to meet up this afternoon. Not much time for preparation (I was out all morning with Mr G), and I was nervous about what I was going to deliver to Andie this time. Anyway, I was happy to see her again; I wanted to see for myself she was okay.

She arrived wearing a hot pink dress, very short, very tight. The first thing she said when she saw me: 'Oh, you're fully clothed! Being mysterious, are we?'

'It's rather chilly today to be wearing just boxer shorts,' I said.

At the beginning she seemed to be in the mood to talk (and I secretly hoped it would be all she asked for). She vented her frustration at being in a padded cell with Chris for a week. 'Can't do this, can't do that; can't go there, can't go here; can't eat this, can't eat that.'

But after all that, eventually she sat on my lap, unbuttoned my shirt and gave me the cue, 'Be gentle, please.'

And that almost sent me to tears – she said it the same way

she had when it had been our first encounter, the start of everything, right on this chair. By now I had endured all the pretending that I could, but I didn't know how to tell her the truth. So I just continued doing the thing that Lucio would: I carried her to bed.

'I missed you,' she whispered as I lay on top of her. 'Whoever you are...'

Why did she have to say that? Was she playing with me? Had she heard my confession when she was semiconscious in the car that night?

I teased her with my tongue – she was pink and in full bloom, as always. But today it was more beautiful than ever. She tasted so sweet, as always, but today she was sweeter than ever.

'Lucio...' she said as she gasped at her first climax.

Gently I turned Andie to her side and nudged her knees to bend. I lay behind her, bonding my body to hers, following her glorious curves. I lifted her leg slightly and entered her. That warm squeeze, I could really feel her and I knew she felt me as she'd never had before. She moaned loudly – her head thrown back, her arm flung out behind her looking for my face. Once she found me she didn't let go, as I thrusted, and withdrew, and thrusted.

Then I withdrew and cried.

'Lucio?' Andie turned completely to face me. 'What's wrong?'

'I'm sorry...' I said. 'I can't...'

'It's okay,' she said. 'You're not feeling well?'

'Andie... I don't want to lose you.'

'Is this about my heart attack? Lucio... I'm fine. I've been staying away from those energy drinks,' she said, trying to get a smile from me.

'Promise me I won't lose you?'

'I'm as strong as an ox. You don't have to worry about me,' she said and put her head on my chest.

And I held her so tight.

'Your heart is beating so fast...' she whispered.

'Andie... I'm sorry... I've never done that before.'

'Heey... I came,' she said bashfully.

'I know I'm just your escort, but I can't help being human, you know.'

She took a deep breath. 'I know. Well, you just have to take my word for it. I'm fine.'

I didn't say anything.

'That night at the hospital you said I reminded you of someone,' she said.

I didn't dare look at her.

'Did I?' I said innocently, playing with her fingers.

'Unlike you to forget?'

'You really want to know?'

'Tell me.'

I stared at her. 'You remind me of the most amazing human being I've ever known.'

She smiled hesitantly.

'My real name is Frederico...'

Andie's eyes widened, her lips parted. 'I... I've heard that name before...' she said. 'In the car before my heart attack... everything was black, my ears were ringing but I heard that name. It's a beautiful name.'

'That most amazing human being, I saw her in Rome... I was just a boy––'

She gasped and quickly pulled the sheet to cover herself. 'You were that boy?'

'You saved my life, Andie.'

She jumped out of bed and put on her clothes.

'Andie, please, tell me you want to be with me!'

'I held you in my arms...' she said. 'This is all wrong!'

'You want to be with me! That night at the hospital, you cried when you had to say *I love you* to Chris. You looked at *me* and cried. You didn't want to say it to him. You wanted to say it to me!'

'I held you in my arms... you were...'

'You thought I was your son?'

She covered her mouth and shook her head.

'I am not your son, Andie.'

'I have to go!'

I grabbed her arm.

'Don't touch me!' she said, and pushed me away. She got dressed, snatched her bag and she ran. She didn't even wait for the elevator; she took the stairs and continued running.

I had seen this would happen even before I made the confession. Who wouldn't run away? I was this creepy boy thief who happened to have grown up and become a gay man and fallen in love with a married woman. What different outcome was I was expecting? Different from the rest, was she? I was indeed blind. And stupid.

ANDREA CURTIN: MY BOY

19 SEPTEMBER 2016

I PUT another blue piece in the top right quadrant of my puzzle, forming more sky above what would be the Trevi Fountain. The quadrants were spread out as four cloud-shapes on my dining table. I was almost halfway there. Which one should I build on next? My auto-pilot hand continued with the top right. Rome – the statue of Ocean and his chariot. Rome – the Colosseum. Rome – two bony legs running across the cobblestone street. Rome – police batons landing on the boy's skeletal frame. Rome – two blue eyes staring at me.

The boy was Rome.

My lover, my confidant – the boy from Rome.

Was that why I'd trusted him so much? Not because he was good, but because deep down I knew him? Those teddy bear eyes. And I'd even thought he could've given me a baby… My God!

I put another piece of the puzzle in – part of Ocean's face.

Then the front door behind me opened slowly.

'Wow! Am I dreaming?' Chris said. 'You, home before me?'

I smiled. 'Like I said, I've been a good girl.'

'Well done!' Chris said and kissed me. He looked at the puzzle. 'And... what have we here?'

'I bought this on the way home. Thought it would be a good distraction, rather than watching telly.'

'The Trevi Fountain, eh?' Chris said. 'And you've been doing this since like what, five? And you're almost there?'

'Oh, still a lot of pieces left.'

'You're not stressing yourself out, are you?'

'No! How can puzzles stress me out!'

'I actually came to your office earlier and Sophie said you'd gone home. I was shocked! I went in unannounced, hoping I could kidnap you and take you to Chinatown for dinner. Since you weren't there, I bought you this: wonton noodle soup.'

'Champion! Thank you,' I said. 'What have you got for yourself?'

'Oh, I had some fried rice there. I was with Ken.'

That fly!

'You wanna go back to Rome?' Chris mused over my puzzle pieces.

'What?' I frowned. 'Oh, no! No!'

'All right, all right, not Rome. Where would you go if I told you we could go tomorrow?'

'Where would *you* like to go? It's not just about me.'

'It *is* about you, Sarina. I want to make you happy,' he said, hugging me from behind.

A hint of orange and perhaps bergamot rose from his skin. I didn't recall such a smell this morning when he'd left. No, he hadn't got a new deodorant or cologne. It was the scent of Pub.

FREDERICO LOWE: AN OFFER

20 SEPTEMBER 2016

ANDIE HADN'T CALLED, hadn't texted.

Mother once told me admitting what you'd done wrong would ease your burden. She said it many times, but the time I remembered most was at the police station in Rome, after I'd got beaten up. I denied having stolen the wallet (I tossed it under the car when Andie was hugging me). Then I confessed. And I got beaten up some more.

Honesty is the best policy? Bullshit!

I should've kept lying. What did honesty give me? Punishment. Did the burden go away? Far from it! The world of pretending was a lot better than the truth.

'What do you want?' Andie's voice croaked when I rang her.

'Andie, I'll do anything to have you back,' I blurted, unprepared. I hadn't expected her to answer.

'I don't want you back.'

'Please give me a chance. I'm begging you. I'm *begging* you.'

'You will do anything?'

'I will!'

'Well, here's what I'm thinking. My husband has been seeing

an escort, or two, or three, I don't know. Before a long night out his wallet is always loaded. If I hadn't used an envelope to pay for my romps, my wallet would've been like his, too. And when he came home he had another man's smell on him. Maybe I smelled like that too after I fucked you.' She paused. 'I want you to give me the name of his current escort.'

'What?'

'You heard me.'

'I can't do that.'

'So you lied.'

'Andie... if I gave you a name it wouldn't end well for either of us, it wouldn't end well for Chris.'

'I don't care. I want the name. Or we're really through. I will leave you, I will leave Chris. You know I could go anywhere in the world, right? You won't ever see me again.'

'And if I do this you will let me see you again?'

'I'll think about it.'

And she hung up.

ANDREA CURTIN: MY TOOL

25 SEPTEMBER 2016

No, it wouldn't end well, as Lucio had told me. But that was the only way. I could've confronted my husband and relied on what Chris had to say. But Chris's words wouldn't suffice and I wanted to make Lucio pay for his deceit. He had been a tool for my sexual mind, now I wanted to use him as a tool for my angry mind.

Almost a week had gone by since I made the offer and Lucio had given me nothing.

Between my desire to execute my plan and my desperation to see Lucio again (there was just something about that boy), I decided to initiate contact. Lucio was quiet for most of the call. At the end of it we agreed to meet at a Kings Cross pub.

I purposely came late. From a distance, outside the pub, I watched Lucio playing with his drink. The skeletal child I'd seen in Rome had become a grown man. And he wasn't just any man: he was the man who made love to me, whose chest had absorbed so many of my tears.

Should I turn around and stand him up? Or go ahead and take the plunge?

I joined him without saying a word.

'This is him,' Lucio said, nudging a small piece of paper to my side of the table.

Pablo – and his phone number.

I could smell him – Pub. His cologne, his cum. But I couldn't imagine his face. Spanish eyes, roundish face, muscular. Maybe a bit like Alban. 'How old is he?'

'Early thirties.'

That old? Had Chris changed his preference?

'What are you going to do, Andie?' Lucio asked.

'Well, I'm going to fuck him.'

'Please, don't,' he begged. 'Please, promise me you won't.'

Mummy, please don't go. I shivered. 'I'm not promising you anything, Lucio.'

ANDREA CURTIN: ALIEN'S NEST

26 SEPTEMBER – 5 OCTOBER 2016

WEARING A TIGHT BLACK DRESS, I felt a sense of deja vu walking along the corridor leading to Pablo's apartment. It felt the same as when I went to see Jake the bang-bang gladiator guy; I might've even worn the same dress then. But my emotions were far from deja vu. This time I wasn't seeking pleasure, I wasn't trying to escape. My challenge now was to put forth the best act for an audience of one: a man who knew my husband better than I did. No tingling feelings, no butterflies. Just anger, imagining the two men together.

Pablo greeted me at the door. He spoke with a real Spanish accent, unlike Lucio, who sometimes put on his Italian accent when he felt like it. Initially I imagined ten years ago he would've looked like Vinnie Conway of Minchinbury Avenue. But, no, Pablo didn't resemble Vinnie, only a fleeting, overthinking glance gave me that impression.

Pablo's sleepy eyes and full lips emanated lust, and the bulge between his thighs hinted an urgent need for sex, although I had only booked him for a massage. As he led me to his bedroom, I almost blurted all of my burning questions: *How do you seduce him? What sort of service does he ask for? What position? How often?*

But I simply smiled when Pablo invited me to lie on the velvet-covered bed. Blocks of purple, gold and magenta around the room swirled like a scene from *Arabian Nights*, and the room's spicy fragrance made my surroundings feel like a hedonistic harem.

But the eroticism didn't translate beyond the four walls. Pablo's speech, his touch felt like I was interacting with a mannequin. Maybe it was too early in the morning for him (10 a.m.), or it might've been just his style. Or perhaps Pablo was a gay escort who didn't really enjoy the company of women.

'Is it good for you, my dear?' Pablo said, massaging my back. A few times he had to go around my bra straps.

'Yes.'

Then he slinked in between my thighs.

He slowly glided his body against mine. I thought he was going to keep his briefs on, but I could feel his naked, hard cock sliding along my lower spine, up and down, up and down, like a capsule elevator running between level 1 and 2, ever so slowly. He was smooth, but somewhat perfunctory.

I shook off my negative thoughts. Now that I'd been with Lucio, I had become hypercritical of any move and gesture – I was comparing Pablo with the best in the business (biased as I might've been), and Pablo didn't come even close. Maybe *I* was the one who hesitated.

'Really tight around the shoulders,' he said seductively.

'Stress,' I said.

'You have to relax,' he said in my ear.

'Make me...' I sighed.

Unexpectedly he turned me over. His knees were on each side of my waist. For the first time I saw sweetness on my escort's face. When I looked down I saw a mighty big, red cock towering up past his belly button. I'd seen it on his ad and had thought it was just the camera angle that distorted the size, but it was truly a big one – bigger than Chris's.

I took the opportunity to fish for some warmth from my masseuse, I needed to start asking questions soon. I pulled his hands over to my breasts. 'Play with me,' I said helplessly.

I started sighing and writhing as Pablo was warming up to me. He even took off my bra. I didn't want him to, but I let him. What he was giving me felt more and more genuine.

'You look like a soldier,' I said and winked. 'I like army men, you know. Next time you should greet me wearing army fatigues, and we can take it to the next level.'

He licked my face.

I giggled, suppressing my dislike.

'Naughty, naughty girl!' Pablo said.

'Are you an army man, Pablo?' I said, as he was rigorously massaging my breasts. In any other situation I'd ask my man to stop, but once again I played along.

'No, but I learned how to be an army man,' he said.

'That's good enough for me,' I said and lifted my thigh, rubbing it on his cock.

Pablo lowered his body and glided on me again, on top of my belly and chest. I hissed.

'Army men turn me on... do army men turn *you* on?' I said it on top of my panting. I wanted him to think I blurted it out of unbearable pleasure.

'What do you mean?' Pablo said.

'Threesome, maybe, next time, with another army man...'

'You are *really* naughty, my dear,' he laughed. 'I have friends who would do that, of course.'

'Do you have army clients?'

'Ooooo... that's a secret!'

'Heeey... you know, it would be more fun if you could hook me up with one of your clients. It would be more... real, you know, like a real affair.'

He trapped me with his body. 'Violet, my dear, I didn't think you were that type.'

'Well, I *am* that type and I am willing to pay a high price for fantasies.'

He looked at the clock. Time was almost up. He rolled over to my side and said, 'No, I don't have army clients.'

Not the answer I wanted, but I sensed he had something more to reveal. I gazed at him. Eye contact and vulnerability gained trust – it always worked in business, and this was no exception.

He continued: 'I... I used to. Very good client. He was in the army for a long time, he's retired now. I liked him. He was good. Very handsome too. Yes.'

'Shame...' I said. I noticed something glum creeping beneath his smile. 'Oh sorry... I shouldn't have asked that.'

'No, no it's okay. It was the past,' he said. 'I have friends, I can ask them, it will be fun.'

I didn't want his friends. But I had to be curious about them otherwise it would be the end of my role play, and it would be the end of Pablo's insights into the life of Chris Curtin. I still needed him so I said, 'That would be awesome. Where do you hang out?'

'We can meet here, or at a pub.'

'A pub sounds good.'

THE MEETING at Back to Back on Oxford St was probably a rare, effortlessly good time for Pablo and his two friends (all drinks paid, their half hour fees paid, and they didn't need to pull their pants down). All they had to do was talk about soldier role play and share their kinky thoughts about having sex out in the wilderness. But it yielded nothing.

Pablo anxiously asked how I wanted to proceed. Desperate to dig more meaningful information about Chris, I had to play the game. But the thought of stripping in front of those sleazy men made me sick. In the end I told Pablo that none of his friends fit my fantasies. I whispered to him: 'I want another man like *you*, Pablo.' And he took it as a compliment. And I now had a trusty relationship with my husband's ex.

After the meeting I rang Lucio.

'You're not telling the truth!' I said.

'What do you mean?'

'Why did you set me up with Pablo? He's no longer with Chris!'

'So the rumours were true...' he whispered. 'I heard Chris had a falling out with him.'

'Is he with you, Lucio? Something smells fishy here!'

'No! Your husband is *not* my client.'

'Then who is he with? I'm sure you know.'

'Please, Andie, you can't blackmail me like this. '

'Oh, I can!'

'Let it go, Andie. Why don't you just leave him?'

'I intend to, but I need a reason.'

Lucio paused. I could hear him breathing heavily.

I asked him again: 'Who is it, Lucio? Or you're not going to see me ever again.'

'His name is Gianni,' Lucio said. 'He's new, but he's very, very attractive. Very much Chris's type.'

I was about to ask what type that was, but I was determined to see for myself.

'YOU MIGHT BE KICKED out of The Nest,' Pablo said to me seductively; he was staring at my outfit: a black patent leather bustier with laces and black patent leather pants, with knee-high red patent leather boots with seven-inch heels.

'You're going to create a storm,' he said.

'That's what I intend to do,' I said, straightening Pablo's bow tie and brushing a few specks off his tuxedo lapels. 'Thanks for sorting out the invitation.'

'My pleasure,' Pablo said. 'But you might meet some army men there and forget about me.'

'Oh, Pablo, my dear, I will never forget you.'

Pablo instructed the cab driver to pull over in front of a club called Maya. From there we went down to the basement, through a short tunnel that ended at a steel door, similar to the one I'd seen at the end of the laneway when the two men attacked me that night.

Pablo looked up at a camera. A few seconds later the door slid open automatically. After we'd walked up two flights of stairs, a man in a purple suit scanned Pablo's member's card.

'And this is Violet, she should be on the guest list,' Pablo said.

Without saying anything, the purple man let us in.

The Nest was exactly as I'd imagined it: a dim brothel with red spotlights moving from one point of interest to another; a G-string-clad DJ, official dancers, and patrons – twirling, sculling, romping, arousing.

I quickly put on my eye mask. Most of the patrons were men in kinky clothes – teeny tiny thongs, chains and leather, head masks and gags, but a handful of them were smartly dressed as if they were at a high-class restaurant. There were a few girls there, all of them wearing costumes; mostly in dominatrix style like me, as advised by Pablo.

'There's an army man,' Pablo teased as we passed a stripper who was wearing camouflage-patterned briefs.

'Ooo yeah, he's hot,' I said.

We walked up to the mezzanine level, which looked down to the main bar and dance floor. Every man and woman turned to me as I walked past a spotlight. Some of them smiled or nodded or raised their glass to Pablo.

'You are creating a storm, Violet,' Pablo whispered.

'Do they know I'm a stranger here?'

'They just haven't seen me with you,' he said.

'Hey, are there any heterosexual men or women here?' I asked.

'I've never come across them, to be honest.'

'Except me?' I said.

He grabbed my waist and turned me like a dancer: 'I reckon you're not that straight.'

'Oooh... you might be right,' I said. 'Let's stay here.'

'As you wish,' he said.

Leaning against the railing, I scanned the floor below, studied the dancers, watched the bartenders, tracked people's movements, and finally I discerned a figure I'd been hoping to see. He was with another man who I could speculate was Gianni. So that was what *Chris's type* looked like. He didn't look like Vinnie Conway, he didn't look like anyone I knew. He was androgynously pretty and distortedly skinny. I wondered how big his cock was that Chris could ever find him attractive.

Both men were dressed in standard clothes. Thank goodness. I couldn't imagine my husband in a silver G-string or leopard thong – he had the body, but he was still *Chris*, Christopher's dad, my other half for almost two decades; he was supposed to be straight, flat, black and white.

The two men kissed.

Mylb – that was what Chris called Gianni, I'd found out. I had turned my husband's phone inside out, although he changed his passcode regularly. I was aware of his cautiousness so I had been acting ignorant. But Chris didn't know he was slow in punching in his passcode. And my peripheral vision was as good as my business instinct. He kept all his text messages and phone logs clean – but what he *also* didn't know was that the back-up ran every day. I found out Mylb was in fact My Little Birdie. His nickname might be cryptic but there was nothing cryptic about the messages they'd been exchanging:

Everything in u is pretty, esp that tight li'l hole of yours

My fist was so deep in you, I could almost grab your heart

9p.m. next Sat, start at the N then we can take it from there

R u prepared for a scorching nite?

Indeed.

A group of girls arrived and hung around next to us. They were all as tall as me, wearing heels and tights, all black, with different degrees of provocativeness. They looked so young, maybe in their early twenties. They were talking quietly and drinking politely among themselves. I played a game with myself, trying to guess who these girls would be come Monday morning: lawyers to be, entrepreneurs, tech experts, media gurus?

Soon another girl joined them. She'd donned a perfect Marilyn look. She stood out from the group, not only because of her white dress, but because she was the only one who dared to look at me front-on. She had lust, and she didn't try to hide.

I knew at some stage Chris would look my way. When that happened, I didn't want him to spot me near a man that he knew. I whispered to Pablo, 'I'll be back.'

'Don't go too far,' he said. 'As my guest you are my responsibility.'

I blew a kiss before I took a couple of steps to approach Marilyn. Just as I was about to infiltrate the circle, Marilyn detached herself from the group.

'Hello, gorgeous,' Marilyn said.

I smiled at her seductively, giving her permission to grab my waist and kiss my lips. Right now I would do anything to keep my sanity – let it be frolicking with a lesbian.

Be careful what you wish for – I had come to see my husband in this light, I got it, but finding Chris in this erotic man cave had pushed me beyond what I could take. And like a gun pointed at my head, I felt I had to decide what to do with him. I couldn't. So I needed an escape. With every pucker, press and push I told Marilyn my story: My husband is down there. Look! He's so into this alien lookalike called Gianni. And I've been fucking another man, who used to be this boy that I saved a long time ago.

I had one eye on Marilyn, another on Chris. I knew energy travelled and the target wasn't too far away. Chris finally looked up. I briefly lifted up my eye mask. Chris raised his wine glass and nodded.

What a fool!

He then kissed Gianni, almost mimicking the action he'd just seen.

Now that Chris was aware of this girl on the mezzanine, I shifted my focus to myself. So this was what it felt like kissing another woman; too soft for my liking. Was Pablo right? Was there was a part of me that wasn't so straight? I let the kiss go on to find out for sure. Much as Marilyn's affection made me feel like the sexiest woman in the building, the chemistry was never forthcoming on my part. It was like kissing myself.

I pulled back a step and gave Marilyn a goodbye smile. I threw a glance at Pablo, who was talking to another man but still keeping an eye on me. I looked down and Chris was still stealing glances at me amidst his frolicking with Gianni.

'Stay with us,' Marilyn said, following me.

I left Marilyn as quietly as I'd come to her. I nudged Pablo to walk to the darker side, hidden from Chris's view. I hugged and kissed him. 'I'm ready to go home.'

FREDERICO LOWE: FOLLOW HER LEAD

5 OCTOBER 2016

Damn Andie! I wanted to forget about her.

I sniffed the white powder off my palm. This time I'd paid for the stuff so it'd better be good! I looked at my diary randomly and tore out the pages of my earlier entries:

2/9/2006 Met with Adam and Frost from year 11. They love me

1/10/2007 Sam and I did it

25/7/2010 – not a career, but I earn heaps more

6/8/2010 – my uniform: tight fake leather briefs

18/8/2011 – this guy Max, we touch each other

12/1/2012 – Pablo, Max and I - weird session

16/2/2012 – Now I know pain.

31/10/2013 I think CJ is addicted to me

And I kept tearing them until:

22/2/2016 – Txt from a woman Andie. She wanted me. So happy.

It hurt to tear our history, it was like tearing my own heart. So I headed to the kitchen with the diary in my hand. I turned on the stove, ready to burn it instead.

But I stopped.

Instead I placed my hand on top of the flame.

Am I still human?

No, I'm just an escort who can't feel the heat.

Human, escort...

Human, escort...

Could I ever be a human being and the greatest escort at the same time?

What humanly thing would make her mine, forever?

What humanly thing did Andie want most in her life?

What could an escort do to make it happen? What could the greatest escort in her life do?

'Arghh!' I groaned.

The heat was real, and so was my idea. I opened my diary again.

13/4/2016 – she wanted to see me but cancelled. Something came up?? An excuse or the truth??? ~~Maybe husband found out~~! We had phone sex, but she told me she wanted a baby and her husband didn't?? untouchable

27/4/2016 – My red hot Andie; happy, relaxed, a bit wild - now I know why she smelled that way

16/5/2016 – Andie cried in my arms. She wouldn't say why, but I knew.

6/6/2016 – Magic. Untying her ribbon was like opening a present. But she still didn't want a massage!!

6/7/2016 – Damn Andie! Something came up again??? I want to see you! Now! - untouchable

18/7/2016 – My Andie, glowing. Something, there's something - now I know that something

3/8/2016 – Andie so grumpy on the phone! PMS

5/8/2016 – ~~(placeholder for allnighter yay!)~~ cancelled - untouchable

I KNEW her better than she knew herself. I *could* give her what she wanted. I knew it like science. I could make her mine that way. All I had to do was follow her lead.

ANDREA CURTIN: SAINT CHRIS

6 OCTOBER 2016

FROM THE NEST, Pablo and I came back to his place where I'd parked my car. I couldn't drive a metre without being distracted by visions of Chris with Gianni. I was worried I might hit someone if I drove home, so I paid Pablo an overnight rate and asked if I could sleep at his place. He cuddled me, massaged my shoulders and made me hot chocolate before bed.

This morning I left after Pablo fixed me an omelette. Chris wasn't there when I got home. He was already on his way to Newcastle to speak at a fitness expo, something about motivation.

I spent a few hours in the office – typing nice emails to my demanding clients while my mouth spitting out curses. I didn't dare answering phone calls, knowing I would say something stupid. Close to 3 p.m. I went home, delegating all my outstanding problems to the ever-patient Sophie.

I shoved another empty can of V in the bin and hurled myself into the sofa. I wouldn't sleep tonight. My heart rate soared, and it would stay this way for a while.

Arms crossed, torso upright like a piece of plywood, I waited for Chris. I was wondering if the talk went well, and what sort of mood he would be in when he walked through the door.

At about 6 p.m. there he was, in a polo and chinos. 'Hey honey!' he said without looking at me as he was busy transferring all his presentation props to his left hand to free the other to latch the door.

I remained silent, waiting for him to look at me. When he finally turned his head, all smiles, he literally jumped as if my wrath had shot him in the chest.

'So, Saint Chris has decided that he needs a good time, too.'

'What?'

'It makes sense,' I said. 'Pablo, Gianni.'

Chris' face blanched, his hands spilling folders, tapes and rolled-up chart paper. 'How did you find out?'

'The Nest.'

'Andrea.' He frowned. 'What did you do?'

'It's not such a secret. Other people know, too.'

'I'm sorry...' Chris slumped onto the sofa.

For the first time he looked small. He was sorry all right, but forgiveness wasn't on my agenda, not tonight.

'You didn't recognise me last night, did you?' I said. 'I was with Pablo.'

'It was you... I saw you!' he said. 'Jesus...'

'Jesus what? Did I look stunning? Or is it "Jesus I never thought that I'd ever get caught"?'

'Andrea, I'm so sorry...,' he said. 'I know it's unfair on you... but this thing, this feeling, it's a dark part of me and I don't want anybody to know.'

'You don't want *your wife* to know,' I snapped. 'Because other people know, Chris – Kenneth, his friends...'

'I'm so sorry...' he said covering his face. 'What did you do with Pablo?'

'You meant, what did he tell me?'

'No, I meant, did you do it with him?'

'No,' I huffed. 'So when you said you didn't want my pussy, you meant it.'

'No, I...'

'How long have you seen those boys?'

He paused as if counting. 'A long time.'

'Did you imagine them when you were with me? When we just got together I wasn't too bad, huh?' I got up and walked to the kitchen. I felt a gagging sensation in my throat. I wanted to wash it off... but water wasn't enough and my energy drink supply had run out and I didn't want booze. So I just stared at the sink.

'Andrea, I did it with boys all the time when I was in the army. I stopped when I met you, when I married you.'

'Back then we were still new, you still cared to pretend. As time went by, when you opened your eyes, you couldn't hide your disgust anymore. "Jesus... this... this thing I'm fucking has breasts and a pussy!"'

He cried. 'I stopped, Andrea. I thought I could change, with you. But I couldn't. A few months after...'

I was dying to complete his sentence but I waited.

'After we lost Christopher's brother, I started seeing those boys,' he sobbed. 'I'm sorry.'

'I understand if your attraction is to boys. I do, trust me,' I said. 'But why the "try-again" charade? Why did you have to make me feel like shit? My husband didn't want to touch me. I kept wondering what's wrong with me? What have I done? All along I thought you were blaming me for Christopher's death, that you were traumatised by what happened to his brother.'

'Andrea, *you* felt that way, and I always told you it was not true for me. And I'm really sorry you had to find out about me this way.'

'And what's worse, you barked so loudly when I asked you

about a gay escort. Remember that afternoon in the city? "Homo dick" and all that?'

'I was trying to deny what's in my head. I didn't want you to know. It made me angry, and it came out like that. I didn't mean it.'

'Hypocrite!'

'Call me that, I'll take it. But please, forgive me. This has got nothing to do with who you are, or what has happened in our relationship. I've always been like this. I just never told you.'

I was about to throw in the name of Vinnie Conway, but Lucio's words kept ringing in my head: *let it go*. And I decided to let it go.

'The two straight escorts that I told you about, well, the truth is, I couldn't have sex with any of them not because I still wanted you. I couldn't do it because they *reminded* me of you!'

Chris shook his head once more.

I continued, 'They reminded me of how meaningless a relationship with a man could be. Flat... straight... superficial... one way...'

'That's not fair!'

'And you were acting like a good husband, so noble, you said things that all good husbands should and would: "I love you, Sarina", "I want you to be happy", "Let's try again." I believed everything you said. But you're nothing more than a cheat!'

'That's so unfair! All these eighteen years you think what we had was just an act? I truly love you, Andrea, that's no lie!'

'You know what, let's call it even. Because I'm no angel either. I fucked that gay escort behind your back, countless times. I couldn't get enough of him. He was *so good. So good!*' I said. 'He made me feel like a woman. With you, I felt like a clueless, pathetic whore!'

I spat the word *whore* in his face. Right then he pushed me against the kitchen bench with his two hands. As the marble edge hit my back, he struck my face.

Almost immediately he pulled back. 'Oh my God... Andrea, I'm sorry... I didn't mean it...' Chris said, reaching out to me. Quailing, I crept sideways to the other end of the bench.

'Get out!' There it went – the fall of the hammer that would make it official: *we're through*.

Chris moved away from me, shaking his head, mouthing sorry again and again as he disappeared from the room.

From the kitchen window I watched his car taking forever to reverse out of the driveway, as if he was waiting for me to go out and shout *don't go*. But I just watched, until the headlights no longer shone on me.

I could fill all the empty space around me with my cries, but I could shed no tears. Instead I reached for the row of drinking glasses on the kitchen shelf.

One... two... I watched the pieces shatter.

Three... four... The shattering sound was more satisfying. The pieces got smaller.

Five... my vision blurred... it was as if the pieces were scattered in front of my eyes.

Six... I held off.

A figure loomed in the splashback. I turned around.

'It's me!' the man said, half ducking, one arm extended to stop me from swinging the last glass at him.

I froze. Those eyes. And I was calm for no reason. 'Lucio... you're not supposed to be here.' I trembled.

'He can't hit you like that!' he said.

'It's none of your business! Were you spying on me?'

'You said you'd reconsider if I gave you the name of the escort. I gave you two names.'

'You want your reward now?'

'Yes. I want you to show me some kind of appreciation, that you'll hold your end of the bargain!'

'Not a good time, Lucio.'

Lucio surveyed the scattered glass on the cook top. He said to me regretfully, 'I told you to keep it to yourself.'

'My fault, my mess, my way.'

'I didn't mean to point the finger at you. It's my mess as much as yours. I've broken every rule I set for myself, for my career. You don't do these things in my line of work,' Lucio said. 'But it was necessary. It was for *you*. And I'd do anything for you. Andie. I don't want to be a beggar. I want to be with you because I want you. I need you.'

Those eyes.

He touched my cheek. 'Come to my place.'

I sighed. I grimaced. But I was just a candle and he was always the flame who melted me. I followed Lucio, who walked briskly to the development site four houses down the road, where he had parked his car.

Inside the car I closed my eyes. It was the place where I'd found a little peace. That familiar smell of French vanilla was no car air freshener. He'd said he'd sprinkled aromatic oil on the upholstery and kept a sheet of paper dipped in it inside the glove compartment. I pulled the paper out and inhaled. I remembered how much comfort Lucio gave me, right on this seat. Tinker Bell, the stars, Christopher... I had been leaning on him then, the only one I could lean on.

Lucio...

Frederico...

The boy from Rome

Campanella...

Does it matter who he is?

Before I could come up with an answer, we had already

arrived at the basement of his apartment building. He swiped his card and the white roller door bellowed.

Lucio helped me out of the car. Anger still raged within me. It surprised me I hadn't insisted I could get up and walk on my own. In the lift I let myself fall to him. On the ground floor the lift stopped. As a woman stepped in, he gently turned my face towards his chest, hiding the spot Chris had hit.

Still in his arms, Lucio guided me to the living room. The armchair, where it had all started. My second home. I wished it to be my forever home, but life's little rules and boundaries would make it all wrong.

'It's not as bad as it looks. I bruise easily, remember?' I said when Lucio studied my lips.

'I'm sorry I forgot to put he ice pack in the fridge... this is all I have,' Lucio said wrapping a small towel around a bottle of cold beer. He put the bottle on the corner of my lips.

'He can't hit you like that. Does he hit you—'

'No, he's never hit me before.'

'He can't do that. I wish I'd been there.'

'You know what? It felt *really* good.'

'Andie, it shouldn't make you feel good.'

'It sealed the deal, you know. It was the end of us. The big Chris and me.'

Lucio repositioned the bottle and moved it up my cheek. 'Why don't you want me any more?' he asked.

'I think you know.'

'I want you as a man now, not as a boy.'

'I was your client, Lucio, nothing more.'

He bowed his head, nodded a few times. 'I, of all people, know that. It's what we swear by. Never fall in love with your client. But life doesn't always bring you what you expect. And what you know often becomes irrelevant very quickly.'

'We have to stop seeing each other. I'm not your friend, I'm not your client, I'm not your anything,' I said.

'Please… I can go back to where we were. We can keep it professional. I can do that.'

'How are you going to do that? Pretend? I can't!'

Lucio sighed.

I said, 'Or maybe that's what you're good at – that's your job, yeah?'

'I never pretended when I was with you, Andie.'

'You lied to me about Pablo. The deal's off.'

'Andie! I didn't lie to you, I didn't know Chris had ditched him. Chris had been hiring Pablo for a long time. I don't know why Chris decided to move on. When I first heard about it I didn't think it was true.'

I would hate to turn on my word. I knew he was telling the truth. But part of me wanted to hold on to his deception and escape having to decide whether I should start seeing him again. I didn't want to decide, I just wanted to let go.

Or did I?

Lucio almost shook me but in the end he just knelt and begged. 'If it makes you feel better, I need the money. I need *your* money because I…' he paused, then hesitantly continued, 'at the moment I have no other clients.'

Away with you, you sad teddy!

I crushed the arms of the chair; wrestling, sinking, resurfacing. 'Okay. This Saturday.'

'No, mid-next week.'

'I thought you needed the money.'

'Please, *next week*. Wednesday.'

'Okay. Wednesday. Just this once, no more.'

We looked at each other, not agreeing nor disagreeing.

FREDERICO LOWE: ANDIE

10 OCTOBER 2016

Five days felt like five months. When I'd told Andie I had no other clients, I'd meant it. I wanted nothing other than having her in my arms again. I gulped my Peroni. This bottle could've been the one I'd put on her swollen lips that night.

A one-liner soon ruined my longing:

Can't meet Wed. Funeral.

'Fuck!' I banged the table.

I rang her.

'A promise is a promise, Andie!' I said.

'I can't, Lucio... please! My uncle died and it's his funeral this Wednesday.'

'Is that an excuse?'

'Lucio! You think I would lie about something like this?'

'Were you close to him?'

'Why is that any of your business?'

'It is my business, Andie. You're playing with me! You *owe* me!'

'He was family. He was my mum's brother. No, I wasn't close

to him, but I have to be there! That's what we do in my family. Do you even understand *family*?'

'Andie. You didn't have to say that,' I told her with deep disappointment. I was as good as orphaned – it hurt to be reminded of it that way and I wanted her to know it.

'Then don't give me your bullshit about my uncle!'

No, she didn't know it hurt, and it wasn't her fault. 'I'm sorry,' I said, rubbing my face. 'I'm sorry. I shouldn't have said that.'

'I'll call you.'

'Your husband will be there at the funeral?'

'Of course.'

ANDREA CURTIN: HOW GREAT THOU ART

12 OCTOBER 2016

UNCLE MO WAS my mother's big brother. She never mentioned him that much. I myself had only met him a few times when I was a kid; the occasion that I remembered was Chinese New Year, we'd gone to his place, and I was wearing a new dress and saying *Gong Xi Fa Chai.* I'd been given a red envelope with money in it. He was the only Catholic in my mother's family and I was told he was quite a figure in the community.

The church was full of people I didn't know, or thought I'd seen but probably hadn't. My parents sat in the front row. I wasn't used to seeing my mother cry, and it was even stranger to see my father comforting her (usually it had been the other way around). Two rows behind them sat Chris and I, who both felt equally out of place.

How Great Thou Art. The voice of the choir carved the church ceiling as the procession was leaving. Chris and I were about fifth in line behind the casket. We were walking along the aisle, his arm hovering at my waist like a lint brush. Halfway between the altar and the vestibule, I turned instinctively. Mingled well with the congregation was a man in a black shirt and grey pants, standing full of respect. His eyes were hidden behind his sunglasses and his head was down, looking at the hymn sheet, although he wasn't singing. No one took notice of him, but to me he was like a coloured zebra among the black and whites.

How shameless can a man be? Turning up at a funeral to collect a debt?

I grabbed Chris's arm and pulled him towards me. As I kept walking with my eyes closed I felt repeated thumps in my heart, in sync with every vibration in my eardrums – the angelic voices saying:

When I in awesome wonder

Consider all the works

Thy hands have made

Lucio...

Frederico...

The boy from Rome...

Such a beautiful creation. A man whose words had comforted me in my darkest hours. I was thankful for his existence. Whoever owned the *hands* that had made him must've loved him, then abandoned him.

Without realising, I shed a tear. Fitting for the occasion, but I knew I had got too carried away with how great the God in this church was. He created me, He created Chris, He created Christopher, He created Lucio, then He watched, He moved the chess pieces, He created bliss, He created conflicts, He created hurt, and He carried on watching until there were no more pieces left to play – He Himself would be the last one standing. I was about to hide my tears but Chris had already noticed me, and his response was simply a frown.

As people were dispersing, Chris and I excused ourselves, blaming my light-headedness to avoid the cremation and the reception at my parents' place. In front of everybody I pressed my head against Chris's chest, my nose still red from crying. Then we drove home in silence.

Later in the evening Chris offered me dinner but I refused. I took a long bath instead. As I was drifting off to sleep with bubbles up to my chin, my phone beeped. I shook my wet hand dry.

My dear Violet, I've got an army guy for us, a perfect army guy. He's available on Tue.

I couldn't help wonder if this army guy was the man eating dinner downstairs. I admired Pablo for his persistence, and at the moment I couldn't find the words to reject him nicely so I deleted the message.

Downstairs I found Chris playing with his bowl of salad. The table looked big with only him sitting at it.

'That was quite a show you put on at the funeral,' Chris said dolefully.

'I had to.'

'Your family never liked me anyway, so why bother? They're probably glad we're separating.'

'Are we, Chris? Separating?'

'Well, we've never said it, but we're doing it, aren't we?' Chris said. 'We're not sleeping in the same bed, we hardly talk, you're there, I'm here.'

'I suppose.'

'I don't know if you still go out with that escort that you raved about, but... I've gotta ask, do you still want to be with me, Andrea? No sex, no child?'

I shrugged.

'So, next step – divorce?'

I shrugged again.

He shook his head. 'I'm going out,' he said. 'I won't be sleeping here tonight.'

I just nodded. My anger towards him had subsided. I

wondered if there was a chance of reconciliation – he and I going back to how we used to be: close, caring, him living his life the way he wanted to, me living my life – how? Would I let Chris carry on with Gianni or whichever escort might come after him? I could see myself being okay with it. Would I find another escort to replace Lucio? Unlikely. What I could see was myself going back to working 60-70 hours a week.

I watched my husband standing beside his car, taking ages to open the door, wiping his face. I couldn't decide what to do next. *Divorce,* he said, but it sounded wrong. Divorce was only for couples who hated each other, and I didn't hate Chris, and nor did Chris me. But it sounded right at the same time. I didn't even care that Chris wasn't sleeping at home tonight. The only thing that was bothering me right now was the thought of me owing another man. It was bothering me because it took priority over my marriage. It was bothering me that Chris's leaving was liberating. I guessed this was what they called 'moving on'. What I desperately wanted right now was to be in that other man's car, just once more, to have those peaceful feelings again, like when he drove me to Minchinbury Avenue.

ANDREA CURTIN AND FREDERICO LOWE: LAST CHANCE NIGHT

12 OCTOBER 2016

I RUSHED to Lucio's car, escaping the jacket he spread over me. I let myself in without saying anything. I didn't even look at him.

The car started purring. Lucio was ready to shift gear.

'No, stay here,' I said, staring at the swishing windscreen wipers.

'Oh? You don't want to go to my place?' he said.

I shook my head.

'That was some guts you had showing up at the funeral,' I said. 'I always keep my promises, Lucio. You didn't have to treat me like a fraud.'

'I'm sorry,' he said. He twisted to reach for something behind the seat. 'I hope this makes it up.'

The smell of French vanilla was taken over by the familiar spices wafting out of the supermarket cooler bag. He'd remembered. I'd only told him about my favourite dish once, when we were in Singapore.

'I bet you haven't eaten all day,' he said softly.

'Lucio...' I said, shrinking into my seat.

'My friend helped me get this. He knows everything about Kingsford.'

My sulky face involuntarily beamed. 'Thank you.' I gave him a peck on the cheek. I rolled my shoulders as I took the plastic container out of the bag. I looked at him as if I shouldn't have. When I opened the lid I found five skewers of satays on a bed of rice cakes with a generous serving of yellow sauce.

'Good?' he asked, watching me take a mouthful – too big a mouthful, but I chewed it all in no time.

'Mm hmm.'

Onto the next one... He tucked my hair behind my ear as a few strands were falling into the dish.

I must've looked like a little girl.

'How old were you?' I asked him as I took a break from eating.

He handed me a bottle of water.

I gave him a *you thought of everything* smile.

'What do you mean?' asked Lucio.

'How old were you when I saw you in Rome?'

Lucio engaged himself in a deep thought, working out the years. Then he said: 'Nine.'

I'd thought he was only six or seven. Chris had been right that the boy looked young for his age.

'I didn't eat much. I grew up slowly,' he said, sensing my disbelief.

'Why were those men chasing you?'

'I stole a man's wallet,' he said. 'Got jailed for three days. Then my mother bribed them and they let me go. But... it got worse after that. My dad beat me up some more when I got home.'

My boy... I regretted I'd asked. My bones ached from thinking about those batons landing on his body. And what would his dad have used?

He shrugged, as if it'd just been what he deserved, or simply something he had to endure.

I didn't want to pity him. Really.

Not tonight.

THE PLASTIC CONTAINER was still on Andie's lap but her hands were off it. Her fingers tapped randomly as if she was looking for something else to touch or hold after I'd told her about what happened to me that day in Rome.

'My father was always beating something or someone. Finally Mother had enough. She dragged me out of Rome. I was scared. But I never stopped thinking about you. I asked her, "Why don't we go to China?" Figured you were from there – that was the only Asian country I knew at the time. She thought I was brain damaged or something. But thanks to her, I found you.'

'So how did you get into this escort business?'

She moved her right hand closer to me, just a tad. She lifted it up and looked at me. I thought she was about to caress my face, but she reached for a tissue instead.

Should I kiss her now? Fondle her breasts? I didn't want to answer her question. But I had to follow her lead. And tonight it was more important than ever.

'I left school early, got into drugs, then my mother started to get sick all the time. When ordinary jobs couldn't support the both of us, I took a job at a massage parlour...'

Andie did her most discreet 'aha'.

'Yes, that's where I honed my skills,' I said, 'but I promise you I was good even before then. One day I decided I needed more money, and I thought, I could be a good escort. It wasn't just about my face and my... you know. I knew I could make people happy. Well, it was sex, but hey, sex is happiness to a lot of people. And I have good self-control, I suppose, so I can take anything that anyone throws at me; with a smile, politely, professionally. And I serve well.'

HE SERVED WELL ALRIGHT. Once again I thought about the database of his brain. What other things did he remember about me?

'Let's go inside,' I said. I packed up the dinner quickly. 'I'll get rid of this in the bin, rather than stink your car.'

The rain pelted on me as I ran back to the house. Lucio wasn't far behind. Once inside I headed straight to the kitchen. I stood in front of the island bench.

Silence.

I was about to tell him to leave. But he grabbed my hand that was still gripping the container with stripped satay sticks and specks of sauce in it. He pulled the container away. 'You want to do it here?'

How could I ask him to leave when I was burning like this?

I glanced at the staircase.

And with that he carried me up as I clung tightly to his neck.

I kissed his lips – saliva, spices, sex – everything on me was on him. I showed all my cards, like a teenager who was too eager, too soon. No other man apart from my husband had ever set foot in this bedroom. Chris hadn't been here in weeks. It felt like I was in someone else's bedroom when I saw Lucio, the boy, Frederico, my escort, my man, lowering me onto the bed... *my own bed...*

Teenager's lust? Oh no... that was a default thing that popped in my brain when I felt the urge. But now it was no teenager's lust – in fact it wasn't any kind of lust. It was my heart bursting. *You're the only one I'll ever desire*, I silently promised again. *I'll never make love to another man.*

But what good would that promise do? I would still break his heart for I would leave him, and my heart would be pierced by its fragments and lacerated eternally.

Lucio spread my legs and twisted his tongue in me. The work of a pro, of a lover, of an obsessed man... I didn't care. This was the last night of the world and I let him do whatever he pleased to please me.

'Lucio...' My throat couldn't utter any other word. Why did that boy have to be him? In that one small window of time, when we were both lying on the cobblestone street, he had felt like Christopher. But alive. Because I had protected him. I had done my duty as a mother. He'd smiled at me – not lying lifeless on the street. After that he became the skeleton walking on two bony legs. Then he became my escort, my lover, my confidant – all that, not as my son, not as a boy, but as a man, whose scent I didn't know whether I liked or disliked, and whose body only had a bit of muscle.

I wanted him.

But I shouldn't. Really.

'LUCIO...' Andie called that name again and again.

I let her. I had to do this her way; it would be the only way. The plan *had* to work.

I felt her warmth on my lips as I moved up her body. She clung to me. We rolled together – she on top, I on top. Then she panted, and panted... Underneath my chest her breasts jolted. This woman was more than the world to me. And seeing she only wanted me, that she was pleasured by me, I wanted to explode. But I couldn't get carried away. I had to intoxicate her the right way.

I lay on top of her. I held her shoulder, and leaned slightly to my left. She liked it this way. Usually I entered her now but tonight my hand had to participate as she was still watching. I had to replace her consciousness with pleasure that she would finally let go of any care about the 'how'.

I watched her head thrown back. I could see her vision fading, she was flying. Every now and then she opened her eyes to find me, and I was always there. So she finally put all of herself in me. It was time. I seamlessly withdrew my fingers and thrust my dick into her – my nice seven-inch tool that never failed to please her. She was so far away she didn't seem to notice. My foreplay had more than just drugged her, she was almost in a coma. Just the way I wanted.

MY HANDS WERE STILL CLINGING tight to Lucio but I kept my eyes closed. I didn't want to see him (those teddy bear eyes, devastating). I just wanted sex. *That's all... I just want sex.*

And tonight the sex was as devastating as his eyes. He asked if it was good. Good? His fingers... in me... How many... I hoped it was all of them. I moved my hips, spurring him to devastate me even more.

And as always the boy delivered. To the stars... where it was always Christmas, it was always summer, it was always with him.

The boy? No... the man... *the man* delivered.

On the last night of the world... and he was the last man on earth... the last man of my heart. And I screamed as I never had before. My fingernails scratched Lucio's back as I felt strange warmth, spreading like fresh lava, inside every tunnel, vein and canal in my body.

I looked at my lover – he was withdrawing, then he threw himself at me. I squeezed him, demanding more.

AND MORE I GAVE HER. Last chance to make her mine...

She bit my pecs, she dug into my shoulders.

So this was how it felt when someone was so close to you. On any other night I would cry and beg right now. Instead I just shed tears silently, like Andie had when we'd first made love – yes it was more than sex, we made love. And just as our first encounter, right now I was hoping I had done enough to make her come back to me.

Andie let out another howl.

And I panted as I released all I had for the last time, for the night – I hoped. I blanketed her, rubbed myself onto her. With each friction I begged her to let me stay.

'Lucio...'

'I'm Frederico.'

I didn't think she heard me.

I quickly got up, went into the bathroom and stood in front of the mirror. To my surprise Andie joined me. She hugged my naked body from behind, feeling my chest, my abs, my pelvis, my balls, my dick and my butt.

And she kissed my back, then observed my reflection in the mirror.

'Go and lie back down, I'll give you a massage,' I said, my eyes growing moist.

She shook her head. She hung on to me.

I turned around and kissed her forehead.

How could I live without her? Those broad shoulders, tiny waist, firm hips, those thighs, those arms...

'Did you know it was me? When I first came to you?' asked Andie.

'I recognised your smell. You looked different but then I saw your eyes... I knew it was you.'

'Do you think it was meant to be, you and I?'

'I would like to believe so.'

'I can't see you again, Lucio.'

'Why, Andie? I thought we were good tonight.'

'I told you this would be the last time.'

'Please, Andie...'

'Lucio, I can't.'

Andie gave me a white envelope.

Two thousand dollars and nothing more – no scent, no note.

'I can't accept this,' I said.

'That's all I can give, Lucio. Good night.'

ANDREA CURTIN: THE MAN IS MY OYSTER

21 – 23 NOVEMBER 2016

I HAD ALMOST HAD ENOUGH of Port Melbourne's salty air. But my appetite for oysters had forced me to stay around.

'Good God! How many have you had?' asked Leanne as I went back to the fish and chips shop for a second round of fresh *and* fried oysters. 'You're preparing for a red hot sextravaganza, are you? Found your new man?'

'You believe that myth about oysters and libido?'

'Of course not, but I had to ask. It's good to change it up, you know. So you don't get too attached,' Leanne commented. Earlier I told her I'd ditched Lucio.

'Have you ever got attached to your escort?' I asked.

'Once. This guy, Julian. He's on Amanda's website – check him out. He's so my type. He's the most generous, gentle, intelligent escort, well, man I've ever known, as a matter of fact.'

'What did you do?'

'I gave myself a couple of weeks to have a mental breakdown, then I killed that hopeless feeling and moved on,' explained Leanne. 'How're you and Chris?'

'Hmm... we're not really talking.'

'He's a good man. He's not a cheater like my Barry, I know for sure.'

'Yeah, he is a good man, my Chris. But I don't know where we're going. We just want different things I suppose.'

Leanne shook her head, questioning herself. 'What did I say? Did I say *my* Barry? Funny that, he's not mine any more and to be honest I never felt he was, ever.'

'So it's all done then, your divorce?'

'Yeah. Official, with the stamps and everything,' Leanne said. 'You've considered divorce?'

'Both of us did, but neither of us has done anything about it.'

'Hmm... I know you'll do the right thing,' Leanne said. 'But of course, if you ever want my help in finding a new man for you, on the side I mean, just let me know.'

'You're a bad influence, you know that?' I gave her a friendly glare. Slowly my glare turned into a frown. I stretched my neck to see past the man standing next to Leanne.

'What's there?' Leanne said and turned around, following the direction of my gaze.

'Huh? Nothing,' I said.

'Oooooooh! I know what you're looking at!' Leanne teased. 'That couple, uh huh, pashing, smooching, yum yum yum... gee, that guy is super horny. Not surprising, being with such a hottie.'

The scene sucked the oyster slime back up my throat. That guy in the distance was Lucio and the woman was a stunner – shiny black hair, all limbs, with curves in all the right places. Although I'd never thought he would be the type who'd admire over-accentuated tits and female assets.

'OTT,' I mumbled and tried to compose myself.

'So many things make you jealous when you're near a beach at sunset,' said Leanne. 'Should we get some champagne? Goes well with oysters.'

'Umm... no thanks,' I said, tugging at her arm so we walked in the opposite direction to the two lovebirds.

That woman is just another client of his.

'You're not having alcohol? What's up with you? You on a shellfish diet or something?'

'I just don't feel like champagne, Lee! I want something... citrusy, very citrusy.'

'All right! Let's find some extremely citrusy drinks.'

I kept tugging at her, one eye still on Lucio who was hugging his Asian hottie really close to him. Now that they weren't kissing any more I could see the woman's pretty face – her eyes were brighter than mine, hair was shinier than mine, her lips were more inviting than mine. Everything on that girl was better than mine. And her stare said: *I'm up for anything as long as I'm with you.*

'Ha! You're still looking at that couple! Loneliness can kill you, I know.'

'I'm not lonely.'

'Andrea, find another guy,' Leanne said, rubbing my arm. 'Err... hold on a sec, I need the loo.'

No matter how hard I tried to play down Lucio's muse for the day, what I saw was fact; he treated that beauty like he loved her passionately, so proudly out in the open, something that 'his Andie' wouldn't let him do. He only kissed at his discretion, and foolishly I thought I'd be the only woman he'd do it with. Or was it just a case of money talking? Had he been paid irresistible amounts of money to give her an authentic girlfriend experience? Would he please her in that position, too? *L'levame*? The more I looked at the two of them, I concluded it was the woman herself who had become irresistible to him. Because that kiss was more than just an escort's kiss; he wasn't Lucio, he was Frederico to her, for when I searched for *European twink* on *backpage*, none of the results were Lucio's.

Pablo dear, *Violet here. Sorry for my radio silence. Family crisis. You free next Sat night?*

Do you still want me to invite that army guy?

I thought for a while and read Pablo's next message:

I know you said no before. Just in case you change your mind.

I pondered.

Send me his photo.

Can't, sorry. But he's handsome, you'll like him guaranteed. He's from overseas, he's only here for a week.

Part of me had wanted the man to be Chris, my Chris who was no longer mine.

Thanks. But I just want to be alone with you.

I'll be at your service, my dear. Should I dress up like an army man?

Whatever you think best. You will always turn me on.

Pablo's hands had never felt so warm. His massage felt like a lover's massage. Right then I believed the lack of warmth the first time I'd met him was my own creation. I had booked Pablo for an hour and I needed every minute of it to be erotic, skin on skin, and...

'Pablo...' I turned around to face my escort.

'Wasn't it good?'

... I needed him to be inside me.

'It was great,' I whispered. 'Now I want you to fuck me.'

'Violet?'

'Is that too much to ask?'

'No, nothing is too much for you,' he said and reached into the bedside drawer.

I moaned as Pablo lay on top of me, inserting his hips in between my legs, and I felt his thick flesh stutter inside me.

'I've never been with a woman like you,' he grunted.

'I've never been with a man like you,' I grunted even louder. I breathed quickly as if I was ready to bite. 'Kiss me.'

Pablo paused, looked at me and smiled.

'Is that too much to ask, or am I not beautiful enough to get a kiss from you?'

'Violet... You're the most beautiful woman I know,' he said and kissed me.

So he kissed me again and again, I welcomed him like he was my legitimate lover. And I consumed all the pleasure I could harvest.

In all my breathlessness I saw a face and I gasped. Then I saw Pablo withdrawing, holding on to his cock and kissing me from the side of the bed. 'I'll be back, just relax.'

I sat up and put on my clothes as I heard the water running behind the bathroom door. I put my face in my hands and wept.

'Hey, Violet...' Pablo sat beside me, hugging me. 'What is it?'

'I saw my husband with another woman.'

'I'm so sorry,' he said.

'Clearly I'm not beautiful enough for him.'

'He's a jerk! You're beautiful, Violet. People are still talking about that mystery woman at The Nest, the one that Pablo was lucky enough to have in his arms.'

I turned to him and smiled. 'But you've never told anybody who I am, right?'

'Of course not. Discreet, always.' He caressed me. 'You still love him, your husband?'

'Maybe.'

'You said his name.'

'Really? I'm sorry.'

'I couldn't quite make out what it was, so don't worry. My guess is he's French.'

I chuckled and shook my head. 'Far from it. What did you hear? Come on, you can tell me.'

'Something like... Louis?'

I took a deep breath.

ANDREA CURTIN: GREEN

21 DECEMBER 2016

TRAVEL BAG, laptop bag, handbag – I was ready to drop them all as I tried to press the elevator button to Leanne's apartment.

'What the hell?' greeted Leanne. 'You look like the Grinch.'

And I retched at the smell of my friend's eggy breakfast.

'Oh shit...' She gave me a look.

I threw myself onto the couch. 'My dream is coming true, Lee! It's coming true!'

'*That* dream?' Leanne said. She gave me a big hug. 'Congrats, hon! Then why are you so miserable?'

'I'm not... I'm just... green as you said. I've been puking all morning.'

'How far along are you?'

'Ten weeks.'

'What? And you just found out now?'

'I did take a test when I first missed my period but it was negative.'

'And you didn't go to the doctor?'

'No, I've had this once before, skipping my period for months when I was a mess, and I've been a mess lately so I thought it was just stress. Who would've knocked me up, anyway!' I snarled at myself.

'Huh?' Leanne frowned. 'I suppose you were a bit funny when we were in Melbourne. All those oyster and citrus cravings.'

'And I don't know why the puking is only starting now.'

'Wait! Go back – *who would've knocked you up*? What's that about?'

It did occur to me it could've been Pablo. But I was sure the condom was still firmly on his cock when he withdrew, and he didn't come. But then again I was in a haze at the time. I scoffed. The doctor said I was ten weeks pregnant, not four weeks. It was in black and white – official pathology results, not some home testing kit with fancy icons.

'I'm over the moon, Lee! But... this isn't how it was supposed to happen.'

'You're not making any sense.'

'It's not Chris's.'

'I kinda figured that out.'

'It's his, L's.'

'Shit! Andrea! Did you let him... you know? No protection?'

'I didn't *let* him! I don't know how it happened. Maybe the rubber leaked or I don't know...'

'But he put it on, right?'

I pressed my lips together.

Leanne growled. 'I told you to watch what his cock was doing!'

'I know... I take full responsibility. I just need to get away from Chris at the moment.'

'Well, he has to take responsibility, too – I mean, L!'

'He's just a kid...' I said helplessly. Lucio had wanted this to happen. *Mid-next week, Wednesday* he precisely said. However he'd planned it – whether he put it on and took it off in the middle of our romp, or never put it on at all. I hated him for his sneaky act, but the bottom line was, he'd made my dream come true. And what would I do to punish him for that?

'Bastard!' said Leanne. 'Have you talked to him?'

'No.'

She looked at me. I shrugged. And I smiled as absurdity took over me. The Lucio effect... the same sensation as I'd felt at Minchinbury Avenue, in his car, when I thought about starting a new life with him.

'I'm sorry, Andrea, I don't want to spoil your happy moment... but... with these guys... they're not father material, babies will ruin their careers. Your L, no matter how he made you feel, will dump you as a client and do a runner, trust me. If you told him he'd probably tell you to get rid of it. Or dance around and say it could be your husband's or someone else's.'

Leanne was telling the hard truth. But there was only so much she knew. Deep down I'd convinced myself there could be a better outcome.

'I need to stay here a while, Lee. I told Chris I was going to Singapore.'

Leanne laughed. 'You're the worst liar! I'll make you some hot chocolate.'

As Leanne disappeared into the kitchen, I reached for my mobile phone. I wanted to vanish, maybe have my baby somewhere west, Adelaide or Perth, or down south in New Zealand.

Just like yesterday, and the day before, and the week before, I searched for Lucio's posts on *backpage*. My heart pounded when his link came up in today's ads: *European twink at your service*. There were some new photos that looked to be professionally taken. He was lying on a red couch, soft light, shadows concealing his private parts. Another one showed him standing in front of a mirror, his dense, dark pubic hair visible. And there was another one of him standing behind a curtain. All nude, but he knew how to hide his assets well. His teasing was still unbearably effective. I wondered how many new clients he had scored, or how desperate his current clients were to see him again after looking at such provocative images.

Then there was the old photo of his teddy bear face – switching between that of a boy and a man. How could I stay mad at him? Although at the moment I still hated him for his sneakiness. Or maybe because I'd been beaten.

FREDERICO LOWE: MY ANDIE

22 DECEMBER 2016

I ZIPPED up my jeans and tucked my shirt in. From the reflection in the mirror I saw my client Lucas admiring my butt. I gave him a marathon full-hour service but I knew he could've kept going.

'I hope you don't mind me taking more of your time today,' Lucas said.

Tousling my hair, I said, 'It's fine, I'm happy to have lunch with you. You're ready?'

Hand in hand we left the apartment. As the elevator took us to the ground floor Lucas told me about his fling with a boy he met in Norway twenty years ago. His account of the sexy Norwegian boy was a bit too private for my liking, but sometimes I simply had to be the good listener for everything.

'So we were in bed, right in the middle of our romp. Oh, his blowjob was amazing, amazing. Then the damn fire alarm blared and out of nowhere the sprinkler rained on us! And there was real smoke, you know, it wasn't just false alarm,' Lucas said enthusiastically. 'It was minus ten outside and we only managed to put on our pants when we were evacuating.'

I laughed. 'Wow... you must've been freezing!'

'We grabbed the doona before we left the room – oh, well, the wet doona that was!'

Our laughter echoed in the lobby as we stepped out of the elevator. I nodded at Billie the concierge while Lucas went on about his Nordic rendezvous. Soon the glass doors to the outside slid open in front of us. Right then I was confronted by a beautiful but unsettling presence; the timing was off, but I was glad she was there. She was pacing back and forth in front of the garden bed that separated the building entrance and the footpath.

'Your apartment is in a great location. Look at this! Out the door and you're in the city,' said Lucas.

We walked right past Andie. I turned my head to escape her glare and led my client out onto the street. I pulled him closer. 'What do you fancy for lunch?'

'Aah... ummm...anything,' Lucas said. He tried to look back but my arm kept pushing him to walk faster.

'Do you like Korean?'

'Did you see that woman?' Lucas said. 'She was *staring* at us. Either she never saw a gay couple before, or she was shocked that a guy like me could be with someone like you.'

'Ah... don't be silly! Any man would be proud going out with you,' I teased him as we walked towards the Spanish Quarter.

So my plan had worked. I knew it would. My calculation was right – the extra days I'd asked for was prime time, and thank goodness the funeral didn't delay anything in the end. But I knew there was still a battle ahead: my Andie wasn't the overjoyed mum-to-be that I was expecting.

Lucas perused the menu presented at the entrance of a Korean barbecue restaurant. 'What do you think?'

I threw him a surprised look: 'Oh... Is it Wednesday today? Or Thursday?'

'Thursday,' Lucas replied.

Now I gave him an apologetic look: 'Shoot! Lucas, I'm so sorry. I forgot… I promised my mother I'd fix her kitchen.'

'Oh, that's a shame,' said Lucas. He shrugged. 'Oh well, this lunch is unscheduled anyway, I shouldn't complain. Good on you for taking care of your mum. It's absolutely fine.'

'Thank you, Lucas,' I said and gave my client a peck on the cheek. 'Have a safe flight back to Melbourne.'

I sprinted back to my apartment. Andie was gone, as I'd expected. I continued running to the back of the building, to her usual parking spot.

'Andie!' I spotted her getting into her car. 'Andie, wait!'

But my voice only made her hurry. As she was spinning the wheel, I jumped in front. The car was barely out of the white line. She reversed and the back wheel bumped against the kerb. She tried to swerve around me, but it was too tight on either side – she would have had to run me over.

Lunchtime traffic soon piled up.

Andie revved the engine.

I stood my ground. The Mercedes rolled forward and the bumper touched my knees. Behind the windscreen, Andie's face had turned red, her hands trembling and her eyes straining.

As drivers hounded and abused us for the hold-up, she opened the passenger door and I quickly hopped in. Before I could close the door she turned the car harshly, entered the lane and drove around to my apartment.

'Card!' she yelled as we arrived at the carpark entrance.

I obeyed. As the roller door opened she threw the card at my face. Soon I was rocked left-right until she pulled over near a storage unit. She got out, walked around to my side, and, as I barely unlatched my door, she pulled it wide open. Then she dragged me out like a rag doll.

One push, and my back was pressed against the hot tinted window of the back door.

Slap! She lashed my right cheek. I closed my eyes. *Stai bene?*

'What's your game, Lucio?!' she said, holding my collar.

Once again I was downed by her strength – this time it wasn't for protection. Her arm muscles swelled against my chest and her face was radiating fury. In front of me was a woman fighting for her honour – *you despicable man, you got me pregnant without my consent!* But somehow her rage seemed forced. Her strength, now I could see, was her desire to have more of me, to have *all* of me.

'I just wanted to make you happy,' I said.

She slapped me once more. 'No! You just want to own me!'

'Andie, it's not like that!'

'What then?' she said. 'You fucking tricked me!'

'Yes... I wanted to own you, but not in a bad way,' I conceded. 'But I know I can't own you. So I just wanted to be the one who made you happy. I wanted to give you what you wanted... a baby, right?'

'Not *your* —' she said then abruptly paused. Lines formed on her forehead.

'"Give it to me," you said,' I told her softly.

She let me go.

'That night, in the car. Minchinbury Avenue – that spot meant something to you. You wouldn't have said that out of nowhere. And you were disappointed when I put on the condom. I saw you.'

'Tell me you've been tested,' she said, her back to me.

'Andie! I wouldn't do that to you.'

'Are you clean?'

For the first time she made me feel like *a sex worker*, like those smart-arse men who hired me for the first time and interrogated me about my health and habits, then demanded the sun and moon in half an hour. And she didn't even have the guts to look at me.

But she had every right. 'Andie, of course I am,' I said. 'That night, I had every intention to get you pregnant, do you think I would make you and the baby sick?'

She faced me. 'Why, Lucio?'

'Isn't this what you want, Andie? Another baby?'

'Yes.... But...'

'I'm not good enough for you?'

Andie leaned back against the car, right next to me. She said, 'One night I was arguing with Chris. I told him I wanted to try it with a gay escort. He didn't like the idea.'

'I'm sorry I tricked you. But I thought this through. It wasn't some spur of the moment thing. I thought, if she wants to stay with her husband and dump me then fine, at least I've made her happy and I will always be in her life through the baby. And if she decides to be with me because of the baby, then I'll be ready, too.'

'What if I decided not to have the baby, and not to see you any more?'

I shook my head. 'That would never happen.'

She closed her eyes.

I moved to face her. I extended my arms slowly and rested my hands on her shoulders. 'The things I've said to you all this time, they're all true. You're beautiful, you're kind, you're naughty, and I want to please you, always. Yes, you paid me, but you are more than just work to me. I make people feel good, that's my job, and I'm happy to take their money for it. I earn it. But with you, you were sent to me... twice... how could I let you go?' I said.

Andie kept a neutral expression. She said slowly, 'One night, out on the streets, Chris and I argued again about me hiring a gay escort. There was something he said to me, in anger. It was hurtful, but it gave me some sort of spark, an unexplainable joy. He said, "Go and have his baby!". Or something like that. I dismissed my feelings straight away. But...now ...'

'You're happy, right?' My eyes, my lips, my hands, everything of mine – they begged her to say yes.

'Do you have a boyfriend?'

'No. I only have you.'

'Was that a client that I saw you with?'

'Yeah.'

'He's handsome,' she said.

'He has three kids,' I said. 'Look, Andie, I didn't mean to ignore you. I was going to come back, but I needed to make an excuse to my client first then...'

'I understand,' she said. 'How about a girlfriend? You disappeared from the escort world for weeks. And I saw you with a beautiful woman down in Melbourne. I saw you two, and I saw us. And that evening I realised "us" was never meant to be.'

Miracle. I smiled for her jealousy, and for the fact that all the stars lined up to get her to be at the same place at the same time when I was with Bee. 'She was just a client. She paid me to fly with her to Melbourne. I decided to stay and work there for a week. Then I took a couple of weeks off.'

'You did things... you did things with her that...'

'It was just an act, Andie, I promise,' I said.

'A kiss doesn't lie. You liked her, didn't you?'

I shook my head. 'No. She paid me extra to kiss her in public. That was her thing.'

'Hard to believe, a woman like her had to pay to get a kiss?'

'She's trans' I said.

Andie gasped, eyes wide, mouthing 'No way!'

Bee was short for Brownsugar, as she'd wanted me to call her. I'd never known her real name.

Andie expressed a little guilt for showing such a reaction. Then: 'I can't compete with her.'

I drew Andie close to me. I looked her in the eye and gave her an honest kiss. When I opened my eyes I observed her parting lips. Now that was a real kiss, Andie. And she stopped pretending to be an ordinary woman. She became the woman I longed for; the one who put her trust in a man who was once her escort, who was once a boy thief. Her hand was on my face. It was like the first time she touched me. Then she asked:

'What should I call you?'

'Frederico.'

'I will have to get used to it.'

We paused for a while.

'Frederico,' Andie said slowly.

The sweetest thing that I'd longed to hear...

And we both cried. We were too close to see each other, we were in each other. At the end of it all we asked ourselves: *what now*?

'I saw you put up some new photos,' Andie said.

I knew she'd notice. 'You like them?'

'Very much,' she said. 'Who took the photos?'

'A friend. He's studying photography and he's very good.'

'Obviously.'

'Did you see my message?'

'What message?'

'On the table, in front of the mirror. There's a notepad there.'

'Wwhhat?'

I held her shoulders. 'I wrote there: *Be mine*.'

Andie shook her head. 'You're impossible!'

'Be mine, Andie.'

'So you do want to own me.'

'I'm yours, too, as much as you're mine, if you want it to happen.'

'My heart is always with you, Frederico. Whether I like it or not.'

'And you know my heart is in you.'

'I understand if you want to continue working, and I'm not expecting you to support me or anything. I...'

She could've come up with a more romantic post kiss-and-make-up statement. I understood her practicality, but I didn't like where she was heading so I didn't let her finish: 'Look, Andie, you may doubt me. I know you can raise the baby yourself, you will be a great mother. And you have a lot of money...'

She sighed. 'I didn't mean it that way.'

'Listen, I'm not just good at giving sex. I know life. I can take care of you, you know, and the baby.' I put my hand on her belly.

'It will be a beautiful baby,' she said.

'Of course. Look at you.'

'I hope he or she has your eyes. You've got the most beautiful blue eyes.'

Andie's index finger followed the arch of my eyebrows. She kissed me, then she hugged me. Her head rested on my shoulder, my arms firmly on her waist.

I would do anything for her.

'Do you want me to be with you when you tell your husband?'

The question took her by surprise.

'You are going to tell him, right?' I said.

'Of course,' she replied. 'That's okay. Let me handle it. I'll be fine.'

'He's not going to hit you?'

'No, no,' she said. 'I'll be more civil. We have been talking about divorce, so I guess it won't come as a surprise.'

'Divorce is one thing, how about telling him you're pregnant?'

'Let me handle it.'

She blinked a couple of times. For now I'd just have to take her word for it.

PART V

THE ATTACK

ANDREA CURTIN: MY CHRIS WHO'S NO LONGER MINE

20 FEBRUARY 2017

EATING for two was a nice excuse for being greedy. I loved food, contrary to what people readily thought – a skinny Asian girl, a fashion slave, too busy to eat. Rushing to my apartment with a grocery bag and a lunchbox, I couldn't wait to relax and enjoy the goodness of my noodles (and fried tofu, and braised beef, and a spring roll) with a cup of jasmine tea.

I swiped my card on the go. These doors always reminded me of my first encounter with Frederico. The scanner didn't quite read the card and I almost kissed the glass. I swiped one more time. As the doors slowly opened, an unexpected presence in the reflection forced me to turn around.

'Surprised you picked an apartment in the CBD out of anywhere in Sydney. I thought you might've stayed with Leanne for a while.'

'What is this about, Chris?'

'Could we go upstairs?'

I looked at my watch. I wasn't sure what time Frederico would come home – hopefully not too soon. Reluctantly I agreed. Chris stayed really close to me all the way to the door, as if I was going to run away.

'You're living with someone?'

I put my groceries – and my lunch – on the kitchen bench. Now the smell of that food made me want to puke.

'Yes.'

'Anything you want to tell me?'

'Chris, we're divorcing, why does it matter who I'm living with? Or anything else about my life for that matter!'

'I just thought you would've had the decency to tell me. Whoever you're with right now, right here. I know you started it while we were still together.'

'Yes I have a boyfriend, but this relationship started when we were separating. So no, you're wrong.'

'It hurts, you know. I even stupidly thought we could be together again, someday soon.'

I felt weak. I hadn't known. 'I thought this was what we both wanted,' I said softly.

'Now, knowing the real reason you left me – it really hurts. Especially when you found out about it in an undignified way.'

'What are you talking about?'

'I know he's an escort. So, after all he did fall in love with you, huh? What did you do? Surely it wasn't just your looks, especially if he's gay.'

While I had been sympathetic earlier, this time he infuriated me. 'So, *your* escort told you, huh? Next time tell him to mind his own business.'

'I just want to know if he's someone I know.'

'You don't know him.'

'What's his name?'

'You don't know him, Chris. And he doesn't know you.'

As we were exchanging stares, the front door burst open.

Frederico beamed at first, then he stopped, as if he'd just interrupted a duel.

'What the hell...' Chris said in disbelief. 'It's you?'

'What? You know him?' I said, frowning at Frederico, then at Chris.

'Leave her alone,' Frederico said. 'If you lay a finger on her, I *will* hurt you.'

'This man is a scumbag!' Chris said. 'Remember a few years ago I told you I had some tax problems? Well, my bad, I lied! I needed the money because this piece of shit was blackmailing me!'

I remembered that time, and I had reminded my husband about it every year. Although now, knowing the truth, I realised I hadn't actually dealt with the tax office myself or even investigated what Chris had told me. I gave him the money, and I'd never asked or followed up where my money had gone.

'My mother was sick!' Frederico said.

'She wasn't sick. She was a junkie!' Chris said.

'Frederico, is this true?' I said.

'What's his name now?' Chris cocked his head.

'I did take a lot of his money, Andie. It's true. But I earned it!'

'Fuck you!' Chris said, restraining himself from swinging at Frederico.

'Frederico, why?'

'It was for my mother, I swear. I had to. I'm sorry.'

'He's known for stealing clients from other escorts, too, if you must know. Ask around if you don't believe me. He's not a good man, Andrea.'

Sometimes Chris got emotional and said things he didn't mean, but had my judgement been so clouded by Frederico's calculated words that I couldn't see past his lies? Never had I thought the encounter between these two men would've happened so soon, this way, here. I'd imagined the time would come to reveal everything to Chris when I started to show, and he would've understood, he would've softened. And then I would've introduced him to Frederico. Now everything was a mess.

Chris approached me and grabbed my hand. He put on his lion eyes, the same eyes he had when he saved me from Jimbo and his footy mates. 'You have to leave him, Andrea! He's bad news. Don't believe anything he says. He's good with words, oh he's good. And those twinkly eyes, manipulation at its best. Trust me, Andrea, whatever he does, he does it for himself!'

'Chris... I can't come with you.'

'You've known me since you were sixteen. How long have you known this guy?'

'That's not...'

'Andrea, I understand why you left me. Believe me, I understand. But leaving me for this scumbag? Please, trust me, you've made a mistake. You don't have to come back to me, just walk away from him!'

'Let me go,' I said, and pulled my hand from his.

Frederico soon stood between me and Chris.

'She's staying!' Frederico said. 'You can go now.'

Chris was about to strike him but I quickly hurled Frederico aside and stood right in front of my ex-husband. 'I can't leave him, Chris.'

'Don't tell me he's the one and that blah blah blah about loving him no matter what!'

'I'm pregnant,' I said. 'It's his.'

'What? Andrea, are you out of your mind?' Chris said.

'Well you wouldn't give it to me!' I started to weep.

Chris shook his head.

'I'm sorry, Chris. I didn't mean to shift the blame to you. I should've told you this that night before I moved out. *That* was my mistake. I know you're hurting...'

'Sarina…' he whispered and squeezed my shoulders.

From the look in his eyes I knew he had given up. I said softly: 'I'm happy, Chris, I'm happy to have this baby, *his* baby.'

And Chris's tears fell. He scooped my chin delicately with his trembling hands. 'Sarina, you're the only person that I love in this world, and I know I couldn't make you happy. I would fight for you, but you've made your choice. I just hope you know what you're doing.'

He kissed my forehead, took a deep breath and let out his sobs. Then he left without looking back.

I closed my eyes and ran to the bedroom. Love had a price, and it hurt me too that Chris was the one paying this time. Right now I wanted to *feel* him, something that I had outgrown. I wished I could feel his arms around me, feel his gladiator chest on my cheek, and feel his breathing, observe his slumber routine. I wished I could whisper how sorry I was and he would've said it was okay. I'd never cried for him before, but as I descended into the darkness that I'd fought to escape from, I did. I choked, for Chris, my Chris who was no longer mine.

A touch on my cheek woke me. I looked up and Frederico was looking back at me, with his own tears.

'Andie…' he said, very, very softly.

After all, I hadn't needed Pablo. Right there was Frederico, a fountain of knowledge about Chris. They went back three years? With the amount of money Chris had splurged they must've seen each other as often as real lovers would.

'Did you do it in my bed?' I asked.

'No. We usually met at a hotel.'

'Usually? Did you do it in this bed?'

'Sometimes he came to my place. Not here. I was still in my other apartment.'

'Yeah, but is it the same bed?'

'No! Andie, look…'

'Shut up!'

I scanned his face – those eyes, those lips. I scrutinised his body. Under his T-shirt there was his chest. His pants were hung from those skinny hips. Behind the inseam there were his cock and balls, and at the back there were those buttocks. They were all better than mine because my ex-husband preferred them.

'Andie, please...'

Chris had those, too. Face, chest, cock and balls. I used to lust over them, but in the end I preferred Frederico's.

'I'm so sorry,' he said, taking my hands.

Rejection and anger exploded in my head, but the explosion didn't quite reach my hands. I watched our fingers interlock. Effortlessly, lovingly. Frederico's fingertips touched my belly and the life inside me made itself clear where it stood in this triangle of sex, lust, madness... and human complications.

It said: that touch gives me joy while I'm safe in your cradle.

Suddenly the triangle looked simple: I was my baby's mother, he was my baby's father, and our baby was everything to us.

Still, there was Chris who didn't belong in this simple triangle.

'He's hurt, you know,' I said. 'He's a good man. And he was my husband no matter what you think. He was good to me. None of this is his fault.'

'I know he's a good man. I knew him, too. I didn't mean to hurt anyone, Andie.'

'But you did.'

'I know. I'm really sorry.'

'Say that to Chris.'

'I can't make it right with him, at least for now. In time, I may have a chance to apologise. But right now, let me make it right to you.'

'Why did I have to meet you?'

Frederico shook his head, begging me not to continue my line of thought.

'Before you came around, Chris was my life, my everything. We married young, I gave birth young. I lost my sons young. I rushed everything. He may not have always desired me, but he stood by me no matter what. And in the end, when I kicked him out of my life, he took it like a gentleman.'

'I'm not the scumbag that he told you I was. What happened between me and him, I can explain, Andie,' he said, sitting next to me.

'I don't want to hear it.'

'But you have to. You have to know my side of the story.'

'I hate you right now. Explanations won't make a difference.'

'Do you? Do you really hate me?' Frederico said.

'All right, tell me your story,' I said.

He heaved a sigh. 'Chris was one of my long-term clients. He was very good to me, very generous. I didn't want to tell you because I knew I would lose you.'

'You schemed really well, Frederico. Now you've trapped me.'

'I didn't mean it like that! I didn't know Chris was your husband back then. I couldn't change the past.'

'Did it occur to you at all that at some stage this would come out? That Chris would eventually realise that I'm with you, and carrying your child?'

'Of course it did! But I didn't have an answer so I just shut it out for now.'

'Yeah... you thought in time you'd find a new strategy to make everything okay,' I said. 'Now it's all a mess because it turned out you didn't have a chance to scheme further!'

'You don't know how much you mean to me, Andie. You would've left me had I told you the truth. You would've moved on to some other escort. Wouldn't you? Wouldn't you?'

'Perhaps.'

'And then we wouldn't have had this!'

'But you lied to me! I asked you. I asked you!'

'Yes, I did lie. I had to.'

'And what about the blackmail? What did you do?'

'It was for my mother. Yes, she was an addict, and she was sick. You don't know what it was like. I was an addict myself, if you must know. I came out of it of my own accord, but my mother almost died. I didn't use the money to buy drugs, I used it for her treatment. She was so screwed sometimes I thought of killing her. But she's my mother. She was the only one who cared about me. I had no money, and Chris struck me as a rich guy. So I did threaten to tell "his wife" about our dealings unless he agreed to hire me as I told him to. I took his money but I earned it. He enjoyed it, Andie!'

Of course Chris did. But Frederico had fuelled it.

'Do you still hate me?' He drew my hand towards his face. 'Slap me. Slap me hard! Let it all out, your hatred. I'll take it.'

I pulled my hand away from him. I closed my eyes. I could hear him taking a couple of breaths. Then, before he took his next breath I swung my arm. My wrist hit the corner of his mouth. How dare he hurt my Chris! His spit wet my palm. It was like he had just kissed it. I grimaced. A tear fell from his left eye.

My fingernails brushed his skin as my hand was leaving his face. I trembled.

And he smiled. This terrible boy from Rome smiled for my slap. I wanted to paint a thief. I could see it – and this time he'd taken more than just a cheap wallet with some Euros in it.

'And is it true you stole clients from other escorts?'

'I was desperate, Andie. It was all work. Please, I'm not a bad person. It was just the situation that forced me into doing things like that. You've gotta understand, Andie, please.'

'You're such a schemer. But I should've known! I should've

seen it in your eyes. You always said the right thing, your timing was impeccable, and...'

'It's the truth, Andie. I don't know what else I can give you. With Chris, I wasn't scheming back then, I wasn't strategising. I simply wanted to save my mother,' he said. 'With this baby, I planned it meticulously, yes. I schemed. But it was because I wanted to make you happy. Nothing else.'

'So it's that simple, huh? Why am I feeling sad then?'

'Because you're hurt, I know. You love Chris, too,' he said. 'No one needs you more than I do. But I don't want to be the one making you miserable. If you want to leave me, I'll understand. But please, try to find something within you to forgive me.'

I looked at my hand. It hurt. It felt like I had a piece of his skin stuck on my palm.

'Please...' he whispered.

Away with you, you sad teddy!

He took my hand once more, pressed my palm against his cheek. The star-shaped scar was next to my thumb. Then he slowly placed my hand on my belly.

I held my breath. In the silence of my head words competed: You fucked my husband. You blackmailed him. Then you fucked me. You knocked me up. And now you want me to forgive you?

No matter how hard I tried to magnify the bad in him, all I saw was a boy thief, caught red-handed, but his crime was somewhat virtuous. What was there to forgive?

'Andie...'

It might've been fate that had brought us together, but what kept us together, what glued me to him, was not fate; it was my heart, I nurtured it to love him *no matter what*. Just as Chris feared.

I sighed, 'What am I supposed to do, Frederico?'

'Forgive me. Please.'

Frederico, a terrible boy from Rome.

'You still want me?' he said, touching my face. He touched my belly.

I stroked his cheek. It hadn't been much of a slap. It had hurt my hand more than it had his face. 'Come here, you sad teddy!' I muttered.

'Thank you, thank you,' he whispered as he put his arms around me.

'In time, maybe we both can make it up to Chris.'

FREDERICO LOWE: THE SCAN

10 MARCH 2017

I PACED in front of my apartment door. By now Andie would be wondering if she was still my priority. With how I felt, I wanted to run away and not come home until she was asleep. But I knew how much this afternoon would mean to her. So I composed myself.

'Sorry I'm late,' I said, huffing.

'Hmm?' Andie was still in her pyjamas.

'Don't we have an appointment?'

'Umm... yes, at two,' she said.

That was why she hadn't called.

'Are you okay?' she asked.

'Yeah... yeah. I thought it was at one.'

'Something happened?'

She asked the question affectionately. Usually when I came home from work exhausted, dejected and regretful, she'd let me be. But occasionally she sensed I was desperate to share my worries. Only when she sensed this she would ask.

'Umm... my client this morning was an old guy and,' I explained slowly, 'he...'

'Frederico? Did he die?'

'No! No!' I said. I could see how she'd reached that assumption. I wanted to tell her what happened but in the end I just said: 'He did something disgusting. I'm glad we don't have to go right at this moment. I'm going to have a shower, okay?'

'Take your time,' she said.

I tossed my clothes into the laundry basket. The shower at Mr G's hadn't done anything. When my underwear was in my hand, I tossed it into the rubbish bin. No detergent would ever wash away the scent of that old man.

Under the running shower I scrubbed myself hard. I almost vomited recalling Mr G losing control of his bladder. I was lying naked on top of him, as he had always requested, and suddenly everything felt wet.

I retched and rubbed my dick. Then I moved on to my balls, my inner thighs, my whole thighs, my backside, and did it all over again. Half a bar of soap gone, my skin red, but I felt clean. I sanded down my body with the towel, then quickly threw it on the floor.

The bathroom mirror steamed up but I could see myself clearly. I hated that face. I hated myself for being who I was. Mr G had his accident because of old age. I was there on top of Mr G because I chose to be. I shouldn't have complained – it was an occupational hazard, my fellow escorts would say.

Angrily I squeezed my Molton Brown tube, but the silver beech smell made me sick. It was the last thing I had smelled on myself before...

The full tube clanked loudly against the metal bin. Then I kicked the bin.

'Frederico, you okay?' Andie said from behind the closed door.

My silence prompted her to enter.

'I just hate the smell of that stuff,' I said when she peeped in.

Andie approached me, touching my chest. 'Tough day, huh?' she said.

'Yeah,' I said. 'I'm okay now. I just needed to get rid of that smell.'

She nodded.

She was about to let me be. 'Stay with me a while,' I said.

And she stayed, with all the warmth that she could give me.

'You still want me?' I asked her.

'Of course!' she said.

'Someday I'll be a normal guy, hopefully, someone that you can truly be proud of.'

'I'm proud of you, Frederico. Truly,' she said. 'I'm with you not only because of the baby. Because I want to be with you.'

I nodded. 'You get dressed, eh?' I said. 'We need to leave soon.'

When I joined Andie in the living room, she was sitting on the sofa in her black dress. At five months, her pregnancy really made her shine. She looked glorious – glorious.

'Ready?' I asked.

She reached out to me smilingly, pretending she couldn't get up.

And I scooped her up and carried her all the way to the carpark.

I WONDERED how many pregnant women there were in the world at this very moment. There were at least a dozen here. But it was the men who really got me thinking. That one standing close to the reception probably owned a lucrative business, the one sitting on the furthest chair was an engineer, or a pilot (and he was holding his stewardess wife), that one in the opposite corner was a banker (could be a fake one, who'd wear a suit and tie to a maternity clinic on a Saturday afternoon?). Then I stopped and looked down at my own lap.

Who am I?

What do I do?

I fucked and got fucked for money. And for something extra I got cuddled or paddled, and today, I got peed on.

Next to me was my wonderful half – the guardian of my heart, the guardian of the creation that bonded her to me. She was happily napping on my shoulder in front of those men – who I could see were secretly glancing at her; at her beautiful face, at her glorious pregnant body. She was more than just my half; she was a whole of me – without her I wouldn't exist today. It should've made me feel better, but I was getting smaller at each glance thrown at her.

I took her hand – it was ice-cold. 'You're freezing!'

She opened her eyes and looked up. 'A bit...'

'Put this on!' I readied myself to lose my canvas jacket, seeing she was only wearing a thin shirt over her dress.

'No, no, I'm just nervous.'

'Why?'

'The baby.'

'Hey, the baby is okay. You don't have to be nervous for that.'

'Andrea Curtin?' a nurse called.

She looked up at the nurse, then turned to me.

'It will be okay,' I said, and helped her up.

As if I was walking her down the aisle, I passed those glancing eyes. Who did *they* think I was? What did *they* think I did? Maybe a handsome geek who earned a bucketload of money having invented something on the Internet.

The exam room was dim. Andie shivered as her body touched the linen. Her ice-cold hand was in mine once more. And she shivered even more when she rolled up her dress to let the lady in white slather the gel on her swelling belly. Earlier the sonographer had introduced herself as Ro.

'You're all right there, Ms Curtin?' Ro said. 'I'll adjust the air con, it is a bit chilly in here.'

'I'm okay,' Andie murmured in between her shuddering. 'Frederico...' she whispered.

I rubbed her hand. 'I'm here.'

When the scan began the monitor revealed a series of pulsing images. All in black and white, grainy, like a damaged movie.

'That's the heart,' Ro pointed out.

'Oh my God...' Andie said.

This time I shivered. The black and white thing there... the thing that I planned, the thing I hoped would make me own Andie, it now had a heart. However grainy the image was, I could see it beating. It wasn't a thing any more. It was living. My flesh and blood. Could it hear me? Did it know who I was? Did it know how I felt right now?

'Everything looks great!' Ro said. 'Do you want to know the sex of the baby?'

'I'm undecided,' said Andie, and quickly turned to me.

'Whatever you want, Andie,' I said.

'Yes... um... yes,' Andie said, squeezing my hand.

'You see this, that's his little...'

Andie got up and turned to hug me with the gel still thick on her. 'Frederico...'

My heart was racing, twice, three times the speed of my baby's pulsing heart. I said: 'He's going to be a beautiful boy.'

'Congratulations, you two!' Ro said. She pressed a button and a polaroid-like photo came out of the printer. Then she wiped Andie's belly with bundles of tissues. She said to the both of us: 'I'm so happy for you guys. From your reaction it seems like you've been expecting a boy?'

Andie blushed. She nodded.

When we came out, half the crowd in the waiting room had changed. I scrutinised the new group of men. They all looked respectable, just like the other men I'd seen before – that one might be a personal trainer, like Chris; that one might be a professor who could solve the most complex problem in the universe. I kept walking with Andie hanging on to my arm.

Mother always said, 'Don't be like your father!' I was never going to be that arsehole. But would I ever be good enough for my son? For *Andie's* son? When I hatched this plan, I thought everything would be perfect. Clearly I hadn't thought of everything.

'When he grows up, what will he think of me?' I asked Andie when we were back in the car.

'Frederico?'

'Imagine him at school, being picked on because his dad is a slut.'

'Frederico, you're not a slut!'

'Am I not?'

Andie inched herself closer to me. She slowly turned and gave me a hug. 'You're my soulmate,' she whispered.

That broke me, and silenced me.

She added: 'I didn't used to believe in that kind of thing – soulmate, some wishy washy celestial phenomenon. But look at us.'

She was carrying the weight of the three of us. No matter how much I tried to contribute, I always came up short.

'Frederico, he's our baby, your baby, he will love you.'

'I'm not so sure, Andie.'

'You're a good man. You make people human again. You fulfil the needs even their loved ones couldn't. It's what you do and that's wonderful.'

With my face in my hands, I said: 'I'm sorry to spoil your happiness.'

'No, you're not spoiling my happiness. Frederico,' she said, nudging my cheek softly so I faced her, 'our son *will* love and respect you, no matter what.'

I shook my head. 'Only you can, Andie. No one else will,' I said. 'No one else will, not even my son.'

'He will, or I'll make sure he does!' she said.

ANDREA CURTIN: AGAINST THE CLOCK

29 MARCH 2017

I STRETCHED LAZILY, slightly annoyed. I had forgotten to put my phone on silent and now it had woken me up from a dream where I'd become an astronaut and gone to Pluto.

I reached for my phone:

Can I call you, my dear? I think you'll like what I have for you!

Pablo! I deleted the message. Luckily Frederico wasn't around.

'Hey!' Frederico greeted me as I emerged from the bedroom.

'Hey... what are you doing topless in front of the computer?' I peeped down his black brief shorts.

And he kissed me. 'Well... I was looking for a job for my mother actually, but I got distracted, and thought there might be one for me.'

'Anything that interests you?'

'Doesn't matter what interests me, Andie. It's what I can do. And I don't seem to be able to do anything. Maybe a kitchen hand, or a waiter, a postman, a bus driver?'

'Are you sick of being an escort?'

He took a deep breath. 'Well... I'm still thinking about the baby. About our son, Andie. I'm ashamed, on his behalf.'

'Frederico...' I said. I pulled his chair back to give myself room to stand in front of him. 'You're the man I chose to be with. You were there when I was in the darkest pit. Don't forget that. You've done things no other person could.'

'I don't know what you see in me.'

I wanted to say that one word that described gratitude, fondness, respect, romance, closeness, longing, honesty, kindness – everything within the space of humanly goodness. I still couldn't find it. In the past I let it slide, this time I told him *all* of those words. He wept. Then he grimaced to stop his tears.

He said, 'I won't be doing this forever, I promise. Besides, I'm only going to get older. Boys like Gianni will soon weed men like me out, and before I know it I'll be a mature escort.'

'Is he that cute – Gianni? Is he that great?' I said cynically. 'I mean, you are handsome and you read people like you've known them all your life. I can understand why your clients are loyal. In fact, you can say Pablo is all right, too; I mean, I can understand why people would want to be with him. But Gianni? He's not attractive at all! Blonde hair, weird tan, disproportionate eyes, bone-thin...'

'A new generation of beautiful men, Andie,' he said.

'Is that so?' I sulked. 'Is Chris still seeing him?'

'Not that I know.'

'Is he back with Pablo?'

'I don't think so. Funny you said people would want to be with him – Pablo. He's actually struggling. His clients are dwindling. It won't be long before I'm in his position,' he said.

'I'm sorry for bringing this up. I didn't mean to make you sad.'

'No,' he said. 'It's reality.'

'Hey, speaking about your mother, how come I've never met her?'

He slumped. 'She's a mess, Andie.'

'Does she know about me?'

'Yes, she does. And yes, she knows about the baby, too.'

'Doesn't she want to meet me?'

'She does,' he said. 'But I don't think it's a good idea.'

'Frederico... I want to see your mother.'

He sighed. 'All right. I'll take you there.' He got up and kissed me. 'I've gotta go. I'll see you tonight.'

He got dressed quickly. As soon as the door closed behind him, I grabbed my phone. What did Pablo have for me? Was he really that desperate for work? Maybe. He wouldn't have otherwise asked me to call him. He'd never done that.

One ring and my call was answered: 'Violet? Is that you?'

'Yes it's me, my dear,' I said. 'I thought I'd better return your call.'

'Oh, thank you, Violet! Well, you'll love what I'm going to tell you!' Pablo said with such enthusiasm. 'Remember Marilyn? The girl you kissed at The Nest?'

Oh no, not her.

'She's having a birthday party next weekend – at The Nest. It's going to be wild and fabulous! She wanted you to be there. And guess what? She's the daughter of one of the club owners and she's offering you full membership. That's rare, Violet! Especially for a woman!'

I closed my eyes. How do you reject someone gently? 'Pablo... I can't. I'm sorry... it all sounds great, but I can't.'

'She knows you're straight. She just wanted to see you again,' Pablo said. 'And if it's not too much to ask, I'd love to take you there.'

His request was polite, but he couldn't hide his zeal; he really wanted me to say yes.

'I'm sorry, Pablo. I've patched things up with my husband. We're back together now.'

'I understand,' he said eventually. 'Have a good day, my dear. If you ever need me you know I'm just a phone call or text message away.'

If I could hug you right now I would, I told myself, something I'd never thought would be in me. I could still see Pub's name clearly on Chris's phone, smell his scent on my ex-husband.

I couldn't help putting Frederico in Pablo's shoes. Frederico was an extraordinary escort and would stay that way forever – to me – but to his clients? When they paid money to satisfy their lust they'd want their object of desire to stay within their imagination, and their imaginations wouldn't align with the consequences of the passage of time. What would happen when his face had wrinkles? Or when his chest softened? And his pain tolerance declined? Those clients would see boys like Gianni as better value, more hip, more invigorating, or simply more 'their type'. By then Frederico would be begging his ex-clients, he would start doing things he'd rather not do. He had promised he wouldn't do it with women any more – maybe he would relax that rule for the possibility of women wanting a more mature escort. I prayed that it would never come to that. Somehow he would find another job that made him content.

FREDERICO LOWE: RAVEN

30 MARCH 2017

TONIGHT I WAS on a double date with Pablo to welcome The Nest's newest sensation: Dr Aqua – the DJ of all DJs, dance guru, and one of Sydney's biggest cocks. Right now the man of the moment stepped out of his DJ booth, onto a circular stage where he performed a sexy chair routine in the rain, wearing all white. I didn't think anyone paid attention to anything else but his bulge. Two songs later the music stopped. He tossed the chair, stood up, swung his right arm up like Freddie Mercury and ripped his clothes. His wet briefs did little to cover up his dick and the spotlight shone a pink shade on it. The Nest erupted.

'They weren't kidding when they promised Sydney's biggest cock,' said Raven, Pablo's client slash date for the night.

'You ain't seen nothing,' seduced Pablo and took Raven's hand to feel his dick. That prompted a steamy kiss between the two.

Raven. He'd been my man of the moment since I'd seen him arriving in Pablo's arms. A basketball-player-like Englishman with the thickest of accents, 40 years old, the owner of a public relations empire all over Europe (and soon Australia). I was warmly cuddled by my client Reggie, who was as cashed up and full of Aussie handsomeness, but I wished I had Raven. Those gorgeous brown eyes, and that electrifying smile.

Raven's eyes wandered my way as he locked lips with Pablo.

Dr Aqua returned to his booth – dry and dressed up. Where had those whities gone? Had he ever went backstage? Maybe he had stripped himself naked and changed costume in front of everyone. I guessed I'd missed the action.

'Hey, I'm going to say hello to my friend there,' said Reggie. He kissed my hand before I let him go. 'Be back in a sec.'

'Another round?' Raven offered to buy us drinks.

'Another Young Henry, mate,' Pablo said.

'Lucio?' Raven looked at me.

Those eyes...

'Peroni?' he said with a huge smile.

I smiled back. 'Yeah.'

'And Reggie?'

'Umm... just get him another chardy.'

'Coming right up,' Raven said. He patted my shoulder as he walked to the bar. His chest brushed mine, spreading warmth all over my body.

Pablo nudged me then casually pointed a Reggie. 'Where did you find Liam Hemsworth?'

'He rang me,' I said. 'Where did you find Raven?'

'Holly.'

'Ah, your old mama-san.'

'Old, yeah but a well-connected pimp,' Pablo said. 'Hey, is it true, you're outcall only now?'

I cringed. 'Where did you hear that from?'

'People.'

I smiled but inside my heart sank thinking about Andie. I no longer invited clients to my apartment. It was our home now, and would be our family home. 'Circumstances, my dear.'

Reggie came back and wrapped his arms around me. He kissed my cheek and rubbed my chest. 'You're my best date ever,' he whispered.

'There we go!' Raven announced his return. He handed everyone's drinks – Pablo first, followed by Reggie, then me.

'Got the same as me again?' Pablo said to Raven.

'Guilty as charge,' Raven said as he stroked Pablo's neck.

'Told you you'd be addicted,' Pablo said and kissed his impossibly sexy client.

We chit-chatted about life in Sydney, how it was brighter here compared to London, and about Raven's country house in Somerset. Reggie invited us to fly to Brisbane and watch a rugby game this Sunday but we all declined. When Raven hinted 'Should we rock and roll?' I quickly offered another round of drinks and rushed to the bar.

'Can I borrow your pen, Ash?' I asked the bar tender. My heart raced.

He gave me it and winked.

So we stayed for another hour listening to Dr Aqua's finale mix. As we hugged each other goodbyes, I slipped a piece of serviette inside Raven's jacket pocket. I had written my phone number on it.

ANDREA CURTIN: MOTHER TO MOTHER

15 APRIL 2017

FREDERICO PARKED the car a few houses away from his mother's house. He tapped at the wheel and pressed his lips together.

'I still don't think this is a good idea,' he said.

'Why? She's your mother.'

'I don't think you'll ever see a mother as messed up as her, Andie.'

'I don't judge, Frederico. You should know that.'

He nodded. 'Please don't be offended if she says something out of place.'

I simply kissed him. I pushed the door wide open, spun myself around and put my feet on the ground, waiting for my driver boyfriend to help me up. He did, with a smile, and a big huff, assuring himself he was ready.

Alexandra Lowe was only nine years older than me, but if Frederico hadn't told me her age, I would've thought she was at least in her mid-fifties. I felt like a liar after telling Frederico I didn't judge. Seeing the woman now, I couldn't help but blame her weakness and bad choices. She could've been a better mother to Frederico, she could've been a better person for herself.

I paused my thoughts. Despite the premature creases around Alexandra's eyes and lips and her yellow teeth, I could see genuine warmth radiating from within her as she smiled. The woman really wanted me inside her home, inside her life.

I cancelled my first impression of her.

'Go fetch some lunch, will you?' Alexandra told Frederico after we were introduced to each other. 'There's a real nice café just around the corner. Indian food if you're into that. The butter chicken is to die for!'

'Sounds good,' I said.

Frederico stood still.

'Don't worry, I won't eat her!' said Alexandra.

He reluctantly left.

'You are okay with what he does?' asked Alexandra with no preamble.

'He's a good man. He makes an honest living, he makes people happy. I know that first-hand. So, yes, I'm proud of what he does.'

'Really? You're the first. Others ran away, you know,' Alexandra said with a degree of suspicion. 'And you're not just okay with it, you're proud. So... you tell people what he does? Proudly?'

'My friends know. As for others, if they ask, I tell them. If they don't like it then it's not my problem.'

'He's so lucky to have you. With your good looks you could've had any man you wanted.'

'I'm lucky to have him.'

'Do you know what you're in for?' Alexandra said.

'What do you mean?' I said, looking intensely at my... mother in law?

'I remember the feeling when I found out I was pregnant. I

was scared, but happy. I was only nineteen,' Alexandra said, full of thoughts. 'Was this baby planned?'

'No.'

'He was your boyfriend at the time, yes?'

'No.'

Alexandra shook her head. 'Huh!'

I knew what was in her head: *you let him do you bareback?*

'Wow... I don't know if your gut instinct was good, or you were just unbelievably naïve. You really trusted him?'

'It happened. It was meant to be.'

'Huh! You were lucky Frederico didn't take after his father. I had a hard time trying to convince Matteo to keep the baby when he found out I was pregnant. Did Frederico tell you about his father?'

I nodded.

'I just kept telling that arsehole "It's a boy!". Being the dick that he was, he said if it turned out to be a girl he would put her up for adoption,' Alexandra said bitterly. 'Frederico will be a good father, I know.'

'He will,' I said.

'I guess it helps that you're not so young. You're wise, you're rich, you know what lies ahead and how to handle the world.'

I looked at Alexandra. I didn't know what Frederico had told his mother. I wanted to tell her about Christopher Jr. But in the end I just said, 'Well, I don't know everything. That's why I need Frederico by my side.'

Alexandra carried on, 'I went to Italy to have a good time, not to get rich or anything; just wanted to live the laid back lifestyle, run away with an Italian lover, but I never thought I'd be so messed up. I had nothing when I came back here.' She frowned at me. 'I used to be a hooker too, you know.'

'There's nothing wrong with supporting yourself and your child.'

By the look on her face I sensed Alexandra hadn't expected such an answer. Perhaps she was used to hearing: *Oh my God, really?*

'I don't mean to be rude, but...' Alexandra said, 'were you ever in the same line of work as Frederico? Is that how you two met?'

'Why do you say that?'

'You seem to be overly comfortable with prostitution.'

'It's work. That's how I see it. Just like what I do,' I said. 'I hired Frederico to have sex with me, so yes, I'm comfortable with prostitution. It doesn't mean I work in the industry.'

'What do you do, Andrea?'

'Ah, umm... I'm in retail.'

'Frederico said you were a successful business woman.'

'I just do what I'm good at,' I replied.

'I was working at supermarkets, at restaurants, but never enough. Frederico needed education, you see. I would do anything for him. And he has been good to me. He took care of me when I was sick, gives me money, buys me food. Look at this place! I can't afford it on my own. You should ask Frederico what I could afford, what kind of life I gave him when we first moved here. It was a shit hole.'

'He's a good man. You've done well.'

'Don't worry, I won't suck the funds for the baby,' Alexandra said. 'I've started working again, and I won't need Frederico's money any more.'

'Alexandra, whatever you've arranged with Frederico, it's none of my business. If he sends you money, that's fine by me,' I said. 'I'm not saying this because I have money myself, but because I care about you and Frederico. And I respect you both.'

'How old are you?'

I looked at her, trying to find what she really wanted to know. 'Thirty-five,' I answered.

'Never married before?'

'Once. Now divorced.'

'No kids?'

I took a deep breath. Alexandra's eyes were on me. 'No,' I replied.

'I won't be the grandmother of your dreams. I'm too messed up to be around babies, I suppose, not a good role model and all. But I'm here for you and Frederico, and I know you understand, right?' Alexandra said. She looked into my eyes, and I could swear she was able to read every story that was written there.

FREDERICO and I decided to have an hour-long city walk before we went back to the car.

As we were approaching Hyde Park, I remembered two years ago, a day after Mardi Gras, on this same stretch of street, when Chris was raging. I'd seen a young pregnant couple standing at that spot across the road – all loved up, full of hope for the future. I still remembered the crushing feeling I had back then. I glanced down at Frederico's hand in mine, then I looked at my swelling belly. Frederico and I had become that couple, and more.

'It's nice to be with you out in the open,' said Frederico. 'We don't have to hide.'

I rested my head on his shoulder.

'You've done well to win my mother's heart.'

'Really?'

'I've never seen her that bright before, in front of anybody. What did you two talk about?'

'Just how we met, she asked whether I was okay with what you did.'

'I see.'

'Frederico, have you ever brought a boyfriend home?'

'Yes, many times,' he said. 'Why?'

'What did she think of them?'

'She didn't mind them, but she didn't feel good, either. Somehow she knew those boys or men would never last. And she was right. I could never sustain a long-term relationship. Everything about me was too vague, too weird, too hard. Sometimes I blamed her for that. She was stoned most of the time. She didn't even know who she was, or who I was sometimes. But she's my mother. She was broken by another man and she doesn't have anyone else. And she brought me to this country, to this city – without her I wouldn't have ever met you again.'

'Don't be too harsh on her, eh?' I said.

He just kissed me.

As spits of rain fell, we arrived at another intersection.

I leaned on Frederico, rubbing my cheek on his arm. He picked up the cue, and he showed those people what I meant to him. He pulled me close, I looked up at him lovingly. He kissed my lips, he kissed my head, smelled my hair, put his hand on my belly, stroked it like he owned it.

'Making the most of it?' I teased.

'Yeah, your belly won't stay this big forever.'

Six months and counting. And he kept showering me with affection that everyone at the intersection would be envious of. I tickled him. And he hugged me even tighter. We crossed the road as one. He was protecting me as if we were under fire.

When we got to the other side, something caught my eye. Not people's attention, not a particular person. A car. One I'd seen not so long ago – it had passed us by slowly then sped off, ten, fifteen minutes before. But, I reasoned, there would be hundreds of white Golfs around the city. So I ignored my silly thought and kept walking.

FREDERICO LOWE: RAVEN

15 MAY 2017

Andie caught me crying behind my hands.

'Work?' said Andie.

'Yeah. Sorry, did I wake you up?' It was well past midnight and since her third trimester she was usually fast asleep at this time (and she'd wake up at around 3 a.m.).

'No, not at all. I've been sweating all night. I'm so thirsty!' she said, grabbing a tall mug from the overhead kitchen cabinet. Her eyes darted between the running tap filling up the mug and me wiping my face. 'I'll be in the bedroom if you need me. I won't be asleep,' she said with the mug in her hand. She half-squatted to kiss my forehead.

I was about to say thank you, but Andie put her finger on my lips. In her breathing, in her own language, she told me she understood. I wanted to share everything, and I could've, because she was strong. But how far could I stretch her strength? In the end sharing my burden would achieve little – those days would come again and nothing would change. One time Andie told me it was like having a secret agent husband: 'I know what you do but don't really know what's going on. But I'm okay with it.' – and I loved her for it.

What was in my mind tonight, for once, was something that I never wanted Andie to know. Yet I wanted her near. While she was still within my reach, I grabbed her hand. 'No, no, please stay with me.'

Andie sat beside me and swallowed two big gulps of water. As I watched, I laughed, 'What a mug! Where did you get that from?'

She quickly turned the mug and then laughed at the illustration: a flock of sperms ran horizontally towards an egg; one had managed to get in and written underneath was 'WE HAVE A WINNER'.

'Oh! I thought I took a plain one,' she said, and put the mug on the coffee table. 'It was from silly Leanne.'

That moment was five minutes of solace, but I still couldn't get over what had happened with Raven in the past few weeks. And tonight it was a climax. We had a drink at a bar and he'd told me he was divorcing his wife. I could've married him. I felt I had been married to him when we made love in his five-star hotel bed.

I looked at Andie and started crying again.

'Hey...' she whispered and hugged me.

It was not only the fear of falling in love. Another kind of fear also lurked inside me – sooner or later Pablo would know. I said to Andie after a long pause, 'I did something that I shouldn't have.'

I withdrew from Andie's hug.

'Were you hurt? You can tell me.'

And now the love of my life was offering me the comfort I never deserved. 'No,' I said. 'It just got complicated. This is why I prefer women clients, you know? They're more, what's the word... Manageable? Someone like you?'

And I started blabbering and fooling myself that I hadn't cheated on her.

'Me? Manageable?' She pinched my cheek.

'No, that's the wrong word, it's... I don't know. More considerate, I suppose, easier to deal with.'

'I don't want you to meet another client like me.'

'Of course not. You're the only one. I won't do it with another woman. I've promised you that.'

'I know. I trust you,' she said.

And I hated myself even more.

'Wine?' she offered.

'No thanks. I'm gonna have a shower.'

'Okay. I'll prepare the bath in the ensuite soon, we can relax for a while?'

'Not too late for you?'

'No, I can't really sleep. And I don't have to start early tomorrow.'

'All right, sounds good then.'

Close to 2 a.m. I joined Andie in the bath. She was already immersing herself in the bubbly rose water.

'You look relaxed,' I said. 'I like it. Not running around worrying about work.'

'Well... my priorities have changed now,' she said and held my hand while I was stepping into the bath.

I massaged her belly. Holding my tears, right then I made up my mind not to see Raven again. I said, 'I'm thinking about doing some study.'

'Frederico, that's great!'

'Maybe psychology.'

'You would be a great psychologist. I don't know how you do it, but it's amazing how well you know people and how you connect with them, and how skilful you are at making people feel good. Well... skilful? Maybe more *wise*.'

'I'm not that good.' I blushed.

'You are, believe me,' she said.

I smiled. 'Don't worry, I will keep working.'

'Look, I'll be happy to support you while you're starting your study, it can be difficult, you know. Once you feel you're set then you can start working again.'

'No, I want to work, always,' I said.

'That's fine, too. I'm just saying, you know, just ask me if you need it.'

'Why are you so good to me, Andie?'

'That's the only thing that I want to do, be good to you, because you've been so good to me.'

And right then I promised myself *again*, no more Raven – in thoughts or in the flesh.

FREDERICO LOWE: ANDIE'S TRAUMA

26 MAY 2017

I WIPED the steamed-up bathroom mirror. I looked terrible. Wet strands of fringe falling untidily on my forehead, wet brows with rebellious hair, sleeping-three-hour-a-night eyes, and – damn... a zit! I tightened the towel knot just below my belly button and leaned forward. I decided to forget about the zit and applied a layer of shaving cream. The mirror started to steam up again. I grumblingly did another round of wiping while sliding my shaving brush along my jawline. Everything had to go – my face had to be hair-free for tomorrow.

I was scraping the straight razor against the left side of my beard when I heard a hiccup – not very loud, but distinct. It soon stopped.

I puckered and carried on.

As I moved on to my chin – a yelp, and a scream.

I dropped the razor and darted out of the bathroom.

'Andie,' I said, kneeling next to her. Her head was tilted backwards, her neck arched over the pillow, eyes dilated, mouth opened wide. I put my palm on the back of her head and caressed her cheek. 'What's wrong?'

She turned her head towards me.

I cradled her in my arms. 'Do we need to go to the hospital? Are you...'

'No, no, it's not that, I'm—' She leapt out of bed, flipped the duvet and swept the length and width of the mattress. In panic she switched on the light and examined the bed all over again.

'Andie, what are you doing?' I said trying to hold her.

But she evaded my grip and pulled her panties down. 'No blood?' she asked me.

I looked at the pink and grey underwear encircling her knees. 'No, no blood,' I said and gently put the panties back on her.

'I dreamt I lost the baby.'

'You've been thinking about it too much. It will be okay, I promise.'

'It was around this time...' she murmured and stopped.

'Around this time what?'

'Ah... forget about it,' she said taking a deep breath. 'I'd better get back to sleep. I have an early start tomorrow.'

I tucked her in and knelt beside her. 'Tell me, please.'

'Christopher's brother... it was around this time.'

Oh, Andie... I reached out my hand and touched her belly. 'The baby will be okay.'

Suddenly a smile. 'Did you feel that?'

'Yes, yes I did,' I said enjoying the soft pulsing kicks under my palm. 'Did I wake him up?'

'Maybe,' she said. 'What time is it?'

'Midnight,' I said. 'Go back to sleep, eh? I'll join you soon.'

'Oh... your beard... you've only done half,' Andrea said gleefully. 'Go and finish off what you need to do.'

I went to the bathroom, thinking. I wiped off my shaving cream and came back to Andie.

'That was quick?'

'I'll sleep with half a beard tonight,' I said.

Andie laughed softly.

'I'm so tired,' I complained.

'You're planning to shave it all?'

'A request for tomorrow's appointment.' My heart started pounding. 'You said you had an early start?'

'Yeah, I have to get a store ready for an afternoon opening. It's in Richmond, I have to be there at six.'

'Are you sure you can't ask Sophie to do it? You will barely have had any sleep.'

'Yeah, maybe. Sophie said that, too. I reckon she'll do it, but I'll miss out.'

'Miss out? Really? A store in Richmond?'

'Well, it's actually a family-owned shop for the blind, like a Braille superstore. We do it for almost nothing, they do good things for the community. Missing out? Yeah, I'll miss out on cuddling those guide puppies. The owners said there'd be about a dozen of them at the opening. Sophie would go. I'll send her a quick text. You'll be here in the morning?'

'Yes, I'll be here in the morning but I'll be coming home late. The appointment is in Glenbrook.'

'Blue Mountains? That's a bit far.'

'Yeah, I know. But he's a good client.'

And my heart palpitated out of control this time. He was more than good – he was irresistible. I could see Raven's text message in my head:

Hey loverboy, it's me, sorry, had to get a new phone. Settled the country house at Glenbrook today. Could we meet there instead of the hotel?

'Just take care of yourself,' she said and lay on my chest and immediately fell asleep.

I kissed her, apologising silently.

Just once more, tomorrow, and he'll fly back to the UK, and that's it.

FREDERICO LOWE: GLENBROOK

27 MAY 2017

Glenbrook was a ghost town when I arrived. I parked right in front of the house Raven had sent the address for. It didn't look like a country house, it was just an ordinary suburban house with a grassless, fenceless yard. One of the rooms was lit up.

At exactly 9 p.m. I knocked on the door.

No answer.

I knocked again.

Still no answer, I went around the back and peeped in the window where the light was coming from. I couldn't spot anyone. I texted Raven.

Hi gorgeous, I'm here. Where are you?

I walked back to the front door and waited for a reply.

Sorry loverboy. getting some wine. Front door is unlocked, let yourself in. C u soon.

The house was almost empty. I wandered inside. A jasmine smell dissipated from the lit-up bedroom. And I liked what I saw. It was just like Raven: he'd prepared it for the night. A double bed with blue sheets, a fluffy duvet and a brown fleece blanket, and two thick pillows for us to rest our heads and chat after we were done pleasing each other.

I couldn't wait to feel his body, kissing it from top to bottom, and caress his full buttocks... smooth and rather cute. Then Raven would turn around, lift me up, lay me gently on the bed and kneel in between my thighs...

I heard the front door open.

'Raven?' I said and walked out of the room.

The floor creaked. I called his name again but there was no reply. The front door was wide open. As I was about to step outside, someone grabbed me from behind and gagged me. Then he covered my head with something dark, it felt like a pillow case, and dragged me along the floor into another room.

In the room I felt another presence. They forced my arms to bend behind my back and soon I was stripped of my pants and underwear.

I didn't know Raven was going to bring someone. And I didn't know he was into this sort of role play. Was Raven even in the house? I could smell his cologne, he *was* one of the men. So I played along.

I writhed as one of them rubbed my dick, rough and fast. That handsome Englishman's hand ... it was hurting me right now, but there was an irresistible reward at the end of it, *there always was with Raven*. My blood rushed.

Once my captors were satisfied with how aroused I was, one of them said: 'Oh yeah, that's what I wanted to see.'

I knew the voice, and it wasn't Raven.

And a punch landed on my groin.

'Piece of shit!' the other said.

I recognised that voice, too, and it wasn't Raven either.

A piece of something struck my thighs this time. Then they came back to the spot they wanted to hurt most – there was a kick, another whack, another kick, and it kept coming – brutal, revengeful and on the same spot.

The first man continued: 'So he called you *loverboy*, too, huh? I gambled with that. I guess he wasn't that creative when it comes to pet names.'

I could hardly stand. A hand tightened the pillowcase from behind my neck, twisting it around.

As I was trying to catch a breath, a fist pounded my mouth...

I had been beaten up before, many times. They were nothing. My father – his fists, his shoes, his knees, his belt – nothing. The Roman police batons – nothing. I could take every blow and not cry, and if it had killed me it wouldn't have mattered. But in this house, where I was supposed to make love to a man I adored – I would plead for the beating to stop.

Andie...

This time I might *really* die for it. Maybe it was better this way, I didn't have to fear falling in love and hurting Andie.

'Raven was mine, Lucio! You fucking thief, you just couldn't help it, *just couldn't help it*!'

I was about to fall to the floor but the man behind me quickly grabbed my arms and forced me to stay up.

'And *your bitch*!' he continued. 'Do you know what she called herself?'

And a big swing of that piece of something landed on the side of my head.

It shook everything in me, for a moment I forgot where I was, stopped hearing anything.

Death.

I'd die now because of my desire for another man.

Andie...

The baby...

No, I couldn't die. I would *not* leave them behind with all this mess.

'Do you like that name?'

What name?

'You don't, huh? Violet. That sneaky little bitch.'

I tried to beg but the two men wouldn't entertain my mumbling behind the gag. They punched my cheeks, left, right, and back to my mouth.

Every blow broke me more. It did, because I resisted – I really wanted to live.

By this time I didn't know how much more I could endure. I just kept begging.

'That's enough, man,' the man who had been hanging on to my body said, and he let me go.

On the floor I scrunched and tried to clutch every part of me that was in pain, but I didn't have enough hands, everywhere was painful.

'No man! Leave him!'

Finally everything stopped.

As the footsteps were leaving me, I let out a cry. I tried to hang on, but in the end I passed out.

In between reality and hallucination, I found myself lying on a lawn. It was bright, almost too bright for my eyes to see. But I wanted to know what was behind that burst of light, so I kept staring at it. A playground. Andie and the baby were there, smiling, giggling, sliding, swinging. They didn't see me. I tried to call them but I couldn't. I fumbled about and groped into my own mouth to pull out the piece of fabric that had been muzzling me.

'Andie...' I moaned.

And she heard me this time. She turned around and walked towards me, with the baby crawling right behind her. She was so close now, she opened her arms, motioning me to get up.

'Sayang...' she said.

'Andie, I can't...'

She knew I couldn't, her gaze told me she felt my suffering. So she pulled me up and she kissed me on the lips. Painful, but soothing.

'I'm sorry, Andie...'

But just like that everything turned dark.

I opened my eyes. The pillowcase was still covering my head but the gag was loose. Panting, out of air, and trembling with stabbing pain, I crawled and slowly made my way to the car. I couldn't sit. I slid myself and knelt, crying in front of the wheel. But I had to get home, I had to.

ANDREA CURTIN: MY MAN

27 MAY 2016

I WISHED I'd come home to Frederico sitting on the sofa, inviting me to snuggle with him, offering me hot chocolate and a massage. Instead I came home just before midnight. I'd ended up going to Richmond; late, but in time for puppy cuddling. Afterwards I was invited to the guide dog academy and spent the evening enjoying a dinner home-cooked by the family.

I drifted off to sleep in front of the TV as I waited for Frederico. I was waking up when a car commercial came on. Mum, dad and bub were happy, enjoying the road trip. The camera zoomed in on the dad – a typical macho but gentle bloke, who was good looking enough to be behind the wheel of a luxurious car (and married to a stunning young mum), but soft enough to be the father of such a precious girl. As my eyelids were shutting, his face morphed into someone I knew well. What was Frederico doing there?

Then I heard my name called. 'Andie...'

I woke up and felt a lump in my throat.

Should I text or ring him? Probably all was going well with this new client so I'd better not.

The front door lock clicked. Frederico! At last.

The door stuttered open... My man was black and blue, bloodied, wearing no pants, trying to get to me with every ounce of energy he had left.

'Frederico...' I ran to him and caught his falling body. 'What the hell happened?'

'I'm sorry,' he huffed, hanging on to me.

'I'm taking you to the hospital!'

'No,' he said and let go of me. He hobbled to the couch, he couldn't sit down. He panted, he held his pain. In the end he leaned on me again.

'We're going to the hospital!'

'No! No police.'

'Frederico, I'm taking you there!'

'Just stay... you're here... Andie... stay... Andie... I'm sorry... don't let anyone in... so bright here...' Slurring and fading, he fell on me completely.

'Frederico?'

His pulse weak, his body cold.

'YOUR BOYFRIEND NEEDS SURGERY, MA'AM,' the doctor said.

'Why? Head injury?'

'No,' the doctor bowed his head. 'He needs penile surgery.'

I gasped.

'His genitals were badly beaten. There's a fracture. It's not a complex procedure. He should be okay, he made it here just in time,' the doctor said.

'Can I see him before the surgery?'

'He's heavily sedated. But you can see him, two minutes.'

I looked at Frederico. He'd called my name when I was asleep on the sofa, that had been real. I touched his hand lightly. 'You'll be all right,' I whispered.

'Miss...?'

'Curtin,' I said.

'Miss Curtin we have to start the preparation,' said a nurse. She looked at my belly. 'I'll get you a comfortable chair. Someone will meet you in the waiting room.'

I dragged my feet along the corridor floor. In the waiting room there was a leather office chair and a male nurse was standing guard next to it.

'This is *your* chair, take it with you wherever you go, don't give it to anyone else,' said the nurse, smiling. 'Do you need anything? Can I get you some tea, coffee?'

V? Red Bull? 'Hot chocolate?'

'Sure.'

The hot chocolate came speedily.

'Can I ring someone for you?' the nurse offered.

'No, thanks.'

'The magazines here are kinda lame...' he said. 'I have a few *Empires* in the back if you're into that sort of thing.'

'You're very kind. But I'll keep myself entertained.'

The nurse nodded and left the room. Five minutes later he was back, with a pillow. 'You should try to sleep, or at least close your eyes. If you need anything I'll be around the corner. Anything, just ask, okay?'

I hugged the pillow tight across my belly and sighed, 'Thank you.'

A HAND TAPPED MY SHOULDER. I opened my eyes, but I fell back asleep – just a dream. Another nudge. I was going to rub my eyes but something was covering my hands and my whole body. The nurse had put on a blanket over me.

'Sorry to wake you up...' It was the doctor.

Oh God...

'The surgery went well,' he said.

I heaved a sigh of relief.

'Can I see him?'

'Of course. He's still unconscious, and will be for maybe a couple of hours.'

I got up and followed the doctor to Frederico's room.

'You should probably go home soon,' the doctor advised. 'We'll take care of him. He'll be fine.'

'No, I'll stay, I'm feeling okay,' I said.

'All right, I'll leave you to it.'

My knees were weak, I had never seen anyone so swollen before. I wanted to kiss him, but there were only a few spots on his face where I could see skin; not enough for my lips. And I couldn't see his star-shaped scar.

A moment later Frederico opened his eyes. He was staring into space, then he cried as he tried to bend his right knee to turn on his side.

I held him in place and he closed his eyes again. I peeped under the blanket and found a drainage bag next to his thigh. The catheter must've hurt every time he moved.

About an hour later he woke up again. He grimaced and tried to muffle his cry, but he couldn't and in the end he forced himself to keep it to soft sobs, then he called my name.

'Frederico, I'm here.'

I could see he wanted to say how much pain he was in, but he just smiled.

'Hey...' I said.

He squeezed my hand feebly, his eyes closed. Then he glanced at me before closing them again. 'Don't worry – 'm used to this – beaten up,' he murmured.

'Don't talk,' I whispered.

His eyelids were shutting.

'You're in so much pain... I wish I could make it go away.'

'I hv... you.'

'Sayang...'

That had always made him smile, but this time it made him weep.

'Hey... don't cry...'

'Sorry.'

'It's not your fault, Frederico.'

'Lv me?' He could barely move his swollen lips.

'I love you. I always will. You will be okay,' I said. 'Please, don't talk.'

But he went on, he couldn't wait to tell me this: 'R baby, 'm the father.' He stopped to swallow his saliva. 'M not a man––,' he cringed as he took a deep breath, 'whatever happn ––r baby.'

'Frederico...'

'Tell 'm ––bout us,' he said, trying to smile in between all the swelling. 'M not a man––'

'You'll always be a man, the best man that I've known,' I said.

'If tis––' Frederico closed his eyes. 'Tis before baby – I wouldn't hv you.'

'We're lucky to have met each other, twice. I will always love you no matter what,' I said. 'But you'll get better, I promise.'

'You so good––' he said, '––to me.'

'Frederico stop.'

'A stranger – thief.'

'Ssshh... Don't talk,' I said as he grimaced at every word.

'Esc––'

And he fell into unconsciousness once again.

FREDERICO LOWE: HOSPITAL DAY 1

27 MAY 2016

ANDIE'S HEAD was resting on the edge of the bed. I felt slightly more awake, although what I was seeing seemed to be bobbing up and down.

Half an hour, an hour, I became more alert, more in pain and bored. I wanted her to wake up; she'd tell me those comforting words. But she needed sleep.

With my free hand I reached for the phone she'd left on the bedside table. Pain pain pain, but I wanted to do it. I took a photo of her sleeping face, next to my IV'd hand. Tapping the buttons one letter every five seconds, I captioned the beautiful image: 'This is love.'

I almost shared it, I wanted the world to know, but I put the phone back on the bedside table, or so I thought. My hand didn't quite make it, and the phone fell to the floor.

'Hey....' Andie said, woken by the noise. 'How are you feeling?'

'You're here,' I said.

Then she saw the phone on the floor. She gave me a look, 'What'cha doing?'

I tried to smile but I grimaced.

'Go home.'

She shook her head.

No, my Andie wouldn't leave my side. But she had to. I continued, 'Rest. Baby.'

She frowned, then finally nodded, rubbing her back and sighing. 'Are you sure you'll be okay?'

'Yeah.'

'I'll be back first thing tomorrow… actually,' she said, looking at her watch, 'in a few hours' time. Ask the nurse to call me if you need anything, anything at all, okay?'

I just closed my eyes.

She kissed me and left.

No… I shouldn't have let her go. I shouldn't! Come back, Andie, stay with me. How could I forget? I was so overcome by my own pain, my own fear, that I forgot about those two men saying *your bitch*.

Where are the police when you need them?

ANDREA CURTIN: THE LETTER

28 MAY 2016

WALKING SLOWLY, I kept turning back to look at Frederico. But I had to go home. My back had been killing me and the bouts of dizziness had made me sway every time I turned a corner.

A taxi was waiting outside. The nurse who had been helping me was there chatting with a security guard.

'Let me get that for ya,' he said opening the taxi door for me.

'Thank you,' I said.

'Get some sleep,' he said. 'Your boyfriend is in good hands.'

I nodded.

On my phone I found the photo Frederico took. I wished I could kiss his hand right now. I didn't want to cry, but I couldn't help it. I was still sobbing hard when the taxi pulled over. It was only the driver's voice that made me realise I was home.

The familiar glass doors slid open. Why did I ever come home? I wouldn't sleep anyway – whether it was in my bed or on the hospital's sofa.

I did a double take as I walked past the rows of mailboxes. A piece of paper stuck out of one mailbox, like a white flag, on a familiar location. Our mailbox.

Bitch! We know where you live. We know there's three of you.

I clutched the paper and went inside the lobby. No one was around, not even the concierge.

Are they already inside the apartment waiting?

Should I run or should I stay?

A man with a backpack walked past me. I clung onto the unattended concierge bench behind me. He looked at me oddly, but he had a card and key; it was unlikely to be him.

When my fingers failed to dial 000, I called the man who was once my protector – I knew he would be again.

About fifteen minutes later a familiar figure loomed at the door. My Chris. He was no longer mine but he was still my Chris.

'What did he do?' he roared. 'Where is he?'

'No, he didn't do anything,' I replied softly. I showed him the letter.

'What's this?' he said and trembled. 'Where is he?'

'He's in hospital.'

'What?'

'He was attacked. And now the attackers... I think they're already inside waiting for me. That's why I'm here... I thought... I thought... at least here there're cameras.'

'Hey... come here.' Chris hugged me.

'I'm sorry. I didn't know who else to call.'

'It's okay, Andrea,' he said. 'You're safe.'

And he looked at my belly. 'You look so beautiful,' he said with teary eyes. He briefly turned around to wipe his face. 'We should go to the police.'

'Stay with me tonight, please,' I said as he walked us out, half his body covering me.

'Of course.'

FREDERICO LOWE: HOSPITAL DAY 2

28 MAY 2016

SOMETHING HAD HAPPENED OVERNIGHT, Andie's face said it all. Ignoring all the pains zapping my body, I extended my arms and hugged her. 'Okay?'

'I'm fine.' A hesitant embrace from her. 'Lie down, Frederico,' she said adjusting the pillows under my neck.

'You okay?' I murmured as the pain almost paralysed me right in the mouth.

'Yes,' Andie said. 'Don't worry about me. How are you feeling?'

'The police?' I said, eyes closed.

'Yes. They came over to the apartment earlier this morning, not long after I got there.'

'Any men come?'

'What's going on, Frederico?' she said. 'Who attacked you?'

I opened my eyes and tried to reach for her face, but I could barely lift my hand. I just looked at her anxiously. I'd never thought those men would harm her. They couldn't harm a woman, they shouldn't, but they might. 'I know them.'

'What?'

'Pablo, Gianni.'

'Oh my God,' she said. 'It's all my fault. I should've listened to you… I should've just let it go. I'm so, so sorry, Frederico.'

Her eyes swelled with tears, her lips trembled. She looked away, shook her head, then paused.

'Not your fault, Andie.'

'Did you tell the police?'

'It's a one-off,' I told her as she tried to listen closely.

'How do you know?'

'Trust me.'

'I got you into this mess,' she sighed.

'No, not you.' I panted for a while then continued, 'It's my fault.'

'I was scared.'

I frowned helplessly. 'Stay safe?' I watched her pupils moving left and right erratically. 'The police stayed?'

'Chris stayed with me last night,' she said, her palm on my shoulder.

I shrugged away from her. I should've been the one protecting her, not that ex-husband of hers!

'He was the only one I could trust. Those men knew I was pregnant.' She trembled.

I let out a hopeless sigh. If there was anyone who could protect her from those animals, it would be Chris.

ANDREA CURTIN: AND HE CALLED ME MISSY

29 MAY 2016

I ARRIVED EARLY this morning and when I entered Frederico's room the nurse was finishing changing his catheter. I didn't want to look, but it was there in front of me – a bag of red, yellow and brown; the colours of his suffering.

'Good morning, Miss Curtin,' said the nurse when she saw me. I pretended I had just arrived.

'Good morning.'

'He looks a lot brighter today,' the nurse said, and left.

Frederico's eyes were shut tightly, tears streaming down his face. His blanket was pulled up and rolled to one side, exposing his feet. The blanket creases showed the trace of his leg movements. Gently I tucked his scrunching feet under the blanket. Immediately he stopped squirming and opened his eyes.

I spread the other half of the blanket over his chest. 'Hey…' I said, dabbing his wet cheeks with a face towel the nurse left on the table. 'I hate seeing you in pain.'

He sniffled. 'It's nothing, Andie.'

'You don't have to pretend with me.'

'It's nothing,' he said. 'You stay safe?'

'Yes. Chris isn't staying any more but the police checked on me regularly. A couple of them came round last night, and this morning.'

'Good.'

'Has the doctor seen you today?'

'No,' he said and pushed himself up a bit. 'I'm hungry... what's that?' he said taking a peek at the flask I was clutching.

'They didn't give you anything to eat?'

'Puree, jelly. Yuck.'

I chuckled. 'I brought you essence of chicken.'

He stared at me.

'Trust me, it's good for you. You can have it now, if you want,' I said. 'It's good for post-surgery. Give you extra strength.'

'Chicken liver?'

'No! No! Not like that. It's just a soup,' I said. 'I remember my mum made this for my dad. He had a ski accident at the Snowy Mountains. His ribs were severely broken. He had surgery and all, and he swore the essence of chicken sped up his recovery.'

Frederico tried to smile.

'And he didn't like jelly,' I said.

He gestured me to give him some to try.

'It stinks a bit, but it doesn't taste too bad,' I said and placed a china spoon in between his swollen lips, trying not to touch any of the bruises.

'Uuh...' he said. 'Nice, warm.'

'More?' I asked.

He gave me a long blink telling me yes.

I gave him one spoonful after another. 'My mum said she had this too after she gave birth to me,' I said. 'Her friends made it for her. My dad wouldn't have a clue.'

Frederico touched my belly and said: 'Teach me.'

I smiled. I was surprised to see the flask was empty.

A knock on the door echoed through the room as I helped Frederico sip some water. I turned around to find a tall, solid man wearing a bright yellow shirt and dark jeans. He looked like an ordinary man, apart from his thinly waxed eyebrows and unusually smooth complexion.

'Lucio...' he said hesitantly, still standing at the door.

'Do you know him?' I said softly to Frederico.

He gave me a long blink.

I let the big man in.

'Bloody hell, Lucio! What did they do to you?'

'Jerry...'

I recognised the name. Of course, the night I was trying to find The Nest – that night *she* called me 'Missy'. And this morning he, too, called me that as he stared at my belly: 'Missy... wow... who knew!'

'Hi,' I responded to him. 'Yes, it's his.'

'Well... Congratulations. So the rumour is true. Well... I knew it was true. I mean, you suddenly went "outcall" only?' Jerry looked at Frederico. 'Something must've been up. I just didn't think it was you!' Jerry turned to me. 'Lucio is lucky.'

I didn't understand why Lucio should be so lucky in Jerry's eyes. Shouldn't lucky mean he was with a beautiful man?

'Lucio, darling, how are you feeling?'

'Okay,' Frederico said, then grimaced.

'Oh Lord, don't speak. I'll do the talking,' Jerry said. 'I take it the police haven't found who did this to you?'

'Jerry...' sighed Frederico.

'Ssshh!' Jerry said.

Before Jerry could say anything further I asked, 'What have you heard?'

'Well... that Lucio was attacked at a house where he was supposed to be with a client. I have no names, but I'm hoping I could know more from... well you, Missy, and also you, Lucio.'

'Jerry don't get involved,' said Frederico.

'To the police we're not a priority. It's never urgent if it comes to cases like this. But this is a hate crime, someone has to deal with it! You know I'm with the Association, right? We have resources to help. You just need to talk to us and we can make ourselves heard, put pressure on the police to do more—'

'Please... no,' Frederico said. 'Please.'

'We can't let them win, Lucio! We have to let people hear our voice!' Jerry said. 'This is why I joined the Association. If we don't stop them, who will? Another escort will be lying in a hospital like you, or worse, maybe dead!'

Frederico closed his eyes, nodding weakly. He tried to draw a long breath but he grimaced.

'You know, Lucio...'

'Jerry,' I snapped, 'I think you should leave.'

Frederico held my hand, holding me back from dragging Jerry out. He said to Jerry laboriously: 'Please... our baby will be born soon. They win, so be it...' He took a break and continued, 'Just... warn the others, okay?'

Jerry sighed and reluctantly nodded. 'I understand,' he said, almost with no sound.

I followed the big man out.

'I know you're watching out for us,' I said just before he stepped into the lift. 'But please, don't try to do anything silly. It might put him in even more danger. Let the police handle it, they've done a good job so far, at least they've kept us safe. You can't keep us safe.'

'I've been watching out for him since he was eighteen. A lost boy, a silly boy,' Jerry said. 'How well do you know him, Missy?'

'I've known him since he was nine.'

Jerry stared at me, lost for words. 'You know who did it, yes?'

'I don't.'

'Someone you were looking for that night? Someone who might be bitter––'

'Are you suggesting it was my ex-husband? He would *never* do that! And I know for a fact he *didn't* do that.'

'Then who did?'

'You're not interested in helping us, you just want publicity,' I said, 'for that Association of yours.'

'What? I care about *him*, and believe it or not I care about you, too,' Jerry said. 'And I care about other escorts out there. I don't give a shit about publicity!'

'I'm heavily pregnant, and my boyfriend is in hospital, so I have the right to be selfish right now,' I said authoritatively. 'I don't care about those other escorts, they're big boys, they put themselves out there, they know the risk.'

'Look, Missy...'

'You want to embark on your own quest? And get him killed?'

'No, that wasn't my intention.'

'Or get *me* killed?' I said. 'Just stay away from us, stop your overzealous overprotective detective instinct bullshit! Aaah...' I pressed my chest. I huffed.

'Hey... Missy, you're okay?'

'Just go. And leave us alone!' I marched back to Frederico's room.

'Hey, what's wrong?' Frederico said.

'No, nothing's wrong. Just had a chat with Jerry,' I said.

'You're... you're red... what did...'

'Nothing,' I said. I took a deep breath. 'Maybe we should tell the truth to the police, Frederico.'

'No!'

'It's all my fault.'

'No, Andie, no. They won't hurt us any more. I swear.'

'I made Pablo trust me, and I can understand why he's mad. I just wish he hadn't thrown it all at you.'

'Andie...'

I sensed trembling under his voice. He was about to say something, something I'd already known; but what exactly?

Frederico held my hand. It felt warm on the top of my palm. 'I stole a client from him.'

'But... that was a long time ago, right?' I knew it wasn't, but I *wanted* it to be about what had happened a long time ago.

'No, recently,' he said.

'You really liked this man?'

He paused. 'I'm sorry, Andie.'

Suddenly a knock on the door. A couple of police officers. I remembered them –Detective Senior Constable Munroe and Constable Aras.

'Good morning Mr Lowe, Miss Curtin,' the older officer, Munroe, greeted us.

'Have you found who did this?' I asked.

'Well, not exactly, but we managed to get some footage of the CCTV at your apartment. I'll let you guys have a look,' Munroe said, motioning his partner to open the laptop in his hand.

A black and white video of the apartment entrance played. There was the hallway to the lobby and on the left and right were rows of the mailboxes. 'As you can see, this man tailgated and hand-delivered that threatening letter straight to your mailbox. Do you recognise him?'

If I was to guess, that man in a hoodie was Gianni – skinny, quick, and his bum wasn't as perky as Pablo's.

Frederico shook his head. 'I don't know him.'

'Do you recognise the jacket? Or the way he moves? Anyone you've met or seen in your line of work, perhaps?' said Aras.

Frederico shook his head once more. 'No.'

'We talked to your client, Mr Glen Bridges, who was supposed to be at the house.'

'That's his name?' Frederico said. 'It wasn't him. Someone else set me up.'

'Apparently so. Mr Bridges denied having another phone, or ever trying to contact you that night. We checked his phone records and the last time he contacted you was ten days ago. Would that be right?'

'About that, yes.'

'The number for the text you received that night belonged to a prepaid account registered to Luther Vandross. We didn't think it was a real name, but is there anyone you know who might've used or mentioned that nickname before?'

'No.'

'The owner of the house where you were attacked said she leased it to a man named Felipe Abasolo. Do you know him?'

'No,' said Frederico.

'Heard the name?'

Frederico shook his head. 'Are you going to track him down?'

'We've tried, but he seems to have disappeared.'

'Don't they have records of his ID and bank account and all that?' I said.

Frederico looked at me.

'Unfortunately not. The leasing was done privately, the owner was desperate for money and this young chap was apparently so charming and trustworthy that she gave the key to him just like that with a bit of deposit money.'

'Huh...' I sighed. I could see how Pablo could've done that.

'All right, Mr Lowe, if you remember anything please let us know,' Munroe said as his partner was packing up. Before he left, he turned to me: 'Oh, by the way, I saw you talking to a man just outside. Are you okay? You seemed a bit...'

'I'm okay,' I said. 'He's just a friend.'

'May I ask what you two were talking about?'

'Leave her out of it,' said Frederico.

I held Frederico's hand and stood up. I turned to face Munroe. 'We were talking about Frederico's other friends wanting to visit him today but I wasn't too happy about it,' I said, straight face, *now go away* face.

And so the two officers left.

FREDERICO LOWE: GIANNI

1 JUNE 2016

IT WAS SO good to wake up in our own bed, free from injections, changes of IV and that catheter. Although now Andie wouldn't be with me as much as she had been at the hospital; she'd gone back to work this morning.

Since my half confession, Andie had not asked any more about it, and nothing more about the incident. She had been caring for me as deeply as someone could, that hadn't changed, but she kept everything to herself. Someday soon I would tell her all about Raven.

The intercom rang. I wondered what Andie might've forgotten.

'It's me, Lucio.' A boy's voice, with an accent I grew up with. Why would Gianni come here?

'Please, I need to see you.'

I hung up.

He rang again.

'I'm alone. Please, there's something I need to tell you.'

I didn't want to see his face, but I was curious what he had to say. So I met him where the mailboxes were, right in front of where the camera pointed.

I stared at him: barely eighteen perhaps even seventeen, naïve, but so *vicious*.

'Lucio...' he said. For a while he examined my face.

'You're looking at a monkey, huh?' I said. 'Your creation.'

'No... sorry...' He started to weep and was about to touch my face.

I flinched and took a step back.

'Could we talk in your apartment?'

I shook my head. 'Tell me here.'

'Please...' He knelt in front of me. When I turned away he clung to my leg. 'Please, let me come upstairs with you.'

A van pulled up in front of the entrance, letting out a group of tourists, including a few kids. Gianni had begun begging hysterically as he clutched my leg. Any minute now the noise would attract the tourists' attention.

'Fuck! All right. Five minutes!' I said.

'I'm sorry about everything. I swear I didn't know he was going to beat you like that,' Gianni said when we were inside.

'Bullshit! You enjoyed it just as much! You pulled that pillowcase so tight, remember that? Did you feel a rush when you did that?'

'No, I swear, I didn't mean to,' Gianni said. 'I made him stop, Lucio. I made him otherwise you would've been dead!'

'Where is he?'

'Pablo went to his sister in Adelaide the morning after. Then I heard he'd left the country. Back to Spain. He's got his boyfriend there, you see. It's so easy for him.'

'Why are you still here?'

'I can't go back to Italy! I have no one there. And I have no one here either,' Gianni said.

'So what do you want from me?'

'I want to apologise,' he said.

'All right, you've done that, so leave.'

'I was at the hospital. I wanted to see you, but I saw the police. Did you tell them about me?'

'No.'

'Thank you,' he said. 'I can't get into police trouble...'

Once again I looked at Gianni. It was a familiar sight – a handsome boy who became an escort, got into a mess, and now he was scared. 'I haven't told them anything and I'm not going to,' I said.

'Thank you,' Gianni said again, giving me a teary stare ... and then, he stripped himself naked.

'What are you doing?'

'You never knew this. I've been watching you, I've been dreaming about someone like you. *I love you, Lucio*,' Gianni said.

'Love? Fuck! You made it sound so cheap.'

'I never wanted to hurt you, it was just... I was really angry at that moment, you know. I was pissed off with you, giving up my name to your girlfriend.'

He approached me.

'Gianni... don't! I love my girlfriend.'

'You like it, too, I can see it. You let me in. I took off my shirt, you didn't stop me. Now I'm naked, you're not really doing anything.'

I took a deep breath. 'Please go, Gianni.'

'Do you know, Pablo didn't believe it when I told him about you and your girlfriend? Well, he sort of knew, but he didn't want to believe it. He had this, I don't know what, something that made him want to protect you.'

'So *you* told him,' I said.

'I'm coming clean, Lucio!' begged Gianni. 'I feel guilty, very guilty. Like I said, I love you.'

'Get out of here!'

'Pablo didn't believe me. He hated me – how could he compete with a pretty young thing like me?' Gianni said, taking a step closer. 'Until he remembered what your girlfriend said when they fucked.'

I held my breath.

'She whispered *your* name when she came. Not CJ's, not Pablo's. I guess she couldn't really control it when she was so turned on. I know Pablo can be good with women. Open your eyes, Lucio. *She* gave you away.'

'You're lying.'

'*She* sent him to beat you up, no? At first Pablo thought it was some French name, but it was *L-u-c-i-o*. You stole Raven, oh Pablo was angry, yes, that made him decide to attack you. But, what really drove him to beat you that hard – *there* – was your girlfriend. He really liked her, you know. The beautiful Violet. But she was a lying little bitch... and no bitch ever crosses Pablo.'

I slapped him.

Gianni didn't move an inch. 'Lucky she's pregnant. But it meant you copped it.'

I closed my eyes.

'She doesn't love you, Lucio. She just likes to use men like us. No woman can ever love you like a man does. Like I do.'

Gianni carried on, 'Do anything to me, punish me, beat me up like I did to you. Or we could...' Gianni reached for my hand and pulled it towards himself, to his bare genitals. 'I could make myself look like her, I could dress like her... If that's what you want?'

I froze. Gianni gripped my hand, forcing me to squeeze that piece of meat harder.

ANDREA CURTIN: ALIEN'S PENIS

1 JUNE 2016

AT AN INTERSECTION HALFWAY between home and work, as I waited for the green light, I watched a woman crossing the road, pushing her pram. She looked to be in her twenties, or could be younger. She had almost no expression. *Isn't she happy? Did her husband leave her to handle everything herself? Or did he have an affair now he thinks she's not as attractive?* Maybe it was simply lack of sleep, I concluded.

'You are crrranky this morning!' I said to my baby. Usually the kicking stopped after I rubbed my belly, but this morning he kept going.

Living in the city, my commute was against the traffic. On a normal day, at this intersection I would've started to revisit my agenda for the day, think about what to say in that upcoming phone call with Mr so-and-so who was paranoid about everything, imagine things that might or might not happen, or simply complain to myself about what I might've forgotten. But right now my head was full of rain clouds, and the eye of the storm was Frederico: his grimace when he walked or tried to get up from a sitting position, or when he had to eat or relieve himself; I wouldn't be there to give him a hand.

And then there was Glen Bridges. I'd known this day would come – him, falling for another man. But I'd kept telling myself I'd deal with it when I had to cross the bridge. Now here I was, in the middle of that bridge, imagining what it'd be like having Frederico loving a man, truly, eternally, like a husband; perhaps in an open relationship (he wouldn't leave me and the baby, of that I was sure).

His face was so clear right now, that teddy bear stare. It would be an act of cruelty to trap a loved one and deny him the most basic needs of a man. Cruelty. Would I have felt the same way if it was Chris? I would've understood Chris had he been truthful, I hadn't changed my mind about that. So, now, with Frederico, the father of my child, I decided I *would* be willing to share. If Frederico wanted to pursue this Mr Bridges, I would understand and make it work.

When the light went green I made a U-turn.

Spending the day on the phone, sitting behind my desk solving puny retail problems – fuck that, not today. I'd rather care for and dress Frederico's wounds, feed him, bathe him, hear every moan and tell him I'd be there for him no matter what. I hadn't said that lately. I had been a silent carer – simply because I didn't know what to say.

I tossed up between ringing Frederico or just turning up at the door and decided the latter.

'Come on! Move!' I said as I got caught behind a P-plater who didn't make the crossing at the notorious red light that could take ten minutes to pass. I honked my horn three times. Funnily at the exact same time I felt three kicks on my belly. I chuckled. 'I know. You want Daddy, huh?'

When I arrived back at the apartment I parked the car

quickly and power-walked to the lift and headed up to our home.

I opened the door to find a boy stark-naked next to the dining table, his cock shiny, curving up; his hand gripping it... and under his hand, my man's hand. It wasn't Mr Bridges' cock, but seeing Frederico in the flesh with another man, I realised, after all, I would *not* share.

'Andie... it's not what you think,' Frederico said, withdrawing his hand. He threw Gianni's clothes at him, 'Get out of here!'

'I know you!' I said to Gianni. That alien lookalike, blonde hair, weird tan, disproportionate eyes, bone-thin... 'You were with my husband that night. Then you beat up my boyfriend, and now you're here sticking out your dick hoping to come all over him? I might just call the police.'

'No, no, please, please!' said Gianni kneeling in front of me, still naked.

'Andie, please, don't,' Frederico said.

I scrambled to find my phone.

Frederico squeezed my hands, 'Please, Andie, just this once, please trust me. You don't want to do this. He was all that you said. But I've been there myself, Andie. I know it's not right, but please, let him go.'

I threw my phone onto the sofa. Gianni was hopping on one leg, putting on his pants. I grabbed a vase from the living room cabinet.

'Get the fuck out!' I shouted and threw the blue china at Gianni. Followed by another vase. 'You bitch!' I shouted. Then a photo frame. 'Fuck you! Get out!' and finally a large crystal sculpture, which left me panting hard from the exertion. I screamed, long, and at the end of it I stopped breathing.

'Andie! Andie!' Frederico said, catching my collapsing body.

A few seconds later I gasped, my eyes widened, and I pulled myself up. 'Don't touch me!' I pushed Frederico away.

'Your face... Andie, we should go to the hospital.'

'No, I'm not having a heart attack, Frederico! I'm having a heartbreak!' I cried, and went into the bedroom.

'Andie, I'm sorry. He came here wanting to apologise. I didn't know he was going to do that,' he said, and was about to reach for my shoulder.

'Fuck you, too! Get the fuck out of my face!' I said, looking at his hand in disgust. By now I was sure I definitely could *not* share.

I lay down and pulled the duvet up to my chin. I turned away and Frederico duly walked out.

The bed smelled like hospital. I looked at Frederico's pillow and noticed a few specks of blood. I uncovered the duvet on his side and I saw bigger spots of blood on the sheet. I closed my eyes. As I was about to call Frederico he carefully stepped into the bedroom as if he could read my mind.

I sniffled and wiped my nose. 'Sit down.'

Frederico sat on the edge of the bed, right next to me. 'You came back; are you feeling ill?'

'I couldn't go to work. All I saw was you, struggling to get yourself food, drink, go to the toilet. You're bleeding again?'

'No,' he said. Then he looked at his side of the bed and said, 'Those were from last night, it was the ointment, not blood. Sorry I stained the bed...'

'Are *you* okay? Do you need to see the doctor?'

Frederico was about to turn to me but he stopped and contorted. He groaned.

'See... you are still in pain,' I said and got up. I held Frederico's shoulders. 'I'll drive you to the doctor. Despite all that just happened, I'm not a monster, you know.'

'I'm okay, Andie,' he said.

I pulled him up gently, stretching my arms as my belly got in the way. 'Lie with me.'

He reached out his hand and touched my cheek. 'I washed them,' he said softly when I threw a glance at his hand. 'Only an hour you were gone, but you don't know how much I missed you.'

I didn't say anything.

He put his hand on my belly when I lay next to him. 'Hello, baby.'

I let him settle and enjoy his moment with his son. After a few minutes, I moved his hand away. 'I understand if you fall in love with another man. I mean, you, me, we're not a natural fit, are we?' I said. 'At the end of the day you'll always come back to where your heart is set to.'

'I swear, there was nothing between me and Gianni. He came on to me. I was slow to say no. It was a sight, I must admit. But I did refuse and ask him to leave. When you came in, he was forcing my hand. I swear. I never wanted him.'

'Do you miss being with a man, Frederico?'

'No.' He answered with no hesitation.

'Huh... really?' I said.

'I am with men, a lot, it's my job, it has nothing to do with love, well, before this happened. I didn't look for it. That client of mine, Glen – I called him Raven – was Pablo's. But he was there, Andie. I felt a strong connection with him.'

'I looked at his photo. He's so handsome I'd probably have fallen for him too, had I known him,' I said. 'Glen-Rowan Bridges, born in Yorkshire, 11 November 1975, founder and CEO of Bridges Global PR. Served in the British Army when he was eighteen until he turned twenty-four. Do you think he loves you, too?'

He sighed. 'Of course not.'

'I can take care of the baby. If you really want to pursue him, you have my blessing. He looks to be a good guy.'

'No, Andie. I want to be with you.'

'Do you feel something is missing, though?'

'No, nothing is missing,' he said, holding back his tears.

'What happened to Pablo? Is he gonna turn up like that, too? I bet he wouldn't be kneeling.'

Frederico cleared his throat and said, 'No, he's back in Spain.'

'Guilt? Fear? Must be. How could a man hurt another like that?'

'Just testosterone, Andie.'

'Testosterone?' I studied his face. There was sadness. He would always try to conceal his sadness, but *this* sadness he put out there, for me to know. 'Yeah, perhaps you're right. I pissed him off like no one ever did. A chick played a trick on him, in bed, in a strip club; he even served me breakfast. Wouldn't he be full of testosterone! I wished he was gunning for me. I swear, I swear if I hadn't been pregnant I would've tracked him down and hurt him bad. Why did he have to attack you?'

'Not like that.' Frederico changed his expression, that sadness was masked once again. 'The attack had nothing to do with you,' he said and reached out for my hand. 'I meant, testosterone – defending your turf. I stole his client, and he was angry. Rightly so.'

'Why are you defending him?'

'Pablo was my friend, but we had a chequered history together. When I started out he was already successful. What was amazing about him, despite what he does for a living, despite his boyfriend staying behind in Spain, was that he could hold a steady relationship – something that I could never do. Do you know he's been with his current boyfriend for more than ten years?' he said. 'When my mother was addicted to meth I needed a lot of money to help her. I knew about one of Pablo's clients who paid excessively well, and I stole that client from him. And I earned a shitload. When he found out, he almost did the same to me then – beat me up and stuff, but he didn't. Then I introduced him to Chris. At the time Pablo was struggling. So we called it even and we became friends again. It wasn't your fault, Andie. But in saying that, I would take a beating for you, any time.'

'Frederico,' I said, 'why are you defending *me*? ... I should've told you this a long time ago. But I did sleep with Pablo.'

Frederico didn't say a word.

'Maybe you already knew,' I continued. 'I did it out of anger. After I saw you with that woman in Melbourne, and your ads weren't appearing any more, I was sure you had started a new life with her.'

Frederico still stayed silent.

'You knew,' I said. 'I'm sorry, Frederico.'

'Is the baby mine or his?'

'It's yours. We used protection, and it turned out at the time I was already six weeks pregnant. The test I did at home returned a false negative, I swear I didn't know. I never wanted him, Frederico.'

He hugged me.

'Now you know, right, why Pablo attacked you?'

'It's got nothing to do with you,' he whispered and wiped my tears. 'I *know* there was nothing between you and Pablo.'

'How do you know?'

'My heart is in you, Andie,' he said. Then he smiled. 'You can't lie to me.' And he kissed me.

'If you ever fall in love with another man, or another woman, please don't let me be the last to know.' I trembled.

'No, Andie.'

'Promise me. I'll understand, believe me.'

'Andie, even if I did fall in love, with whoever it may be, you would still have my heart. I wouldn't leave you, ever,' he said. 'Unless you want me to, or you want to leave me.'

I looked at him. 'No, I can't leave you, Frederico, you have my heart.'

We kissed and hugged until the bed swallowed us and our bodies ached from arching awkwardly. We both failed to pull ourselves up and in the end we laughed at our clumsiness.

PART VI

OUR BOY

ANDREA CURTIN: MY BOYS

27 JUNE 2017

I RELUCTANTLY KISSED FREDERICO GOODBYE. Inevitably, he had to go back to work and I didn't want to be the nagger who stood by the door with a clipboard and checked the *cans* and *can'ts* for him.

A few minutes later the door burst back open.

'I can cancel if you don't want me to go,' Frederico said hurriedly.

I gave him an appreciative smile. I'd already made him reject a couple of massage jobs earlier today. He had said it was okay, but I knew he'd only done it for me. I hadn't made peace with myself because of it; *selfish, paranoid, irrational.* For this evening's job though, I sensed he actually didn't want to go, but this time I simply said, 'It's fine.'

He knelt in front of me. 'It's only dinner. I know this client well, and it's just around the corner from here. I'll be okay.'

'Of course,' I said, and caressed his face, his cheeks bony from the weight loss. Most of the bruises and cuts had healed, and those that were still giving his skin a tinge of pink and green were concealed well with make-up. 'Go.'

'I'll keep my mobile on, just in case.'

He rushed out as quickly as he came in. This time the door stayed shut.

I paced the room, walking like I was in a cat suit; everything felt so tight especially around my breasts and belly.

I skimmed through the gifts from the baby shower scattered on the living room table – a set of Ralph Lauren blankets and linen from Leanne, Tiffany & Co sterling silver baby spoon and fork from Karin, six sets of baby clothes and socks from Lil' & Chic Dubai (yes, the store I'd helped set up, back when I'd wished I could've bought the merchandise for my own baby); most other gifts were still pretty much untouched.

I lay on the sofa and turned on the television. My fingers obsessively pressed the *CH* button up and down: *Survivor*, *MasterChef*, *CSI: Miami*, NutriBullet on TVSN, the Colosseum! Now that this terrible boy from Rome was with me, the memory of the city didn't feel depressing. So I watched the group of historians and engineers reconstructing how the Romans transported animals from underneath the structure up to the open arena, making them *magically* appear during a gladiator battle. Down in the hypogeum (I was there!), a civil engineer was analysing the indentations on the walls, and explaining how they gave a tell-tale sign that an elevator of some sort was used. Based on this research they'd built a wooden elevator (offsite, because the space underground was impossibly tight). Then they used a crane to put the elevator in place. The elevator swayed as the crane hoisted it up, metre by metre ... it was too heavy... it was going to fall...

Out of nowhere drowsiness crept over me. I wanted to see how the project ended, but my eyes gave in and I fell asleep.

As my head drooped towards the edge of the sofa, I woke up. The first thing I saw was a wolf, walking gracefully through the elevator gate, out onto the arena and reunited with its handler.

I looked at the time: just past 10 p.m. I should've asked what time Frederico would be back. Dinner shouldn't take more than a couple of hours. But maybe they'd gone for a drink? He hadn't mentioned it though. But he didn't have to; if that was how the night panned out, he would have to go with the flow. I got up to fetch a glass of water. The drowsiness crept in again, and despite my anxiety I fell back asleep on the couch.

Noises from a car commercial roused me. My weighty eyelids slowly opened: a family was on a road trip, mum, dad and bub. When the camera zoomed in on the dad, he morphed into someone I knew well.

Not again!

'Sorry... sorry... did I scare you?'

'Frederico...' I touched him. He was okay.

He took off his jacket, loosened his tie and sat next to me. 'You all right?'

I nodded as my heart rate slowly got back to normal. 'How was dinner?'

'It was so formal. I didn't have to talk much, or do much,' he said.

'I'm glad you're home.'

'Me too,' he said. 'Let's go to bed.'

'What time is it?'

'About 10.30.'

I pondered. I didn't want to go to bed. Tonight I wanted to be with him in a different way. 'How's the sky?' I asked.

Frederico looked at me thoughtfully. 'It's pretty clear.'

'Would you?'

He smiled and helped me up. 'I'll get the picnic rug so we can lie down. Dress warm, eh?'

THE MIDNIGHT SKY above Bouddi was as clear as the universe could give us, clearer than when we were here the last time.

'This is perfect,' I said, lying next to Frederico on the woolly rug. 'Look! That bright star!'

I reached across to find his hand. I told him, 'I was worried about you, you know.'

'I know. But really, you don't have to,' Frederico said. He took a deep breath. 'It was hard tonight, I must admit. At the restaurant, I kept thinking: I can't do this any more.'

'Hey, you don't have to stop just because of me. I'm sorry if I've been all over the shop today. One of those days when I was just feeling funny,' I said, although today was a bit on the extreme side of 'funny'. 'When you're back to one hundred per cent you might feel differently.'

He hadn't healed fully. On a bad day he would hide in the bedroom and curl in bed, crying. Sometimes I came in and tried to comfort him, sometimes I just turned away as it was hurting *me* too much. No painkillers, no hug, no words would ever make him okay (despite him saying with a smile: 'I'm better now that you're here').

'Well, maybe it is my injuries, but, I just can't do it anymore. Even a simple dinner like tonight was such a drag. And I think Jeff knew. He was kind about it, knowing that I had been *sick* – well, that was what I told him.'

He paused to play with my fingers. Then he continued, 'What you said a while back, about pretending... you're right, that is what I do. And I can't do it any more.'

'I said that because I was confused,' I said. 'But sometimes you just have to pretend. It doesn't mean you're a bad person. You're a good man, you're a good escort, you change people's lives.'

'You're biased.'

'Of course I am, but I was your client once, remember?' I sat up and loomed over him, becoming his sky. 'You will be okay, it's just gonna take time.' I positioned myself to kiss him, but pain suddenly hit me, as if a rope had been tightened around my waist and someone was tugging the other end of it. I held his hand tight. Then I squeezed it, then crushed it. 'Frederico...' I cried.

'Andie?'

I hurled myself back and lay flat on the rug, staring at the starry heavens, breathing through my mouth.

'Frederico... he's coming...'

'What? It's early.'

'I know... but he's definitely coming!'

'Come on, let's go to the hospital.'

'No... if I stand up he will come out! He will! Please,' I begged. 'Please... I don't want to lose the baby.'

'You'll be okay, just lie there,' he said and made a call.

I should've known. Christopher had been early, like this. But he could still wait until we were at the hospital. He even waited until Chris made his flight back from Melbourne.

'Frederico....' I cried. 'Tell me everything will be okay...'

'Of course everything will be okay,' he said. My head was cradled on his lap, and his hand never let mine go. 'The paramedics are coming, hang in there, Andie.'

I was scared, as scared as the day Christopher was born. My mum drove me to the hospital as Chris was in the air, probably the most nervous flight he'd ever been on. When Chris was by my side, he didn't know what to do. The big man was holding my hand, but his mind was somewhere else, making me even more frightened. When the time came I cried for my mum, callously kicking my husband out. Despite the drama, both Chris and I were thankful for that decision; we told each other things wouldn't have gone well if we'd been together in that room. I remembered that conversation clearly; I was cradling Christopher Jr. and Chris was hugging me.

Then there was the stillbirth. It was in the middle of the last trimester and it had felt like the end of the world. This was almost like that. The drowsiness – now I remembered I had slept almost the whole afternoon that day, and I simply couldn't control it. This was really like that...

Only, at this very moment, I wasn't alone in bed – I was lying in the sand, star-gazing with my man, twelve years my junior. Right now he didn't know what to do either, just like the big man, but I wanted him by my side, I needed him to be. When he said it would be okay, *it would be okay*.

I tried to keep my breathing under control, I counted the stars above me, and the brightest one looked even brighter. With that I could feel an unstoppable momentum in me. My son he couldn't wait to see the world.

Frederico wiped the dripping sweat off my forehead.

'Frederico...'

My son couldn't wait to see that beautiful face.

I was about to scream, but I looked at that face. A star had been carved out of my man's cheek, and now the stars in the sky had formed a halo around his crown. I didn't need to scream, I had him, very near, and he knew my pain, so I just softly cried and let go.

A looming siren. Then three paramedics tore the night with their torchlights. There was no time to talk about the state of affairs, as soon as the female paramedic knelt in front of my spread legs, a cry echoed through the night.

The most beautiful sound.

I never thought I'd ever hear it again. It was the cry of my baby, mine, not some other woman's. It was his – the boy I saved, the man who had my heart; *my* man, not someone else's man.

I forced myself to sit up. 'Is he okay?' I whispered, trembling, panting.

'Yes, he is.' Frederico hugged me.

'Ooooo! It's a beautiful boy!' one of the paramedics said. She quickly wrapped the baby and handed him over to me.

'Our boy,' I cried. I couldn't see much of him. But I knew he was perfect; a tiny bundle, wriggling as much as a newborn could do, crying hard in my arms. What was he trying to say, I wondered. I glanced behind me. Frederico caped me with a blanket and himself. His hand shivered as he touched the baby's face.

'He's got strong lungs!' said the other paramedic.

'We'd better get you guys to the hospital, just to make sure everything is okay.'

'Are you feeling okay, Andie?' Frederico said.

'Yeah. Hold him.' I let Frederico take over as the paramedics helped me get on the stretcher. I watched the tears streaming down Frederico's face. He was smiling, trying to say something to the baby. As awkward as his cradling looked, the baby settled and stopped crying.

Inside the ambulance fatigue started to overwhelm me. Frederico was still holding my hand. Every now and then he looked at the baby inside the cot.

'Is he okay? He's so quiet...' I murmured.

'He's okay,' the paramedic said. 'I think your husband just sent him to sleep.'

Frederico took a peep and smiled. 'He just puckered. So funny,' he said. Then he gazed at me and he kissed me.

His kiss felt different this time. It wasn't the usual passionate, burning kiss, nor was it the deep kiss he gave when he was grateful that I was there for him; it was like a conclusion, a victory. *He* made this happen; I resisted him with all my might, but he knew better. Clairvoyant, like Leanne said to me once; he could see the future and once again he never lied when he said everything would be okay.

'Did I tell you you look handsome tonight?' I teased him.

'No. Must've been the shirt, huh?'

'Maybe... but I think it was because you look so ready to welcome our son.'

'I certainly wasn't ready!'

We both laughed.

'You won't ever know how much you mean to me, Andie,' he whispered. 'You saved my life, and more, you gave me a chance. A lifetime of showing you how much you mean to me, or telling it to you – it won't be enough.'

And I smiled. I whispered back, as softly as he did, 'I would save you again and again.'

'And I would make you happy again and again.'

I WATCHED Leanne playing with baby Luca as he wriggled inside his cot.

'Imagine, this is my first time in the maternity ward, ever,' said Leanne. 'I've not seen that many babies. But he's so cute, so cute.'

'Pick him up,' I said.

'Umm... no thanks, I'm happy where he is now. I don't wanna drop him or anything.'

Leanne the clown! 'No, you won't drop him,' I said.

'You know I'm not the most handy with cradling another human being, right?' she said. 'I don't want to traumatise him. He might get a bad perception of women when he grows up.'

'Geez, Lee! Where did that come from?'

She laughed at herself, and with that baby Luca cried.

'See! See!' Leanne said.

'Oh, chill out, he's just hungry,' I said and picked him up.

'Gosh your boobs are...'

'Well, mummies' boobs are like these.'

'Not that I've seen! As I remember them, they looked rather intimidating,' she said, and laughed at her own remark. 'Yours look delightfully perky.'

'Lee!'

'So where's Mr Handsome?'

'He went home to get a few things for me.'

'Morning,' Frederico suddenly entered the room. He wasn't expecting Leanne, who was crouching to pick up a pack of tissue she had just dropped. 'Oh... hello there.'

'Oh...' Leanne was stuttering. 'Um... hi there.'

'There's Mr Handsome,' I said and winked at Leanne. Then I looked at Frederico. 'You've met Leanne?'

'Ah yeah, briefly, at the baby shower,' he said.

'Congratulations,' Leanne said. 'He's very beautiful.'

'Thank you,' said Frederico. 'So he's hungry again?'

'Yes,' I said.

'I'd better go,' Leanne said. 'I'll come back tonight.'

'Hey...' Frederico said and kissed me then baby Luca. 'I've got something for you,' he said and showed me a flask.

'Nooo... is that?'

'Yes, essence of chicken. I didn't make it, your mum did. I rang her yesterday and stopped by their place this morning.'

'Ooh... thank you,' I said. 'When are they coming?'

'Soon,' he said. 'Your mum needs to pick up your dad from the airport, then they'll head here.'

I looked at baby Luca, who had fallen asleep. 'He doesn't like to have big meals, just frequent meals,' I said and put him back in his cot.

'Is it time to feed you now?' Frederico said, with a bowl in his hand. He carefully used the porcelain spoon to scoop the soup and feed me.

'Oh so good!' I said absorbing the flavour and warmth.

'It sure works, too. I know it first-hand,' Frederico said.

I was ready for the next spoonful but Frederico withdrew and manoeuvred the spoon left and right like an aeroplane.

'Frederico you're going to spill it!' I squealed.

And as the spoon arrived at my mouth, a figure loomed at the door. A big man with a big bouquet of flowers.

'Chris?' I gaped.

'Sorry, I'll come back later.'

'No, no, please,' I said.

Cautiously he stepped in. 'Congratulations,' said Chris, and gave me the flowers with stiffly outstretched arms.

'They're beautiful, thank you,' I said.

'Let me get those.' Frederico took the flowers and put them on the window sill next to Leanne's.

'So my mum rang you, I take it?' I said.

'Umm...' Chris murmured.

'Actually, Andie, I texted him,' said Frederico.

'Oh...' I said.

'I'll go, I'm sorry, I shouldn't have just come here like this,' said Chris.

'Chris, no, please stay.' I held his hand.

'I'll leave you two,' Frederico said, and kissed me.

'You can stay, Frederico, please, don't feel...'

'You two talk, okay?' Frederico left.

'Andrea... he's so beautiful,' Chris said, staring at baby Luca.

'Luca Curtin-Lowe,' I said.

And Chris cried. I stood up and hugged him.

'You decided to keep your surname?'

'Yeah, you're always a part of me, Chris.'

'We could've,' Chris said, gently rubbing Luca's cheek with his finger. 'But I'm happy for you. Honestly.'

'Pick him up.'

'Ooooh... you are sooo precious,' he whispered with teary eyes. Baby Luca glanced at the big man. Chris's arms must've felt like a huge pillow to him. 'I hate to bring this up... but I still remember the feeling when Christopher was born. Just like this. It just wasn't meant to be, was it? Maybe in our next lives.'

'You were a good dad.'

He nodded in sadness.

'You can still be a part of our lives, Chris,' I added. 'You're welcome to visit us, any time.'

He was about to put Luca back in the cot, but he decided to carry him a little longer. A grin formed on his face. An old grin, a genuinely happy grin, which I hadn't seen since Christopher Jr. had been gone. Then carefully he lowered Luca back into his cot.

Chris asked, 'Were our lives back then really bad?'

'No. I think we were just learning. Sometimes the hard way. And in the end I'm here and... you're here, although we're not together any more.'

'Did you ever love me?'

'I did, Chris, I did. We had what we had.'

'Does he take good care of you?' Chris asked, looking at the door, checking on Frederico.

I nodded. 'He's not a bad man.'

'A man who makes you happy is never bad,' he said, helping me climb back into bed. He pulled up a chair. 'I stopped seeing those men, you know.'

Selfishly I was glad; he could've splashed out and got into money trouble again, I could see that. But he's a man, too. 'Maybe you need a partner,' I said unconvincingly.

He sighed. 'It feels wrong.'

'Why?'

'Men... liking them makes me feel like a failure.'

'Chris, you're not a failure. What would I have been without you?' I said. 'Do you remember?'

'I'm sorry I couldn't make you happy.'

'You did.'

'I'm just like this, I hate being like this, you know! I hate it because it made me incapable of making you happy.' His voice trembled.

I hugged him. 'Who you are made me who I am. I had my happiness with you. We had Christopher. Not for long, but during that time the three of us were unstoppable.'

'I may desire men sexually, but I love you more than anything in this world. I've never even loved a man,' he said.

He kissed my forehead. His tears trickled over my face.

'There's nothing wrong with wanting to be with a man, Chris,' I said. 'You can't hate yourself for it.'

'Love is a funny thing, isn't it?'

'Yeah, it is.'

'I'm selling up. I'm moving to Queensland, most likely Brisbane, but maybe the Gold Coast.'

'Chris... really?'

'It's not the same without you,' he said. 'I need a new start. Perhaps someday I will learn to understand love. In time I will feel good about myself, about my life. I just need to keep reminding myself that you're happy now. Although not with me.'

'I'm sorry I hurt you.'

He shook his head. 'No, you never hurt me.'

Hand on heart he said: 'I hurt you. Because I never wanted you to know. Never. Even after we lost our sons, and you went through hell and thought I didn't want to touch you because I blamed you, I let you think that way. Of course I said no. But I just said it, you know, flatly – never fiercely. I never gave you an explanation. I just let the ambiguity linger.

'Because I never wanted you to know who I am; who your

husband was. The army made me good at pretending, and I succeeded covering myself for a good part of our marriage. You didn't hurt me. I hurt you.'

I shook my head and was about to say––

But he shushed me and continued, 'I tried my best to be a good husband to you. I know I failed, Sarina. I know. But I tried.'

I sat up and fell onto him. I hugged him tight. I felt the push-back from his muscles, but I hung on.

'Don't cry, honey, don't,' he said. He gently pushed me away, asking me to look him in the eye. 'We've done the right thing. Seeing you with Luca, seeing you with... with him, Frederico, it's like a huge weight has been lifted off my shoulders. Lying, pretending, cheating on you – I didn't want a life like that. But when we were together it was like that. I did it to myself, Andrea. I was riddled with guilt all the time. But you copped a lot of pain. I'm so sorry.'

'I understand, Chris, believe me. There's nothing to be sorry about,' I said, squeezing his hand.

'Like I said, love is a funny thing. Sometimes you can't be together, even if you love each other. You know that I love you, right?'

'I do, I do, Chris. And I still love you. Not in the sense of, you know, husband and wife, but I love you as someone that I've shared my life with, who has made me a better person. And I hope I will still share my life with you even when we're apart.'

'I like the sound of that.' He nodded, stooped to kiss Luca, then looked at me with a content smile. He hugged me once more, then left.

ANDREA CURTIN: INFERNO

1 AUGUST 2017

BABY LUCA SMILED at the sight of Frederico. For hours I'd been trying to send him to sleep but the bub simply refused. Today was the first time he'd spent his late morning feed without Frederico's caressing fingers, and his afternoon nap without his dad's (rather out of tune) version of 'Old MacDonald'. And during bathtime Luca had made it clear my *blob blob* bubble-making was a fail. What could a five-week old understand about tunes and bubbles?

'So how was work?' I asked Frederico as I buttoned up baby Luca's top.

'Yeah, all right.'

He tried to escape my glance.

'It was bad. I used to wait tables but I have forgotten how to do it,' he said.

'It might take time but I'm sure you'll be fine,' I said. 'Luca was cranky all day. Not seeing you, I suppose.'

Frederico cradled Luca and rocked him gently as I watched on: how did he do it, what shook Luca's little princely attitude away? A special touch perhaps, or had Luca built more than just a father-son bond with Frederico? After all, although it takes two to make a baby, in all fairness I could say Frederico *made* Luca that night, the last night of the world.

I smiled at Frederico, as happily as Luca did.

I remembered the first proper smile Christopher Jr. flashed at me, not those coincidental ones when he was caught moving his lips wide or when he had trapped wind. His whole face lit up, and so did mine. And Chris was by my side then.

I turned my head slightly to escape Frederico, blocking him from reading my thoughts: Chris and Christopher, was the bond between them as strong as Luca's and Frederico's? I supposed it was, but I'd never paid attention. I was too caught up in all the scary things about being a teenage mother. But Chris had always been there. I remembered those nights when I'd cried almost as loudly as Christopher had. Chris would've told me: 'Go to sleep, Sarina. Change of the guard, I'll keep watch tonight.'

Perhaps it wouldn't be fair to compare – both Chris and Frederico equally wanted the best for me, the best for their sons. Guilt was still within me. Christopher's death, leaving Chris. I missed Chris in a way that I didn't understand. I wondered how he was doing in Brisbane, whether he'd found the love he deserved. Knowing Chris, he probably hadn't.

'Oooh... you can't stop smiling, can you!' said Frederico excitedly as he tickled Luca's belly.

He must've gone on to say something, or ask me something, as I was back to staring at the wall. 'Andie? Andie?'

I quickly turned to Frederico. 'Oh, sorry.'

'You okay?'

'Yeah. I was thinking about what I had to do tomorrow. What did you say?'

'I said Luca's smile looked a bit different. See! See!'

I chuckled at that little face. 'Yeah, that's a real smile.'

A few more seconds of smiling, a few minutes of rocking, and soon off to sleep Luca went.

'What have your arms got, seriously, he falls asleep just like that,' I said snapping my fingers. 'Always. Since he was like... ten minutes old. Remember that night at the beach?'

'Andie, of course I remember. How could I ever forget! The happiest day of my life, no doubt, but honestly I'd never been so scared,' he said.

I'd never heard him say he'd been scared that night, and to me he had never looked scared. But what man wouldn't, when his woman said the baby was coming out *now now* and they were out star-gazing in the middle of a national park?

'So what's the secret of your arms?' I said.

'You should know. You've fallen asleep on me many times,' he said.

'True.' Maybe because they were just nicely cushioned; however you lay on them you felt safe. And they smelled like... like him, and they were warm, like they had been heated.

Frederico put Luca in his cot. 'My arms are better with babies and ladies, not so good with dishes.'

I laughed at his remark, while keeping watch on my man wrapping a blanket over Luca. 'You tired? You want to have a shower and go to bed?'

'Let's sit down for a while,' he said, and guided me to the living room. 'I missed you.'

'I missed you too,' I said. I gestured him to lie flat on the sofa and put his head on my lap. I played with his hair. 'You smell like saffron,' I giggled. 'So, tell me the scoop.'

'Apart from me being clumsy, well, everyone was nice. Customers were nice, the ladies were hitting on me,' he said, winking at me.

'Hmm?' I pinched his nose.

'And someone gave me this,' he took out a name card from his shirt pocket. 'Not sure what the guy was on about.'

'Oh, talent management?' Andrea said. 'Inferno. Very bold.'

Frederico fiddled with his phone to look at their website.

'What the...' Frederico sighed.

Got the looks? Got the right tools? Let us help you get out there!

'Oh! Fuck him!' said Frederico looking at all the naked actors and models posing on the website. He threw his phone to the other end of the sofa. 'Am I really only good at sex?'

'Frederico, you're a sexy guy, you should take it as a compliment. But he was pretty rude, I suppose, just leaving you with a card without saying anything.'

He got up. 'I'm going for a run.'

'Frederico! Wait...'

But he was gone, running in his white shirt, black pants and black loafers.

FREDERICO LOWE: SAD LADY

2 AUGUST 2017

THE COUPLE at table 9 hadn't spoken to each other since their mains were served. Despite the lunchtime crowd dispersing around them, they hung around. The man maintained his upright sitting position while the woman curled into her chair, her meal pretty much untouched.

'Frederico! Break time!' my boss said as I cleared table 12.

I wanted to know when or if the couple would eventually talk. Earlier the man had complained (to his lunch companion, not to any of the waiters): 'What's this crap? Hate Italian food! You can't even feed a bird with this pathetic amount of food.'

The woman had then apologised and asked if he would like to try something else. He refused and then he stared at her meal: 'Seriously, I was surprised you ordered that. Isn't it too much for you?'

She'd shrugged. 'I thought this one would be quick so you didn't have to wait for my usual risotto.'

Sad, I thought as I left table 12.

I opened my locker and found a text message waiting. Andie.

Got this accounting puzzle. My accountant is overseas. I'll be late. Baby Luca is fine tho, happy to be in the office

From the staff room I watched the table 9 woman walking out to the back garden carrying a pack of ciggies while her man was having coffee. She stood near the bin at the back entrance wiping her face.

I stopped typing to Andie and approached the woman.

'Are you okay?' I said. I realised how tiny she was.

'Yeah,' she said, rubbing her eyes, the ciggie between her fingers remained unlit. 'This dry air is making everything feel... well, dry.' She looked at my name badge. 'Thanks for asking, Frederico.'

I left her be, but I couldn't help feeling for her. I'd seen that sad face on Andie last night, when I'd come home after my inferno run, when I'd ignored her and locked myself in the bathroom.

The woman wrote something on a serviette and tucked it under a saucer. Her man was already past the door leaving her to settle the bill. I casually cleared the table. *Thanks F*, followed by a lipstick mark, clear and full, and a phone number.

'Frederico! What are you doing?' my boss marched towards me from behind the counter.

'Umm... nothing,' I said, juggling the spoons, cups, saucers, teapot, and water jug. 'Hey... Braden... umm... is it okay if I leave ummm... now? I'll make it up tomorrow. I'll do the full shift. I know I've only been here a week, I don't want any trouble, I just need to leave early today.'

Braden Quinn, the 60-year-old restaurateur frowned. I didn't usually speak that quickly. He was Irish, but he cooked like an Italian. And I thought he would run a business like an Italian, too, with an Irish touch, and he wouldn't be happy with my request. I readied myself to give him more reasons but Braden simply said: 'Your baby all right?'

A pause.

'Frederico?'

'Uhh...yeah,' I said. 'I just have to get him from my partner's office.'

Braden smirked. 'Go. See you tomorrow. One and a half shifts. Yes?'

I TIPTOED to Andie's private office. Under the dim light, in an oversized armchair, she fed Luca. Every now and then she kissed Luca's forehead and caressed his cheek as the baby put his furled fingers on her breast.

I had made my Andie happy, look at her. Years ago I would've said this was a happy ending, but now it was a happy beginning. Look at her. Look at them. *My family*.

That sad face was gone, but I didn't know how she felt about me after last night.

'Is that you, Rach?' Andie said.

'Only me,' I said, coming out of hiding

'Frederico!' Andie gaped. A gape like she'd been praying for me to turn up, as if nothing had happened last night. 'Are you on a long break or something?'

'No, I finished for the day.' I glanced at the new photo frames on her desk: Christopher Jr side by side with baby Luca.

'Don't you think they look nice?'

'Yes. They're beautiful together.'

'It makes me happy. Remember when you came here that night, I told you it made me scared looking at Christopher's photo, it was like... uhh...'

'Hey...' I said and put my arm around her.

'I will never get over it, you know, but I'm okay with it, that was what I thought was amazing. Just because I'm with you, I'm okay.'

She was what mattered most in my life, and she always made me feel I was the most important thing in her life. *That* was amazing.

'Luca is enjoying the change of scenery. He's been smiling all day, *and* eating a lot too.'

'Noisy so-and-so!' I commented at Luca's enthusiastic suckling.

'Oh tell me about it!'

'I saw your text. I thought I could take Luca if you want.'

'Frederico... you don't have to. But if you really don't mind, I've been trying not to get too stressed with him around. But it's so hard...'

'Of course I don't mind,' I said. 'I'm sorry about last night.'

'Shh! Don't worry about it.'

'See what I've just bought.' On the way here I stopped by a baby shop and got a wrap-around baby pack.

'Oh, Frederico! I'd always wanted to have one of those!'

I put it on slowly.

'You've done this before?' she said.

'The shopkeeper put it on me. I think this is right, yes, now give me Luca.' Luca looked at me, chin up. Cradled, tucked in, he smiled as brightly as he always did. 'You like it? Yes you do!'

'My God you're the sexiest dad ever,' she said. 'Let me take a photo of you two like that.'

And we boys happily posed for her.

I put my arm around her and said, 'Okay, I should leave you to it.'

'I hate this, why don't the numbers add up?' Andie said and scrunched her forehead.

'You'll work it out, I'm sure,' I said and kissed her. 'I'll see you at home. Take your time. I'll wait for you.'

Old MacDonald has a farm, E-I-E-I-O... And in his farm he's na na na, E-I-E-I-O-...

'Oh!' I didn't expect to see anyone at the reception. 'Hi there!'

'Oh hi, you must be Frederico,' said the woman in her overly-warm clothing, with a suitcase in tow. 'I'm Andrea's client. Rachel.'

She knew my name. How many times had Andie spoken about me that her client remembered?

'This must be Luca,' she said. 'How old is he now?'

'Five weeks,' I said.

'In the photos he looked like Andrea. But I must say he looks like you in the flesh,' Rachel said, looking at me, almost admiring. 'Andrea and I, we go back years. She helped me set up my first store in Dubai, babywear. That woman has guts. I knew it wasn't easy for her at the time. Babies made her sad. But look at this beautiful little guy. You two have done well. *You* have done well.'

I looked into her eyes. I knew Andie had told her everything. And for the first time in my life I could truly say I was proud of myself.

ANDREA CURTIN: THE HAMMOCK

2 AUGUST 2017

'YEEEEESSSS!' I finally got the numbers to tally up.

Without wasting a second I zoomed home and jumped at Frederico, who was relaxing on the sofa. I looked at his lap. White smudges all around his pants.

'You smell like Luca,' I said.

'Ahhh yeah, I spilled some of his powder.'

'You bathed him this afternoon?'

'Of course I did. Wine?'

'Yes please.'

'Have I ever made you sad?' he asked, handing me a glass of pinot.

'Frederico what is it?'

'I saw a couple earlier today. I thought they were going to have a romantic lunch, but in the end the woman actually cried.'

No, Frederico had never made me sad. But this woman had made *him* sad.

'How could a woman cry when she was having lunch? At a nice Italian restaurant?' he asked me.

'Did they have an argument?'

'The man, her husband or boyfriend, he was rude. He complained about Italian food, and had a go at her because she couldn't finish her meal. The woman was tiny. That calamari is one of the smallest dishes we have,' he said. 'Or maybe she had lost her appetite – who could blame her? I mean, if you don't like Italian why go to an Italian restaurant?'

'Perhaps because she picked it,' I said.

'Is that a guy thing?'

'I never had that with Chris, but Leanne's husband was like that. When he said *up to you*, he really meant *read my mind and do what I asked you to do*. And if it was really up to her, things didn't usually end well and she got blamed for it. I guess that was partly why they separated.'

'Really?' he said. 'I understand why a man can be a loser like my father, you know, it was just *in him* to hit my mother and me, and get angry at everything. But... for a guy who lunches with his woman, to see him make her so sad, in front of other people, I can't understand that!'

'I guess some men are like that.'

'Have I made you sad, Andie?'

We look into each other's eyes. And I shook my head. 'No, you've never made me sad, Frederico.'

'Did I make you sad last night?'

'No,' I said. 'Honestly, don't worry about last night.'

I touched his star-shaped scar and kissed it. 'So what happened to that woman?'

Frederico told me she had written him a message on a serviette, with her phone number and sealed it with a kiss. 'Huh! Occupational hazard for being a kind, handsome waiter.' I made light of it.

'Are you jealous?'

I stared at him. 'Depends on what you did with it.'

'I threw it away like other serviettes.'

'No, I'm not jealous, you silly! It's just *in you* to try to make people happy. But if it happens every day I'll be nervous.'

Frederico winked at me. 'We'd better do something about it then.'

'What do you mean?'

'I might need a ring or something, so people know I'm taken.'

'Well, if someone wanted to hit on you, they'd hit on you, ring or no ring.'

'True. And, I must confess, the shopkeeper at the baby store was kind of hitting on me, too. I showed him baby Luca's photo, with you in it. I told him –'

'Oh it was a guy?'

'Yes, and he's one hundred per cent gay. So I told him you were my wife.'

Oh... that was what he meant by a 'ring'. I said to him: 'Frederico... you're not saying we...'

'Oh, no I'm not suggesting we're getting married. I was just rambling,' he said and rummaged his pocket. 'I've got us these.'

A couple of braided bracelets, in ivory, six-cord wide, no buckle, just a couple of loose strings to tie at the end.

'Nothing special,' he said. 'But I thought it would be nice to have something that shows we're together.'

'Frederico this is so sweet!' I gave my right hand and Frederico slowly encircled my wrist and tied a knot right on top of my pulse.

Then he gave his hand to me, and I did the same.

When we were both wearing them, he took my wrist and pressed the knot with his three fingers. 'I can feel you,' he said.

'And I you.' With my fingers on his bracelet I took a deep breath. 'I won't forget this moment.'

'Just trying to be romantic. I'm Italian, what can I say,' he said. 'Might not always go with your clothes, but I thought a neutral white would be ok.'

'I love it. I won't take it off.'

'Really?'

'Yes. It means a lot to me.' I kissed his wrist.

'Am I meant to just please people? Or pretend to?'

'You are much more than a people pleaser, Frederico. You're the love of my life, you're the father of my child, you're the one that I lean on and you never let me down,' I said putting my palm on his cheek. 'You will start your course next month. You will be a brilliant psychologist. And then you won't just be pleasing people, you'll be *helping* people.'

A smile on his burdened face.

'It's a long way to get there, but you'll get there,' I said. 'Frederico, you know I'll support you, right? If the restaurant job doesn't work out, or if you're unhappy with it, I will support you. Anything you do.'

'I know. I know. But I'm a man, I need to work.'

'Do you miss escorting?'

'Yeah, sometimes, ironically I do miss pleasing people that way,' he said. 'But I don't want to go back there. Andie, I'm okay with waiting tables. As long as I have you and baby Luca to come home to, I'm happy.'

'Why don't you want to go back there?'

'It's not right, with the baby.'

'Luca will understand, if that's really what you want.'

'Honestly, Andie, I don't want to fall in love.'

This had always been in the back of my mind.

'I won't be strong enough to resist,' he added.

'But you could fall in love anywhere, Frederico.'

'I know, but when you're both naked it is completely different,' he said. 'I don't want to go there.'

'Okay.'

'But I will always please you. That will never change,' he whispered and kissed me while his hands were unbuttoning my shirt.

'Frederico...'

'I think I'm ok now,' he said.

'Are you sure?'

'I tried it in the bathroom yesterday. It was okay.'

I smiled and kissed him.

'Just be gentle,' he said.

'No *llévame*?'

He chuckled. 'Nnno, not yet.'

I welcomed his body; warm, cushioned with a bit of muscle, blanketed by a forest of hair. Behind the smell of Luca's powder I caught a whiff of his body scent.

'I saw that,' he said.

'Saw what?'

'That look when you smelled me.'

I chuckled. 'I like the way you smell.'

'Like a baby?'

It was sweet like cider. 'No, *your* smell.' I crawled on top of him. 'It turns me on... so manly...'

This time he chuckled. 'Hey... maybe we can... you know...'

'What?'

'Have another one.'

'Seriously?'

'Yeah. What do you think?'

'You're still keeping track?' I teased him.

'No, I kinda know, you smell different when... you know... when it's coming. I trained myself when I was still your escort. I'd know when to expect you to cancel our appointment, and when you got horny again. And when you'd be moody and all that.'

I pinched him. 'You are terrible!'

'I wanted to be perfect for you always.'

'You're always perfect,' I said. 'I guess we'll have to wait until Luca is old enough.'

'Of course.'

'So, you'll tell me when it's a good time to make a baby then?' I winked at him.

'How about letting it all flow. When it happens, it happens.'

'I like that, Sayang...'

And we were one once more, without a past, without a goal. It was like lying in a hammock together; the rhythm, the swing, the speed, all driven by our one body, the gravity and the wind.

'About that ring —' Frederico said quickly, then stopped.

'You're still thinking about it aren't you?'

'Wouldn't it be nice? Just a thought. Again, I'm Italian, I can't help it.'

I didn't plan to remarry, but the way he delivered the line made me think *maybe*.

And we silently and noisily continued with our affair. He still had it. The boy, the escort, the man, *my man*, he still sent me to the moon, to the stars – where it's always summer, it's always Christmas, and it's always with him.

INSPIRATION PHOTOS ON PINTEREST

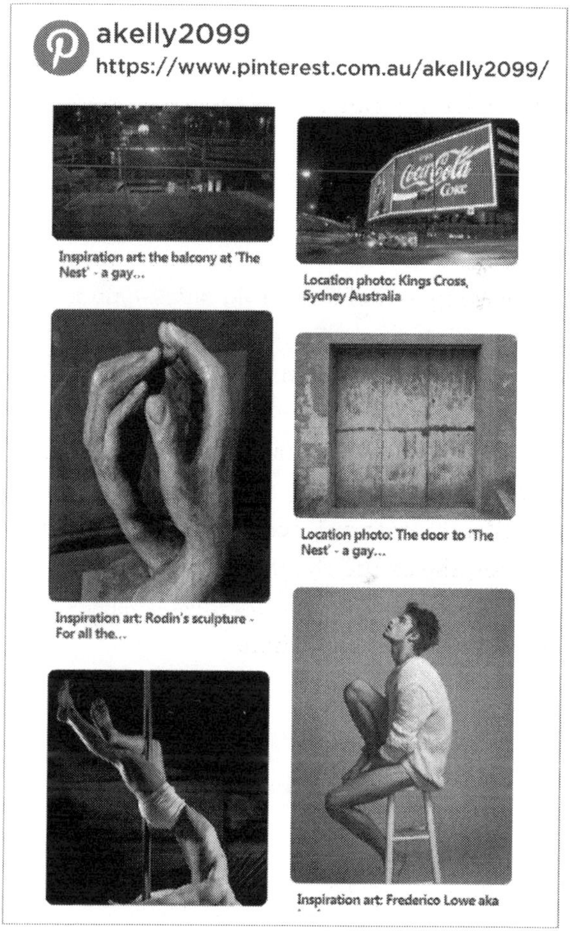

How did you enjoy the story?

Let us know and leave a review on Amazon.

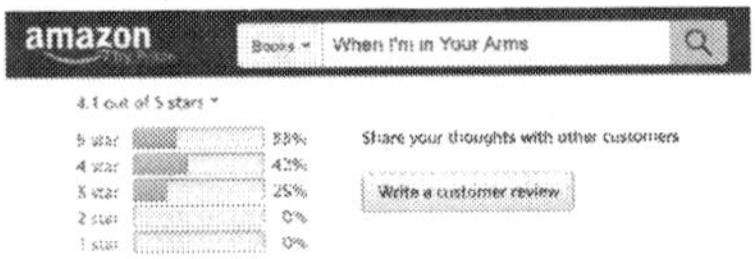

OTHER WORK BY A KELLY

She falls for a man who loves men.

"Amazingly unique love story that will stick with you long after it's over!" *MSquared Book Blog*

18593539R00231

Made in the USA
Middletown, DE
30 November 2018